IN A TIME OF DARKNESS...

...WHEN ALL SEEMS LOST...

...A RAY OF HOPE REMAINS.

THE AUSCHWITZ ESCAPE

JOEL C. ROSENBERG

TYNDALE HOUSE PUBLISHERS, INC.
CAROL STREAM, ILLINOIS

Visit Tyndale online at www.tyndale.com.

Visit Joel C. Rosenberg's website at www.joelrosenberg.com.

Designed by Dean H. Renninger

Library of Congress Cataloging-in-Publication Data

Rosenberg, Joel C., date.
The Auschwitz escape / Joel C. Rosenberg.
pages cm
ISBN 978-1-4143-3624-4 (hc)
1. Holocaust, Jewish (1939-1945)—Fiction. 2. Auschwitz (Concentration camp)—Fiction.
3. Concentration camp inmates—Fiction. 4. Escaped prisoners—Fiction. 5. Jewish fiction. I. Title.
PS3618.O832A94 2014
813′.6—dc232013044075

ISBN 978-1-4143-3625-1 (sc)

Printed in the United States of America

21 20
7 6 5 4

To the memory of all those who were murdered at
Auschwitz and throughout the Holocaust—
may you never be forgotten.

To the remarkable spirit of those who survived the Shoah—
may your lives and your witness be forever honored and blessed.

To all those unknown souls whose faith compelled them
to risk their lives to rescue Jews from a terrible evil—
may your love be an example followed by others.

CAST OF CHARACTERS

GERMAN

Weisz Family

- Jacob Weisz, young Jewish man originally from Berlin
- Avraham ("Avi") Weisz, Jacob's uncle
- Ruthie Weisz, Jacob's younger sister
- Dr. Reuben Weisz, Jacob's father
- Sarah Weisz, Jacob's mother

Siegen Residents

- Hans Meyer, Jacob's friend
- Naomi Silver, Jacob's neighbor
- Herr Berger, tailor
- Eli Berger, his son
- Herr Mueller, baker

Auschwitz Officers

- Rudolf Hoess, Auschwitz commandant*
- Colonel Klaus Von Strassen, director of security
- Josef Mengele, Auschwitz doctor*
- "Fat Louie," camp guard

FRENCH

Leclerc Family

- Jean-Luc ("Luc") Leclerc, assistant pastor in Le Chambon
- Claire Leclerc, his wife
- Lilly Leclerc, their elder daughter
- Madeline Leclerc, their younger daughter
- Philippe Leclerc, Jean-Luc's brother
- Monique, Jean-Luc's sister
- Nicolas ("Nic"), Monique's husband
- Jacqueline, their daughter

Others

- Pastor Chrétien, Jean-Luc's colleague
- Pastor Émile, Jean-Luc's colleague
- François d'Astier, former French ambassador to the U.S.
- Camille d'Astier, his wife

AMERICAN

- Cordell Hull, secretary of state*
- Colonel Jack Dancy, military aide to President Roosevelt
- William Barrett, senior advisor to Secretary Hull
- Sumner Welles, undersecretary of state*
- Henry Stimson, secretary of war*
- Harry Hopkins, secretary of commerce*

BELGIAN

- Maurice ("Morry") Tulek, commander of a Resistance cell
- Micah Kahn, Resistance member
- Marc Kahn, Micah's brother, a Communist
- Henri Germaine, Resistance member
- Jacques Bouquet, Resistance member
- Léon Halévy, Jewish refugee

---

*Real historical figures

AUSCHWITZ PRISONERS

Jewish Prisoners

- Maximilian ("Max") Cohen, Romanian, works in "Canada"
- Abigail ("Abby") Cohen, his sister, works in the clinic
- Lara, woman on the train to Auschwitz
- Mrs. Brenner, woman on the train to Auschwitz
- Marvin Eliezer, man on the train to Auschwitz
- Leonard Eliezer, Marvin's son
- Josef Starwolski, Polish, works in the records office
- Otto Steinberger, Czechoslovakian, registrar
- Abraham ("Abe") Frenkel, Czechoslovakian, registrar

Others

- Leszek Poczciwinski, kapo in charge of "Canada"
- Gerhard Gruder, block senior
- Stefan, bakery worker
- Andrej, bakery worker
- Janko, bakery worker

POLISH

- Jedrick, farmer
- Brygita, his wife

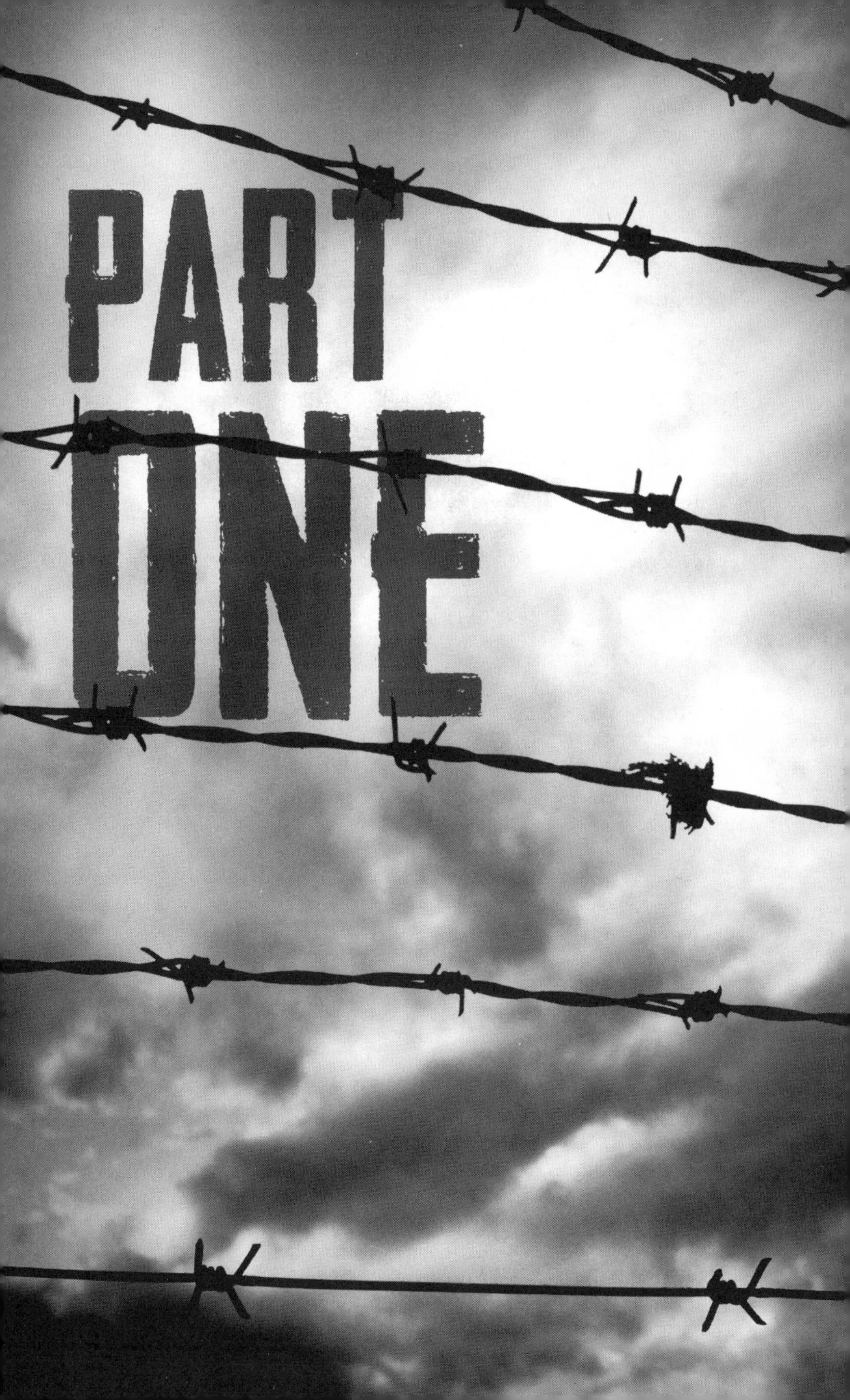
PART
ONE

IT SEEMED THAT A PRODIGIOUS CLOUD OF TOXIC, NERVOUS,
AND PARALYSING GAS HAD ENGULFED THE COUNTRY.
EVERYTHING WAS UNRAVELLING, FALLING TO PIECES
AND BEING THROWN INTO PANIC LIKE A MACHINE THAT WAS DRUNK,
EVERYTHING WAS TAKING PLACE AS IF IT WAS PART OF
AN INDESCRIBABLE NIGHTMARE.

ANDRÉ MORIZE

1

MAY 12, 1940
SEDAN, FRANCE

"Evil, unchecked, is the prelude to genocide."

It was a phrase Jean-Luc Leclerc had once read in an old book. It had caught his eye, and his subconscious had filed it away. At the moment he could not even remember who had written the book or what its title was, but neither was important. The book was forgettable; the phrase was not. Now, try as he might, he could not get it out of his head.

He felt as though every molecule in his body were shaking. Evil was on the march, and though everyone around him seemed bound and determined not to believe it, there was no question in his mind the Nazis were coming for them, for the people of France, all of them, with all their murderous fury, and he desperately feared the bloodbath that was coming with the jackboots and the broken cross.

Not that anyone was listening to him. And who was he, anyway, to think he knew what fate lay in store for his country? He was just a kid, really, only twenty-eight years old, and when he looked in the mirror every morning, he didn't see anyone special. He didn't stand out in a crowd. He was of average height and average build, with sandy-blond hair and bluish-green eyes set behind round, gold wire-rimmed glasses that made him look a bit more studious, even intellectual, than he really was. He'd always wanted to grow a beard—a goatee, at least—but even his adorable young wife teased him that his efforts were never quite successful. He had no great office or title or power, no money or fame or renown. He had no direct access to the political class or the media. He was, instead, a nearly penniless son of five generations of farmers. A Protestant in a nation where Catholics were by far the majority, he was a lowly pastor—actually merely an *assistant* pastor—in a little country church in the little country hamlet of Le Chambon, in the south of France, which no one had heard of nor probably ever would. Why should anyone take him seriously?

There was no reason, he told himself, but that didn't mean he was wrong.

To the north, Winston Churchill was warning that Hitler wanted to take over the world. The new British prime minister had been saying it for years. No one had listened. Now *der Führer* was on the march, and France was not ready. Not the people. Not the politicians. Not the press. Not even the generals.

In Paris, they said the Germans would never dare to invade France. They said the Nazis could never penetrate the Maginot Line, the twenty-five-kilometer-thick virtual wall of heavily armed and manned guard posts and bunkers and concrete tank barricades and antiaircraft batteries and minefields and all manner of other military fortifications designed to keep the Germans at bay. They'd convinced themselves Hitler would never try to move his panzer divisions through the forests of the Ardennes. Those forests were too thick, too dense, too foreboding for anyone to move tanks and mobile artillery and armored personnel carriers and other mechanized units through.

But Jean-Luc Leclerc knew that they were wrong.

"Luc? Luc, are you listening?"

No one actually called him Jean-Luc. Not since he was a little boy. His parents, his siblings, his grandparents—they all called him Luc. Now, though he still felt like a kid at times, theoretically he was "all grown up." Married. Two small daughters. A mortgage. A parish. Ever-growing responsibilities.

"Luc, are you even hearing a word I'm saying?"

Suddenly he realized his sister, Monique, was trying to get his attention, and he was embarrassed. "Yes, yes, of course; I'm sorry—what do you need?"

"Would you turn out the lights and bring those napkins and forks?" she asked with a warm smile as she stood in the center of the cozy kitchen and lit the candles on an exquisitely decorated and no doubt scrumptious homemade birthday cake.

Luc did as he was asked and followed his sister into the dining room, singing with the others and trying his best not to let his fears show on his face. He was not there to ruin his niece's birthday party. Little Jacqueline stood there in her pink dress and shiny brown hair and black leather shoes. She didn't know war was looming. She knew nothing of Herr Hitler's invasion of Poland the previous September. Nor did she know anything of Hitler's invasion of the Low Countries—Belgium and the Netherlands—three days earlier. The adults had shielded the children from their worries over their older brother, Philippe, who lived with his family in Brussels, the Belgian capital. Jacqueline didn't know they had not heard from Philippe since the German invasion, that Luc feared Philippe was dead. All she knew was that she had a houseful of family and friends and a cake with candles and a new doll from her beloved Uncle Luc and Aunt Claire and her cousins Lilly and Madeline. She was so innocent, he thought as he sang, so unaware of the darkness that was settling upon them all. At least she had an excuse. She was only four.

What was her parents' excuse? Monique was thirty-two. Her husband, Nicolas, was thirty-six. They were a sharp, attractive couple, well-educated and by all measures worldly-wise. They'd both been to university. She had studied nursing. He had been to the Sorbonne and had become a gifted physician. They were well-read. They had a little money socked away. They had interesting friends in high places all over Europe. How could they not see what had happened to Philippe? How could they not see the grave danger they were in? Why did they not flee while they still could, away from the border, to Le Chambon to be with Luc and Claire?

"... Happy birthday, dear Jacqueline; happy birthday to you!"

With that, the room erupted in applause and smiles and laughter and great joy. Jacqueline looked radiant, and Luc knew that his wife, Claire, and their two daughters would have loved to be at his side. Claire had made the doll and written the card, and Lilly and Madeline had colored it and made it special for their beloved cousin. But despite their protests, Luc had forbidden them to come. The Belgian border was no place for his family. Certainly not now.

As Jacqueline made a wish and blew out the candles and Monique cut the cake, Luc dutifully distributed the forks in his hand and then stepped back into the kitchen to get a couple bottles of cold milk.

Then, without warning, the house was rocked by an enormous, deafening explosion. The blast wave sent everyone crashing to the ground. All the windows shattered. Shards of wood and splinters of glass flew everywhere. Plates and glasses smashed to the floor. Terrified parents grasped their children, trying to shield their small bodies with their own as they covered their heads with their hands and hid under the table and behind overstuffed chairs.

Before they knew it, smoke and dust filled the room, pouring in through the shattered windows. Luc fully expected to hear people screaming and crying, but for the moment everyone seemed too stunned to do anything but cough and choke.

"Is everyone okay?" he asked, covering his nose and mouth with his shirt.

There was a low murmur as parents checked their children and themselves and then indicated that but for a few cuts and scrapes, they were mostly all right.

Luc checked himself as well. He, too, seemed fine—physically, at least—so he got up, dusted himself off, and moved toward the front door. "Wait here," he told the others. "I'll see what's happening."

"I'll come with you," Nicolas said, standing and grabbing his leather satchel of medicines and supplies.

"Nic, what are you doing?" Monique asked. "Come back here. You can't leave us."

"People may be hurt, darling," Nic replied. "Don't worry. It'll be okay. I'll be back soon."

It would not be okay, and everyone in the room knew it. Tears streamed down Monique's face as she clutched their daughter in her arms. Nic leaned down, kissed them both on the forehead, then headed for the door.

Luc couldn't help but admire his brother-in-law's commitment to his oath as a physician. As he went to follow Nic, he heard Monique whimper, "What's happening? Someone tell me what's happening."

Luc knew full well what was happening. The Nazi attack had begun.

He was petrified. He had been certain the Germans were coming, but he'd thought it would take at least a week before the invasion of France actually began. That was why he had come. That was why he had driven through the night from his home in Le Chambon to his sister's home in Sedan. Not for a party. Not for cake. But to implore Monique and Nicolas to pack up their belongings and come with him, away from the border, away from the danger, to Le Chambon, where they would be safe. All day he had made his case. All day he had pleaded with the couple, but they had refused to listen. They had a party to prepare. They had Jacqueline to care for. They had patients to attend to. They couldn't leave. It was out of the question. Besides, they argued, Hitler would never invade their beloved French Republic. Why would he? It would be an act of suicide, they said.

Now, as he opened the front door and stepped out of the narrow, three-level house not far from the river Meuse, Luc was horrified by the scene before him. To his left lay a flaming, smoking crater. Moments before, it had been a police barracks. Now the stench of burning human flesh was unbearable. Thick, black smoke billowed into the late-afternoon sky. People were rushing to the scene from all directions. Nicolas sprinted off, helping people carry a few survivors into a nearby church just up the street. The bells in the steeple began ringing furiously, sounding the alarm and calling people to action.

Luc could hear the sirens of fire trucks and ambulances approaching from the west. He knew he should rush to his brother-in-law's side and help the wounded and the wailing. But for a moment he hesitated—not because he didn't want to help but because he wanted to understand what was truly unfolding.

He turned to his right, looking toward the east, and what he saw nearly knocked the wind out of him. It was a sight apparently lost on all the people around, for they were riveted on the death and destruction that had already been wrought. They couldn't see what was coming. But Luc saw it, and he stood there unable to move.

The eastern skies were filled with planes as far as the eye could see. Nazi planes. Fighters. Bombers. Hundreds upon hundreds of them. Like a plague of locusts, the Luftwaffe was coming. And that was not all. Out of the thick, dense, supposedly impassable and impenetrable forests of the Ardennes now emerged German mechanized divisions and swarms of infantrymen, armed to the teeth—more than he could possibly count. Jean-Luc Leclerc had never been so scared.

The Germans were advancing quickly, and there was no one to stop them. The northern end of the Maginot Line was many kilometers away. The bulk of the French forces were positioned along that line, waiting for a frontal German attack that Luc now realized would never come. The Nazis had achieved what the generals and politicians in Paris said was impossible. They had carefully navigated their way through the Ardennes. They had used the trees as cover to keep French reconnaissance planes from spotting them. And now they were launching a devilishly clever sneak attack. They were outflanking the French forces. They were about to skirt right around them and attack them from behind.

It was now clear that the little town of Sedan—with a population of less than eighteen thousand people—was one of the Germans' first targets. How long would it take them to overrun and consume the town? How long would it be until everyone was dead or a prisoner of war? Once the Nazis controlled the bridges across the Meuse River, they could pour their forces into France, annihilate her armies, and march on Paris.

How long would it take them to occupy and enslave the entire country?

2

All color drained from Luc's face.

His body felt numb. His mouth went dry. He had to warn the others. But it was as if his throat had constricted. Try as he might, no sound came forth. Just then, he was startled by a high-pitched whine off to his left. Then another and another. He looked up and saw that the German planes were now overhead and were unleashing their ordnance. It seemed to be happening in slow motion. He could see bomb-bay doors opening. He could see the long black dots spilling out and raining down toward the town and the paltry few French units that flanked Sedan. Down came the bombs. They were getting larger and larger. They were reaching terminal velocity. He knew he should run. He knew he had to hide. But he could not. He just stood there frozen in place.

One by one, the bombs began to land, closer and closer until one scored a direct hit on the church. The force of the blast sent Luc sprawling backward, nearly crushing him against a brick wall and leaving him crumpled on the ground. The sound was deafening. He had never heard anything so loud.

More bombs fell. He watched a young woman—running for her life—thrown through the plate-glass window of a patisserie. He saw others disintegrate before his very eyes as the bombs kept falling and the carnage grew.

Adrenaline began coursing through his system. Luc's first thought was the church. Nicolas was in there. He had to pull him out of the wreckage and get him back to his family. He started heading for the church, but as he approached the roaring flames, he watched in horror as the steeple collapsed, then the roof, and then the walls imploded as yet more bombs decimated both the church and the buildings around it. The Nazis were carpet bombing Sedan, and soon whole portions of the town were blazing infernos.

Nicolas was dead. There was nothing Luc could do to save him now. That much was clear. But what of his family?

Luc turned and ran back into the house. He could hear screams, and he began shouting for people to follow him. Some listened. Some did not. But he couldn't wait. They had no time to spare.

Scooping up Jacqueline in his arms, he grabbed Monique by the hand and ordered her to come with him. She was sobbing, asking for Nicolas. But Luc didn't dare tell her. Not yet. He feared she would not come if she knew he was dead. They had to leave now. They had to get to his truck. They had to flee Sedan before the Nazis entered the town.

"Follow me!" he shouted, though he could barely hear himself over the successive explosions and the raging fires.

Out of the corner of his eye, he saw two fathers grab their families and pull them toward the door. Their families followed the three of them into the streets, now littered with fallen bodies and body parts. The wounded and the frightened were everywhere, and people huddled against walls that were still standing.

Luc was running now. His truck was parked two blocks away. It was a pickup, almost new, and unless it had been hit, it would run. He could fit all of them in the back—and at the moment that was all that mattered to him.

"Don't stop!" Luc shouted to his ragtag team. *"Keep moving."*

Just then he spotted a German Messerschmitt in the sky ahead of them. It was firing its machine guns and seemed to be aiming right for them. He ordered everyone to dive into the alleyway beside them, and they all took cover just as the fighter roared by, killing all those who remained in its path. Then came another explosion, just behind them. Luc pressed his body down on Monique and Jacqueline, doing everything he could to protect them. But he knew they couldn't stay pinned down. He could hear the German tanks rumbling up the road from the east. The Nazis were approaching far more quickly than he'd expected. They had to keep moving.

Checking the group for injuries, Luc decided they were okay for now. He quickly ducked his head out of the alleyway to see if the coast was clear. It was, but he could also see the flaming wreckage where Monique and Nic's house had stood moments before. It had taken a direct hit, and now it—and all the souls who had stayed inside—were gone.

"Come on, everyone. We need to go now," Luc ordered. "Turn to the right. Run for the park. Don't stop. Don't look back. My truck is the red one. When you get there, jump into the back. I'll be right behind you. Go!"

One by one the group climbed to their feet, moved to the corner, and sprinted for the truck.

All but Monique.

"I can't leave Nic," she cried. "We have to find him."

Luc hesitated but only for a moment. He had no choice. He had to tell her. He set Jacqueline down, then said bluntly and without emotion, "He's dead."

"What? No. He's helping people."

Luc grabbed Monique by the shoulders and stared into her eyes. "Monique, listen to me. Nic is dead."

"No, no, he's—"

"Listen, Monique. Nic is dead. He's gone. He was trying to help people. He helped carry a wounded man into the church. I was about to follow him there myself. But before I got there, the bombs began to fall. They destroyed the church. They killed everyone inside. I watched it happen. I'm sorry. But he's gone."

Just as Luc feared, Monique collapsed in his arms. She was sobbing uncontrollably, crying, *"No, no, no!"*

Luc set her down gently, then glanced across the park. The rest of the group had reached the truck. They were waiting for him. They were counting on him. He again scooped up Jacqueline in his arms. Then he pleaded with Monique to come with him. They had to go, but she would not budge. She collapsed in a heap on the ground, wailing.

Luc turned and started toward the truck. Jacqueline screamed, *"Mommy, Mommy!"* The girl struggled to break free, to go back to her mother, the only parent she had left. But Luc held his niece tighter and ran all the faster.

As he approached the pickup truck, a 1939 Ford import, he could see everyone huddled in the back. He could see the horror in their eyes, the shock that he could be so heartless as to leave his own sister in a war zone and rip her little girl away from her. But he had no time for sentimentality or explanation. He reached the truck and quickly handed Jacqueline to one of the mothers who knew her best. Then he raced around to the other side of the truck, fumbled for his keys, unlocked the cab, and jumped into the driver's seat. Three seconds later he was gunning the engine, and they were off.

One explosion after another ripped through Sedan. Those residents who were not dead were running for their lives, heading for the countryside on the flimsy premise that they could outrun the Nazi war machine. Anyone with a car or truck was on the move as well, with whatever valuables they'd had time to grab. But now vehicles clogged every available street out of town and were sitting ducks when the Luftwaffe came swooping down to strafe them with 20mm cannon fire.

Luc, however, was not following them. Instead he raced back to the corner where he had left his sister. Reaching the spot, he slammed on the brakes, jumped out—leaving the engine running—and ran over to Monique, who was still weeping and shivering against a brick wall. With no time to be gentle, he grabbed her by the arms and pulled her to the truck, and then, opening the passenger-side door, he pushed her inside and slammed the door shut.

Back in the driver's seat, he slammed his own door and hit the gas.

"Hold on!" he yelled to the people in the back, then turned to Monique and ordered her to do the same.

He began driving but could see that to the west, the road heading toward the main bridge across the Meuse was jammed with cars and trucks and motorcycles of every kind. There didn't appear to be any way out. He dared not get stuck in a traffic jam. Nor did he have any intention of letting anyone in his care be captured by the Nazis. That was a death sentence, he knew. So he jammed the truck into first gear, then second, and raced along the eastern outskirts of town. Perhaps the town's other bridge—Pont Neuf—was not yet jammed. It was their only hope, but they hadn't much time. As he sped down one side street after another, zigzagging his way through the town, he could see the enemy forces rapidly approaching from his right.

Bombs continued dropping all around them, and Luc found himself drenched in sweat. Just then he heard an artillery round go whizzing over the truck. A split second later a small grocery store erupted into flames. Distracted, he made a wrong turn. He headed into a cul-de-sac and didn't realize it until he had gotten to the end. Screeching to a halt and praying everyone in the back was still safe, he threw the pickup into reverse, did a K-turn, and retraced his path. When he got back to the cross street, Rue de Pierremont, he took a hard left, heading once again for Pont Neuf.

The good news was that at the moment there was no one else on the street. It was deserted as far as the eye could see. Luc breathed a sigh of relief, but that was premature. Screaming erupted from everyone in the back of the truck. Just then Monique unexpectedly stopped crying. She craned her neck to see what the commotion was about and then went white as a sheet.

"Luc, behind you!" she shouted, the first words she had uttered since Luc put her in the truck.

Luc quickly glanced in the rearview mirror and gasped. A German tank was bearing down on them. He was stunned to see it already in town and even more stunned that it was no more than a hundred meters away. Machine-gun fire opened up behind him and with it came more screams. Trying to take evasive action, he began swerving back and forth across the empty boulevard, but he knew it wasn't enough. Rounds of ammunition kept hitting the tailgate of the truck and even the cab, forcing him to duck down repeatedly even as he fought to maintain control of the vehicle.

He hit the gas, trying to open up the distance between them and the tank. But he knew he had to get off this road. The machine guns kept firing, and he suddenly realized they were heading straight for a complex of army barracks near the heart of the town that was experiencing a withering bombing campaign. He glanced back again and saw the tank lowering its cannon and preparing to fire.

Saying a silent prayer that God would have mercy on them all, he again shouted for everyone to hold on, then slammed on the brakes, downshifted, and took a hard left turn onto some boulevard whose name he did not catch. As he did, he heard the tank fire and felt a projectile go whooshing behind them. The resulting explosion rocked the vehicle, but they kept on driving, weaving through streets that were completely empty. This sector of Sedan was now a ghost town, and Luc hoped the bridge was just as clear.

Moments later, they came around the bend. He could see Pont Neuf ahead. It wasn't empty. Indeed, the roads leading to it were filling with vehicles. More and more people were heading this way, but the traffic was moving, and they weren't far from the bridge now. The road shook from one explosion after another. German planes roared overhead, and Luc wondered where the French air force was. Why weren't the Nazis being engaged? It would take time for ground forces to launch a counteroffensive and try to hold—or perhaps retake—Sedan, but why weren't the Germans being countered in the air?

Finally they reached the bridge. A flash of panic rippled through Luc's body. He wondered what would happen if the Germans bombed the bridge while they were on it. But the thought passed quickly. The bridges were the very reason the Germans had targeted Sedan. Hitler's forces weren't going to bomb them. They were going to do everything they could to protect them.

Crossing Pont Neuf didn't turn out to be the problem. The problem was the other side. As he came around a bend, Luc found the road clogged with vehicles of every type. Now a new fear gripped him. No traffic jam had prevented their crossing the Meuse River. But one still might prevent them from successfully fleeing the German forces, which were at that very moment overrunning the town.

Seeing so many red taillights ahead, Luc slammed on the brakes. They came to a full stop. They were just idling there while the Nazi forces pressed their attack, closing in on the bridge with every passing moment.

Luc had to make a decision. He knew he could not hesitate. He could not ponder his options. There was no time to weigh pros and cons. Every second wasted brought death closer. He made his choice and didn't think twice. He was going to get these people out of harm's way. He was going to get them to Le Chambon. He was going to hug Claire and his girls before the night was through. That was all there was to it.

So he gunned the engine and turned the wheel hard to the left. He hopped a curb and accelerated. He began driving over people's lawns, through their backyards, across their fields. No one was around to stop him. Everyone on this side of Sedan had already evacuated.

After a few minutes, he came to the end of a cornfield and found the main road heading south. At first he was glad to reconnect with a real road, but he found it just as clogged as all the roads behind him. He didn't think twice. He veered into the lane of oncoming traffic and gunned the engine again. In any other circumstance, it would have seemed like an act of lunacy. But in this case there was no oncoming traffic. The lane was empty. Not a soul was heading north toward Sedan and the Belgian border. Why on earth would they? His fellow Frenchmen were following the rules, staying in the southbound lane. They weren't even thinking of using the northbound one. Luc could think of nothing else.

3

MAY 12, 1940
SEDAN, FRANCE

Colonel Klaus Von Strassen stepped out of the command car.

Under the cover of darkness and flanked by German soldiers bearing submachine guns at the ready, the Nazi officer slipped through the back door of a schoolhouse on the eastern edge of Sedan to see the nearly three dozen prisoners—men, women, and children—sitting in orderly rows on the floor. They had been forced to strip down to their underwear. Their feet and hands were bound tightly with ropes and chains. They were blindfolded and gagged. They sat shivering in the cool night air, thick with the smell of gunpowder and burning human flesh.

At thirty-five, Von Strassen was the youngest officer in General Heinz Wilhelm Guderian's notorious Nineteenth Panzer Corps. He was also arguably the most ambitious. He hailed from a proud German military family. His father had been a decorated general in the Great War. His grandfathers and great-grandfathers on both his father's and mother's sides had been high-ranking generals as well. As they headed into France, Guderian had put him in charge of rounding up, interrogating, and processing prisoners of war. At this Von Strassen excelled. No one on the general's staff was more efficient or more ruthless. But while Von Strassen appreciated his commander's confidence, he also felt insulted by the assignment. He had far grander ambitions. He wanted a panzer division of his own. He wanted to lead armies into battle. That's where the action was—and the glory.

For now, however, there was a job to be done, and Von Strassen was nothing if not fanatical about following orders and honoring the chain of command.

Removing a small flashlight from his coat pocket, he shone it around the room and surveyed the pitiful lot before him. He motioned impatiently to his adjutant and was handed a small stack of identification papers, which he quickly riffled through. Von Strassen concluded immediately that there was no one of value in the bunch. No military men. No intelligence officers. No one who likely had any information that could be of use.

"Stand up if you're a Jew," he ordered.

No one stood.

"I'm only going to say it one more time," Von Strassen growled. "You're all going to be sent to a prison camp—a labor camp, a work camp. You will remain there, serving the German war effort, until the war is over and *der Führer* decides your fate. But if you are Jewish, you will be treated specially. You will be treated differently. So you must stand to your feet if you are a Jew."

Still no one rose.

The colonel turned to his adjutant. "Have all the men stand," he ordered. "Have them drop their pants. Then we will know who is a kike and who is not."

It took only a moment, but soon all the men were standing, their bodies trembling, their knees shaking. One by one, they removed their underwear. Von Strassen shone his flashlight at their private parts. Three were found to be circumcised—a father, his teenage son, and his six-year-old son.

"Away with them," Von Strassen spat. "Send them to Auschwitz."

4

MAY 13, 1940

The German bombers kept coming.

In town after town, Jean-Luc Leclerc could hear the air-raid sirens. But he refused to stop, refused to take shelter. He had one mission, and that was to reach Le Chambon, no matter what it took. He desperately wanted to hug his daughter Lilly, only six years old, and her sister, Madeline, not quite four. He wanted to hold them and never let them go. Even more he wanted to hold his beloved Claire. Surely she had heard about the German invasion. She was constantly listening to the news from Paris and London on the radio. He couldn't imagine the anxiety she was going through.

Finally, just after two in the morning, he reached his objective. As he pulled into the driveway of the farmhouse his parents had left him when they passed away a few years before, he could hear his two dogs welcoming him home. He could see lights coming on inside, and before he knew it, Claire was opening the front door, wrapped in a bathrobe and wearing no makeup. Her already-pale face went completely ashen when she saw all those who were in the pickup truck with her husband. Their clothes were torn. Their hands and faces were covered in blood and dust. They looked as shell-shocked as they felt. What's more, they were hungry and thirsty and exhausted and grieving their families and friends and the town they had left behind.

"I heard, on the wireless," Claire said without missing a beat. "It's all anyone is talking about. Thank God you're okay. Come in. All of you, please come in. We will get you something to eat and give you a place to sleep and a hot bath. Come in; don't be shy. You're with friends here."

Luc herded them all inside. In the commotion, he didn't get a hug or a kiss from Claire after all. She was too busy scrambling to help the others. It did not bother him in the slightest. He knew they would be alone together soon enough. For now she was doing what she did best—serving those who needed her most. She was remarkable that way, Luc thought. It was a gift she had, and he loved to see her use it. He stood in the doorway for a moment, watching her comfort each guest and get them settled in the living room or the dining room. She looked up, and he caught her eye. She winked at him, and he returned the favor.

The girls, he assumed, were surely tucked in bed and asleep. He would check in on them in a minute. First Luc turned and walked outside to the truck. He opened the passenger-side door and gently put his hand on Monique's shoulder. She was sound asleep, her arms wrapped around Jacqueline's frail little body, the pink party dress all ripped and dirty and covered in blood.

"We're home, you two," he whispered. "Come on, let's get you inside."

After some initial resistance, Monique finally roused, and Luc got them inside and settled upstairs in the room that once had been Monique's when they were growing up. Now it was a guest room, quiet and cozy and safe.

Luc went to fetch them some fresh towels and brought back a pot of tea and some fruit as well. Monique nodded her thanks but said nothing. She just began to weep softly again. So Luc held his eldest sister until both of them heard Jacqueline stirring on the bed, asking for her daddy. At that, Luc gave Monique a kiss on the forehead, slipped out of the room so the two of them could be alone, and closed the door behind him.

He peeked in on Lilly and Madeline. They were fast asleep, cuddled together in the same bed, holding their little blankets and stuffed animals. Lilly's right arm was draped over her younger sister. Luc said a prayer over them, then kissed them both and quietly slipped out of their room.

As he came down the stairs, Claire appeared around the corner, a load of towels and fresh linens in her arms. She gave him a quick kiss and a weary smile. "Was that Monique and Jacqueline you just took up?" she asked.

"Yes. I put them in the guest room, if that's okay."

"Of course," Claire said. "But will there be enough room for Nic? Actually, come to think of it, where is Nic? I haven't seen him yet."

Luc looked down at his feet. Then he told her the awful truth.

5

Luc finally collapsed into bed just after four o'clock in the morning.

He knew he would have to be up soon. As soon as the sun peeked its head above the wooded hills behind their home, he and Claire would need to care for their own children as well as make breakfast for all their guests.

There was so much to do, so much to decide. How long would everyone stay? They certainly couldn't go back to Sedan, but could they really stay here? Monique and Jacqueline could, of course. But how could they house and feed and care for the others? Hopefully most of them had relatives in safer parts of France and could go there. That might take some time to sort out, but at least it would be a start. But for right now, it was too late. Both Luc and Claire were physically and emotionally spent, and they needed a little shut-eye.

It was not to be. No sooner had both of them closed their eyes than they were awakened by someone furiously pounding on the front door.

The two bit their lips and forced themselves out of bed. As they threw on their bathrobes and slippers, they speculated—in whispers, so as not to wake up the others—as to who could possibly be calling on them at such an hour. Luc figured it must be Pastor Chrétien or Pastor Émile—his colleagues at the church—or maybe the mayor, come to check on them and see if there was anything he could do to help. Surely they all would have heard the news on the wireless about the invasion of northern France. But Claire said no. Why would the pastors or the mayor come so early in the morning? Surely they would wait for daybreak, wouldn't they? No one in his right mind would be pounding on their door in the wee hours of the morning unless it was an emergency, she insisted. Then the same thought hit them both at the same time. What if it was the police or even the army?

The pounding continued. Ever more fearful that the whole house would be awakened by the racket, the couple made their way quickly to the vestibule.

When they opened the door, they were startled to see not the pastors or the mayor but a family on their porch. There was a father who appeared to be in his late forties or early fifties. There was a mother, too, not much younger, and three children—two boys and a girl—none of whom seemed older than fifteen or sixteen. Luc had never seen any of them before. Indeed, he had never seen anyone like them. Not in these parts. The father had a full beard, carefully groomed and going gray. He was dressed in a black suit and a black fedora with a white shirt and polished black leather shoes. The mother wore a dark-blue silk blouse, a black skirt that went down to her ankles, and a pretty silk scarf over her head. The children were fairly well dressed too, all of which seemed a bit out of place on the porch of a farmhouse before sunup. But what was most striking about them was not their clothing but the fear in their eyes.

"Monsieur Leclerc?" the father asked, his voice tired and gravelly.

"Yes, that is me," Luc replied. "Do I know you?"

"No. But my name is Léon Halévy. I know your brother in Brussels."

"You know Philippe?" Luc asked, startled by the connection.

"Of course, and Muriel and little Simon."

"Are they safe? Where are they now?"

"I do not know," Mr. Halévy said. "We are Jews. My father owned the building where your brother and his family rented a flat. When my father passed away a few years ago, he left the building to me. I became your brother's landlord. We've known the family for years. But when rumors of the Nazi invasion began several weeks ago, we made preparations to flee. We begged Philippe and Muriel to come with us. They are,

I must say, our dearest Gentile friends. But they did not think Hitler would really do it. We pleaded with them, 'Come with us. There is no more time.' But they refused. I'm afraid we could not wait any longer. Last Tuesday we fled the city. It broke our hearts to leave our friends and our home, but we simply couldn't take a chance on being captured by the Germans. We hear they are sending Jews to work camps all over Europe."

Luc looked at Claire. He could hardly believe what he was hearing, yet sadly it all rang true. He had been writing to his brother for months, urging him to bring his family to Le Chambon. But like Monique, Philippe would have none of it. He said he didn't have time to read Hitler's manifesto, *Mein Kampf*. He was not a "political man," he said. He had no time for rumors of war or invasion. He was a violin teacher. He had his classes, he had his lessons, he had his students to think about.

Looking back at the man, Luc asked how they had found their way to Le Chambon.

"Your brother spoke of you all the time," Mr. Halévy replied. "He spoke of this little town. He loved it so. He spoke of his childhood here. When we fled Brussels, we started for Switzerland, but we don't know anyone there. Then my wife thought of Le Chambon. She thought maybe we could find shelter here. This is why we have come. Is that true? Might you take us in, at least until we can figure out what to do next?"

Luc tensed. He wanted to say yes. He couldn't imagine saying no, not to any family that was fleeing the Nazis and especially not to a family who were friends with Philippe and Muriel. But neither could he bear to look over at Claire. The house was full. They had no idea how they were going to care for all those who had already come. He could only imagine the enormous burden she must be feeling, and now this? It wasn't fair to her. As much as it pained him, he would have to say no. They weren't running a refugee center. They were just putting up a few people for a few days. That was all.

But before he could utter a word, Claire spoke. "Of course you can stay with us, Mr. Halévy. Come in; please come in."

6

Luc felt he was living in a nightmare.

As the days passed, the group staying in his home settled into a routine of sorts. Night after night, the group gathered for dinner around the radio. Luc would invite Mr. Halévy to read a psalm and then say a blessing for the food as they all bowed their heads. Then Lilly and Madeline would serve baskets of freshly baked bread, and Claire would serve the meal, often one of her homemade soup recipes since money was tight and soup went the furthest. As they ate, they would listen to the latest news from Paris, as well as from the BBC in London. None of it was good. Not ever.

On the night of May 15, they listened in shock to details of Holland surrendering to the Nazis. By May 28, Belgium had formally surrendered too, though they had long since been overrun. They listened in silent horror to report after report of German forces blazing and murdering their way through northern France and moving steadily toward their beloved Paris. They couldn't imagine the Germans actually seizing the capital, but on the night of June 10, the BBC reported that the French government had begun evacuating Paris. Four days later, they wept upon hearing reports of the Nazis entering and occupying the capital. Soon the French were signing an armistice with Hitler. Prime Minister Reynaud was stepping down. Before they knew what was happening, the eighty-four-year-old Marshal Philippe Pétain, a puppet of Adolf Hitler, was suddenly the head of a new French government operating not out of Paris but out of the town of Vichy. To make matters worse, they heard reports that Hitler's forces were heading to northern France, now known as the Occupied Zone, while allowing Pétain to administrate the center and south, ostensibly now known as the Free Zone, though it could hardly be truly free with the jackboot of *der Führer* on their necks.

In the meantime, none of the folks who had come from Sedan with Monique and Jacqueline had departed. Nor had the Halévy family from Brussels. Homeless and shell-shocked, none of them seemed to know where else to go or what else to do. The Europe they had all known, the Europe they had all grown up in and loved, was gone, in the hands of a madman who was now attempting to conquer Britain and North Africa as well.

Luc and Claire gathered in their bedroom late at night, after each day's work was done, after everyone else had gone to sleep, after they themselves had washed and changed and gotten ready for bed. Together, they got down on their knees and prayed. They thanked the Lord for having mercy on them all, for saving their lives and providing for their essential needs. They asked for mercy for their country and the whole of Europe. They took turns praying for specific family members or friends.

Most of all, they pleaded with the Lord for wisdom. What exactly were they supposed to do with a houseful of people? How were they supposed to care and provide for them while meeting their own needs? They had no idea. A pastor's allowance didn't go far. Monique had money, but it had probably all been stolen by the Nazis by now.

Still, there were some glimmers of hope. Luc's fellow pastors were becoming a great support. They had no problem with caring for so many people. To the contrary, they were thrilled. In a wonderful answer to prayer, Chrétien and Émile and their wives brought over bushels of fruit and vegetables to help feed everyone. They brought fresh clothes so the group didn't have to wear the same things day after day.

One morning, Émile showed up with new identity papers for each person and a plan to move most of them in with other families, including his own, to lighten the burden and not draw so much attention to Luc and Claire, lest the authorities start asking questions.

Chrétien showed special kindness to the Jewish family. Hearing rumors that Jews throughout Nazi-occupied Europe were being forced to wear yellow stars, he brought them new papers that said they were French citizens and Gentiles, and he brought them clothes to make them look like locals. One afternoon while visiting Luc and Claire, he smiled and declared, "What an honor to be chosen to care for God's chosen people."

Luc reflected on that for the next few days. He hadn't really thought about it as an honor. It just seemed the right thing to do. The Bible commanded him to love his neighbors. Weren't these his neighbors, even if they didn't believe the same things he believed?

Then one day he heard the whistle of the daily one o'clock train pulling into the station. A few minutes later, he heard more pounding on his front door. To his astonishment, there were three families—more than twenty people total—standing on his front porch. They were dressed much as the Halévys had been dressed the night they arrived, and they had that unmistakable look of fear in their eyes.

"We've heard you take in Jews," said one of the elders of the group. "Is it true?"

This time, before he'd even taken time to think about what he was doing, Luc heard himself saying, "Of course. Come in; please come in."

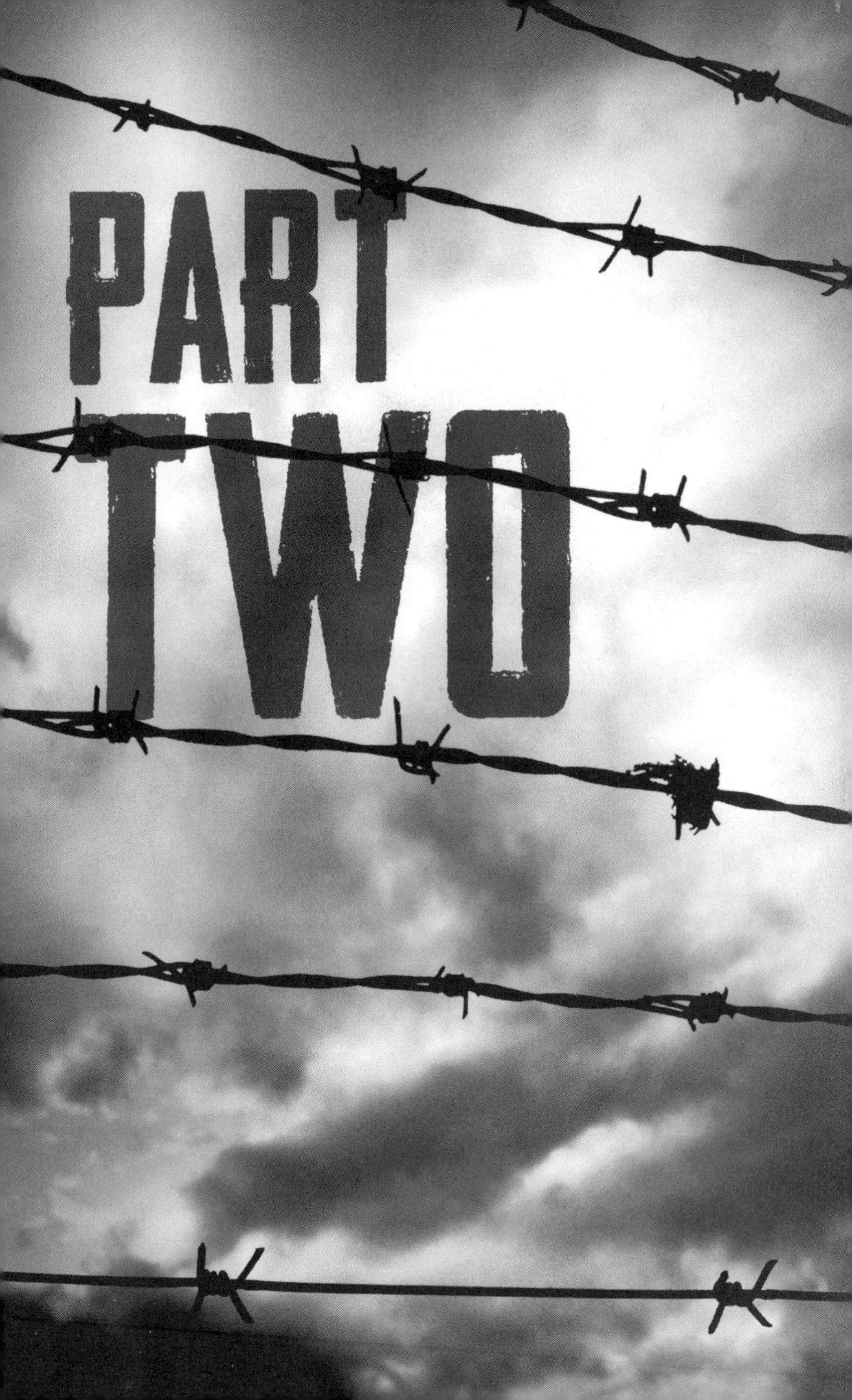
PART
TWO

7

TWO YEARS EARLIER
NOVEMBER 9, 1938
SIEGEN, GERMANY

Jacob Weisz feared the power he held in his hands.

The power to shatter. To wound. To take a man's life. But his uncle Avraham assured him he was doing nothing wrong. To the contrary, Avi insisted, this was his duty, and this was his moment.

"There is a time for every activity under the sun," Avi explained. "That's what Solomon said. A time to give birth and a time to die. A time to kill and a time to heal. A time for war and a time for peace. It's not for us to choose our times, Jacob. But we must be ready when they come."

His uncle's words sounded wise. They might even be right. But they didn't help. Not here. Not now.

Jacob gripped the walnut-wood stock of the Mauser rifle. It felt heavy and cold in his hands. He didn't want to do it. He had never wanted to. But who was he to talk back? He was just a boy, only seventeen. His days were not his own to plan. Neither was his destiny.

Jacob could feel his heart beating wildly in his chest, and try as he might, he could not slow his breathing. He wiped the perspiration from one hand, then the other, then steadied his grip on the Karabiner 98.

He had no idea where the rifle had come from. It simply seemed to appear one day in the little cabin in the forest, his uncle's "home away from home." Jacob had never asked him where he got it, nor would he.

Slowly, Jacob pulled back the bolt until he heard the single round lift from the magazine. Then, as carefully and as quietly as he could—trying to remember everything his uncle had taught him—he pushed the bolt forward until the round entered the chamber and the bolt locked into place.

Jacob lay absolutely still, flat on his stomach on the cold, hard ground, covered in leaves, deep in the woods on the leeward side of the mountains near the little town of Siegen. It was a place he knew well. He'd grown up on these slopes. He'd spent every summer hiking and jogging up and down the entire range, alone and with his uncle. He knew every cave, every outcropping, every coppice. It was one of the joys of his childhood, a season that was now hurriedly setting like the sun over the ridge just above him.

Though he didn't understand it all, Jacob understood that a terrible darkness was falling upon the land. Just a few years before, Adolf Hitler and his Brownshirts had surged to power. Now they held Germany by the throat. The Gestapo was rapidly creating a cruel and brutal police state that treated all but true Aryans like dogs and swine.

That was certainly true for Jews like the Weisz family. In just the last few years, they and all of the Jewish families in Germany had been stripped of their citizenship and denied many of their most basic rights. Jacob's father, an esteemed professor of German history, had been summarily fired from his prestigious post at Frederick William University in Berlin. The Weisz family had been forced out of their beautiful, spacious home in the suburbs of the capital. They'd had a big red *J* stamped on their official papers and had been denied permission to leave the country. So they had left Berlin and made a new home in Siegen.

But the trouble hadn't stopped. Longtime family friends had begun to avoid Jacob's family. He'd seen his father openly mocked in the street. Jacob, too, had been taunted, spat upon, even beaten up once by a gang of Brownshirts. His parents forbade him to retaliate or to do anything that could provoke further hostility. But now Uncle Avi said the time to fight back had come.

"It's time, Jacob," Avi had said. "You're no longer a boy. You're becoming a man. What are you now—five feet eight, 160 pounds?"

Jacob shrugged and mumbled, "Something like that." Actually, he was now five-ten, 170 pounds. But he was not one to correct his elders.

Ominous thunderclouds hung in the late-afternoon November air. A storm was coming. It was not the first of the season, but Jacob sensed it would be fierce. The shadows around him were growing longer. The temperature was growing colder, and now the soaring, bushy, aromatic pine trees were swaying in the breeze.

Jacob could faintly detect the smell of a wood fire off to the east, off toward Siegen, and he imagined it wafting to him from his very own home. He wondered, if only for a moment, what his mother and Ruthie were preparing for supper. Ruthie was only nine, but she was Mama's little helper and already an accomplished cook. His mouth began to water.

Maybe they're making veal schnitzel. Maybe latkes. Maybe even some apple strudel for dessert. His favorite. Could it be?

Jacob pictured them cooking and talking and laughing together in the kitchen, as they loved to do so often. He could see his father stoking the fire, then easing into his rocking chair. Maybe he was sitting down to a good book. Jacob hoped so. A pall seemed to be settling over their country and their home, and Jacob ached for the clocks to be turned back, for life to return to the way it had been before Hitler's rise to power, when things were simple and sweet and calm and quiet.

Jacob liked things quiet, and now he wished he were back in the three-story house his uncle owned on Rubensstrasse. How he longed to be sitting around the hearth, sipping hot tea and listening to Papa tell tales of adventures in faraway lands. Sometimes his mama asked Jacob to get out his grandfather's violin and play something from Beethoven, Bach, Mozart, or Mendelssohn. In a perfect world, Jacob would finish high school and go to a conservatory to become one of the world's great violinists. He dreamed of attending the National Conservatory of Music in Leipzig, founded by Mendelssohn himself. He dreamed of holding an actual Stradivarius in his hands. But it was not a perfect world. Far from it.

And suddenly he could feel his uncle's immense disapproval.

Focus, Jacob, he could hear Avi saying, though not a word was spoken. The only sound was a hawk downrange and the slight rustling of Jacob's target just ahead. *No distractions. No confusions. Just clear your head and focus.*

Jacob closed one eye and squinted with the other. He'd hesitated long enough. He didn't want his uncle to think him cowardly or indecisive. He was a good boy. Good and quiet and obedient and true, and he knew the sooner he did it, the sooner it would be over. Looking through the scope, he adjusted for the crosswind and pulled the trigger.

The explosion echoed across the mountains and down the Westphalia valley. And for a moment, Jacob's heart seemed to stop.

"You missed," his uncle sighed.

Jacob watched helplessly as the red deer scampered away and every bird for a kilometer scattered and screeched. And suddenly he felt cold and lonely. He hated to let anyone down, least of all his uncle. But once again he had.

Only a few weeks had passed since his uncle had begun teaching him to hunt. His skills were improving, and he knew he would get the hang of it eventually. But he also knew that hunting for food wasn't his uncle's primary objective. Avi wanted Jacob to know how to defend himself and his family. But Jacob had been uneasy about all of it from the start. His father forbade any discussion of guns, much less the handling of them. His mother would smile and say if God wanted Jews to hunt for their food, he would never have created butchers. Little Ruthie was too young to care. But Avi was insistent that Jacob learn to handle a weapon—and in the process tell no one.

"Az men krigt zikh miten rov, muz men sholem zein miten shainker," Avi had said when he first put the rifle in Jacob's hands.

The old Yiddish proverb could be roughly translated as, "If you're at odds with your rabbi, make peace with your bartender." His uncle offered no explanation, but as Jacob had chewed on its meaning, he had concluded that Avi meant something like, "Always be prepared" or "Have a plan B." The problem was, Jacob didn't want a plan B. He didn't want life to change. He wanted things to be the way they had always been.

"I'm sorry," he said at last, handing over the rifle and a handful of unused bullets.

"You should be," his uncle said. "Do you want your family to starve?" Avi didn't laugh. He didn't smile. He wasn't joshing. He was deadly serious.

Then, without saying another word, he turned toward the path and headed back down the mountain.

Jacob stood there in the forest alone, chilled to the bone, stinging from his uncle's rebuke, covered in mud, and fighting back tears.

8

Jacob said nothing on the long hike back to the cabin.

For the first half hour or so, Avi was silent as well. He seemed uncharacteristically sullen, his thoughts far away. But eventually the burden on his heart seemed to lift, if only for a while, and he relaxed. He slowed his pace, let Jacob catch up, and then began to talk. That was a good sign, Jacob thought, for Uncle Avi always talked when he was in fine spirits.

As he talked, Avi seemed to forget the fact that his nephew had missed everything he had fired at that day—two rabbits, a pheasant, and the deer. He seemed deeply satisfied just to be teaching his brother's only son to hunt. For the better part of the next hour, he told stories of how he had learned to shoot from an uncle of his and how Jacob's father had refused to go hunting, regarding it as beneath his station. Never one to miss an opportunity to teach his young protégé, Avi kept shifting from German to Polish to Slovak to English and then back to German—all languages Jacob knew well or in which he was steadily becoming proficient.

Jacob was good at languages. With a remarkable memory, he picked them up quickly even if he used them infrequently. Small talk had never been his strong suit.

"Enough of all that," Avi said, patting Jacob gently on the back. "Let's get this place squared away and then get you back home as quick as we can. I can only imagine what your mother and Ruthie are cooking up."

Jacob moved immediately to the kitchen to wash the few dishes in the sink. Then he watched silently as Avi pulled back the tattered carpet and pried up several floorboards. Under the floor was an enormous steel trunk about five feet long and several feet wide, sealed with a large combination lock. Avi bent down, dialed in the combination, and opened the trunk, revealing a stash of four additional Mauser rifles. He quickly replaced the fifth rifle in the trunk and closed and locked the case. Then he opened a smaller steel box, where he stored the spare rounds.

Soon Jacob was folding and storing their blankets and pillows. Then he tidied up his growing collection of history books, novels, textbooks, and encyclopedias in the range of languages he was expected to master. Each was a precious gift from Avi. Jacob's parents had no money to buy books anymore. Indeed, ever since his father had been fired from the university, they had barely enough money to make ends meet. Avi, on the other hand, was never without plenty of reichsmarks, and he was the most generous man Jacob had ever met, especially when it came to Jacob's education.

More than four years had passed since Jacob last stepped into a government school. His formal education had come to an abrupt end when *der Führer* had risen to power as Reich Chancellor in 1933. It was then that Jacob's father, the renowned Dr. Reuben Weisz, had been "relieved" of his duties at the university. Soon the family had lost their house, their savings, and most of the people they once thought were their friends.

That's when Avi had stepped in to help. He'd offered his elder brother the opportunity to manage the metalworking shop he owned in Siegen. And he had invited his brother's family to live in the town house on Rubensstrasse at a reduced rent.

A proud man, Dr. Weisz had initially turned down the offer. He was a scholar, not a tradesman or a clerk. This was Germany. He was lettered. He would teach. He would write. He would publish and support his family along the way. But soon it became painfully obvious that these were no longer options for Jews in Germany. How Uncle Avi continued to own and run several businesses, Jacob had never understood.

He dared not ask. He was simply grateful. After all, it had soon become painfully obvious that the Weisz family had no options but Avi's metal-working shop. So they said yes and moved 414 kilometers southwest of the German capital, just over five hours by car, to the picturesque little town of forty thousand souls on the river Sieg.

Jacob had feared everything about the move and the hardships on the road ahead. To his surprise, however, it hadn't been nearly as bad as he'd feared—difficult, to be sure, but bearable. His mother taught him mathematics, literature, and language at home during the day. His father taught him German history and world history and culture in the evenings. And whenever he could get away from his factories, Uncle Avi came and took him up into the mountains to hike and to fix things and learn to work with his hands.

Jacob climbed into the passenger seat of the gray two-door Adler Standard 6 as Avi locked up the cabin. Soon they were wending their way through the thick growth of trees and carefully proceeding down the mountain.

"So, young man, is there a *fräulein* that has caught your eye?" Avi asked out of the clear blue.

Jacob was grateful night had fallen. Perhaps his uncle wouldn't see his face turn red. He shrugged as if the answer were no.

"Nonsense," Avi said. "A fine-looking young man like you, Jacob? Strong. Tall. Good face. A kind and gentle soul. You must be driving all the girls at *shul* crazy."

Jacob's mouth went dry. He knew his uncle was just teasing, but he hated being put on the spot. Especially on this subject. So he mumbled something and hoped the topic would change quickly.

The truth was, though he was loath to admit it, a young girl had caught his attention. Naomi Silver. She was also seventeen. Her family lived just around the corner, over the clock shop that her father owned. She, too, loved playing the violin. In fact, her teacher was the same as his, and her biweekly lessons finished just before his began. She was even more shy than he was. They rarely talked. He certainly had not made his feelings known to her. But every now and then she would catch his eye as she walked out of her lessons, clutching her violin by her side, and she would smile at him.

There was only one problem. Well, two, really. One, of course, was that he had never gotten up the nerve to talk to her, even though he sensed that she respected him, perhaps even liked him. The other was that his friend Hans Meyer was interested in her too—and Hans was much better looking and much more outgoing than Jacob. Plus, he had a motorbike. It was his brother's, actually, but Hans often "borrowed" it and really got girls' attention when he did.

Jacob had never confided in Hans how much he liked Naomi. But earlier that week, Hans had told Jacob that he liked her and was planning to invite her to an upcoming concert. Inside, Jacob was devastated, but characteristically he had kept his feelings to himself. No one knew what Jacob Weisz was really thinking. Not Naomi. Not Hans. Not his family. Not even Uncle Avi, though Avi seemed to understand Jacob better than most.

Fortunately, before Jacob was forced to reply, the sedan rolled off the gravelly mountain path. He saw Siegen as they came around a bend, and when he did, his eyes went wide. The night air was filled with a strange and eerie glow. He could see flames shooting twenty, thirty, maybe forty feet into the moonless sky, and not just from one building but from dozens. "What is it, Uncle?" he gasped. "What is happening?"

At first Jacob was merely bewildered. But he quickly grew scared. There was madness in the air, a sense of frenzy he had never seen or felt before. As they entered the outskirts of Siegen, Jacob could see people running from all directions. People he knew. Neighbors of theirs. He assumed, of course, they were rushing to put out the fires, but the deeper they drove into town, the clearer it was that this was not the case at all.

As they turned up Hundgasse Street, they found their way blocked by a crowd—at least a hundred strong—gathered in the middle of the street in front of Herr Berger's shop. Herr Berger was Siegen's tailor. He was a fine, sweet man and a devout Jew. His son, Eli, was also a tailor and a close friend of Jacob's father as well as the cantor at their *shul.*

The crowd was shouting, screaming obscenities, their faces contorted. They were pounding on Herr Berger's front door, demanding he come out, but to no avail. Then someone in the crowd threw a stone through the shop's front window. Someone else lit a torch and tossed it into the shop, and it, too, began to be engulfed by flames, like so many other shops nearby.

Flames leaped from the structure. Billows of thick, black smoke poured forth. Then suddenly Herr Berger came rushing out the front door. He fell to his knees before the crowd, pleading for mercy. But the mob gave him none. They descended upon him in a blind rage, punching and kicking him as he shrieked in agony.

Jacob was aghast. Herr Berger was old, in his late seventies at least. He was growing frail, and his hearing was beginning to fade. But he was a hard worker, meticulous in his craft, and Jacob regarded him as one of the kindest men in the town.

"Why, Uncle?" Jacob asked. "Why are they doing this?"

Abruptly, Avi pulled the Adler around a corner onto a street that, for the moment at least, was as quiet as it was deserted. Avi slammed on the brakes and shut down the engine. Then he turned sharply and stared into Jacob's eyes.

"Because he's a Jew," Avi whispered. "They're killing him because he's a Jew."

9

"Stay here," Avi ordered, jumping out of the car.

"Why? Where are you going?" Jacob asked, seeing a look in his uncle's eyes he'd never seen before.

"Just stay here," Avi insisted. "If you're in danger, run straight home. Don't worry about me. I'll find you later." He slammed the door and headed for the mob.

Jacob couldn't comprehend what was happening. His uncle wasn't actually going to try to save Herr Berger, was he? Avi was unarmed. He was vastly outnumbered. It was suicide.

Jumping out of the car, Jacob raced up the street, then grabbed his uncle and swung him around. "Uncle, stop!" he said.

"Get back in the car," his uncle ordered.

Nearby, Jacob heard what he thought was more windows being smashed, but when he turned to look, he saw a group of wild-eyed teenagers not much older than himself tossing fine china, lamps, and other valuables out a second-story window. It was the flat owned by Mrs. Lowenstein, Jacob realized, the grieving widow of Rabbi Lowenstein, so recently departed due to a massive heart attack.

"Kill the Jews! Kill them all!" someone shouted.

"Go back to the car, Jacob!"

"No, Uncle, we need to get off the streets now. We need to—"

"I'm not going to say it again," Avi ordered, his voice low and fierce. "Go back to the car, now."

"I beg you, don't do this thing," Jacob pleaded.

"You wouldn't have me act to save this man's life?" Avi asked, his countenance signaling a brutal combination of anger and disappointment.

Jacob didn't know what to say. He didn't want to sound cold or callous. He wasn't a mean, heartless person. He did feel compassion for Herr Berger and for Mrs. Lowenstein, too. But none of that overrode the sheer terror he felt at that moment. Nor did it override his absolute certainty that if he didn't stop his uncle from this act of madness, they would both be dead in minutes.

"Please, Uncle—take me home," Jacob finally said, staring at his muddy boots.

"No, you answer me," Avi growled, grabbing both of Jacob's shoulders and forcing his nephew to look him square in the eye. "You're really telling me you wouldn't act to save a man's life?"

Jacob tried to look away, but Avi wouldn't let him. He tried to answer, but the words would not come. He was trembling. His eyes were filling with tears. He hated confrontation. He was tongue-tied and embarrassed. He feared that at any moment the crowd would be finished with Herr Berger and would come rushing around the corner looking for new victims for their pogrom.

"I don't . . . I just . . . ," he stammered, confused and defeated. "I'm sorry, Uncle—I . . . I don't know . . ."

Again he looked down at his boots. He genuinely expected his uncle to slap him, drag him back to the car, and lock him in. But something else happened, something he did not expect.

"Actually, you do know, Jacob," Avi said, his voice suddenly gentle and curiously warm, his grip on Jacob's shoulders now loosening. "Didn't you just try to save my life?"

At that, Jacob looked up into his uncle's eyes. But before he could reply, he heard a voice calling them into a doorway. He was startled by how close it was and how familiar. He hadn't realized anyone was nearby.

"Herr Mueller?" Avi said, squinting in the darkness. "Is that you?"

"Get in here, you fools," the voice said.

Avi quickly obeyed the older man, and Jacob followed, stepping off the street and into the man's bakery.

Standing before them was Herr Mueller. He was as pale as a ghost. "Something has happened," the baker said. "Something terrible."

"Yes, we know, Herr Mueller," Avi replied. "We just saw the mob and we—"

"No, no, something worse," Herr Mueller said. "Something unspeakable."

The man's hands were shaking. Beads of perspiration gleamed on his forehead. His eyes were red and moist and somewhat glazed.

"The whole town," he said, his voice quivering. "They've all gone mad. They've burned down the synagogue. They're attacking the shops, the ones owned by Jews. They're beating anyone they can find, anyone who is a Jew. And now I have to show you. You must come. I carried her from the street, where they left her . . ." His voice trailed off.

"What?" Avi asked. "What is it?"

But Herr Mueller would not—or could not—speak anymore. Trembling, he took Avi and Jacob by the arms. He led them through the darkened front room of the bakery, past all its cases of pastries, pies, cakes, and strudels. They passed through the darkened kitchen, all its surfaces covered with a fine dust of flour and yeast. Into the back room, a storeroom of sorts. When they arrived, Herr Mueller took a small flashlight from his pocket and turned back to them one last time, then switched the flashlight on and pointed it at the crumpled body of a little girl, no older than ten.

Jacob gasped, his right hand involuntarily covering his mouth as he staggered backward. Avi gasped as well but took two steps forward, trying to get a better look.

"What happened?" Avi asked, his voice quavering.

The baker said nothing.

"Is she dead?" Avi asked.

Herr Mueller nodded.

"Are you sure?" Avi pressed, though for the moment he seemed paralyzed, unable to reach down and check for himself.

Jacob, too, was stiff as a board, unable to move, unable to react at all. But he did not have to ask who the girl was. Though she was lying facedown on the dirty tiled floor, a pool of blood around her, he already knew. He knew this pale-blue dress, trimmed with white lace. He recognized it, even torn and covered in blood. He knew these black patent-leather shoes. Jacob could not see her face, but he didn't need to see it. Indeed, he didn't want to see it. He knew immediately who it was. This was the dress Herr Berger had made for a discount. These were the shoes that Frau Bloom had special-ordered from Munich. He recognized the gold bracelet on the girl's right wrist as the one Mama had given her on her ninth birthday.

Avi finally leaned down and carefully rolled the little girl over.

Instinctively, Jacob covered his eyes and looked away. But finally he looked back and winced. There was no mistaking the bitter truth.

This was his sister, Ruth.

10

Ruth's eyes were frozen open in a frightful, glassy stare.

Jacob suddenly became extremely ill. He turned away and vomited. His vision began to blur. His head began to spin. His eyes filled with tears. He was about to cry out in anguish, but Herr Mueller saw him and grabbed him and covered his mouth.

"No, my son!" he whispered. "You mustn't cry. Not here. It's too dangerous. Go to your family. Tell them what happened and get them to safety."

Then he turned to Avi. "When the madness ends, I will bring her body, washed and wrapped in linens. We will make for her a proper burial, I assure you. But for now you both must go. You don't have much time."

Avi hesitated, but only for a moment. There was nothing they could do for Ruthie now, and Herr Mueller was right. They had to move before the mob turned on them. He ordered Jacob to follow him and then broke into a sprint, back to the car, with Jacob close on his heels.

As shops and houses went up in flames, as the wrenching cries of Jewish mothers and fathers rose into the night, they both jumped into the Adler. Avi gunned the engine and sped down the shadowy streets of Siegen faster than Jacob had ever seen him drive. He said nothing on the journey. His face showed no emotion. Not anger. Not grief. Not confusion or fear. Shock, perhaps, but Jacob was in no position to assess his uncle's reaction properly, for he was in shock as well.

Finally they pulled onto Rubensstrasse and parked in front of number twenty-three, the three-story walk-up Avi had purchased before the *Weltkrieg*, what the rest of Europe was calling the Great War. It was a simple but sturdy house; Jacob's family had rented it from Avi for nearly five years. But as Jacob forced himself to open the car door and stepped out onto the cold sidewalk and made himself walk up the stone steps, he knew in his heart and his soul that their lives would never be the same.

Jacob opened the front door and immediately saw the anxiety in his parents' eyes. They rushed to him, but he could not make out what they were saying. Though they were standing right before him, it was as if their voices were miles away. He perceived they were asking something, but he didn't know what. He tried to focus, tried to concentrate on the sounds or at least the movement of their lips. But he couldn't. His father was pleading with him to talk. His mother was shaking with fright. They were demanding something from him. But it was all murky and indistinct. It was as if a fog had descended upon the room. Jacob couldn't hear, couldn't think, couldn't reason, couldn't speak—that is, until he heard Avi speak up behind him.

"I'm so sorry, but Ruthie is dead," Avi said.

Then Jacob watched as his mother collapsed to the floor and let out a shriek. It was loud and shrill and piercing and could, Jacob was certain, be heard for blocks. Jacob had never heard a human being make such a sound. It was an unnatural, grief-stricken wail—utterly pained, lost, and devoid of hope.

11

After two days, the violence ended, and the fires were extinguished.

Some sense of order began to be restored, though every Jewish family was deeply shaken and fearful of what might happen next. For the next seven days, the Weisz family sat shivah. They mourned and wept and tried to make sense of their loss.

Hans Meyer and his family from the other end of the street stopped by one day to sit with them. Another time the Silvers from around the corner, including Naomi and her sisters, came. Jacob was grateful for their thoughtfulness, but he could not make eye contact with Naomi. He was stricken with grief, unable to process what had just happened, much less able to articulate how he was feeling about it.

Few spoke more than simple condolences. Jacob just looked down at the floor and nodded when spoken to. What was there to say? Still, when the rare visitor came with hard news, Jacob found himself determined to eavesdrop on the conversations of his father and his friends—and Uncle Avi, during his occasional visits. He had hoped that the horror they had endured in Siegen was somehow an isolated incident. What he found, however, was just the opposite.

One businessman who came to see Dr. Weisz from Vienna told them the anti-Jewish rampages had occurred all throughout Germany, Austria, and Czechoslovakia. What's more, it seemed as if they had all been coordinated. The man from Vienna said he'd heard that at least ninety Jews had been murdered. Then Father told him that their Ruth had been murdered that night, though they still weren't certain how it had come about exactly.

"Ninety-one, then," the man said softly, respectfully. "I did not know. I am very sorry. I will tell the others. She will not be forgotten."

A few days later, a friend of Jacob's father came through town from Dresden, bringing even more ominous news.

"Have you heard what Frick has done?" the man asked.

"Minister Frick?" Jacob's father asked. Jacob knew he was referring to Wilhelm Frick, the German interior minister.

"Who else?"

"No, we've heard nothing."

"With Herr Hitler's consent, he just passed a new ordinance," the man said. "It's a law called the Regulations against Jews' Possession of Weapons. Effective immediately, no Jew in Germany has the right to own, possess, or carry a gun. All weapons and ammunition in the possession of Jews must be turned over forthwith. Any Jews caught with a handgun or rifle will be imprisoned and fined."

"And?" Dr. Weisz asked. "I'm no sportsman. Are you?"

"No, I'm not," the man from Dresden said. "But don't you see? These attacks on our communities are just the beginning. Now Hitler is disarming us, and when we are completely defenseless, he will come for us, for all of us. Mark my words."

Jacob was frightened. He wished Uncle Avi were there. He would understand. But it was clear that his father did not see the seriousness of the threat, even after Ruth's death. Dr. Weisz grieved over his daughter, to be sure, but he absolutely refused to believe it represented the policy of the Third Reich.

Jacob found himself deeply troubled by the news but even more so by the realization that his father still seemed so unwilling to face up to the dangers Hitler posed to the Jewish people—not just in Germany but throughout Europe. He still seemed to think this was a brief anomaly, not the beginning of a far greater evil.

Toward the end of December, a rabbi from Berlin, a dear friend of Dr. Weisz from his days at the university, came through town and stopped for a very brief visit. He said guardedly that a new word was being used in private Jewish circles in Berlin to describe the attacks on the Jews on November 9 and 10—*Kristallnacht*, the Night of Broken Glass. The rabbi said Siegen's synagogue hadn't been the only one burned to the ground. A total of some 265 synagogues had been burned, and an estimated 7,500 Jewish businesses had been ransacked.

"*Der Führer* even ordered his Brownshirts to desecrate Jewish cemeteries all over the country," the rabbi said. "You should pack up your things and take your family out of Germany before it's too late."

Dr. Weisz was aghast at the notion of leaving the Fatherland, and he remonstrated with his friend for even proposing such an objectionable notion. "The Weisz family are good Germans," he insisted. "We will never leave our home. You should be ashamed of yourself for even suggesting such a thing."

The rabbi argued with him at length. He said he and his family were leaving for England within days. He was urging every Jew he could find to get out before the end of the month.

Jacob found the man's arguments compelling, but as usual he kept his thoughts to himself, and the rabbi left as quickly as he'd come.

Day by day Jacob was becoming more frightened. But his father seemed to be in a state of denial. Rather than read the news or discuss it, he instead began to read novels, retreating into a fictional world for hours and days on end.

Then the most troubling news—at least to Jacob—came to their home.

This time it came not from friends and neighbors but from Uncle Avi. He said he'd heard that upward of thirty thousand Jewish men had been arrested by the Gestapo and the SS.

Jacob blanched when he heard the number. But his father seemed to believe neither the number nor the source. "Arrested? Arrested for what?"

"For being Jews—what else?" Avi said.

"Thirty thousand? That's ridiculous."

"It's a fact, Reuben."

"Says who?"

"I heard it from one of my suppliers, a goy from Wiesbaden," Avi replied. "His son is high up in the Gestapo. Tells him everything. The man was practically bragging about it."

"Why would he tell you?" Dr. Weisz asked.

"He doesn't know I'm a Jew," Avi said.

"How's that possible?"

"He thinks I'm Catholic. Remember the crucifix I asked you to get me a few years back from your priest friend in Berlin?"

"Of course."

"It's hanging in my office in Cologne," Avi said. "And I've never gone by Avraham Weisz there or in Lüdenscheid. There I'm Allen Dirksen."

"And people believe you?"

"Why shouldn't they believe me?"

"I've never heard anyone call you Allen Dirksen."

"You've never come to Cologne or Lüdenscheid."

"That's because you keep me working like a slave in the factory here."

"Now you know why I do that."

"How much longer do you think you can keep that charade going?"

There was a long pause. "I don't know," Avi said finally. "But honestly, Reuben, that's why I've come."

Jacob had long before stopped slicing the carrot in his hand. His ear was pressed to the door between the kitchen and the living room, trying to catch every word, every syllable.

"What do you mean?" his father said.

Jacob heard Avi get up, followed by the sound of the shades being drawn. "I think we need to leave Germany."

"Not this again. That's ludicrous."

"No, it's not. We need to leave soon—now, before this gets any worse."

The argument that ensued that night was as intense as any Jacob had ever heard between his father and uncle. At one point, it got so heated that Dr. Weisz ordered Jacob to go up to his room, a cozy little nook in the attic.

Jacob hadn't been sent to his room without dinner since childhood. Defiant, he went only as far as the landing on the second floor, where the master bedroom and Ruthie's bedroom were situated, along with a bath. There he sat crouched, perfectly still and quiet, straining to hear every word that was spoken.

"Don't you see, Brother?" Avi pleaded. "They do not want us here. We are not safe."

"Nonsense—we're Germans," Dr. Weisz shot back, fuming but careful not to let himself be heard by the neighbors. "Faithful, proud, loyal citizens of the Fatherland."

"That's not how Herr Hitler sees it."

"His days are numbered."

"They're not," Avi said. "His power is growing. He's gained full control of the army. There are rumors he wants to seize Czechoslovakia and maybe all of Poland. He's already grabbed the Rhineland and the Sudetenland. Who's going to stop him now? The French? They had their chance. They blinked. The British? Chamberlain is clueless."

"You underestimate Chamberlain, Avi."

"Do I? Look at the mess he made in Munich."

"What about Roosevelt?"

"What about him?" Avi replied. "Brother, please, you don't really think the Americans are going to save the day, do you? They don't see how evil Hitler is. One of their biggest magazines is making him a cover story, naming him Man of the Year. And besides, the Americans have their own troubles. Their economy is sputtering. Isolationism is rampant. You really think Roosevelt is focused on our problems? And even if he knows what we Jews are facing here, do you really think he's going to lift a finger to help us?"

"You're a fool, Avi!" Dr. Weisz replied. "What you're saying is treasonous. I will not have you bring such poison into this house!"

Moments later, Jacob heard a door slam, and all was quiet.

But it was not over. It had only just begun.

12

JANUARY 1939
SIEGEN, GERMANY

As the new year began, Avi began coming to Siegen late on most Friday afternoons.

Often he would bring a basket of fresh fruit or vegetables or a new book from London or Paris that he'd bought on the black market, and then he would sit and chat at length with his brother.

"How is Sarah today?" Avi would ask, dutifully inquiring after his sister-in-law.

On that subject there wasn't any good news to report. The death of little Ruth had plunged Jacob's mother into a deep depression. Most of the time she refused to talk at all. For months now she had locked herself away in her bedroom, rarely willing to emerge even for meals.

As it was all too painful to discuss, Jacob's father would turn the conversation to other things, and invariably the two brothers would find themselves arguing over politics. Jacob would always try to look and sound busy as he worked in the kitchen, preparing the Shabbat dinner. Yet as he peeled potatoes and diced onions, he listened carefully to all the men were saying in the other room. He was stunned by how rapidly it seemed the Reich was rushing toward another European war. He was sympathetic to his uncle's argument that they should all leave Germany soon. And he was deeply dismayed that his father refused to see the handwriting on the wall and what it bespoke of the fate of Germany and its Jews.

"Reuben, have you ever heard of the Dachau camp?" Avi asked one night.

"No," Jacob heard his father say.

"Buchenwald?"

"No."

"Sachsenhausen?" Avi pressed.

"No, why?"

"That's where they've been sent, all of them."

"Who?"

"The Jews."

"What Jews?"

"The thirty thousand they arrested during *Kristallnacht*. They've been sent to work camps, except I hear they're not just work camps. They're slave-labor camps. Supposedly they're building things for the military, so *der Führer* has everything he needs to take Germany into another disastrous war."

"Don't be ridiculous, Avi," Dr. Weisz said. "This isn't Egypt under the pharaohs."

"Reuben, don't you see what's happening?" Avi asked. "Hitler is turning on the Jews. Haven't you read *Mein Kampf*?"

"No; why should I?"

"Because everyone else in the country has."

"It's just political propaganda."

"Maybe so, but Herr Hitler is pretty honest about what he thinks of us. You should read it, Reuben. Here, I've brought you a copy. Read it, and then promise me you'll let me help you, Sarah, and Jacob get out of the country while we still can."

"Don't say such things, Avi. You're going to get us all arrested."

"Think about it, Reuben—look what's happened in just the past few years. Don't you see? They're coming for us soon, Reuben. *Kristallnacht*? That was just the start of it."

"Enough!" Dr. Weisz bellowed. "That is enough, Avi. How many times must I warn you? You are talking nonsense, and you will get us all killed. Now speak no more of such things, or get out of my house!"

At the end of January, Jacob's father became very ill.

Out of nowhere, it seemed, he developed a hacking cough, a raging fever, and intense pain in his lungs. He couldn't work. He couldn't eat. He just stayed in bed, wheezing and groaning, so much so that Jacob's mother moved into Ruthie's old room so as not to catch whatever her husband had.

All the responsibilities of the house—cooking, cleaning, shopping, paying the bills, and caring full-time for both his bedridden father and his reclusive mother—now fell to Jacob. He had no time for his personal studies. He had to drop his violin lessons. He never got to see Naomi Silver's smile anymore or ride his bike with Hans or any of his other friends.

And then came news that Berlin had decreed all Jews in Germany and Austria must obtain special government-issued identity papers marking them as Jews and have those papers with them at all times whenever they left their homes.

By early February, Uncle Avi had found a young doctor he trusted and brought him from Cologne. When his examination was complete, Dr. Eisenberg gave his diagnosis: pleurisy, which he explained involved an inflammation of the lining of the lungs and chest. Jacob had never heard of such an ailment, but it wasn't difficult to see by Eisenberg's body language and how he was talking in such hushed tones with Uncle Avi that this was very serious indeed. The doctor prescribed medicine that couldn't be purchased by Jews—not through normal pharmacies, anyway. But within days, Avi miraculously found a way to get a small bottle of pills from a friend of his.

For the next few weeks, Jacob cared for his grieving, shut-in parents. He made sure his father took his pills. He cleaned his bedpan. He helped him take sponge baths and did all the laundry and even brought an occasional treat from Herr Mueller at the bakery.

And bit by bit, day by day, his father began to recover. Even his mother began to emerge from seclusion. There were bad days, to be sure, and setbacks aplenty, but by the middle of March, Jacob could clearly see rays of hope. His father and mother were sleeping in the same room again. They were taking their meals together. They were sitting by the fire and letting Jacob read to them, sometimes from Kafka, sometimes from Dickens.

And then, without warning, life went from hard to catastrophic.

13

MARCH 15, 1939
WASHINGTON, D.C.

William Barrett set down the phone and stared out the window.

It was an unseasonable, bitterly cold day in Washington. A light snow was falling, and the heater in Barrett's small office at the State Department was not working. He had asked his secretary to ring for someone to come fix it, but so far, no one from engineering had shown up. Barrett, therefore, was working in his overcoat and gloves. But today these were the least of his worries. He stood, swallowed the last drop of cooling coffee from his mug, and knocked on the door of the adjacent office.

"Come in."

Barrett opened the door and stepped into the large, spacious corner office of Cordell Hull, the U.S. secretary of state.

"What's the matter, Bill?" Hull asked, looking up from the stack of papers on his large oak desk. "Looks like you've seen a ghost."

"It's the Czechs, sir," Barrett said.

"What about them?"

"Hitler's forces just crossed their border."

Hull was aghast. "Germany has invaded Czechoslovakia?"

"I'm afraid so, sir."

"This is confirmed?"

Barrett nodded.

"Very well," Hull said. "Get the White House on the line. I need to see the president."

14

MARCH 15, 1939
SIEGEN, GERMANY

It was Avi who brought the news.

Germany had just invaded Czechoslovakia. Would the Allied powers retaliate? If so, war was coming, and with it, changes none of them could contemplate.

Avi rarely came on a weeknight, but he was in Siegen to check on the small factory he owned, the metalworking shop his brother was still too ill to manage. This time, however, he did not provoke a fight over politics. Rather, after bringing a fresh bottle of pills, he politely asked if he could "borrow" Jacob for a few hours and was granted permission.

Jacob climbed into the Adler. "Where are we going, Uncle?" he asked.

"Where do you think?"

The roads were largely deserted but for seemingly endless caravans of military vehicles transporting troops and equipment presumably toward Prague.

Soon they broke off the main road and headed up into the mountains, arriving at Avi's little cabin under a full moon.

Jacob chopped firewood out back while Avi warmed some beef stew from scratch and baked some fresh bread. Then Jacob built a roaring fire, and the two pulled up chairs and ate in silence by the stone fireplace, listening to the crackling flames and watching the sparks pop and settle like fireworks.

In time, Avi turned to his nephew and dropped a bomb. "The Resistance could use a young man like you."

Jacob nearly choked on a piece of bread. "*What?*"

"You heard me," Avi said quietly. "About a year ago, a dear friend of mine asked me to join. He could see war was coming. He knew I had contacts and resources, and he asked for my help. I said yes immediately."

"Why?"

"If he isn't stopped, Herr Hitler is going to destroy this country, Jacob," Avi said without emotion. "He's dragging us into a war we can't afford and can't win. First the Czechs. Then the Poles. Then the rest of Europe and the world. You mark my words. This is going to be the death of our nation."

Jacob said nothing. But in his heart he knew his uncle was right.

"For the past year, I've been stockpiling rifles and ammunition," Avi continued.

"But . . ."

"But what?"

"But . . . you're . . ."

"I'm what—a Jew?" Avi asked.

"Yes, of course a Jew," Jacob whispered, glancing toward the door, though he knew there wasn't another soul for miles.

"And?"

"And Jews can't own guns," Jacob whispered again. "It's forbidden. You could go to prison. Or worse, you could be sent to one of those slave camps you keep telling us about. Is that what you want?"

"Why can't Jews own guns?" Avi asked.

"Because *der Führer* forbade it."

"Yes, but why?" Avi pressed.

Jacob had no answer. Avi did.

"To make us passive, Jacob. To make us helpless. How can we resist Herr Hitler and the SS and the Gestapo if we cannot fight back? And how can we fight back without weapons and ammunition?"

Jacob was silent.

"Last time you were here, I had five rifles," Avi said. "Now, under these very floorboards, I have almost a hundred. For the past few months, I've been recruiting a network of trusted operatives—men of various ages, professions, and skills. Quietly, in the shadows, we've been training. Now that Hitler is on the move, we're going to begin to move as well. I'm asking you to join us."

"Me?" Jacob asked, genuinely stunned. "What could I do? You've seen me shoot. I'm terrible."

"You'll get better—I guarantee it," his uncle replied. "You're a natural. It's in your blood. But more important, you're strong and fast and smart and discreet. You remember everything I tell you. I know when I tell you to do something, you'll do it quickly and completely without me having to worry about it again. And somehow when you're in a room, you have a way of not being noticed."

"I don't think of that as a positive, Uncle," Jacob said softly.

"Well, I do," Avi replied. "In intelligence work, that can come in very handy."

For the next half hour, they discussed the nature of the underground resistance movement that was growing in Germany, its goals and objectives and the risks of joining. Avi mentioned no specific names or places or operations. He spoke in generalities but made it clear to Jacob that this very conversation—the same he'd had with dozens of men, and a few women, throughout the country—was punishable by hanging or by a firing squad.

"I'm not asking you to join because it's going to be fun," Avi said somberly as their fire began to die down. "I'm asking you because Hitler is coming for us. He's coming for the Jews. *Kristallnacht* was just the start. It's going to get very ugly from here on in. You and I don't have a choice. It's fight or perish—what do you say?"

"Fight?" Jacob asked. "I thought you wanted us to flee. You keep telling Papa we must leave Germany. We must go to England before it's too late. You've been knocking heads with him for months."

"I have," Avi conceded. "That's true. But the door is closing, my son. Indeed, it may already be closed. Jews can no longer get on a train or plane and leave the country. The only way out is to escape secretly. I myself considered fleeing in January, but your mother was . . . well, you know . . . and then your father fell ill."

"So joining the underground was plan B."

"It's become plan A."

"Because you really think we can't get out? You really believe we've missed our chance?"

"I do," Avi said softly. "That's why I brought you here. Your parents are on their feet again. They can't run. But soon they'll be able to function on their own. That will free up time for you. Now is your moment, Jacob. The Resistance needs you. I need you. What do you say?"

Jacob suddenly stood. He did not answer but rather cleared their dishes and washed them in the sink.

"Your father doesn't see what we see," Avi said after a long silence, as if he knew exactly what Jacob was thinking. "You know that. You've heard us arguing. You've heard what he's said. He doesn't see it. That breaks my heart. But there's nothing more I can do about it. If he won't save himself, we're going to have to take matters into our own hands."

"But if I join you, what will happen to them?"

"I can't give you answers, Jacob," Avi replied. "I can't promise you they'll be safe. I hope they will be. But I don't really know. All I can do is tell you the truth, which is this: the moment of reckoning is at hand. I've made my choice. Now you must make yours."

"But really, Uncle, what about them?" Jacob pressed. "You said fight or perish. Mama and Papa cannot fight. They haven't the notion or the strength. Are they just going to perish?"

Avi said nothing.

Jacob grabbed a dish towel and wiped his hands dry. "No," he said firmly, turning to face Avi. "I can't just leave them. I'm all they have. They've been through so much. They need me."

"They don't have to know," Avi said. "In fact, it would be better if they didn't."

"You want me to put their lives in grave danger without even telling them?" Jacob retorted. "That's even worse."

"Jacob, listen to me—they're already in grave danger," Avi said. "They're Jews. So are you. So am I. We're marked men, Jacob. We're going to be arrested. We're going to be imprisoned. We're going to be sent to slave-labor camps. We're going to disappear, and no one will care. If we do nothing, that's our fate. There's no way around it. The only question is whether we decide to fight back or be like lambs to the slaughter. I'm not afraid to die, Jacob. But I'm not going down without a fight. Are you?"

15

SEPTEMBER 1, 1939
WASHINGTON, D.C.

The Nazis invaded Poland on a Friday.

At 2:50 a.m., President Roosevelt was awakened at the White House residence by a phone call from William Bullitt, the U.S. ambassador in Paris, with news that German planes were bombing Warsaw and that German panzer divisions had punctured the borders.

"Well, Bill, it's come at last," the president said. "God help us all."

A few hours later, the president met in the Oval Office with Secretary Hull, Undersecretary Sumner Welles, Secretary of War Henry Stimson, and Harry Hopkins, the commerce secretary and one of Roosevelt's closest confidants. William Barrett, Hull's senior advisor, sat in on the meeting to take notes.

"What's Chamberlain saying?" the president asked.

"I'm afraid he's dithering, Mr. President," Hull replied. "Downing Street is in a panic. Churchill is pushing the PM to declare war, but Chamberlain won't do it."

"Good heaven—the man has no spine," Roosevelt snapped. "Is he just going to let the Nazis take over all of Europe? Is that his plan? What about the French? Will they declare war?"

"Not without the British," Welles said. "Paris doesn't want to be out there all by themselves."

"Are the French even ready for war?" the president asked.

"They say they're ready to defend themselves," Stimson replied. "They've built their Maginot Line—at considerable cost. But to launch an offensive war against Hitler at this point? I'd say it's doubtful at best."

A disaster was brewing in Europe. They could all see it. As to what they should do about it, that was a different matter altogether.

16

SEPTEMBER 1, 1939
SIEGEN, GERMANY

All of Siegen was buzzing.

War had finally come. But what did this mean for them? Where would it lead? How would it end? For the Gentiles of the town, the news brought a somber mood that settled over them. But the Jews of Siegen were gripped by a spirit of fear. Jacob's mother wept on and off throughout the day. His father sat alone in the living room, in his favorite chair, smoking a pipe and reading a novel, and spoke not a word.

Jacob waited for Uncle Avi to come. He would bring news and words of comfort. Yet to Jacob's surprise and deep disappointment, Uncle Avi did not come for Shabbat dinner. Was he ill? Was he safe? Jacob had a thousand questions. His parents, however, had no answers, or at least they kept them to themselves.

When it came time to share the dinner Jacob had prepared, his mother refused to come out of her room. His father dutifully lit the evening candles, but they did not pray or read any Scriptures. The only prayer that night was the silent and recurring *Why?* that Jacob kept asking God. They ate without speaking.

Saturday was eerily quiet in the Weisz home, even as trucks filled with soldiers roared through the streets, presumably on the way to the front or to reinforce other borders.

Sunday, September 3, was quiet too. Jacob tried to study but had a difficult time concentrating. He tried to read one of his father's novels but had little interest in anything but the crisis now at hand. He cooked for his family and cleaned the kitchen after each meal and straightened the house and tried to stay busy.

Around nine o'clock, he and his father turned out the lights, said good night to each other, and went to their bedrooms.

Jacob had not changed into his nightclothes yet. He wasn't tired. He had no interest in sleeping. He had too much on his mind. He wanted to talk to someone. Anyone. The world around them was collapsing. Everything they knew was being ripped away. Shouldn't they do something? Shouldn't they go somewhere? Shouldn't they at least try to leave Germany? What was the worst that could happen?

He finally kicked off his shoes, lay down on the bed in his clothes, and stared up at the ceiling. Where was Uncle Avi? Was he in trouble? Had he been captured? Was he even still alive?

What was the Meyer family doing tonight? Was Hans all right? Were they really planning to flee the country? Hans had confided in Jacob that his parents were seriously considering going to Palestine. Lots of Jews were going there, Hans said, to escape from Herr Hitler and to build a new Jewish homeland. Hans had sworn Jacob to secrecy. Even to utter such things could get a Jew arrested these days, Hans had reminded him. But Hans need not have worried. Jacob was as silent as the mountains, and his word was his bond. Jacob would take Hans's secrets to the grave if need be. Yet somewhere deep in his heart, Jacob actually contemplated the idea of running away with the Meyers, be it to Palestine or anywhere else. To stay in Germany was becoming more foolish with each and every passing day, Jacob could see. Why could his father not see it too?

A selfish thought suddenly popped into Jacob's mind. If Hans and his family did leave, Jacob would miss them very much. But then again, Hans would no longer be in a position to court Naomi Silver. Jacob pondered that for a moment. Maybe in such times he should not let himself be so shy. If time was running out, maybe he should talk to

Naomi. Maybe he should even bring her a gift. Perhaps even tell her his feelings for her. What if events continued to go from bad to worse? What if he never talked to her and then never had the chance to? What a waste that would be, and how bad he would feel. What's the worst that could happen if he started to smile back at her when she smiled at him—or talked to her before violin class?

But then another thought entered his heart. What if the Silvers were planning to leave as well? What if one night they just up and disappeared? Wasn't that possible? That got Jacob wondering how they were taking the news of the German invasion of Poland. What did it mean to them? What were they going to do? He wondered, too, what Naomi was doing at that very hour. What was she thinking about? Was she able to sleep? Or was she tossing and turning and staring at her ceiling too? Was there any chance she was thinking of him?

Suddenly there was a sharp knock at the front door. Startled, Jacob sat up and glanced at the clock. It was just before ten. He quickly put his shoes back on and was prepared to head downstairs when he heard his father get up and answer the door. Then, to his surprise, he heard his mother get up and head to the front door as well. Quietly, he crept down the stairs and crouched on the second-floor landing.

"Who is it?" his father asked.

"It's me; open up," came the urgent reply.

The voice was unmistakable. It was Uncle Avi.

They let him in and shut and locked the door quickly behind him.

"What is it, Avi?" Jacob's mother asked. "You look like you've seen a ghost."

"We must go," Avi said. "All of us. We must go now."

"Not this again," Dr. Weisz said. "Avi, I told you—"

But Avi persisted. "Reuben, listen to me. My friends in the underground say thousands of Jews are being rounded up, all over the country. This is it. They're being sent to labor camps. We've run out of time."

"Underground?" Jacob's father whispered in horror. "Do not utter such a word in this house. Are you mad?"

Jacob could not stay upstairs any longer. He crept down the next flight of stairs, step by step, as quietly as he could, and peeked around the corner to see precisely what was happening and hear everything more clearly.

"Hear me out, just for a moment—I've made all the preparations," Avi continued, pulling an envelope from his jacket pocket. "Everything you need is in here. False ID papers, passports, train tickets to Switzerland. My car is parked around the corner. You have ten minutes. Pack some clothes—just the basics—and your valuables, but nothing more. I will take them to my cabin. And tomorrow, we will make our move."

At this, Dr. Weisz became livid. He was clearly incensed that his younger brother had taken the liberty—indeed, the risk—of having false papers made on their behalf. Jacob watched in silence as his father and uncle argued in hushed voices so the neighbors—and, God forbid, the SS informants who lurked everywhere—wouldn't overhear. His mother slipped away into the kitchen, presumably to put on a pot of tea. But Jacob had no intention of going anywhere. He wanted to hear everything. He knew his uncle was right. He was grateful Avi had made such preparations to get them out of Germany. Now he silently begged God to make his father agree and let them all escape while they still had a chance, however slim.

"Jacob, what are you doing here?" his father said suddenly, for the first time noticing his son spying from the stairs.

"Well, I, uh—I just came down to—"

"Quiet," his father ordered in a sharp whisper. "You want the neighbors to hear you? Go to your room. This isn't for you."

"But, Papa, I—"

His father glared at him. "I gave you an order."

Jacob's hurt turned to a flush of anger, but he held his tongue. A son's flagrant disobedience was only going to inflame an already-volatile situation. He turned away from his father, nodded to his uncle, and went to the second-floor landing.

"All the way up, young man," his father snapped, knowing his son all too well.

Jacob's fists tightened. But again he said nothing and did as he was told. When he reached his room, he slammed and locked the door behind him, his one act of defiance—and a childish one at that, he told himself.

His heart was racing. He needed fresh air. He wanted to get out, to run. But he was trapped in the attic for now, so he lay on his bed and again stared up at the exposed rafters above him. Outside, lightning flashed, and thunder shook their house. Then the downpour began. He looked out his only window, but it had already fogged up. He wiped it clear, if only for a moment, and saw the deserted streets filling with water and mud.

Jacob was furious at his father, but he forced himself to calm down and start to think clearly. Then the thought struck him. What if his uncle persuaded his parents to leave? Time was fleeting. He had to be ready.

He jumped up, pulled out the suitcase he stored under his bed, and began to pack everything he would need for the journey ahead. Two sweaters, two pairs of pants, a couple of T-shirts, and some underwear. As many pairs of socks as he owned. A pair of dress shoes, a dress jacket, and two ties. Then he put on his usual shoes, tied up the laces, put on a black sweater and a winter coat, and sat on the bed, waiting for his father—or better yet, his uncle—to knock on the door and say it was time to leave.

Ten minutes went by.

Then fifteen. Then twenty.

Unable to stand it any longer, Jacob got up, quietly went over to his door, unlocked it, and tried to open it without any creaking. He held his breath and listened for yelling, for voices, for any sign of life and movement. He heard nothing.

Taking a chance, he went to the bathroom, grabbed his toothbrush, and crept down the stairs to the second floor. If caught, he would say he was just going to wash up before bed. And then he heard the door between the kitchen and the living room open.

"What happened to Avi?" he heard his mother ask.

"He left."

"But I made you both some tea."

Jacob heard his father mutter something. The man clearly was not interested in tea. He was pacing.

Jacob heard his mother set down the tray of teacups and sit in her creaky rocking chair. There was a long, awkward, painful silence, broken only by the sound of their ornately carved grandfather clock ticking monotonously in the corner.

"What's in the envelope?" his mother asked at long last.

Jacob strained to hear every word.

"The papers he had made."

"I thought you didn't want them in this house."

"I don't."

"Well?"

"He wouldn't take them back."

There was another long silence, and then Jacob heard his mother speak again. "Maybe he's right."

"Who?"

"Avi."

"About what?"

"Maybe we should join my parents in London. They begged us to go with them. Now Avi is—"

"Sarah, please; don't start this nonsense. We may be Jews, but we're also Germans. Loyal Germans. This all will pass in due course. Herr Hitler's days are numbered, and everything will be restored to how it once was."

"And what if it isn't?"

"You must have faith, my dear."

"My faith was shattered the day they killed Ruth," Jacob heard his mother say. "Your brother is right. We should leave now, before they kill our only son, as well."

But Jacob's father would have none of it. "It's getting late. We should get some sleep."

Not wanting to be found on the landing, Jacob scooted up to his room and blew out his candle but left the door ajar in case there were any other tidbits of conversation he might overhear.

There was no way he could sleep now. He couldn't even change into his nightclothes. There was no space in his tiny room to pace, so yet again he lay on his bed, listening to the rain pelting against the roof and window, his mind churning with one question after another. Where was Avi going now? Was he going to leave Germany without them? Would he really leave and not say good-bye?

Jacob felt cold and lost and scared.

– – –

Soon Jacob saw himself running through the woods at night.

He was alone, running in the moonlight, and finally he reached his uncle's cabin. The lights were off. The Adler was not there. He saw himself pounding furiously on the front door, but no one answered. Where was Avi? Would he ever see him again?

Suddenly Jacob sat bolt upright in bed. He was covered in perspiration and realized he'd been having a nightmare. Now he could hear heavy pounding on the front door. He could hear his father scrambling down the stairs, shouting, "Just a moment; just a moment."

He didn't remember ever having fallen asleep, but as he wiped the fatigue from his eyes, he glanced at the little clock on his dresser, the one he had bought from Naomi Silver's father. It said it was 3:09 in the morning. Jacob was confused. He was still dressed, still had his shoes on.

Outside, the rain persisted, cold and blustery.

The pounding continued. *Avi,* Jacob thought. *It must be Uncle Avi. He's come back to get us.* But he was wrong. Dead wrong.

17

"Where is he?" bellowed an angry voice Jacob had never heard before.

"Where is who?" Jacob heard his father reply.

"Where is Avraham Weisz? He is to be placed under arrest."

Jacob's heart was racing. He moved to the window. He heard boots marching on the street below, and to his horror he now saw several black cars parked out front. It was the Gestapo. They had come for Avi.

"Arrest?" he heard his father say. "On what charge?"

"Sedition. Treason," came the reply. "Don't play stupid with me, Dr. Weisz. Your brother is a leader in the Jewish underground. Now where is he?"

"I don't know. Really, I don't. He was here last night. But he left hours ago. He should be back in Cologne by now."

"I have men waiting for him there," the Gestapo agent said. "But I don't expect him to return. The word is he is leaving—leaving tonight—with you."

"I don't know what you're talking about."

"I will give you one more chance to tell the truth, Dr. Weisz."

Jacob moved to the top of the stairs. He wished he were at his parents' side. He could hear his mother crying. She was already in such a fragile state. Jacob feared the trauma this would now induce. And then his heart nearly stopped as he heard the unmistakable sound of someone chambering a round in a Luger.

"If I find you are lying to me, Dr. Weisz . . ."

"Please, no—I beg of you, have mercy," Jacob heard his father plead.

"I don't know where he is. Truly I don't. But yes, he's planning to leave the country."

Jacob gasped. He, too, was afraid, but he couldn't believe his father was so quickly betraying his very own brother. And then it got worse.

"He brought us papers," his father continued. "False papers, passports, train tickets—here—here they are. All of them. We told him we didn't want them. We're loyal Germans. We're—"

"Silence!" the Gestapo agent ordered. "You are Jews, not Germans. You are dirty, filthy kikes! How dare you claim to be loyal to *der Führer*?"

Now Jacob heard soldiers smashing furniture and lamps and dishes. Were they just trashing the house for no reason, or were they hunting for something else, something more than the papers?

"Now, Mrs. Weisz, where is your brother-in-law?"

There was no reply.

"I'm going to count to three, Mrs. Weisz. If you don't tell me, I'm going to shoot your husband in the temple, right in front of you. Do you understand?"

Jacob could hear his mother becoming hysterical now, pleading for mercy that was never going to come.

"And then, if you still won't tell me, I'm going to shoot you. Have I made myself clear? One . . ."

"No, please, I beg of you. Don't do this thing."

"Two . . ."

"We don't know. He was here, but he left."

"Three."

"We don't know where he is now. He could be anywhere. He could be—"

Jacob heard the gun go off and his mother scream in terror.

"Did you think I was lying, Mrs. Weisz? Did you think I wouldn't do it? Now, I will count to three one more time, and you will tell me what I want to know. Ready?"

All the blood had drained from Jacob's face. Tears were streaming from his eyes. His trembling hands covered his mouth. He didn't dare move, didn't dare make a sound. He couldn't believe what was happening. He wanted to race down the stairs. Maybe with the element of surprise he could tackle the Gestapo agent. But how long could he last? He knew he would be shot by the other agents within seconds. How he wished he had one of Avi's rifles. How he wished he had become a better shot.

"One . . ."

Jacob's mind searched desperately for answers.

"Two . . ."

What should he do? Jacob wondered. What *could* he do?

"Last chance, Mrs. Weisz. Where is Avraham?"

She was weeping, begging, pleading, but to no avail.

He had to do something, Jacob told himself. He couldn't just let them kill her.

"Time's up, Mrs. Weisz. I am very disappointed."

Suddenly Jacob heard his mother scream at the top of her lungs. "RUN, JACOB—RUUUUUNNNN!"

And then the gun went off again.

Jacob heard his mother's body drop to the floor. For a split second he froze, barely able to make sense of the nightmare unfolding below. But then he heard the sound of heavy boots coming across the living room floor and heading up the stairs. Instinctively he jumped up, ran back to his room, threw open the window, and jumped out onto the roof.

In the driving rain, the tiles on the slanted roof were slick. Jacob lost his footing almost immediately and started sliding toward the street three stories below. Grabbing the edge of the brick chimney, however, he stopped his fall at the last minute. Then he pulled himself to his feet and leaped to the roof of the house next door.

Behind him he heard several shots ring out. He glanced back and saw a Gestapo man standing in his window, aiming his Luger at him and firing again and again.

Without thinking, Jacob turned now and began to run. He was scared of slipping in the rain and falling ten or fifteen meters and breaking every bone in his body. But he was even more scared of being shot down like a dog. He had no choice. It was flee or perish.

So he was running now atop his neighbor's roof, and soon he was leaping from roof to roof. He could hear yelling and more gunfire. But he would not look back again. He could not. There was no time. He knew every step could be his last. He raced down the entire block, twenty-two houses in a row.

Soon all sound faded away. He couldn't hear a thing. Not the dogs barking. Not the sirens wailing. He didn't notice the whole neighborhood was now awake. He didn't see every family he knew peering out their windows. None of it registered. Adrenaline was coursing through his veins. All he could think about was escaping certain death.

At last, Jacob reached the final house on the block—Hans Meyer's house—and didn't hesitate for a moment. He slowed to a halt, crouched down, grabbed hold of the storm drain running along the edge of the roof, and holding it for dear life, swung down until his feet crashed through the window of a room much like his own, a window situated on the third floor in a little attic bedroom. It was the room Hans shared with his older brother, Wolf.

The expression on Wolf's face was one of shock and a touch of anger, Jacob thought. Hans was shocked, too, but he actually burst out laughing. Hans laughed when he was nervous.

Jacob had no time to sit and talk. He shook the glass shards off of him, threw open the bedroom door, and raced down both flights of stairs, nearly knocking over Hans's father as he blew through the living room and out the back door.

Moments later, he was dashing across Rubensstrasse, down a dark alley, and over to Tiergartenstrasse. He turned right, staying in the shadows, close to the houses, running toward the auto repair shop about halfway down the street. He knew the place well. The shop was where Hans's brother worked as a mechanic and where he kept his motorbike. Jacob knew the keys were hanging on a nail in the wall of the main office.

Reaching the back of the shop, Jacob picked up a rock and smashed out a window. He used the rock to scrape away the remaining glass, then climbed inside the shop, found the key, hoisted up the main garage door, and started the motorbike. Soon he was zigzagging through the streets of Siegen until he found the main thoroughfare and headed toward the mountains.

There was no question where he was going, only whether he had enough petrol to get there. He had no money. He had no change of clothes. He had no idea if he'd find Avi when he got there. But he was alive, and for the moment at least, he was free.

It took nearly an hour to reach the cabin. Fearing SS patrols and possible Gestapo roadblocks, Jacob did not take the usual route. To be even more careful, he didn't drive straight to the cabin. Rather, he parked and hid the motorbike several kilometers away, then proceeded to hike through the woods in the glow of the moonlight, just like he had done in his dream.

After nearly twenty minutes of walking in driving rain that showed no signs of letting up, Jacob thought he smelled smoke. Coming up over a ridge less than five hundred meters from the cabin, he suddenly saw enormous flames leaping into the night sky. Standing around were at least a half-dozen Gestapo men holding submachine guns and laughing among themselves.

Jacob just stood there, staring at Avi's cabin being consumed by the blaze. What had become of his uncle? Had he been captured by the Gestapo? Had he been tortured and killed? Was he in the cabin, being burned alive?

A thousand cruel thoughts engulfed his mind. Dimly he thought perhaps he should drop to the ground, so as not to be seen. But he didn't move. He was completely stunned by the scene before him, numb from grief, and in danger of slipping into shock. Everyone he loved was gone. Everything he knew was over. Where was he supposed to go now? What was he supposed to do?

Just then, someone grabbed him from behind. Before he knew what was happening, a gloved hand was over his nose and mouth, and his legs were kicked out from under him. He hit the ground hard and found himself lying face-first in the mud. The gloved hand tightened its grip. He couldn't move, couldn't scream, couldn't even breathe.

"Don't make a sound," someone whispered in his ear. "Just listen carefully, and do exactly what I say."

18

Jacob's captor finally rolled him over.

Jacob closed his eyes and braced for impact. He waited to be struck—or shot. When nothing happened, he slowly opened his eyes. The shock of what he saw overwhelmed him, but he finally exhaled. His heart started beating again. For the face staring down at him was Avi's.

"Follow me," Avi ordered. "Keep your mouth shut, and don't look back."

Immediately they were on the move, away from the burning cabin, away from the Gestapo agents. But they were not returning to get the motorbike. The roads were not safe. If they were going to get away, it was going to be on foot.

The journey was more grueling than anything Jacob had experienced before. Racing through the mountains, fording rivers, traversing open fields, they kept moving all night, stopping only occasionally to scoop some water from a stream or listen to see if anyone was following them or near them at all.

As dawn came, Jacob was exhausted. But the two men did not stop moving. They were not running now. They were walking, but Avi set a brisk and steady pace. Jacob wanted to stop. He wanted to ask Avi if they could rest, even for a little while. But he had been told not to say a word, and Jacob knew their very lives depended on his obeying. At least the pain in his feet and in his belly from lack of food and the fatigue permeating every fiber of his being kept his mind off the fact that he would never see his parents or his sister again. And at least he was reunited once again with Avi, and this gave him a measure of comfort, however small. Avi would know what to do. He would know how to get them out of Germany, out of danger, and to their relatives now living in London.

For three days and nights, Avi and Jacob stayed on the move. Avi did allow for a few breaks. And they did stop a few times to take brief naps. But only brief ones, and then they were moving again.

On the fourth day, Avi and Jacob slipped over the German border into Belgium. They were not safe, Avi told him in hushed tones, but he had friends who could help them.

Along the way, when they were high up in the mountains or moving through a thick forest, Avi allowed Jacob to talk, and to both of their surprise, Jacob spilled his guts. He told his uncle everything that had occurred after Avi left the house on Sunday night. Jacob explained what had happened when the Gestapo came and how both of his parents had been shot, one after the other. He explained how his mother's last words were for him to run and how he had run for his life, reached the motorbike, and raced immediately to the cabin. As he and Avi compared notes on all that had transpired, Jacob found that though they grieved, they did not cry. They had lost everyone dear to them except each other. But fear was a tonic that somehow calmed their nerves and focused their minds.

Soon they were deep inside Belgium and holed up in a barn behind a farmhouse, hiding in a loft under bales of hay.

"So where exactly are we?" Jacob whispered as the sun began to rise.

"Zellik," Avi whispered back.

"Where?"

"A little village northwest of Brussels."

"How little?"

"Don't know—too small for us to go wandering around in daylight, that's for certain."

"You know anybody here?"

"One guy."

"Who?"

"You're about to find out. Come on. It's time."

Avi climbed out of their hiding place and brushed himself off, then brushed pieces of straw off Jacob. Moving quickly and quietly, they sneaked to the side door of the barn, made sure the coast was clear, then sprinted for the farmhouse. When they reached a cellar door, Avi began knocking with some sort of a code.

Moments later, someone with a rifle opened the door. They entered and the door was closed and locked behind them. They were immediately directed to a young boy, no older than ten or twelve, who proceeded to lead them through a labyrinth of farm equipment and supplies to a small, enclosed workshop, guarded by two burly men with rifles. "Wait here," the boy said, and he scampered inside the workshop.

A minute later, a tall, gaunt, pale man—probably in his early to mid-fifties—with thinning blond hair, tattered work clothes, a brown felt cap, and a kindly expression emerged from the workshop. He lit up when he saw Avi, and the two gave each other a bear hug.

"Morry, this is the nephew I've been telling you about."

The man put out his big, calloused hand. "You must be Jacob." He spoke with a thick French accent.

"I am," Jacob replied, surprised to be known. He shook the man's hand with a sturdy, firm grip, just as his uncle had taught him.

"My name is Maurice," the man said. "Maurice Tulek. My friends call me Morry, but I let your uncle call me Morry too."

The two men laughed, but Jacob didn't find it funny. He didn't see any humor in the moment. His pain was much too fresh.

Avi explained that Maurice was a Jew. Originally from Bourgogne, Maurice had moved to Brussels several years before, joined the Resistance, and was now commander of a critically important cell. Avi briefed his friend on the latest situation inside Germany and on the death of Jacob's parents, then asked Morry to lay out the plan for Jacob's training.

"Training?" Jacob asked, dumbfounded. "I thought we were going to England."

"England?" Morry said. "No, no, no. You're not going to England. We need you here. We have to be ready."

Frightened and confused, Jacob looked to Avi, but rather than correct his friend, Avi confirmed the plan.

"Morry's right," Avi said. "We're not going to England, Jacob. We're needed here."

"But I thought . . ."

"No, Jacob. We cannot run. We cannot be selfish. We cannot think only of ourselves. The Jews of Germany are in danger. So are the Jews of Belgium. We need to help *them* get to England and America and Palestine."

"But, Uncle," Jacob protested, "you said *we* had to get out. You said that *we* had to get to someplace safe."

"Things have changed," Avi calmly replied. "Everything has changed. You and I can't fix what happened to your family. But we can help other Jewish families in Siegen and beyond. After all, Jacob, if we don't help them, who will?"

Jacob said no more. He stared into his uncle's eyes, searching for any sign that the man could be persuaded, but there was none to be had. Instead Jacob saw a deep and fierce resolve. Indeed, his uncle seemed electrified by the opportunity to save lives.

At one level, the whole notion seemed ludicrous, even suicidal. Yet in a way that he could not explain even to himself, his uncle's intense sense of conviction about the matter struck a mystifying yet riveting chord deep in Jacob's soul. Finally he shrugged and nodded, and as he did, Avi and Morry beamed with what appeared to be joy, a rather odd emotion to be feeling under the circumstances, Jacob thought.

"Very good," the Frenchman began. "I will personally oversee your training. You two must both get in much better shape. Physical conditioning is critical. Then we'll cover setting up safe houses, forging documents, Morse code, building and fixing and operating all kinds of radios, surveillance, weapons training, hand-to-hand combat. But we don't have much time. We're expecting the Germans to invade by the end of the year. You sure you're up for this?"

Jacob looked at his uncle, then to Maurice Tulek, and nodded. "I'm ready."

"Good," Maurice said. "Then let's get to it."

19

The Nazi invasion didn't happen by the end of 1939 after all.

The German seizure of the Low Countries—Belgium, the Netherlands, and Luxembourg—didn't occur until May of 1940, and Jacob was grateful for the extra months of training and conditioning.

Maurice, Avi, and Jacob used the time to recruit and assemble the rest of their team of young Jewish insurgents.

Their first recruit was Micah Kahn. A twenty-six-year-old Belgian Jew, Micah was a medical doctor and the son of a military physician. Tall and handsome with slicked-back dark hair, a brilliant mind, and an athletic build, he possessed an uncanny gift of leadership that could persuade just about anyone to do just about anything.

When Avi first met Micah and his equally sophisticated older brother, Marc, at a café in Brussels, he sensed their potential immediately and tried to recruit them both. Both were passionate in their hatred of the Nazis and fearful for the fate of Belgium. Marc, however, had decided to become a Communist and was committed to working with the Reds to overcome the Nazis. Micah, on the other hand, had become increasingly sympathetic to the Resistance—even more so after the invasion, when he was forced by the Nazis to stop practicing medicine and start wearing a yellow Star of David, which he considered degrading and humiliating. He didn't commit to becoming active in the Resistance, though, until a number of his friends began disappearing. Rumor had it they had been arrested by the Gestapo, tortured, and either killed or shipped out to various concentration camps. Micah couldn't be certain exactly what had happened in each and every case, but he was sure about one thing: he had to do everything in his power to save his fellow Jews.

Once Micah was in, he was all in. He became like a brother to Jacob, and Avi taught him everything he had learned from Maurice. Micah then set about recruiting two of his childhood friends, Henri Germaine and Jacques Bouquet, to join the Resistance, even though neither of them was Jewish.

At twenty-two, Henri was four years younger than Micah but just as tall, though somewhat thinner, with wild, curly hair that gave him a look reminiscent of a young Albert Einstein. Henri and Micah had grown up in the same neighborhood—just around the corner from one another, in fact. They met on their grade school playground and became good friends despite their difference in age. They had remained close ever since.

In some ways, the two were cut from similar cloth. Like Micah, Henri had a father who was a doctor in the Belgian military, and he, too, had a brother who was six years older. Henri found Micah's love of books and music and films absolutely compelling, and it resonated with his own love for the arts and for new ideas.

Micah had often invited Henri to join him in games and hikes and outings of all kinds growing up, so Henri always felt included in Micah's world. Over the years, though he himself was not Jewish, Henri also got to know Micah's family, and he developed both an appreciation for Jewish wit and a sympathy for the Jewish people, given all the ridicule and persecution they faced. With the rise of the Third Reich came a commensurate rise in Henri's antipathy toward Herr Hitler and his Nazi forces. Many of the friends Micah lost to the Nazis were friends of Henri's, too. So when Micah asked him if he wanted to do damage to the Reich that was crushing their country and destroying their futures, it was not a hard sell.

Micah also brought Jacques, who was the same age as Micah and just as brilliant—perhaps even more so. A fanatic about mathematics, he also loved art and poetry and music and films. Indeed, in many ways he had competed all his life with Micah to know more and accomplish more as well as to laugh more and have more fun. Growing up with Micah and Henri, Jacques had developed a love for adventure and for the outdoors.

Whereas Micah was the leader and Henri was the professor, Jacques was the class clown. Mischievous and full of life, he was always playing pranks yet narrowly escaping getting caught by teachers and other authorities. And though he was no more Jewish than Henri, he, too, was very fond of the Kahn family and their Jewish friends. He abhorred the Nazi goose-steppers and the ugly anti-Semitism of the times.

In Avi's and Jacob's eyes, these three young men were ideal recruits for the Resistance. They proved to be fast studies, hard workers, and exceedingly brave. They were also natives of Belgium, and this Avi prized above all. They knew Brussels in particular, inside and out, and they not only had excellent contacts throughout the country but seemed to excel at making new contacts that proved equally valuable.

Jacob had never had friends like this in Siegen. His friends were not as interesting, not as well-read, and not nearly as committed to a common goal against a common foe. But here, in the danger-drenched climate of Nazi-controlled Europe, it was a combination that quickly bonded these four young men to each other and to Avi.

At first the team's primary goal was helping Jewish families escape the Third Reich. Together, they helped more than three hundred families pass through Belgium. Some went to England, and some made it to Canada. Jacob and his new friends provided safe houses, basic provisions, clothes, and false documents along the way.

Once the invasion occurred, however, Maurice Tulek redirected them from rescuing Jews to other tasks considered more vital to the Allies. For the next several years, they gathered critical intelligence on German troop movements, blew up fuel depots, stole Nazi uniforms, and sabotaged lorries. Once, Avi and Jacob were ordered to attack a police station and grab any uniforms they could. They captured two police uniforms, two pistols, a small box of ammunition, and a money box with over ten thousand francs inside. What's more, they escaped with a bonus neither of them had expected—a stash of six thousand food-ration coupons, which they promptly gave to Morry to distribute among the various Jewish Resistance members scattered throughout the country.

The fact that they had not yet been caught was a source of many arguments among them. Some attributed their good fortune to dumb luck. Others to their great skill and cleverness. Jacob wondered whether it was the hand of divine Providence. Regardless, each of these men loved the game, and they played it exceedingly well.

They rarely stayed in the same place two nights in a row. It was harrowing, thankless work, but Jacob was proud to be doing it and grateful to be at the side of an uncle he so deeply admired.

And then one day, without warning, they were blindsided.

20

FEBRUARY 2, 1943
HERSTAL, BELGIUM

The second of February fell on a Tuesday.

Jacob remembered it distinctly because it was his twenty-second birthday, and he was annoyed at being awakened by his uncle at 1:17 in the morning. But Avi had no time to be sentimental. He ordered Jacob to hightail it with him through a bone-chilling winter night to get to some safe house they'd never been to before and make it there by the top of the hour.

Jacob had been hoping to sleep in a little and maybe eat a half-decent meal before sitting down to plan the sabotage of a radio tower near Antwerp, an operation scheduled for the coming weekend. But none of that was to be. Instead Avi insisted they risk their lives by defying the Nazi curfew to get to a top-secret "emergency" meeting with Maurice Tulek and three other underground cell commanders, none of whom Jacob had ever met.

"Gentlemen, thank you for agreeing to meet with me, and especially on such short notice," Avi began as they huddled in the uninsulated attic of a farmhouse on the outskirts of a town called Herstal. "A few hours ago, I received credible intelligence that the Nazis have moved a total of nineteen trainloads of Jews—mostly women and children, but also men, especially the elderly—out of Belgium to a concentration camp in Poland, a camp known as Auschwitz."

Jacob, silently grumbling at his uncle, had been half-asleep as the meeting began. But the man now had his full attention. Was this true? Where had Avi gotten such intel?

"The nineteenth train departed the Mechelen camp on the fifteenth of January," his uncle continued. "According to my sources, some sixteen thousand Jews have been deported to date. This would be bad enough, but there are reports that Auschwitz is not simply a slave-labor camp, as it has been described. At least one Nazi official in Brussels has privately told colleagues that Auschwitz is a 'slaughterhouse' or a 'death factory.' Some believe the Nazis are systematically killing Jews there by the hundreds, maybe by the thousands."

"Come on, Avi, those are baseless rumors," Morry sniffed. "The Nazis are killing Jews—how did you put it—'*systematically*'? Rubbish. What would be the point? They need Jewish labor to build and run their factories. They need Jewish hands to produce *matériel* for the German war effort."

"Maybe yes, maybe no," Avi replied. "I agree it sounds incredible. But this much we know for certain: our own people are being shipped out of Belgium to the most feared camp the Nazis have. What exactly happens at Auschwitz? I have no idea. But I've just learned that Kurt Asche—Hitler's personal representative in Belgium on the 'Jewish question'—is making plans as we speak to fill a twentieth train with more Jews and send them to Auschwitz as well."

"When?" asked one of the cell commanders.

"I'm not yet sure," Avi conceded. "But very soon."

"You're not sure because you can't get reliable information?" another cell commander asked. "Or because Asche hasn't decided yet?"

"To be honest, I'm not sure about that either," Avi said. "At the moment, we believe they have about eight hundred Jews in the transit camp. I'm told when they get to fifteen hundred, the twentieth train will depart."

"How do you know this?" Morry asked.

"I have two reliable sources. One is inside Asche's headquarters," Avi replied, referring to the Gestapo's feared Avenue Louise compound in Brussels. "The other works at the prison at Boortmeerbeek. They are both patriotic Belgians. Both are civilians who have been forced to work for the Nazis. Neither knows of the other, but their stories match, and I have great confidence in these sources. Neither believes Asche has made a final decision on timing, but both believe that it's possible the decision could have already been made and simply not yet communicated down the ranks. Either way, they are terrified. At first, both thought the Jews were just being sent to work camps. But they, too, are beginning to hear whispers of ghastly things happening at Auschwitz."

"Why are they talking to you?" one of the commanders inquired.

"One is doing it for money," Avi said bluntly. "The other is stricken with guilt. He no longer wants to be part of organizing these convoys. Indeed, he's actually planning to flee his post and try to leave the country, too, though we've begged him to stay."

"Begged him to stay?" Morry said. "What on earth for?"

"Precisely for the reason I have gathered you all to discuss: I want your permission as representatives of the Jewish Defense Council to attack the twentieth train and set these captives free," Avi said. "I need my source to remain in place at least until we can get all the intel we'll need for the attack. Then he can go. In fact, I'll personally do everything I can to help him get out of the country."

The commanders were incredulous.

"Attack a heavily guarded train full of Jewish prisoners?" one asked. "Have you lost your mind, Avi?"

"Of course not—have you?" Avi retorted, his face flush with anger. "They're *Jewish* prisoners. Isn't it our job to save them—or some of them, at least—if we possibly can?"

"Not if it's a suicide mission," the commander shot back. "How do you plan to do it?"

"I'd like twenty-two men," Avi said. "Two experts in explosives to blow up the tracks. Two snipers plus another half-dozen trained marksmen to take out the SS troops and provide cover. I'll also need a half-dozen men with bolt cutters and wire cutters and the like to open up the train cars, and a third half-dozen to drive the getaway cars."

"That's preposterous—it'll never work," another commander said. "First of all, we don't have twenty-two men we can spare. And even if we did, you'd get them all killed, not to mention yourself."

"And what if it does work?" the third commander said. "What then? You'd put the entire Resistance movement in jeopardy. The Nazis would be humiliated. They'd turn the country upside down to catch us. And when they find us, they'll crush us. And then what? How are we going to save Belgium when the Resistance is no more? No, Avi, it's foolhardy and reckless. I cannot give my permission."

Jacob had never seen his uncle so angry. First Avi excoriated his superiors, telling them to wake up and confront reality. Then he pleaded for a fundamental change of perspective. Hitler was rolling over the Allies. *Der Führer* was gaining ground, picking up speed, putting more and more of Europe under the jackboots of the Reich. The Jewish Resistance was too small to save Belgium. This they had to admit, he said. They were, he argued, wasting precious time and manpower helping the Allies gather intelligence. It was time to save Jewish lives. They certainly couldn't save them all. But they could save some, and therefore it was their sacred duty to do so.

"What does the Talmud say?" Avi asked, his voice becoming quieter now but even more impassioned. "'Whoever destroys a soul, it is considered as if he destroyed an entire world. And whoever saves a life, it is considered as if he saved an entire world.' Your job, gentlemen—my job, the job of all in the Jewish Resistance—is to save lives, lives that will otherwise be destroyed by Herr Hitler and his thugs. Please, I implore you: Let us hear the cries of our condemned brothers and sisters. Let us come to their rescue. Let us not waste another second doing anything else. Is not this why God has spared our lives thus far?"

The room grew silent. Jacob's eyes turned to Maurice Tulek. So did everyone else's. Jacob could see the argument on both sides, but he was moved by his uncle's passion. It was the same passion that had moved

Avi to try to save Herr Berger's life during *Kristallnacht*, the same passion that had moved him to argue so vehemently with his brother to leave Germany before it was too late. And it was that passion—that deep and abiding sense of moral conviction—that had persuaded Jacob his uncle was right.

To Jacob's shock, however, Maurice Tulek came down on the side of his fellow cell commanders and against Avi. Their mission, he said, was to gather intelligence on Nazi troop strength, locations of arms caches, and the like, and to feed that intelligence to the Allies. The sooner the Allies won, the more Jews who would be saved. A mission such as the one Avi was proposing, Morry felt, would threaten the entire Resistance in Belgium.

It was a risk that could not be afforded. The answer was no.

21

Jacob felt betrayed.

It had been his love for these men, his admiration for their courage and for their willingness to risk their lives to do what was right, that had so inspired him and given him the motivation to keep going against all odds. Now all of that was lost. His faith in the Resistance was rattled at best, if not shattered altogether. As he and Avi sneaked back to their own safe house—this time the basement of a warehouse on the west side of Brussels—Jacob felt the will to continue steadily draining from his heart.

Avi said nothing. He seemed focused entirely on their safe return home. Nothing more. Nothing less. Nothing else. When they finally got there, Micah, Henri, and Jacques were sound asleep on their tattered old mattresses on the cold cement floor. Jacob glanced at his watch. It was nearly four. They had to be cleared out of the warehouse by seven. Yawning, he quietly pulled off his boots, climbed up onto the top level of the room's only bunk bed, and pulled a thick wool blanket over himself. Avi, however, did not go to bed. He just sat on a wooden stool and stared at the floor.

"Uncle, what are you going to do?" Jacob whispered when he could take the suspense no more.

"What would you do?" Avi replied.

Jacob was caught off guard by the question. "Me?" he asked. "I'm not a commander."

"Someday you will be," Avi replied. "Maybe someday soon."

"I'll be dead or the war will be over long before that," Jacob sighed.

"Don't be so sure. God has given you a quick mind and a good heart, Jacob. Don't underestimate what he could do with you."

Jacob said nothing, but he mulled his uncle's unexpectedly kind words.

"So what would you do?" Avi asked again.

Jacob stared up at the ceiling. "Let it go, I guess," he said at last. "We have to follow orders."

There was a long silence. Several minutes went by. Finally Avi got up, came over to the bed, and settled in on the lower bunk. "You would really send all those Jews to die at Auschwitz?"

"Before today, I had never heard of Auschwitz."

"It's a concentration camp in southern Poland."

"Okay."

"A death camp."

"Morry says that's only a rumor."

"What if it's true?" Avi asked.

"What if it isn't?" Jacob replied over the snoring of the Belgians.

"Are you prepared to take that chance?" Avi pressed. "The rumors come from people in a position to know what's really happening. What if they're right?"

"What choice do we have?" Jacob said. "You said it yourself. We'd need more than twenty men. We don't have them. We'd need rifles, but you gave them all to Morry. All we have left now is a single pistol and a handful of bullets. I see your point, Uncle. I do. But if the council isn't going to back you, then it's a suicide mission."

Avi said nothing for what seemed like several minutes, and Jacob thought that maybe, just maybe, he had won the day. He breathed a bit easier and finally closed his eyes.

But Avi was not yet done. "What if our Ruthie were being sent to Auschwitz? What if your parents were on the twentieth train?"

22

FEBRUARY 3, 1943
WEMMEL, BELGIUM

By nightfall the next day, their little team had relocated.

Wemmel was a small town north of Brussels. Huddled in the attic of an elderly couple sympathetic to the Resistance, Jacob and Avi feverishly worked on their plan.

When they explained the situation to Micah, Henri, and Jacques, all three men had instantly agreed to help attack the train as soon as possible. "Of course we'll help," they'd said when Jacob asked for their support. "Don't you know us by now?"

As Avi listed out the questions to which they needed answers, the supplies they'd need, and the enormous challenges that lay ahead, Jacob couldn't help but look at these men with affection. He'd never imagined having true friends like these, men so ready and willing to risk their lives for a cause greater than themselves. It might not have restored his faith in mankind, but it certainly moved it in the right direction.

One important fact emerged that night: Micah was Avi's source for the intelligence he had shared with the members of the council. Avi didn't actually know the two people he had referred to in the meeting. Those were Micah's contacts. But the more Jacob heard about them, the more confidence he had in Micah's assessment of their trustworthiness.

For the next few weeks, Micah pressed these contacts hard for more information. Which train would they use? What night were they leaving?

Exactly how many prisoners would be on the train? Nothing could be left to chance. They had to have precise, actionable intelligence. The mission was already likely to cost all of them their lives. They needed at least a shred of hope that they could succeed, and that came only with knowing exactly what they were up against and whether the plan Avi had developed could really work under those specific circumstances.

There was plenty of critical work to be done. Most important, they had to find a site to attack the train. Since they no longer had any access to cars or trucks, it couldn't be far from Brussels. It had to be close enough that they could reach it by bicycle. It had to be near public transportation. Once they'd helped the Jewish prisoners escape the train, those who weren't gunned down by the Nazis had to be able to travel quickly to Brussels or Antwerp or some other nearby city. Micah's intelligence indicated that all the Jews were still wearing street clothes, not prison uniforms, and they hadn't been captive for more than a few months—only a few weeks in some cases—so Avi felt certain they had a real chance at blending into society and using public transportation without immediately getting noticed and arrested.

The point of attack had to be near a curve in the track, Avi said. As hard as they'd tried to get some, they didn't have explosives. Thus they couldn't blow up the train or the track. Nor could they cut the track ahead of time. It was inspected daily. If they couldn't figure out a way to make the train stop, they at least had to take advantage of a curve, where the train would have to slow down from hurtling along at roughly thirty kilometers an hour to a manageable six or seven kilometers an hour. Only then would Jacob and his fellow freedom fighters be able to rush forward, jump on the train, cut the chains and wires securing the cattle cars, open the doors, and help the people jump out.

Furthermore, the site had to be isolated enough that no one could witness the raid or the escape. Ideally, it needed to be near a forest to provide cover for the team to hide until the train arrived, cover for Avi as he fired at the guards with their one pistol, and cover for the prisoners as they fled.

The longer Avi made the list of requirements, the less confidence Jacob had that this could actually be done. But he didn't voice his concerns. He didn't say much of anything. He judged this wasn't the time to express doubts, however real they were. After all, Avi was right: What if his sister or his parents had been forced onto such a train? Wouldn't he want people to do everything in their power to try to set them free, even if they failed?

Each man on the team was given a list of duties. Avi would be responsible for finding the right attack spot. Micah would work his contacts for more information. Henri and Jacob would gather bicycles, pliers, and wire and bolt cutters. Jacques would be in charge of gathering bags of cash and then distributing fifty-franc notes to every prisoner and directing them through the forest to various train and bus routes.

On Friday, April 16, they gathered for dinner, though everyone but Avi was too nervous to eat.

The good news was that their intelligence channels were working. All the pieces were coming together. According to Micah's sources, there were now just over 1,600 Jews in Mechelen. Commander Asche and the Gestapo were ready to go. The plan was for the prisoners to be loaded into cattle cars on the evening of Monday, April 19. Train 801 would then pull out at precisely 10:00 p.m. No later than 10:30, the train should pass the site Avi had chosen.

The bad news was that none of them believed their current plan was sufficient. They needed a way to stop the train, even for a few moments. Only then could they effectively cut the chains and wires and get people out of the cars. The Belgians were adamant that trying to open the doors while the train was still moving—even at a slower rate—simply wasn't realistic.

Jacob looked at Avi, expecting him to be angry. But he was not. Or at least he didn't give the appearance that he was upset, just exhausted. He calmly told his men they had until lunchtime tomorrow to come up with a plan to stop the train, though he had tried for weeks and hadn't come up with anything convincing. He wolfed down some soup and bread and a glass of wine and then said he was going to bed. He had a meeting with Morry in the morning. He told the men that they should plan to meet again at noon for a final review of the plan.

With that, he retired for the night. The younger men were on their own.

They spent half the night considering ways they might be able to bring the train to a halt.

Unfortunately, not one of the ideas floated seemed realistic. They had no way to sabotage the train engine. They had no explosives. They could steal a vehicle and park it on the tracks, perhaps with its hood up to make it look like the engine had stalled. But the site Avi had chosen didn't have a road close to it or a crossing near it, and it would be very suspicious to have a car in that area. What's more, stealing a car or truck or some other kind of vehicle bore its own set of risks of getting caught. The operation was going to be difficult enough. Potentially losing one of their team members during the botched theft of a vehicle would make it impossible.

At one point, Jacob suggested he lie down on the tracks. But Micah reminded him they were dealing with Nazis.

"They're killing half of Europe," he said. "Do you really think they're going to stop an entire train of prisoners in the dead of night to avoid cutting some poor sap in half? They probably won't even see you in time."

23

In the morning, Jacob awoke with a new idea.

"How do you make a train stop?" he asked.

"If we knew that, we wouldn't have been up until three," Jacques snapped.

"But how does one normally stop a train?" Jacob pressed.

The three stared at him blankly.

"Trains stop at stations, and they stop for obstructions on the track," Jacob continued. "The only other reason they stop is if they see a red light, correct?"

The men shrugged.

"So let's get a light—a red light," Jacob said, his excitement rising. "We'll put it in the middle of the track. In the darkness, the engineer won't know why it's there. He'll just do what his training tells him to do."

"Stop," Henri said.

"Exactly."

"What kind of light?" Micah asked.

"I don't know," Jacob said. "How about a hurricane lamp? You know, the old kind with oil and a wick. We can get some red tissue paper and cover the glass around it. From a distance, it might look like a railway lamp."

The four of them looked at each other and decided it just might work. What other choice did they have? Time was running out. Henri volunteered to help Jacob find the lamp. Jacques would acquire the tissue paper. Micah agreed to go out and scrounge up something for lunch, and then, as planned, they'd all meet again at noon with Avi, who had left early that morning as promised.

When noon came, they were huddled back in the attic with a loaf of bread, a few small apples, and a jug of wine. They now had a hurricane lamp and the requisite paper. But Avi was nowhere to be found.

At first they weren't worried. They ate together and talked excitedly about the mission ahead. But when Avi wasn't back by one o'clock, and then two o'clock, Jacob grew concerned. By three thirty, they decided to go out and look for him. But by the time the curfew fell at eight o'clock and they were back together in the cramped and drafty attic, they still had not found him.

Jacob reported that he had gone to see Morry, who confirmed that he'd had breakfast with Avi. The two had met and discussed several upcoming operations. Jacob said Morry gave no indication that he knew about the operation scheduled for Monday evening, nor had Jacob alluded to it. Morry said Avi had left around ten that morning and indicated only that he had "a few errands to attend to."

Suddenly there was a knock on the attic floor. Micah opened the hatch and peered down at the old man who was safeguarding them in his home.

"Someone just dropped this off," the man said, his voice gravelly from years of smoking. "Didn't stay. Didn't leave his name. Said it was for you. Then he was gone."

The old man handed up a sealed envelope. Micah took it and looked it over. It had no writing on either the front or the back. Out of respect, he handed it to Jacob, who quickly opened and read the short note within.

A. captured by Gestapo. At Avenue Louise now.
Being moved to M. tonight. All we have.

Jacob's stomach tightened. He stared at the paper in his trembling hands. It wasn't possible. His uncle was the shrewdest, most careful man Jacob knew. How could he have been arrested? What had gone wrong? Worse, was he now being tortured in the basement of the Gestapo's headquarters? Was he really being transferred to the Mechelen transit camp? If so, that could only mean one thing.

"He'll be on the train," Jacob said softly. "They're sending him to Auschwitz."

24

APRIL 19, 1943
BOORTMEERBEEK, BELGIUM

The brutal truth was that they were not yet ready.

They were, as one of them put it so bluntly, "badly equipped and underprepared." But there was nothing more they could do, and they were now out of time. They had never envisioned running such an operation with just the four of them. Avi's original concept, after all, had called for twenty-two armed men. But though none of them said it aloud, each of them knew they absolutely had to succeed. For Avi's sake, not to mention the other 1,600 souls who would be on that train.

At precisely seven o'clock Monday evening, they set out on bicycles for the same destination. They went in different directions, of course, and took different routes, to see if any of them was being followed and to shake their shadows if at all possible.

Jacob knew the plan cold. If he was being followed, he was supposed to stop at a café, have a cup of coffee, and return to the safe house. But there was no way he was going to abort this mission. Not with his uncle's life at stake.

Detecting no one on his trail, to his great relief, he pedaled for more than two hours, covering some forty kilometers, before he finally reached the stretch of track that Avi had chosen. It was about a kilometer from the Boortmeerbeek train station, secluded and desolate.

In his backpack, Jacob carried the lamp and a thin red scarf, having worried that the lamp could become too hot and burn up the tissue paper. Seeing no one and hearing nothing but the wind rustling through the trees and some birds off in the distance, Jacob hid his bicycle under some bushes on the far side of the woods. Then he hiked back through the trees and found a perch from which to eye the tracks.

Soon he saw the others arrive, one by one. They gathered and quickly went back over the plan, though they didn't dare speak above a whisper. Then Jacob decided it was too dangerous to be anywhere near each other and ordered everyone to retreat to their predetermined positions and wait.

When Jacob's watch struck ten, he climbed down from his lookout in a tall pine tree and sprinted the fifty yards or so between the edge of the woods and the tracks. At a point just past the bend, Jacob pulled the hurricane lamp from his backpack, lit it, set it in the middle of the tracks, and wrapped it with the red scarf he'd brought. Then he walked back along the tracks about twenty yards and turned to look at the lamp. It wasn't bad, he thought. It might even work.

Jacob stood there longer than he should have, taking in the beauty of the pastoral scene around him. For a moment, it was possible to forget the world was gripped in a terrible, bloody war. Here there were no tanks or troops or bombers or barbed wire. The moon above was full. The stars were out in all their twinkling glory. There wasn't a cloud in the sky, and the temperature was falling quickly. Jacob figured it was hovering around the freezing mark and was likely to drop further over the next few hours. He drank in the lovely scent of the pines, swaying in the breeze now coming from the east, and then he thought he detected a trace of smoke in the air. It was faint at first, then grew stronger, and as it did, his thoughts drifted back to Siegen.

He closed his eyes and remembered hiking in the mountains with his uncle. He could suddenly see and smell and taste all the wonderful meals his mother and Ruthie used to prepare, the roasts and the pastries, and the life he had grown up with—the life he cherished so dearly—all came rushing back.

Then he heard the piercing wail of the train whistle. His eyes opened instantly. His heart began to race. He looked behind him. He couldn't see the engine yet, but he could feel the ground trembling ever so slightly beneath his feet.

He glanced at his watch, not understanding what was happening. Train 801 was too early. How was that possible? German trains were never early, never late, always exactly on time. In his peripheral vision he saw Micah waving frantically for him to get moving. He immediately jumped off the tracks, ran down the slight embankment and across the field to the forest's edge. There he retook his position as the shrill whistle grew louder and the ground shook all the more.

Hiding behind a tree, Jacob saw in the distance a single engine pulling a single tender. This wasn't the 801. It was a false alarm. But he just stood there, fixated on the wrong train, frozen with fear.

The lamp.

He couldn't leave it on the tracks. They didn't want this train to stop. They needed it to roll through, and quickly. He was too far away. Could he get to the lamp and get it off the tracks and get back into the woods in time? Suddenly, as he was about to move, he saw Micah save the day. He sprinted to the tracks, grabbed the hurricane lamp, and then sprinted back for the woods, just in the nick of time. Moments later, the train rushed past. It slowed, but thank God, it did not stop.

Drenched in sweat and freezing in the breeze, Jacob castigated himself for the mistake he'd just made. He'd nearly blown the entire mission. He'd nearly cost Avi and 1,600 other people their lives. A wave of guilt and depression washed over him, but before he knew it, another train whistle cut through the night.

Turning to his left, he now saw the enormous steam engine that had to be the 801. To his relief, Micah was ready. Once again, Micah ran up the embankment and put the lamp on the tracks, then disappeared back into the trees.

Less than twenty seconds later, train 801 came barreling down the line, huffing and puffing and sending great belches of soot into the night sky. Jacob tried to push his failures out of his mind, but now he feared the ruse wouldn't work after all. What if the train slowed but didn't stop? What if the SS troops on the train saw the lamp for what it was—a Resistance plot—and radioed for backup? The forest could soon be crawling with troops. They would all be dead within the hour.

Yet even as those thoughts flickered across the transom of his mind, the train began to brake right in front of him. The horrendous screeching of metal on metal grated upon Jacob's already-frayed nerves. It took longer than he'd expected for all thirty cattle cars to come to a stop, but the instant they did, gunfire erupted from his right. That was it. That was the signal.

Jacob put his head down and bolted for the train as more shots rang out in the night.

Micah's job was to use the one pistol they had and keep firing in hopes that he could stun the SS guards in the lead cars into thinking they were being attacked by a superior force spread out through the woods. Hopefully that would buy the rest of the team just enough time to free the prisoners in the cattle cars before the soldiers, armed with machine guns, began to return fire.

To his left, Jacob saw Henri reach the last car in the line. Seconds later, Jacob scrambled up the embankment and reached his designated car, six from the rear. He immediately set about cutting the wires, then slid the cattle car door open. Turning on his flashlight, he peered at the stunned, pale faces huddled inside.

"Get up—now!" he shouted in Dutch and then in French. "Run for the woods! We are the Resistance, come to set you free! Run, you fools—run now or die!"

He could see the panic and confusion in their eyes. But he remembered Avi's words not to wait for them to move. They had to open as many cars as possible before the counterattack began. There was not time to tell the people that Jacques was in the woods, ready to give them each a fifty-franc note and directions to public transportation that would get them to Brussels, Antwerp, Charleroi, and beyond. If they obeyed Jacob's commands, jumped off the train, and began running into the woods, they would find Jacques, or Jacques would find them. For now, Jacob had to keep moving.

Gunfire again filled the night. Micah was doing his job flawlessly, and Jacob found himself intoxicated by the adrenaline surging through his system. He broke open a second cattle car and then a third. He screamed at the people to flee, and mostly they did. But when the latest group of prisoners heard the SS machine guns open fire, everyone froze in place.

Knowing they had only moments to break free, Jacob jumped up into the train car, yelling, *"Snel, snel, springen, vluchten!"* He grabbed some of the younger men in the car, pulled them to their feet, and pushed them toward the door, yelling at them to jump and run for their lives. He moved through the train car, turning to the older folks and begging them to move quickly, for there was not much time. He knew they were scared, but if they wanted to live, they had to run. Deeper into the cattle car Jacob moved, and just then he heard someone behind him shout his name.

The sound took a second to register, but when he turned, Jacob began beaming. "Uncle!" he yelled, seeing Avi standing outside the cattle car. "You're safe!"

"I am, and I'm so proud of you," Avi shouted back over the intensifying gunfire. "Any chance you've got some extra pliers?"

Jacob smiled wider. He did, in fact, have an extra pair, and he now tossed them to his uncle, thrilled to see him again and glad to have extra hands. They still had some twenty cars to open. It didn't seem possible, but Avi's help would make a huge difference.

Just then, however, Jacob saw an SS soldier swing around the side of the cattle car. He heard a burst of machine-gun fire. He saw the flash from the muzzle, and then he watched helplessly as Avi was repeatedly hit by bullets and fell down the embankment and out of sight.

"Get back!" the soldier screamed in German, his voice brutal and guttural. "Get back, all of you, or you will be shot like dogs!"

And then, before Jacob fully realized what was happening, the door of the cattle car was being slammed shut and locked, and before long, the train started moving again. The people around him huddled in fear, but Jacob ran to the door and struggled frantically to open it. He began hacking away at the door with the wire cutters in his hands, but it was in vain.

Panic-stricken, he pulled himself up to look through a tiny opening near the roof of the car. He could hear more shooting. He could see Jewish prisoners running. Some were falling, cut down by the SS. But he couldn't see Avi. He couldn't see Micah, Henri, or Jacques.

And then they were in darkness, and he couldn't see anything at all, and a terrible, sick feeling permeated Jacob's body.

He was trapped and alone, and headed for Auschwitz.

PART
THREE

25

APRIL 19, 1943
LA ROCHELLE, FRANCE

Hundreds of kilometers away, Jean-Luc Leclerc was also on a train.

His journey from Le Chambon to the seaside port city of La Rochelle, overlooking the vast expanse of the Atlantic Ocean, had already taken him the better part of a day. It was a risk to travel so far from the safety of his home, away from Claire and the girls, away from the church and the hundreds of Jews who depended on them for their very lives. It was an especially great risk to travel to a city that housed a U-boat base and thus was crawling with Nazi soldiers and Gestapo agents.

Luc had become the overseer of the clandestine refugee project that now engulfed the entire town. It was he who greeted the new Jewish families that seemed to arrive every few days on the one o'clock train through the once-sleepy hollow of Le Chambon. It was he who learned their stories, made them feel welcome, and assigned them to someone's home. It was he who then took them there personally and introduced them to the owners of that home and made sure they got settled quickly and quietly and discreetly.

It was Luc who arranged for the families to get new identity papers and who briefed them on the protocols he and the other pastors had developed to help the refugees become integrated into the schools and the shops and the patterns of life in the little French village. It was he who got them different clothes to wear and gave them pointers on looking and sounding like Gentiles—like Protestants.

He was always respectful of their faith, or lack thereof, and their habits and customs and traditions. The fact was, he was completely fascinated with God's chosen people, and he did everything he could to make them feel comfortable and safe. But to make them truly safe, he told them candidly, was to erase any evidence that they were Jews. Not for the sake of the people of Le Chambon, but to prevent the Vichy police from finding them and turning them over to the Nazis.

Quite simply, Luc loved what he did, and he was good at it. That was why it was dangerous for him to leave. He knew so much. He knew the people personally. He loved to visit them and talk with them and learn their stories and introduce them to his family and invite them over for picnics and hikes and other family events. Luc knew how to make the system work. He was methodical and detailed and could anticipate problems and try to solve them before they metastasized. He was artful at mediating conflicts, and he was—usually—rather patient and good-humored about it all. This was why the elders at the church didn't want him to leave. Not on this trip. Not on any. It was Claire who had insisted, and after much prayer, including several days of fasting, he concluded that she was right.

It was dark and late, and there was nothing to see out the window of the steam-propelled train as it chugged ever closer to its destination. As the whistle shrieked into the night, signaling their imminent approach to the station in La Rochelle, Luc closed his eyes and thought back to the meeting in the basement of the church building just twenty-four hours earlier.

"We are reaching our capacity," Luc had explained. "It's a true miracle what has happened so far. But I'm not sure we can sustain this."

"What do you mean?" Chrétien, the senior pastor, asked. "I've heard no complaints so far."

Luc laughed. "That's because we have a town full of saints. You keep preaching Christ's command that we love our neighbors, and everyone is trying to obey. You keep preaching through passages about caring for the widows and the orphans and feeding the hungry and clothing the naked, and people want to be found faithful to our Savior. But with all due respect, sir, there is a point of no return. We're a town of three thousand people. So far, we've given shelter and care to more than five thousand people over the last three years. They haven't all been Jews. But most of them have. And they haven't all stayed here. But a lot of them have. And our people, God bless them, have quietly done their bit, and much, much more, because they want to. Because they know it's the right thing to do. And the last thing they want to do is complain. But we're reaching the breaking point. We need help."

"What kind of help?" asked Émile, who in addition to his duties as a pastor also filled the role of director of the elementary and secondary school run by the church. "Chrétien has raised money from our brothers and sisters in Marseilles and elsewhere. But money is tight. You know that."

"Yes, of course," Luc said. "Actually, I'm not speaking of money. We grow our own food, and God has surely provided abundantly, beyond what we could ask or desire. And we sew our own clothes, so it hasn't been hard to give our surplus to the new families. That is all well and good, truly."

"Then what?" Chrétien asked.

"We need to find another community, somewhere in France, that will partner with us," Luc explained. "We need a place that truly loves the Lord and loves his Word and loves his people and will welcome them with open arms. We need to be able to send people who come to us to this other community, a community full of people who aren't already overworked and overwhelmed."

"You're saying the people of Le Chambon don't want to do this anymore?" Chrétien asked pointedly.

"No, sir," Luc replied. "They are honored to do what they do. But we cannot ask them to do more. We need to find a partner community, a place where we can send those who come to us, a place where we can be sure that these dear people will get the same kind of love and prayer and attention that we give them. To be frank, gentlemen, I fear many more Jews are coming. We've already seen a pickup in the numbers in recent months, and I think that's only going to accelerate. We need to reproduce what we're doing here. We need to do it fast. And we need to do it quietly, without the Vichy government catching wind of it."

The two elders sighed.

"You may be right, Luc," Chrétien conceded. "So what do you propose?"

Another sharp blast of the train whistle, and Luc could feel the train slowing. He opened his eyes and saw the deserted and poorly lit platform approaching. A thick fog had rolled in off the ocean, giving the streetlamps an eerie, unnatural glow. Luc used his sleeve to wipe moisture from the window. He peered out into the night and hoped Claire's brother was there to meet him. He, too, was a pastor. His congregation was located in a wooded hamlet about thirty kilometers south of La Rochelle. Having grown up there, Claire was convinced it was a perfect place to set up another operation to rescue Jews fleeing from *der Führer*. Luc thought she just might be right. They would know soon enough.

The train lurched to a stop. Luc grabbed his overnight bag and stepped out into the sultry night air. He strolled slowly along the wooden platform, letting the other passengers—not that there were many of them—pass him by, meet those who had come to receive them, and depart. Not seeing Claire's brother, he worked his way down a flight of stairs to the parking lot.

He never saw them coming.

He was jumped from behind by two men whose faces he couldn't see. They threw him to the ground, kicked him repeatedly, nearly breaking several of his ribs. Then a black hood was thrown over his head, and someone smashed a large blunt object into the back of his skull.

When he awoke, he was bound and gagged and blindfolded, with no idea how long he had been unconscious, who had grabbed him, or where he was.

Someone pulled the rag out of his mouth, and Luc coughed and sputtered and then began to breathe deeply of the salty night air. They were still in La Rochelle, he concluded, not far from the coast.

"How long have you been harboring kikes?" a voice demanded.

The language was French, but the accent was most decidedly German, which told him he was in the hands of the Gestapo. Luc said nothing.

"How many filthy Jews have you stashed away?"

Still Luc remained silent.

"How many Jews have you hidden from *der Führer*? Who paid you to do it? How much?"

The questions kept coming, one after another, one after another, like bursts from a machine gun. When Luc refused to answer, someone punched him squarely in the nose. He could hear the crunch as he felt excruciating pain explode through his entire head and radiate throughout his body. He felt blood running down his face. But still he refused to talk.

"When did Pastor Chrétien start harboring Jews? When did Pastor Émile start helping? Why do you do it? Why did you choose to betray your race? What's in it for you?"

Luc was determined to keep his mouth shut. He didn't want to lie, and he certainly did not want to tell the Gestapo the truth. But he was rattled at the unexpected mention of his fellow pastors in Le Chambon. These were his elders, his mentors. How did the Germans know about any of them? They had all worked so hard to be discreet. The whole town had. They didn't talk to outsiders about what they were doing. Why would anyone say a word? And to whom would they say it? How, then, had the Gestapo zeroed in on them?

Suddenly it occurred to Luc that Chrétien and Émile had probably been arrested as well. Indeed, it might not just be the three of them, he realized. There were so many others in Le Chambon who were intimately involved in rescuing the people of God from the labor camps or even just from the humiliation of being run out of their towns and villages for being different. Some were doing much more than he and

Claire, Luc thought. Surely if he had been dragged in by the Gestapo, others far more important than he had been arrested too.

The Gestapo man was screaming at him again. But Luc could barely hear him. The most vile obscenities were being hurled at him, but rather than recoil, Luc felt an involuntary smile slowly spread across his bloodied face. How was it possible that he, of all people, was worthy of being cursed and beaten like his Savior? It made no sense, but it gave him a strange, unspeakable joy.

It was then that the heavy blows started raining down on him again, and before he realized what was happening, he had blacked out once more.

26

APRIL 19, 1943
AUSCHWITZ-BIRKENAU CONCENTRATION CAMP, POLAND

Colonel Klaus Von Strassen nodded, and the deed was done.

Upon seeing the "go" sign from Von Strassen, the prison guard pulled the lever, the trapdoor immediately opened, and another Jew twisted and writhed in the cold night air.

Von Strassen watched as the young boy—no more than fifteen or sixteen years old—kicked violently and strained at the ropes wound tightly about his hands until his eyes bulged and then rolled back in his head and the life drained out of him.

"What did this one do?" the guard on the platform asked as he cut the boy down.

"He was a Jew," Von Strassen said, lighting up a cigarette. "Does it really matter?"

Just then, Von Strassen's adjutant came running up to him and breathlessly announced he had a phone call in the operations center.

Von Strassen strode quickly down the street and ran up the stairs to his corner office on the third floor, where he took the call.

"Yes, this is he. . . . Yes. . . . *What?* . . . How is that possible? When? . . . How many? . . . You're certain? . . . What time? . . . Yes, yes; I will inform him at once."

Von Strassen told his young aide to stay close to the phone and to inform him of any updates. In the meantime, he was heading for the commandant's office and would be right back.

"You mean his home?" the aide asked.

"No, his office."

"Would he still be there?"

"You're new, aren't you?" Von Strassen asked.

The young man nodded.

"I suggest you learn not to ask stupid questions."

Internally, Von Strassen was seething. He had no interest in helping to run a prison camp. He wanted to be on the front lines. He wanted to be leading a panzer division. He longed to have raced across the North African deserts with Field Marshal Rommel, the Desert Fox. He was desperate to get a forward command, but here he was, stuck in southern Poland, on the most godforsaken spit of land he could possibly imagine.

On the outside, however, he willed himself to maintain his composure and do the tasks set before him with such excellence that his worth to the Third Reich would not be overlooked much longer.

He headed back downstairs and across the courtyard. For now, he had to be content as the chief of security for the Auschwitz-Birkenau concentration camp and its adjacent complex of forty-five subcamps.

Two minutes later, Von Strassen stood outside the commandant's office and knocked sharply on the door.

"*Ja*—come," came the irritated reply.

Von Strassen picked some lint from his uniform, slicked back his hair, arched his back, and took a deep breath. Then he opened the door, entered, and—standing erect—gave the Nazi salute and a hearty "Heil Hitler!"

Rudolf Hoess did not look up from the mountain of papers on his desk. It was late, and he looked weary and annoyed. Von Strassen knew the forty-two-year-old camp commander had no desire to be working by flickering candlelight on the insatiable requests coming from Berlin for more-detailed reports. Von Strassen had no doubt that Hoess certainly would have preferred to be around the corner, back home with his five sleeping children, in bed with his wife, Hedwig. But orders were orders, and Hoess prided himself on being loyal to *der Führer* above all. The fit, stern-looking Baden native with close-cropped black hair seemed driven to continue impressing his superiors as he had for the past several years since being personally directed by Heinrich Himmler to turn this old Polish army base into "the largest extermination center of all time." Von Strassen, in turn, felt driven to help Hoess in every way he could, assuming that success for the camp commandant would undoubtedly redound in his favor.

"Heil Hitler," came Hoess's perfunctory reply. His attention was still riveted on the reports he was preparing. "Why the urgency, Colonel? Surely you have better things to do than bother me at such an hour."

"I beg your pardon, Herr Commandant," Von Strassen replied. "I would not interrupt you if it was not urgent, but I just spoke to Commander Asche in Brussels."

"And?" Hoess continued signing forms and putting them in his out-box for his secretary to handle first thing in the morning.

"He has troubling news to report, I'm afraid."

"Get to your point, Colonel," Hoess ordered. "You're trying my patience."

"Yes, sir," Von Strassen said and then delivered the disturbing news as succinctly as he could. "It would appear that train 801 was attacked by a small group of Resistance members not long after it left Boortmeerbeek."

Hoess stopped writing and looked up. Von Strassen certainly had his attention now.

"Commander Asche says more than two hundred prisoners escaped," the colonel continued.

"Two hundred, you say?" Hoess asked. "How is that possible? Wasn't there any security on that train?"

"There was, Herr Commandant," Von Strassen replied. "They returned fire. At least one of the Resistance members was killed. The rest fled into the woods. The police in the area are on full alert, as is the army. They are doing a massive search of the city. Roadblocks are up. Troops are covering every bridge and rail station. Local citizens are being notified that if they harbor any of the fugitives, they will be hanged. Commander Asche is confident all the escapees—and the criminals responsible, no doubt all Jewish vermin—will be caught and shot. The rest of the Jews, he said, are still on their way."

"How many?"

"About 1,400, sir."

Hoess glared at Von Strassen. "In ancient times, you would have been shot for such news," the commandant fumed. He stood and began pacing his spacious office, its walls lined with bookshelves filled with volumes on history and military strategy that Von Strassen privately doubted Hoess had ever read. "You should thank *der Führer* that we run such an enlightened empire."

"Yes, Herr Commandant," said Von Strassen, undeterred, at full attention, his back ramrod straight, ready to do whatever Hoess requested.

The commandant of Auschwitz-Birkenau walked to the window. "When I began in the SS, there were no escapes, or nearly none," he said in a melancholy, almost-wistful manner. "When I was the deputy at Dachau, escapes were exceedingly rare. And why was that?"

"I don't know, Herr Commandant," Von Strassen said. He was in no mood to play twenty questions with his superior.

"Because the head of security and the guards he commanded knew they would be severely punished if anyone got away," Hoess explained. "When I ran Sachsenhausen, we cracked down even more. An escape was considered the most serious crime there was, and I treated it as such. I insisted that absolutely everything be done to prevent an escape, and I was merciless with those who refused to take this point seriously. That's why I brought you in last year, Colonel. You know that, don't you?"

"Yes, sir."

Hoess now turned and faced Von Strassen. "You must close the gaps, or there will be hell to pay. You must improve the discipline of your men to always stay sharp and never let their guard down, even for a split second. You must also instill the fear of God into the prisoners so that they do not think even for one moment that an escape will be tolerated. And you know why, right? You know why we can never allow any of these prisoners to make it out alive, do you not?"

"Yes, sir," Von Strassen said. "Absolutely, sir."

Hoess locked his gaze on his security chief and walked directly to him, stopping only inches from his face. "The world must never know the things we do here, Colonel. Never. Do I make myself clear?"

"Yes, Herr Commandant. I shall do my best. You have my word."

27

"Who are you?" someone asked.

It was still pitch-black. Jacob was still bracing himself against the cattle car door, trying to maintain his balance and process the magnitude of what had just happened, when someone called out in the darkness. It was the voice of an old man. He sounded scared.

Just then the train came out of the shadows and moonlight again filtered into the car. Jacob saw that the cattle car—which had been packed with as many as eighty or ninety people—was now only about half-full. Most of those who were left were sitting on their trunks or suitcases or on the floor, which was covered in hay. A putrid odor suddenly caught his attention, and he noticed a bucket in one corner, overflowing with feces.

He scanned the faces of the forty or so souls around him. Most appeared at least sixty or older. There was one family—a father, a trembling mother, and three small, pale, shell-shocked children, a boy and twin girls.

"Who are you, young man?" an older man's voice asked again.

To his left, Jacob saw the man who was speaking to him. He was standing, leaning against one of the walls of the car, and looking straight into Jacob's eyes. Jacob figured him to be in his seventies, at least. He was thin, of medium height, and wore rumpled slacks, a shirt, a gray cardigan sweater, and gold wire-rimmed glasses. He had a weathered but gentle face and kindly blue eyes, and he wore a dark-brown felt homburg that made him look a bit distinguished but also somewhat like the grandpa Jacob always wished he had known. Jacob tried to determine why the man was asking and how he should reply. His first instinct was to lie, but what good would that do him? These were not his enemies. Indeed, these might become his only friends.

"Jacob," he said at last. "My name is Jacob."

"Jacob what?" the man asked over the monotonous *clickity-clack, clickity-clack, clickity-clack* of the tracks rushing below them and the whistle of the wind whipping by outside and occasionally finding its way into the car.

"Weisz, sir—Jacob Weisz."

"Are you Jewish?"

Jacob hesitated a moment but finally nodded.

"And you're with the Resistance?"

"Yes."

There was a long silence. Jacob looked around at all the faces staring at him. He wondered what they were all thinking, but in the shadows they were inscrutable.

"Well, Jacob Weisz, that was a brave thing you just did," the old man said. "Brave, indeed."

Several people nodded at that, but none of them relaxed. None of them smiled or grinned or even looked appreciative. Then again, why should they? They hadn't escaped. Their friends and relatives and complete strangers had, and they were left behind.

"Are you of the Weisz family in Antwerp?" another man asked, this one off to his right.

"No, sir," Jacob said. "I'm from Germany—Siegen, to be precise."

"I would stop that," the first old man said.

"What?"

"Precision."

"I'm sorry—I don't follow," Jacob said.

"Stop answering questions with precision, young man," the older man repeated. "It's not going to help you where you're going. In fact, I'd lose your name entirely. From this moment forward, you're no longer Jacob Weisz."

"Why not?"

"Do you really need to ask?"

Jacob said nothing.

"The SS has paperwork. They know the names of everyone on this train and everyone in this car. And there's no Jacob Weisz on their list, is there?"

"No, sir."

"Of course not, because you didn't come with us. So if there's no Jacob Weisz on their list, then that means you're with the Resistance. And if you're with the Resistance, that means they're going to shoot you or hang you the second they figure that out. Do you understand where I'm going with this?"

Jacob nodded as the dreadful reality of what was happening began to sink in.

"My son was on this train," the old man continued. "When you opened the door and told us all to flee, I pushed him out before he could say no. I pray to God that he got away safely. His name was Lenny . . ." The man began to choke up, his eyes filling with tears. ". . . Leonard Eliezer. He was about your age. And now that's your name. I'll be your father, and you'll be my son, and maybe, just maybe, we'll get through this thing together."

Jacob was deeply moved by this unexpected act of kindness, and he thanked the man profusely.

But the old man was not finished. "Do you have papers?"

"Yes, of course," Jacob said. "My wallet, my ID."

"Dispose of them immediately."

"What?"

"You heard me. Right now. You need to purge yourself of everything that ties you to your past."

Jacob knew the man was right, but still he hesitated. In his wallet weren't just wads of fifty-franc notes. His most precious possessions in the world were the pictures he had of his mother and father and Ruthie and his uncle. They were the only ones he had. How could he throw them away?

"Do you want to live or die, my son?" the man asked bluntly. "Keep it all, and you die. Get rid of it all, and who knows—you might die, but perhaps you will live."

The people around him were clutching their most valuable possessions, their family heirlooms and keepsakes, all tucked away in their trunks and their bags. They didn't have to part with theirs. How was it fair that he had to part with his? Yet what choice did he have? Nothing about this war was fair. Nothing about being Jewish was fair. The only question that counted was whether he wanted to live or not, and he did.

Jacob pulled out his wallet, kept the money he had on him, and tossed everything else out the slit at the top of the train door.

"Now the pliers," the old man said.

Jacob reluctantly pushed them through a crack and watched them disappear.

"Now, come over here, and I'll teach you everything you'll need to know about being my son. First of all, my name is Marvin. Marvin Eliezer."

With that, the man stuck out his hand. It was wrinkled and thin, but Jacob took it gratefully. He was surprised by the warmth and the strength of the man's handshake and by the lump forming in his own throat.

"Mr. Eliezer, it is an honor to meet you," Jacob said.

"Not Mr. Eliezer," the man corrected. "From now on you call me Papa."

28

For the next sixty-one hours, they rode in near silence.

Some hummed or sang quietly to themselves. Others talked in low whispers. Some recited their ritual prayers. But all Jacob could do was think about escaping the nightmare to come.

He remonstrated with himself for throwing away his wire cutters so quickly. In the end, Mr. Eliezer might turn out to be right, but Jacob berated himself for acting rashly. He hadn't done what Avi and Maurice Tulek had taught him during their Resistance training. He hadn't remained calm. He hadn't carefully thought through every move and countermove and then taken decisive, considered action. Instead he had panicked, and it might cost him—cost all of them—dearly.

As they rode the nearly 1,300 kilometers from Brussels to the small Polish town of Oświęcim and the concentration camp known as Auschwitz, the people in the train car who had food with them graciously shared it with those who did not, Jacob among them. Their water supply, however, was used up quickly. Occasionally train 801 stopped and the cattle car door noisily slid open. One man was selected from among the prisoners and forced out of the car at gunpoint. Surrounded by SS guards with machine guns, the chosen man from each car was told he had three minutes to fill up a bucket with water.

During one stop, that man was Jacob.

The moment he stepped out of the car and onto the train station platform, his first thought wasn't water but escape. As he stood in line behind two dozen other men, he nervously eyed the guards and the growling German shepherds straining at their leashes. He calculated his odds of breaking free. But after only sixteen of the men ahead of him had had time to fill up their buckets from the tap, one of the men suddenly jumped from the platform. He bolted for a nearby field but was cut down in a hail of gunfire. As bad as that was, Jacob noticed the man was not yet dead. He writhed in agony until an officer walked over to him, pulled out a Luger, and shot him in the face.

At once, the SS guards on the platform began beating the men with wooden sticks to get them back in their cars. Not trying to protect a bucket filled with water, Jacob was able to shield himself from the worst of the blows and made it quickly back into his car. Then the door was slammed shut and locked behind him. The whistle shrieked twice, and Jacob had to apologize to all the dehydrated people in his car who had been expecting him to bring them water. But at least he was still alive, he told himself.

And now, cold and thirsty, Jacob felt the train begin moving again, out of Belgium, across Germany, and into the heart of darkness, and all the while the thought of escape slowly faded away.

29

"Has anyone gotten a letter?"

Jacob woke abruptly, realizing he had dozed off and must have been asleep for several hours. The question had been asked by a grossly overweight but pleasant-enough-sounding middle-aged woman.

"Did anyone receive a letter in recent months from friends or relatives who have been sent to a camp?"

At first no one answered the woman. The lack of responses, however, did not dissuade her.

"Listen," she said. "I got this letter from my sister. She was sent to Auschwitz several months ago."

Jacob listened as the woman began to read.

"'Dearest Lara, I miss you terribly and long to be reunited with you, to see your face and hear your infectious laugh. Do not be sad for me, though. Life here at Auschwitz is hard but fair. I have a good job working in the bakery, though I wish I could remember your recipes for your famous *Blechkuchen* or your luscious *Apfelkuchen*.'"

The very mention made Jacob's mouth water for his mother's own fabulous sheet cake and apple cake—and of course the strudel he loved so much.

"'Please pray for the war to be over soon and for Germany to be victorious,'" the letter continued. "'I want to come back and see you and hear all about what you're doing and the fun you're having. Please give Mother and Father a kiss on the cheek for me. Tell them I miss them so. Yours for eternity, Marion.'"

The woman evidently named Lara finished reading and kept staring at the page, but no one said a word.

Embarrassed for her that she had been so vulnerable to a train car full of strangers, only to be ignored, Jacob thanked her and said how nice it would be for the two of them to be reunited.

"Yes, yes," the woman said, not seeming embarrassed in the slightest. "Still, it is a bit odd, I must say."

"Why is that?" Jacob asked.

"It is peculiar—yes, that is the right word—it is peculiar that my sister would ask me to kiss our parents and tell them she misses them."

"That doesn't seem so odd," Jacob said.

The woman turned and stared at him. "It wouldn't be if our parents were alive and well. But they died in a house fire seventeen years ago."

The shock of what she said caused Jacob to physically pull back from her. He could hardly imagine feeling more ill at ease than he already did, but something in what she said triggered a wave of revulsion inside him.

But before he could understand why he felt this way or ask her about the discrepancy, a gray-haired woman bundled up in a lovely fur coat suddenly sat up and spoke for the first time. "I, too, received a letter."

Jacob looked over at her. "What is your name, ma'am?"

"I'm Mrs. Brenner," the woman said. "Just before Chanukah, the police arrested my husband for not wearing his yellow star. He'd simply gone outside to fetch a bottle of milk. He didn't think he needed to wear the star then. An officer was walking by, and he started yelling and beating him without mercy. I came running from the house to see what was happening, only to find blood streaming from my poor husband's head and hands. Before I knew it, he was put in chains and taken away. And then in January, they sent him to Poland, to this place called Auschwitz."

Everyone in the car now was riveted to Mrs. Brenner's story. Jacob knew they all had loved ones who had suddenly disappeared, snatched off the streets, never to be seen again. And now each had his or her own personal story of being arrested, given no trial, given barely enough food and water to survive, and now being thrown into a cattle car and moved across the continent with no idea what really lay ahead.

"I got a letter just ten days ago," Mrs. Brenner said, coming to the point of her story. "My husband said he was fine, adjusting well, eating well, making friends, and so forth. He told me how much he cared for me and longed to see me—everything I wanted and needed to hear. We've been married thirty-two years, my Otto and me, and . . ."

Now her eyes filled with tears. She put her hand over her trembling lips, and to Jacob it seemed she was trying desperately not to suffer the humiliation of weeping in front of complete strangers.

". . . this is the first time we have ever been apart from each other for so long," she said after regaining a measure of control and wiping her eyes.

Then she pulled his letter out from her handbag.

"But this is the part I found odd," she said as she donned a pair of reading glasses and scanned the piece of stationery until she found the exact line. "Yes, here. He writes, 'I am terribly sorry I was not there for your birthday. Please forgive me. Has there ever been a February 9 that I wasn't there? I will make it up to you, my love. In the meantime, buy yourself something nice and tell yourself it's from me. And then ask Madeline to take you out for tea and make a day of it. Live it up. Life is short. But you are worth it.'"

She stopped and stared at the page, and tears began to well up once again. She dabbed them with a pink handkerchief and took several deep breaths, then looked up and turned to the woman named Lara.

"Madeline was our daughter, our only daughter," Mrs. Brenner explained. "But she died while I was giving birth to her. And that was twenty-six years ago. It was the most devastating period of my life. Our marriage almost ended. Why on earth would Otto bring up such a painful memory—and do it so disrespectfully? It makes no sense, and I've been haunted by it ever since. And now I hear your letter, and it sounds as strange as my own."

Jacob suddenly remembered something bizarre that Maurice Tulek had told him and Avi a few weeks before. Morry had received a letter from his brother, Pascal, a revered member of the Resistance, who had been arrested and sent to a camp. Jacob couldn't remember if Pascal had been sent to Auschwitz or Treblinka or Bergen-Belsen or some other camp, but the point was that Morry had been thrilled to hear from Pascal, thrilled to know he was alive and even allowed to write letters. But Morry had been troubled by the postscript his brother had written: "Please visit Mother and Father and tell them I'm so sorry and that I love them dearly." When Avi had asked what was so troubling about that, Morry said their parents had been dead for nearly a decade.

At this point, the car was filled with the sounds of other people fishing their own letters out of billfolds and pocketbooks and comparing them with one another. It soon became evident that nearly everyone in the car had received such a letter, including Mr. Eliezer. All of them contained these strange anomalies. Everyone was talking about why their friends and relatives would say things so odd and disturbing in the midst of otherwise kind and heartfelt correspondence.

Deeply troubled, Jacob, too, pondered the mystery. He slowly moved through the car, eager to overhear what the others were saying and asking questions now and again.

And then he knew.

"They're warnings," he said aloud.

"What do you mean?" asked a middle-aged man in the back of the car.

"Your friends, your neighbors, your loved ones, they're sending you—they're sending all of us—a warning," Jacob said, trying to keep his voice calm and steady though his heart was pounding and he felt gripped by a new wave of fear. "The Nazis forced them to write those letters, to say that they were fine, that all was okay. But what's the theme of the anomalies you're describing? They're all references to people you know who have long since died. The guards at the camps, they must read all these letters. They're no doubt on alert for any language that could give people on the outside a true sense of what's happening inside these concentration camps. But the guards would have no way of knowing the people mentioned in these letters are dead. To them, it must all seem like perfectly normal language, so the letters are cleared. But your loved ones are sending you coded messages. They're telling you that all is not well. They are not fine. And they're warning us not to come."

Mrs. Brenner gasped. So did others. Some scoffed and told Jacob he was crazy. But for most, his analysis rang true.

Jacob knew in his heart that he was right. The rumors were true. They were headed to a death camp. And they would not be coming out.

30

"To sleep, perchance to dream . . ."

As the train continued its monotonous journey toward southern Poland, Jacob found himself awake earlier than most, surprised he had slept through the night. Anxiety and thirst had, in the end, given way to exhaustion, and not just for him but for everyone in his car.

He had dreamed for the first time in months, and in his dream he had asked Naomi Silver to go to the movies with him, and to his astonishment, she had said yes. Now, as he rubbed the sleep from his eyes, the faint whisper of a smile was still on his lips. He could still vividly see the navy-blue dress she was wearing, the one with the small white polka dots. It was the dress she had worn the last time he'd seen her walking into *shul*, the last time she'd smiled shyly at him. He hoped the others were dreaming of something just as pleasant. He hoped they all had a place to escape and hide when the demons came.

Checking his watch, he was surprised to see it was nearly seven in the morning. It was Thursday, April 22, and if his calculations were correct, they would be arriving in the next few hours.

He thought about Uncle Avi. Was he alive? Had he somehow survived the multiple gunshot wounds Jacob had helplessly watched him receive? Was it possible Micah and Henri and Jacques had been able to get him to safety and even now were nursing his wounds and saving his life?

And what of them? Had any of them survived the gun battle? Were they now safely on their way to England? Or were they dead, their bodies still lying beside the railroad tracks?

And what of all the others, the prisoners they had set free? How many had made it off the train, and what had become of them?

Soon those around Jacob began waking up as well. Some used the bucket in the corner to relieve themselves while others graciously created a cordon around them, providing a slim measure of privacy. When Mr. Eliezer awoke, he fished through his luggage and gave Jacob several pieces of matzo and an apple.

"It's all I had in the house when they came to get me," he said.

Jacob was deeply grateful, and they blessed it and ate it together.

Some of the folks in the car, Jacob noticed, had clearly been arrested and beaten and given little or no notice that they were being sent to a slave-labor camp. Like him, they had no luggage, no trunks filled with personal possessions, no food or other provisions. Others on the train seemed as if they were going on holiday to the country for the summer. That was certainly the case with Lara and Mrs. Brenner. They had several trunks each and more food than anyone else. Jacob didn't pretend to know how such differences in preparation had come about, but he was heartened in no small way to see those with food and other provisions being so generous to those without.

Lara, for example, had a big basket of cookies she had baked herself, and she readily shared them with anyone who wanted one. To Jacob, in fact, she gave two, insisting he needed to put "some meat on his bones" and thanking him for letting so many escape. She told him she had been planning to take the cookies to a wedding, but when the Gestapo came for her, they said she had only ten minutes to gather whatever she needed.

Jacob looked at the men and women around him. Some read books they had brought with them, though there wasn't much light, even well after the sun rose. Others tended to their knitting or played cards or tic-tac-toe or other games on the train walls.

In time, however, they all heard the piercing shriek of the train whistle and felt the train begin to slow. This was it, Jacob realized. They had arrived.

31

APRIL 22, 1943
AUSCHWITZ-BIRKENAU CONCENTRATION CAMP, POLAND

What Jacob saw overwhelmed him.

He stood peering through the small, thin opening at the top of the door. Before him was a sprawling complex, surrounded by barbed-wire fences and enormous guard towers with soldiers aiming .50-caliber machine guns and sniper rifles at them. Just ahead were row upon row of three-story brick buildings that looked like army barracks or dormitories. In the distance, he saw an enormous smokestack, several stories high. Thick, black, acrid smoke was belching out of it, and occasionally flames shot out of the top as well. The building below it seemed too small to be a factory of any kind, and Jacob wondered what in the world it was.

Before he knew it, the side door of the car was opening, and he and the others were blinded by a flood of sunshine they hadn't truly seen or experienced in nearly three days. To Jacob's shock, he thought he heard music—a Viennese waltz, no less.

As Jacob's eyes adjusted, he could see heavily armed soldiers shouting at them. They were demanding everyone leave their belongings behind and move rapidly onto the platform and down the wooden ramp. There, they were split into two groups—men on one side, women on the other. Those who dallied were immediately clubbed by the soldiers, who were continuously spewing vile obscenities. And then, sure enough, behind the soldiers, down in the courtyard, Jacob actually spotted a small orchestra, including a whole string section, playing the most beautiful music as if everything were well and they were all on holiday.

Jacob grabbed Mr. Eliezer's hand and pulled him to his feet and toward the door.

"My bag," the old man cried.

"Leave it," snapped a guard, who used a truncheon to bash the old man in the ribs.

Jacob's blood boiled. His hand balled up in a fist, but Mr. Eliezer quickly recovered and insisted he was all right. The guard moved farther into the train car to beat others, and as he did, Mr. Eliezer now took the lead, pulling Jacob toward the rest of the crowd, where they fell in line behind the others who had disembarked first.

"Play the game, my son," he whispered, "or you won't make it to lunch."

Jacob said nothing. He did as he was told, but his instincts and training prompted him to start wondering about escape. The Nazi show of force, however, made any such notion seem far-fetched at best. The easiest way out, presumably, would have been to stow away on the trains they'd just arrived on, but that was clearly impossible. The cattle cars were being thoroughly searched by armed guards and dogs, even as men arrived to remove the luggage, packages, and personal effects and then clean and disinfect each car and put fresh hay on the floors.

Heavily armed soldiers were everywhere. There were hundreds of them. And now, as Jacob looked more carefully, he noticed there was not just one barbed-wire fence ringing the perimeter but two. Even if a prisoner could break free and get over—or under—the first fence without getting shot, there was no way he could get over or under the next fence before being shredded by bullets.

Jacob's attention shifted to more pressing matters at hand. Why in the world were they being sorted? The single-file lines moved steadily, but Jacob and Mr. Eliezer were near the back, and with hundreds of people ahead of them, the process took a while. At the head of the line were two men wearing lab coats—doctors?—each carrying a clipboard and flanked by several assistants. One set focused on the men, the other on the women. Beside them were two men in uniforms, one of whom seemed to be making all the decisions.

The man directed some people to the right. Others he directed to the left. Anyone standing in the line who dared to speak was ordered to be beaten without mercy. Anyone who didn't stand perfectly still was beaten. Any man who so much as glanced over at the women was beaten—not simply tapped or swatted but savagely struck again and again and again. As Jacob watched, at least a dozen men and two women were beaten to death, one within just a few meters of his position. He had seen death over the past few years, even close-up, but never anything like this. He stared aghast as bizarre, emaciated men wearing black-and-white striped clothes and matching striped hats emerged out of nowhere. They gathered up the broken, bloodied bodies, stacked them on a cart like they were cords of wood, and wheeled the cart around a corner and out of sight.

Jacob felt sick to his empty stomach, but he forced himself not to vomit, afraid this might trigger a beating. Fearful of looking to the left or the right, he looked up and let himself be distracted by the weather. It was, he couldn't help but notice, quite a lovely day, in particularly stark contrast to the mood and the moment. The southern Polish skies were a bright and dazzling blue. There wasn't a cloud in sight, and the spring sun was warm and friendly on his face. A slight breeze made the flags with the swastika rustle and clang on their poles every now and again and also felt, dare he say, refreshing.

At least he wasn't boiling or freezing. But Jacob's intense thirst was now growing painful. Aside from the juices of the apple Mr. Eliezer had given him on the train, Jacob hadn't put any liquids in his mouth since Monday evening before they'd left for the mission, and he was now feeling the effect. Still, he was young and strong and determined to maintain a brave composure in the face of the evils that now awaited him. He wondered how much longer the elderly and infirm were going to hold up under such conditions. Surely they would be given food and water now that they had arrived. How else could they be useful slaves in a slave-labor camp?

Suddenly the direction of the wind shifted, and Jacob picked up a whiff of an odor more foul than anything he had ever experienced before.

It was smoke, but not ordinary smoke. This wasn't the scent of burning wood or leaves or even trash. What was it? he wondered. Where was it coming from? Perhaps, he thought, it was from the giant smokestack he had seen earlier.

32

With every step forward, Jacob's trepidation increased.

He was nearing the front of the line, with his "father" right behind him. The orchestra was now playing an upbeat piece Jacob recognized as being from *The Bartered Bride*. Once again he tried desperately to resist the urge to vomit.

What if the camp guards knew he wasn't Leonard Eliezer? What if they knew exactly who he was? Or what if they at least suspected him of not telling the truth? What if they interrogated him? He had spent hours memorizing every fact and detail Mr. Eliezer had taught him about his son. But now he felt flustered, and his stomach ached in fear.

As he edged closer to the front of the line, Jacob could now see the uniformed man in charge very clearly. He was of average height and build, with short dark hair and a sturdy jaw, a patrician nose, and cold, dark eyes. He stood completely still, his head cocked back slightly, his chest puffed out. Considering how deferentially everyone was treating him, Jacob concluded he had to be the camp commander. He hadn't interrogated anyone yet. But this man clearly had the power of life and death in his hands. Jacob had already seen him order men and women beaten to death and watch without flinching. What else was he capable of? Jacob wondered.

For the moment, the uniformed man was still sending some people to the right and some to the left, though as of yet no one had actually said which direction was better and which was worse. Actually, no one—not any guard, nor the doctors nor their assistants nor this commander—had said much of anything. They hadn't explained what going right or left meant, and the simple fact of not knowing gnawed at Jacob.

At first he'd wondered if people were being separated based on height or weight or their last names, but eventually he concluded that the people being sent to the left were those over sixty years of age, along with anyone who seemed sick or walked with a limp or had any other obvious infirmity or defect. Those sent to the right seemed to be younger and healthier and sturdier.

That was it, Jacob decided. They were in a work camp, after all. Those going to the right must be assigned to more physically challenging jobs, while those on the left were undoubtedly assigned to something a little less demanding.

"Name?"

"Uh . . . I'm . . . Lenny . . . er, Leonard," Jacob stammered, finding it strange to say for the first time aloud. "Leonard Eliezer."

"He's my son," Mr. Eliezer added, a bit too eagerly in Jacob's view. He feared for the man's safety, and sure enough, the guards instructed him to shut up and wait his turn, but to Jacob's relief his new father was not beaten.

Jacob felt protective of this man who had been so kind to him and who had thought so clearly and given him such wise counsel. He hoped the older man would be sent to the left and assigned a lighter workload. Indeed, he hoped he would too. He didn't want to be separated from the only man he knew at Auschwitz, even if they'd only met a few days earlier.

An assistant to the man in the white lab coat traced down through the names on his clipboard until he found the right name and put a check mark next to it. The young assistant nodded to the doctor, the doctor whispered something to the commander, and the commander said, "Right," pointing for Jacob to follow the younger prisoners.

Disappointed, Jacob nevertheless did as he was told, though he walked slowly enough to hear the fate of Mr. Eliezer a few moments later. "Left."

Jacob's heart sank. He knew he was about to take a serious and possibly fatal risk, but he couldn't help himself. He quickly glanced back and made eye contact with the old man. Then he smiled and mouthed, "See you soon."

Mr. Eliezer put his hand on his heart and mouthed back, "Be well."

And then the old man was marched around the corner of a building, and Jacob could see him no more.

Quickly regaining his focus, Jacob followed those ahead of him through the doors of a three-story redbrick building and into a large room. Jacob got the odd impression he was in a school cafeteria. There were no food or beverages, nor were there any plates or cups or utensils. There were, however, lots of tables.

At the first table, a soldier ordered the prisoners to turn over all valuables and said that anyone holding back any valuables would be beaten. Reluctantly Jacob handed over the wad of francs he'd been keeping in his pocket and was forced to remove and surrender the watch his father had given him for his bar mitzvah.

Jacob proceeded to the second table. There sat a gaunt older woman, probably in her fifties, a prisoner to be sure, flanked by an armed soldier. She was filling out index cards that she took from a large metal filing box.

"Name?"

"Leonard Eliezer."

"Eye color?"

"Brown."

"Hair color?"

"Brown."

"Condition of teeth? Open your mouth."

Jacob complied.

"Fine. Past illnesses?"

Jacob just stood silently.

"What have you been sick with in the past?"

"Colds, coughs—I don't know," Jacob said.

"Measles?"

"No."

"Mumps?"

"No."

"Pneumonia?"

"No."

"Scarlet fever?"

"No."

"Age?"

"What?"

"What's your age?" the woman repeated, annoyed. "How old are you?"

"Twenty-one."

"Date of birth?"

"February 2, 1921."

The woman looked up at him. "That would make you twenty-two, wouldn't it?"

Jacob felt his face grow red. "Yes, sorry, twenty-two."

The woman stared at him for a moment, then went back to her work. "Occupation?"

Jacob drew a blank. What was he supposed to say? Member of the Jewish Resistance? Document forger? Attacker of Nazi trains? He had no idea what his occupation was. He'd never really thought about it. The woman asked again. Suddenly he remembered Mr. Eliezer saying his son was a metalworker, so that's what Jacob told the woman, though he worried about getting caught in a lie. He'd never worked one day in the metalworking shop owned by his uncle and managed by his father. What if they assigned him to a metalworking shop and he didn't know what to do? They'd beat him for sure.

The woman next asked about his education, and he said, "None." With that, she handed him the card and sent him to the next table.

There, a far more attractive woman about his own age took his card and scanned it without looking up. "Name?" she asked.

Jacob paused for a moment, taken aback by seeing someone so beautiful in such a dreadful place. She struck him as a sliver of light in a pitch-black dungeon. She was slender and shapely with lovely auburn hair.

"Name?" the young woman asked again, still not looking up.

"Oh, it's right there at the top," Jacob replied, pointing.

She looked up from the card, and Jacob was mesmerized by her large, sad brown eyes. But then, feeling self-conscious, he immediately looked down at his shoes.

"Do you think this is a joke?" she asked, lowering her voice and leaning toward him.

"No, no; I'm just saying that it's right there on the—"

"I'll ask the questions, if you don't mind, Mr. Eliezer," she said. "That is your name, correct? Leonard Eliezer?"

Jacob glanced quickly at her, nodded, then looked away.

She asked him for more personal data and carefully wrote down his answers. She asked him for his most recent address. She asked him for the names and addresses of family members he would want to write to assure them that he was okay. Fortunately, Jacob remembered most of what Mr. Eliezer had told him and cobbled together enough material to give her. He watched as she wrote on the back of his index card, admiring her penmanship and suddenly wondering what it would be like to hold her hand.

The moment was shattered by a wooden club crashing against the back of his skull. Jacob staggered forward in immense pain. He tried to stabilize himself by grabbing hold of the table, but the table moved with him, and he nearly lost his footing. The young woman yelped and jumped back, and the guard behind him started cursing him and telling him to move along and stop wasting time.

Jacob grabbed the back of his head and felt blood there but did as he was told. As he went, he caught one last glimpse of the young woman. She looked scared but also sad for him. That's what he told himself, at least, and then he stepped around the corner, following the crowd.

What had he done wrong? Jacob wondered. He had simply admired the woman's hands. Was that a crime in this place? How could it be? It had to be something else. Maybe he had spoken too slowly or too softly. Maybe that had made it seem he was conspiring with the woman or being too friendly. Whatever it was, it had earned him a severe blow and now an excruciating headache.

In this new room beside yet another table was a scale. Jacob was told to strip down and put all of his clothes, including his underpants, into a large wooden box. Then he was told to stand on the scale to be weighed, after which his height was measured. In this room there were only men. Still, Jacob was embarrassed and cold and bleeding, and he feared he might black out at any moment. And then he joined a long line of naked men who were being tattooed.

"Your number is 202502," a soldier told him while a prisoner tattooed the number into his left forearm with a new wave of searing pain. "You will remember this number. You will memorize it. You will answer when it is called. You have no name any longer. Just a number. Any prisoner who forgets his number or doesn't respond when his number is called will be shot. Do you understand?"

Jacob did not understand. He had no idea what the man was talking about. He couldn't believe what was happening. But he nodded and was sent forward to the next table. There, a prisoner shaved all the hair off Jacob's head until he was completely bald. At the next table, all the hair on his body was shaved off. Then a soldier directed fifty naked men at a time to enter a shower room at the end of the hallway. As always, Jacob did as he was told. What else could he do? Even the slightest hesitation could result in a beating—or death.

The doors shut, and Jacob waited.

33

They waited several minutes.

They stared at the showerheads, waiting for the water, but none came. Jacob tried not to look at anyone or touch anyone, though given the crammed quarters, that was almost impossible. Shivering, his skin covered with goose pimples, his knees knocking with cold and fright, Jacob vigorously rubbed his arms, trying to warm them up. He pressed his legs together over his privates. Then he closed his eyes and waited for the warm water to take away the terrible chill.

Just then the pipes began to creak and groan. He could hear them in the wall and in the ceiling. Jacob opened his eyes and looked up at the showerhead. Instinctively he opened his mouth and waited to drink in the first wave. He was severely dehydrated and aching with thirst. But then a strange and discomfiting thought crossed Jacob's mind, though from where he did not know.

Don't drink the water. You'll get dysentery.

Jacob closed his mouth and cocked his head to one side. What in the world was he thinking? The notion was so odd and yet so clear that he actually turned and looked around to see if someone had spoken the words aloud. But no one was talking or making eye contact with others.

As the pipes kept groaning, he again looked up and opened his mouth. Yet again he was nearly overcome with the thought that he shouldn't drink the water. He closed his mouth and looked around again. Nearly everyone around him stood with mouths open. Apparently he was the only one who had any misgivings.

Just then water began to flow. But it was not hot. It was not even warm or lukewarm. It was freezing cold, and it was coming at them with the intensity of a fire hose, pummeling their shivering bodies and causing grown men to cry out in pain. Jacob covered his face with his hands, trying in vain to deflect the frigid waters away from his head and chest. He noticed others attempting to drink in every drop and decided he should too, unbidden thoughts notwithstanding. But just before he could open his mouth, the water stopped flowing. The shower was over as quickly as it had begun.

Now the doors behind them were opening. Guards were swinging their batons and forcing the naked men out of the frigid shower room and into another room that was even colder. Each man was handed a pair of underpants, a zebra-striped prison shirt, a matching striped cap, one pair of prison trousers, a pair of socks, and a pair of wooden shoes. They had only seconds to put the clothes on. Then everyone was given a colored triangle to wear on their chests. Most of the men in this cohort received yellow triangles, marking them as Jews. Gypsies were given brown triangles. Those accused of being homosexuals wore pink ones. Those marked as political prisoners wore red ones. Those regarded as antisocial prisoners wore black ones.

Moments after being given their triangles, they were divided into small groups and told which barracks they had been assigned to. Then the doors at the far end of the room were opened, and the guards cursed at them and forced them to march double-time to their barracks. Though he hated where he was, Jacob was actually glad to be running. He needed the exercise. He needed to get his muscles moving again. He needed to get his heart pounding and blood circulating, and the movement was raising his body temperature, and for this he was grateful.

But his gratitude evaporated almost instantly.

Straight ahead Jacob could see the enormous smokestack he'd glimpsed from the train. It was still belching out the thickest, blackest smoke he'd ever seen, and the smell emanating from it was so ghastly he twice vomited on the road, as did several of the others.

Staring at them as they ran were small groups of prisoners. All of them wore the striped camp clothes that Jacob was now wearing. The clothes seemed far too big for them. These prisoners, who had obviously been here for a while, weren't merely gaunt. They were emaciated, with too little skin stretched over too many bones. They were dead men walking. Living skeletons. These men were being starved to death. That was the only explanation. Some of them were jaundiced. Most simply were gray. Their eyes were sunken and lifeless. Jacob had never seen anything like it, and it unnerved him.

Then they rounded a corner and headed through a muddy field, and Jacob's eyes went wide. On both sides of the path they were running down were large ditches filled with reddish-brown water. Sticking up from the ditches were hundreds of human heads. These were not skulls. They were heads with eyes and lips and noses and flesh. Some of them seemed freshly beheaded. Others were decomposing. Again Jacob began to vomit, but there was nothing left in his system. These were dry heaves, excruciatingly painful, and they still had a half mile to run.

Eventually they reached a street lined with three-story redbrick buildings on both sides, all surrounded by high fences and more barbed wire, and stopped running. A cruel-looking man wearing a black triangle—"antisocial"—stepped forward and introduced himself as Gerhard Gruder. He was their block senior, he explained in a short speech peppered with vulgar language. Gruder wasted no time in bragging to the new men under his command that he had been arrested for raping and killing five women, though he seemed to relish telling them he had only been convicted of three.

He then told them there was one sin above all others he would not tolerate: laziness. To him, laziness was a capital offense, and he proudly declared he'd already sent nineteen men from his barracks to the gallows that month. In fact, he said, just the previous day he had caught a fifteen-year-old boy sleeping in during morning roll call.

"They hanged him at midnight," Gruder said. "Tonight, that could be you."

34

That first day seemed interminable.

But Jacob couldn't afford the luxury of feeling sorry for himself. He refused to let himself think about Avi or the rest of his family and friends. Not yet. Not now. He knew he had to watch and learn and get every step right the first time, every time. He knew now his very life depended on it. Not the quality of his life, but whether he would live at all to see another day.

At one point, he watched as a camp guard beat an older man to death. The man's offense? He hadn't removed his cap and saluted soldiers a full three meters away before he passed them on the street.

Another time Jacob saw Gruder throttle a boy for asking where the toilets were. The same hour, Gruder punched another man in the face for not saying, "Yes, sir," and "Thank you, sir."

Those who cried out when they were beaten were beaten harder. Those who walked too slowly were subject to twenty lashes. One man who asked when they might be given some water disappeared from their group and was never heard from again. The list of unwritten rules was slowly but brutally emerging, and Jacob took careful mental notes. No questions. No complaints. No disrespect. No laziness. No second chances. No mercy.

At seven o'clock that night, a gong sounded, and prisoners returned from their jobs all over the camp. Roll call was taken in a nearby courtyard. The process took almost an hour. Every number was called out. Every tattoo on every arm was properly accounted for. Only then were the men told they would be allowed to eat dinner.

Jacob breathed a sigh of relief. His mouth began watering. He told himself not to get his hopes up. It wasn't going to be schnitzel and apple strudel, he knew, but he was desperate to get some calories into him, and he thought he was ready to eat anything.

He was wrong.

Jacob was stunned by what they set in front of him. A chunk of spoiled salami. Two slices of rotten cheese. About three hundred grams of black bread, which for some reason had dust and bits of wood shavings in it. And a cup of brown, putrid, scalding water that Gruder mockingly called coffee. Some of the men pushed the food away in disgust. Jacob was inclined to do so as well, but the thought of all those emaciated men gave him pause. Was this it? Was this all the food he was getting? If so, what choice did he have? If he didn't eat this, he'd soon waste away, and if he wasted away, he'd soon be dead. And Jacob did not want to die.

He closed his eyes for a moment and made a decision: he would live. He would not give up. Somehow, he would survive this place. He'd escape if possible, but no matter what, he would survive. The Nazis had taken away his name, his clothes, his dignity. But only he could give away his will to fight, and he resolved not to do it. He would eat. He would put aside his pride. He would swallow whatever they set before him. He would steal food when he could. He would find a way to survive, whatever it took.

Feeling good about his decision, knowing Uncle Avi would approve and would have decided the same if he were here, Jacob opened his eyes and reached for the salami. It was gone. So was the bread. His entire dinner was gone, and so were the men of his barracks.

More scared than angry, Jacob jumped up and raced out of the dining hall and into the street. He spotted his comrades turning a corner and broke into a sprint to catch up with them.

Fortunately, Gruder was in the front and hadn't seemed to notice Jacob was missing. He was about to lead them into a barracks building marked *Block 18* when one of the men broke away from the group and began running for the fence. Gruder yelled after him, warning him to stop, but the man would not listen. He didn't make it thirty yards before he was shredded to pieces by machine-gun fire.

Jacob shuddered, and not only because of the cruelty of what he'd just witnessed. He realized he could have been shot for running to catch up with his group. He had discovered another unwritten, unspoken rule—two, perhaps: no running, and stay away from the fences.

Shaken, the men clattered up the stairs to the second floor without saying a word. Gruder ordered them into the first room on the left. It was packed with three-tiered bunk beds. Each bed had a thin mattress topped with a single neatly folded, thin, green wool blanket.

The problem became immediately obvious: there weren't enough beds for all the men under Gruder's command. As that fact dawned on the men, everyone began to push and shove to get a bed and blanket of his own. Jacob managed to scramble to the top of a bunk in the far corner of the room just as Gruder began cursing and screaming at them all. He said every man had to be in a bed immediately. There could be no exceptions. In most cases, that meant at least two men—and sometimes three—would have to share a bed. There simply were not enough for every man to have a bunk of his own.

Before he knew it, Jacob found himself with a thin, wild-eyed, and somewhat-odorous man in his forties as well as a pleasant enough but shell-shocked young man about his own age. Neither introduced himself. Neither made eye contact. The older man grabbed the blanket for himself, leaving Jacob and the other boy without any covering whatsoever. What's more, the older man kept kicking and pushing the other two away from him. Just before Gruder turned the lights out, Jacob saw the older man was wearing a black triangle. The antisocial label fit him perfectly. The younger man had a yellow triangle. He was a fellow Jew.

Jacob noticed there was a coal-fired stove in the middle of the room, but there was no coal and no fire. The windows were covered with steel bars. The floor was littered with hay, reminding him of the cattle car they had arrived in.

When the lights went out, Jacob noticed how cold he felt and how exhausted. Yet he could not sleep. Not with this lunatic pushing and kicking him. Not with men moaning and crying all around him. Not with some snoring instantly and loudly, and others finally feeling free to talk to one another or to themselves. Not with his stomach grumbling and his mouth parched. Not with the fear of what the night would hold and what tomorrow would bring. He remembered the letters people had read on the train. He thought about the hidden warnings so many had tried to give to their loved ones. He could almost see the angel of death hovering over this place. It was not passing over. It had come here to rob, kill, and destroy, and for the first time in his life, Jacob was scared to close his eyes. He didn't know if he was more afraid that he might never wake up, or that he might.

He stared up at the ceiling in the pitch-blackness and tried to think about something—anything—other than death. He wondered who all these men were. What were their names? He didn't want to be mad at them. They obviously didn't want to be there any more than he did. Where were they from? How had they been caught? What were they thinking? Did they know anyone here? Were any of them in the Resistance? Was there anyone he could trust?

There were no answers, for tonight at least. Jacob certainly wasn't about to start asking questions. But maybe in the days ahead, if he listened carefully, he could get to know the men in this room, which of them might be enemies, and who, if anyone, might become an ally.

35

At 4:30 a.m., Jacob was awakened by a loud gong.

Moments later, Gerhard Gruder was standing in their doorway, demanding everyone get up, fold their blankets, and use the facilities. Having decided to do everything Gruder ordered first and fastest, Jacob leaped over his two comrades, jumped down to the floor, and led the crowd to the lavatories.

What he found were only twenty-two toilets and forty-two sinks for the nearly three hundred men who lived in Block 18. Worse, the guards gave each prisoner less than a minute to do his business, even though many of the men were starting to experience severe diarrhea.

Those who delayed were beaten. Those who resisted were beaten more. Those who complained to Gerhard that they were suffering dysentery were beaten worst of all. Jacob backed away from the melee. Having had so little to eat and drink, he had hardly any business to attend to and no desire to get his head pounded in. He suddenly remembered the strange voice he thought he had heard in the showers and found himself grateful for not having drunk the freezing-cold water. He suspected the water—probably in combination with the spoiled salami—was the cause of the stomach problems these men were having.

Back in the bunk room, Jacob found that Gruder was handing out small crusts of bread, barely more than a few crumbs. Jacob relished every morsel and couldn't believe it when it was gone so quickly. How could he get more? He was tempted to grab some out of the hands of others, but he had to assume that was a sure way to get beaten, if not by Gruder then by a fellow prisoner.

Then someone dragged in a barrel of some steaming liquid, and someone else handed out small metal cups. Jacob took his immediately and was given half a liter of something pale and frothy that was described as tea but looked more like sewer water. Fortunately it did not smell, nor did it taste as bad as it looked. Jacob swallowed it as quickly as he could and then stuck his cup back through the throng of men. In the confusion, someone ladled another portion into his cup, but before Jacob could get it to his mouth, the angry, wild-eyed man he'd bunked with the night before grabbed it from him and pushed him away.

Jacob's blood boiled. He balled up his fist and was ready for a fight, but then he thought of Mr. Eliezer's admonition to keep his cool. This was no time for a fight, unless he was planning to commit suicide, and he was not.

The gong sounded again. It was time for the morning roll call. Jacob trailed the crowd down the stairs and into the courtyard and followed Gruder's barking orders to the letter.

At precisely 5 a.m., the men lined up in rows of ten, block by block, surrounded by hundreds of guards with machine guns at the ready. Once again, every prisoner's number was called out one by one. As each man shouted, "Here," his number was checked and double-checked against two separate lists. Jacob noticed that each block senior individually inspected his men to make sure each prisoner was present and accounted for. This, Jacob assumed, was done so that someone couldn't shout "here" for a friend when his friend was really still sleeping or going to the toilet, much less escaping.

Block 18, it soon became clear to Jacob, was mostly comprised of relatively new arrivals. The men in the roll call all looked reasonably healthy and well-fed. Next door in Block 17, the men looked like they were on the verge of death. The same was true of the men from Block 16, on their other side.

And that's when Jacob noticed the block seniors weren't simply counting the living. They were counting the dead, as well. At that moment, several seniors and their deputies from Block 15 were actually carrying out of their building the corpses of five men, each of whom had presumably died in his sleep. To his astonishment, Jacob watched as the corpses were stacked up against the front wall of their building. The block seniors then read out the tattooed numbers of each of the men so they could be checked off the master list. Then the bodies were loaded on wooden carts by men who didn't look like they were long for this world either, and they were wheeled around the building and out of sight.

36

When the roll call was finished, another gong sounded.

This was the signal for the men to rush to their labor detail and head off to work. Of course, neither Jacob nor any of the men in Block 18 had been assigned to a labor detail yet, so their block senior explained the procedure.

"Work begins precisely at 7:30 every morning, except Sundays," Gruder began. "If you survive until Sunday, I'll explain that to you then. In the meantime, each of you better come to terms with the fact that you're at a labor camp. You will give every ounce of energy you have for the Reich, or you will be punished severely. No exceptions.

"There are many types of jobs. Among them, the construction squad, the roofing squad, the roadworks squad, working at the timber yard, the fishponds, handling trash and sewerage, working in the clothes room, helping in the motor works, or serving as *Sonderkommandos*. Some of you will be assigned to the medical clinic or as clerks and record keepers, though most of those jobs are handled by women. You are men. You were strong and healthy enough to pass the initial inspection, so you'll be expected to show us what you are made of. Don't expect to be block deputies or seniors anytime soon. All of us have been here at least two years, and frankly, I don't expect most of you to make it to summer. And don't waste your time thinking about how to escape this place. It's impossible. The only way out is through the chimney."

With those depressing words, Gruder gestured to a dozen men who had been watching from the perimeter of the group, and they stepped forward. Gruder introduced them as work-detail bosses, calling them kapos.

The kapos wore green triangles on their clothing.

These, Jacob would soon learn, were the real slave masters of Auschwitz. They were prisoners who had somehow proven their loyalty to the camp leadership and had been assigned to run the work details in return for better living conditions, better clothing, and more and better food.

As soon as Gruder was finished speaking, the kapos swooped in and grabbed whomever they wanted, swearing at them and telling them to fall in line and do what they were told or they were going "to the ovens." Jacob had no idea what that meant, but he was not about to ask questions.

Suddenly he was slapped on the back of his head by a nasty, brutish-looking kapo who told him he was going to be a *Sonderkommando*. It was another term he had never heard before today, but he said nothing.

Jacob dutifully followed along with two others from his block. One of them was his wild-eyed bunkmate, who for some reason had wound rags around both of his hands. The man was a lunatic, Jacob decided. He wanted nothing to do with him and stepped behind the kapo to be as far away from this creep as possible.

Jacob had no idea what a *Sonderkommando* did or what the duties entailed, but he was determined to work hard and prove his worth. After all, he thought, if Gruder could make it through two years and earn a promotion, so could he. But no sooner had the thought crossed his mind than the wild-eyed man broke away from the group. Screaming at the top of his lungs, he ran down an alley to their right. He was headed straight for the fences.

Jacob suddenly understood what the rags were for. They weren't to keep the man's hands warm. They were to try to blunt the pain of the barbed wire as he climbed for freedom. He really was crazy, Jacob realized as he watched the man run and heard the kapo and Gruder yelling. But he had to give the man some credit. He was tall and he was fast, and for a split second Jacob wondered if he might actually make it. In some strange way, Jacob wanted him to. He was for anyone who could escape this hellhole.

Moving in a blur, the man reached the end of the alley before the guards could open fire. Then he made a running leap and grabbed for the top of the fence. Suddenly the scene erupted with sparks and flames. No one had told them the fence was electrified. Nevertheless, thousands of volts went ripping through the man's body, thoroughly frying him before he could have possibly known what hit him. The man's head and hair burst into flames, and a moment later, his charred, smoking body fell from the fence into a smoldering heap on the ground.

Even from fifty feet away, the smell was horrific. Jacob nearly began to gag again, and then it hit him. *That* was the smell! It was the same odor coming from the big smokestack. It was the smell of burning flesh, human flesh. Was that where they were taking all the bodies? Were they actually cremating all the people who died in this camp? Was that what Gruder had meant when he said the only way out was through the chimney?

"Quit staring—let's move," the kapo snapped at Jacob and the other recruit. "You'd better pray I find someone else or you'll be working till midnight every day."

Jacob couldn't tell if the man was kidding, but he doubted it. He didn't look like a man capable of humor.

As they walked, another kapo strode up beside them and walked with them for a stretch as they headed toward the squat little building at the base of the great chimney. He was staring at Jacob and finally asked, "What's your name, son?"

Jacob wasn't sure whether he should answer or not. Was that allowed? Which was worse, to answer or to remain silent? "Uh, my name is Leonard, Herr Kapo," he said at last. "Leonard Eliezer."

"No, it's not," the man replied.

"Pardon?" Jacob asked, his anxiety spiking.

"You're Avi's nephew," the man said. "Right? Aren't you Avi Weisz's nephew?"

Jacob stopped in his tracks. All the color drained from his face. How could this man know him? And what did that portend?

"I . . . uh . . . I don't know what . . ."

He was so flustered, he couldn't finish a sentence.

The first kapo now turned and berated this interloper, but it quickly became clear to Jacob that this other kapo, the one who had approached him and somehow actually knew him, outranked the first.

"This man's coming with me," the second kapo declared, grabbing Jacob by the arm and walking him down a side alley to a large building marked *Canada*.

The first kapo put up a fight, but only briefly. Then he turned to his remaining recruit, grabbed him by the scruff of the neck, and insisted, "Don't even think about it. You're not getting away."

The penalty for lying in this place had to be death, Jacob told himself. They seemed to kill people for far less. Was that where this man was taking him—to the gallows or to the wall to be shot?

Jacob stumbled as they walked. His knees felt weak. Despite the cold, he was sweating profusely. He wanted to be back with the other kapo, working, keeping his head down, staying anonymous, staying alive. But this was not to be. The kapo manhandled Jacob into the building, past two armed guards, up some stairs, and into a small, cluttered office, where he was pushed into a chair and told to stay put and not touch anything.

The man left. Jacob was trembling. He looked around for a way to escape, but there were no windows to the outside, though there were windows looking out over what appeared to be a gigantic warehouse. From Jacob's angle, however, he was sitting too low to see much through the windows, and he didn't dare stand or move at all or make a noise. He spotted a phone on the desk, but whom was he going to call in Poland? He didn't know a living soul in this country, and even if he knew how to make a long-distance call to Germany or Belgium—and even if he believed the call would not be monitored by the Gestapo—whom was he going to call in either of those places? His family was dead. His friends were on the run. He was utterly alone in the universe. That was the pathetic truth. No one knew where he was. No one even really cared. And even if they did, there was nothing they could do to get him out.

He had entered hell itself. Who knew exactly what the afterlife held, but how could it be worse than this? Here they worked you to death or starved you if they could. Here they beat your brains in for sport. Here you were nothing—not a name, not a soul, just a number, and a worthless one at that. Here a German rapist and murderer had more value than an innocent Jew. He had come to a place with no hope, no life, and no way out but the chimney.

Maybe the wild man was right—live free or die as quickly as you can.

37

Not two minutes passed before the kapo stepped back into the office.

He handed Jacob a wanted poster. On it was his uncle's name and photograph and personal details—height, weight, date of birth, home addresses, all three of his business enterprises, and several aliases.

"That's your uncle Avraham Weisz, is it not?" the man said.

Jacob just stared at the paper in his hands. He knew the look on his face betrayed him. He couldn't very well say he didn't know him. Not now. And what if his uncle was still alive? So he nodded and kept staring at the photograph. It was grainy and out of focus and badly reproduced, but there was no question—that was Avi.

"So that would make you Jacob Weisz, would it not?"

Jacob winced and nodded, refusing to look at the man, but rather staring down at the wood floor.

"It's okay, Jacob," the man said. "I've heard a great deal about your uncle. He was a hero among my circles of friends. We all mourn his passing."

Startled, Jacob looked up at the man. "So it's true?" Jacob asked tentatively. "He's really dead?"

"Didn't you see it yourself?"

"I saw him get shot," Jacob confirmed. "I was hoping he had survived."

"I'm told he died instantly," the man said. "You should be glad he did. If he'd been captured by the Gestapo after what you all did . . ."

The man's voice trailed off, and Jacob was glad he did not finish. He was right, of course. To have been captured under such circumstances would have been a nightmare. If Avi had lived, he would have been tortured mercilessly, and if he had survived that, he'd have been sent to certain death in Auschwitz.

"How do you know about him and about me?" Jacob asked.

"My name is Leszek Poczciwinski," the man said. "I have—well, again, let's call them 'friends'—who work in various parts of this camp and outside this camp too. I help these men when I can. They help me when they can. One of them works in a particularly sensitive position here in the camp. He came to me early this morning and told me that Commander Asche in Belgium, a man with whom I believe you are familiar, recently telephoned Rudolf Hoess, a man with whom you will become acquainted. Hoess is the commandant here at the Auschwitz-Birkenau death camps. Commander Asche wanted Hoess to know about a raid by the Jewish underground on train 801, which he said occurred not far from Brussels. Asche provided the details of the raid and a list of the Resistance members who were involved. Overnight, a special courier came from the Gestapo with a copy of the file on the incident. My friend saw a portion of the file. He only had access to it for a moment, but he saw that the three Belgians involved in the raid appeared to have fled the country. The report also said that one Avraham Weisz was killed in the raid and that his nephew, Jacob, was on the run but believed to still be in Belgium."

Jacob couldn't believe how much detail this guy had on him. Who was he? And who were these "friends"?

"How did you know it was me?"

"I didn't," Poczciwinski said. "But I'd heard so much about the exploits of your uncle that I was intrigued when I finally saw a picture of him. I studied that picture carefully. I was fascinated by it. You might say it was seared into my psyche. And then I was walking down the street this morning and you walked by. Do you realize how much you look like your uncle? Anyway, I put two and two together and took a calculated risk. You should have seen the look on your face! And now here you are. Welcome to Auschwitz."

Jacob wasn't sure what to say.

"And welcome to the Canada command," Poczciwinski added. "I just saved your life."

"I don't understand."

"You were about to become a *Sonderkommando*, right?"

"Yes."

"Do you know what they do?"

Jacob shook his head.

"They remove corpses from the gas chambers."

"The what?"

"The gas chambers."

"What are you talking about?"

"Haven't you heard?"

Jacob shook his head again.

"The Nazis are exterminating the Jewish race here at Auschwitz," Poczciwinski said, now sitting on the edge of the desk. "That's what this place is for."

"Really, sir, I don't understand," Jacob said. "I mean, obviously people are dying, but . . ."

"No, Jacob, they're not just dying," Poczciwinski insisted. "They're being systematically liquidated. That's what's happening here. The Nazis are methodically murdering the Jews by the thousands. Actually by the tens of thousands."

"How?"

"They march them into special rooms that look like showers, and then they pump in poison gas—it's called Zyklon B—and within a half hour, everyone in the showers is dead."

Jacob just stared at him for a few moments. That wasn't possible.

"They sent me into the showers," he finally said. "I didn't die."

"When you first got off the train, were you sent to the right or the left?"

"To the right."

"There you go."

When Jacob didn't respond, Poczciwinski kept talking. "Everyone who was sent to the left yesterday was gassed, Jacob. They're all dead. They've all been cremated. All that's left of them are ashes and smoke."

"Everyone?"

"Everyone."

"What about Mr. Eliezer?"

"Gone."

Jacob felt sick to his stomach.

"You don't believe me?" Poczciwinski asked after a pause. "I understand. I didn't believe it at first myself. But it's true. They kill the weak. They force the strong to work. When they become weak, they kill them, too. And then another train comes, and it all begins again."

Poczciwinski let that horrible reality sink in for a moment. Then he turned to more practical and immediate issues.

"You're lucky I found you," he said. "Otherwise you would have been up to your waist in dead bodies. Pulling out their gold teeth. Prying off their gold crowns and fillings. Loading them on carts. Wheeling them next door to the crematorium. Watching them be shoved into ovens. And then hosing down the gas chambers of the blood and the urine and the excrement so they're ready for the next shipment of unsuspecting victims."

Jacob was too stunned to speak. A thousand questions flooded his brain, but he didn't know which one to ask first. So he just said nothing.

"Go ahead, son. It's okay."

"Why do they do it?" Jacob finally asked.

"Who, the Nazis?"

"No, the *Sonderkommandos*."

"What choice do they have?" Poczciwinski asked with a shrug. "They want to live. Plus they're fed better. They get extra bread. A little extra jam. Occasionally some decent meat—you know, the kind that's not spoiled. The kind that you might actually serve to a dog. It's not much, but it's more than everyone else gets. But it's no life. The *Sonderkommandos* get extra food, but they don't live that long."

"What do you mean?"

"They go crazy. It doesn't take long. They throw themselves against the fences. Or they're rounded up every eight to ten weeks and shot by the guards and thrown into the ovens themselves."

"Why?"

"The Nazis know a man can only take so much. They try to shoot them before they go crazy."

"Why not assign them another job?"

"To keep them quiet."

Jacob didn't understand.

"Not everyone knows what's happening here, Jacob," Poczciwinski explained. "That's part of the Nazis' plan. If everyone in the camp knew all the sinister details of what happens here, they might revolt. Then who would do all the work? And what if someone escaped? God forbid. They might tell the Jews on the outside what was really happening here, that this isn't a slave-labor camp but a death camp. Would any Jew in his or her right mind actually get on a train bound for a camp if he knew—not suspected, not heard rumors, but actually knew for certain—that it was an extermination camp? Would you?"

Jacob just stared at him.

"Of course not," Poczciwinski said. "You'd fight back. There would be massive revolts everywhere. And that's what the Nazis are afraid of. The only way for Hitler and the SS to kill every Jew in Europe—and believe me, this is their plan—is to keep the Jews and the rest of the world from knowing what's really happening here. That's why they take every precaution to prevent word from getting out. That's why the security here is airtight. That's why they go to such extraordinary lengths to prevent anyone from escaping. All the fences. All the towers. All the guards and dogs. Huge fields of land mines around the camp for dozens of kilometers. Thousands of soldiers on alert twenty-four hours a day to hunt down and kill anyone who does manage to break out for a few minutes or a few hours."

"Has anyone ever gotten out?" Jacob asked.

Poczciwinski shook his head. "Close to eight hundred people have tried," he said. "Not one of them made it. Then again, there's a first time for everything, right? Maybe the first will be you."

38

Leszek Poczciwinski stood up from the desk.

He was taller than most of the men Jacob had seen in the camp, probably around six feet, and seemed in good physical shape, considering all he had been through. Though by nature his build was slender, he was not gaunt. He wasn't starving. Like everyone else, he wore the zebra stripes, but for some reason his seemed to fit better. They weren't baggy or falling off of him. They almost seemed tailored or at least carefully chosen.

One thing was sure: he was not Jewish. He wore a red triangle, meaning that he was a political prisoner. His piercing blue eyes betrayed a sharp intelligence, and they showed no hint of fear. Jacob wasn't sure if that should be reassuring or a cause for concern. How could one not be afraid in such a place?

Leszek pulled two glass bottles of apple juice out of a cooler and set one on the desk. The other he opened and began to sip. He did not offer the second bottle to Jacob. Instead he pointed through the window to the warehouse below and began to speak once again.

"There," he said, motioning Jacob to come and look, which Jacob dutifully did. "That's the world I oversee, young man. And believe me, of all the jobs in this godforsaken place, this is the one you want."

Jacob looked out over the expanse and saw shelves filled with every kind of clothing imaginable. Other shelves were piled with blankets, comforters, and sheets, while still others were filled with jars of fruit and canned vegetables, boxes of jams and jellies, bottles of syrup and cooking oil, and bags of rice and flour. And this was just the beginning. In one area were piles of household goods—shaving kits, ladies' makeup supplies, combs and brushes, sewing kits, flashlights, personal mirrors, and the like. In another area there were stacks of lamps and sets of china, pots and pans, and all manner of cookware and kitchen supplies, save knives or anything else that could be used as a weapon. In yet another area was an enormous mound of shoes and boots and slippers, and on and on it went.

Jacob was amazed by how plentiful everything was. As he stared in wonder, for the first time he felt a bit more hopeful that things could actually get better. Perhaps the guards were just punishing everyone for a while. Perhaps all this roughness was just for a season, to make everyone more humble, more pliant, more willing to work hard, and then conditions would be eased. Here, after all, was tremendous plenty. People didn't have to starve. They didn't have to suffer cold or heat.

He stole a glance at the bottle of apple juice now sitting in a small puddle of water on the desk. His mouth was watering. He wanted to grab it and drink it down as rapidly as humanly possible. He was becoming desperate, but it had not been offered, and Jacob kept telling himself to be careful. He didn't know this man. Perhaps he was being tested. He didn't dare fail the test.

Then Leszek explained that everything in this place had been taken from the prisoners upon their arrival at Auschwitz. Nothing had ever been returned to them, and nothing ever would be.

"Most of this is sent back to Berlin, to be distributed among the families of Nazi soldiers serving on the front," Leszek explained. "But no matter how much we ship out, the place is always bursting at the seams. Every few days another train arrives. More Jews. More luggage. More booty. The SS guards steal what they want, so long as they don't get caught, then make us catalog the rest. And it all gets shipped out in due course."

"All of it?" Jacob asked, his hopes suddenly dashed.

"Every bit," Leszek confirmed. "And you're not even seeing everything here."

"What do you mean?"

"I'm talking about the gold and the silver and the cash and the jewelry," Leszek said. "All of that is kept separate, under much more security than here."

"How much are we talking about?" Jacob asked.

"Millions, tens of millions, maybe more. I couldn't say exactly, but the Jews are coming with everything they have, and Hoess and his men are taking it all away."

"And it all goes to *der Führer* in Berlin?"

"I'm sure his inner circle is getting their cut. If I had to guess, I'd say most of this Jewish treasure is being stashed away in Swiss bank accounts, not in the central bank in Berlin. But that's just a guess. And Hoess's men don't miss a thing. They rip the rings off fingers. As I said, they pull the gold fillings and crowns right out of people's mouths. They want it all."

Jacob backed away from the windows.

"Young man, welcome to Canada," Leszek said gently, waiting a few moments and then adding, "That's what people—long before me—nicknamed this place. Canada."

"Why?"

"I don't know exactly. I guess they think of Canada as a land of great bounty and natural resources. Anyway, the name stuck. I'm the kapo that runs this place, and I need a new man. I'd like you to come join me."

"Why?" Jacob asked, wondering if he looked as perplexed and troubled as he felt.

"I want you to survive, Jacob," Leszek said bluntly. "I've heard of the work your uncle did in Germany and in Belgium, and I could use someone with your background. Now, let's be clear. I'm going to work you hard—very hard—but I'll also take care of you. I'll give you extra food, make sure you get some coffee you can actually swallow, and I'll watch your back. All I ask is that you watch mine. Only the strong survive here. And only people who have enough to eat and drink stay strong. Only those with inside jobs stay strong. Only those who help each other and build true friendships and alliances stay strong. I'm giving you a chance to survive and hopefully to help some others survive too. So what do you say? Can I count on you?"

Jacob reminded himself that he didn't know this man from Adam. Yet somehow Leszek knew an awful lot about him, or at least about Avi. Was he trustworthy? How could Jacob know for sure? It certainly seemed like this man was part of the Resistance. How else could he know such things? But he hadn't said as much. Not definitively, anyway.

Then again, what if he was actually an agent working for the SS? What if he worked for the Gestapo or directly for the commandant? Wouldn't that make more sense? How else would he have gotten such a plum position of working inside this treasure trove?

Still, if the Nazis knew Jacob's real name, why go to such lengths? Why not just arrest him, torture him until he spilled whatever secrets he had, and then hang him? Of course, he didn't know that much about the Resistance network. Avi would have been the real catch. He was a big fish in the Resistance. Jacob was a minnow, and he couldn't imagine the Nazis didn't know that. Why, then, go through this charade?

"May I ask you a question?" Jacob said at last.

"Of course."

"Why don't you just turn me in?"

"Whatever for?"

"Wouldn't they reward you for turning in a member of the Resistance, even one as insignificant as me?" Jacob asked.

"They might," Leszek said.

"Then why not do it?"

"I'm not here to help the Nazis, Jacob. I'm here to save every life I can—Polish, Jewish, whatever."

Jacob considered that for a moment.

"But isn't it against the rules to give a prisoner extra food?" he asked.

"Yes."

"What happens if you get caught?"

"They'll probably hang me," Leszek said. "They'll probably hang you, too. But here's the thing, Jacob. I've survived here two and a half years. So who knows? Maybe today my number will come up. But if they catch and kill me, I want it to be for something that matters. And saving lives matters to me."

"You've been here two and a half years?" Jacob asked, having a hard time believing that.

Leszek nodded. "I got here in September of 1940."

"How long do most people last?" Jacob wondered.

"Two months," Leszek said. "Maybe three."

"Then how did you make it so long?"

"I made friends."

Jacob just stared at the man, but Leszek didn't strike Jacob as someone who often told tales or cracked jokes. He had an air of confidence about him, though he didn't wear it on his sleeve. Conflicted though he was, Jacob decided he had little choice but to play the charade out and see where it led. Maybe he would only live another few days or a few weeks or three months at best. But wouldn't that be better than dying today? After all, every added hour gave him more time to plot his escape. And there was no question in Jacob's mind that he was going to escape. The only questions now were how and when. Working here in Canada with Leszek, he calculated, might just give him access to the supplies and the cover he'd need to find a way out.

So Jacob finally nodded and forced himself to say yes and thank you to the opportunity he was being offered.

He put out his hand, and Leszek shook it firmly and smiled. "Again, welcome to Canada."

Then, and only then, did Leszek pick up the bottle of apple juice and hand it to him. Jacob took it, stared at it, and then gulped it down before Leszek could change his mind.

Nothing had ever tasted so sweet.

39

"Excuse me; I'm here to pick up a box for Canada."

Jacob desperately hoped he had come to the right building. Auschwitz was not a place that was forgiving of errors. He glanced back at the paper in his hand, on which Leszek had scrawled down the building name and number. Jacob had asked several prisoners, and they had all pointed him here. Though he hadn't actually been able to find a name or number on the front of the building, he had nevertheless entered the low, squat structure adjacent to the great chimney, ever spewing its putrid black smoke.

"Which box, boy?" said a prisoner working behind the counter. "I don't got all day."

"I really don't know, sir," Jacob conceded. "I'm kind of new here."

The man sniffed in disgust and went off muttering and cursing but came back in a few minutes with a huge box filled with eyeglasses of all shapes and sizes.

"That what you come for?" the man grunted, clearly at the end of whatever shred of patience he'd ever had.

Jacob had no idea. But as he stared into the box at all the different kinds of spectacles, one pair caught his attention. Sitting to one side of the wooden box, nestled up against the edge, was a pair of gold wire-rimmed glasses. Jacob instantly knew he had seen these before. He reached for them and picked them up. He examined them carefully and finally set them down. These were Mr. Eliezer's glasses, the very ones his "father" had been wearing on the train. Jacob felt a sadness so haunting and so palpable he thought he might actually be able to reach out and touch it with his hands.

Leszek was right. He wasn't lying or telling ghost stories. The old and the infirm were being exterminated in Auschwitz. Mr. Eliezer had been murdered. He had done no wrong. He hadn't hurt anyone or caused any trouble. But Commandant Hoess had ordered him to be slaughtered anyway. One day Mr. Eliezer was alive and well and trying to save Jacob's life. The next day he was sent to a gas chamber, and his body had been burned to ashes in an oven right next door. Now all that was left were his spectacles. All that was left of any of them in that cattle car were their glasses. Reading glasses. Sunglasses. Everyday glasses. That was it. Lara was no more. Mrs. Brenner was gone too. They were all dead. These kind ladies who had taken care of him and given him food to eat on the train, they were all gassed. Murdered. The gold in their teeth ripped out. Their naked bodies set on fire.

Jacob grabbed the box of glasses, which was heavier than he would have expected, and left quickly, back to the Canada command. It was about a six-minute walk, and Jacob kept his head down. He did his best not to make eye contact with anyone else, though he was careful to doff his cap at every soldier within a hundred kilometers. He didn't want to see anything else that was happening. He didn't want to be noticed by anyone else. He just wanted to finish this job and disappear. Maybe Leszek would take pity on him, allow him to sit in some quiet place to grieve all that he had seen.

That, however, was not the case. When Jacob returned successfully with the box of eyeglasses, Leszek told him to count and catalog everything in the box. Then he showed Jacob where in the warehouse to store them. After that, he took Jacob up to his office and gave him an apple and a large piece of bread with butter and raspberry marmalade. Jacob thanked him profusely, then sat down on the couch and devoured them quickly.

He battled mixed emotions. He felt guilty eating when his friends were dead. He felt guilty eating when so many others were literally starving to death. But he was determined to survive, which meant he had to eat whenever he could, wherever he could, as much as he could. There was simply no other way.

When Jacob was finished and had wiped his hands and face clean and washed down the serendipitous treat with a cup of coffee, Leszek sent him out to meet a train that had just pulled in. This time, however, Jacob was not alone. He was sent with a tall, skinny Jewish kid who apparently was one of Leszek's trusted deputies.

"Name's Max," the kid said as they left the warehouse and headed to the train platform. "Max Cohen. It's Maximilian, actually, but no one calls me that. Even my father didn't call me that. My mother did, but I couldn't stand it. I begged her to call me Max, but she wouldn't hear of it. 'Cause I was named after her father, and she loved her father, and I can understand why. He was a great rabbi in Bucharest. That's why she married my father, 'cause he was a rabbi too. Lots of rabbis in our family. They want me to be a rabbi. Studied Torah most of my life. Guess that was a waste. Not a lot of openings for camp rabbi here, you know? Besides, it seems like every other person you meet here is a rabbi. So you're Jacob—er, I mean, Leonard. Right?"

Jacob just shrugged and kept walking.

"So what's your story?"

"I got on the wrong train."

Max nearly laughed but restrained himself, not wanting to draw undue attention. "So, what, you're a joker or something? Got on the wrong train? Yeah, guess you did. Where were you really headed? To Paris for the weekend to see your girl?"

"No."

"Then what? Going to visit your rich uncle in London?"

"I'd rather not say."

"Oh, sorry; it's secret, huh? What are you, part of *la Résistance*?"

Jacob just glared at him.

"Okay, okay, relax," Max said. "Guess you're not a big talker, huh? But you're Jewish, right? I mean, you're wearing the yellow triangle and all, right? So we're cousins, right?"

Jacob said nothing.

"Ever think of becoming a rabbi?" Max asked.

"No."

"Is your family religious?"

Jacob shrugged again.

"Not very, huh?" Max said. "Did you go to *shul* growing up?"

"Sure."

"Did you have a bar mitzvah?"

"Of course."

"Where are you from?"

"Siegen."

"Where's that?"

"Germany."

"Near Berlin?"

"No, closer to Belgium."

"Parlez-vous français?"

"A little."

"So how do you have a girlfriend in Paris if you don't speak French?"

Jacob just looked at Max until Max slapped him on the back and told him not to be so uptight. "Relax," he said. "It's going to be fine. Now come on. Let's go to work."

An enormous train with at least forty cars had just pulled in. Jacob figured there had to be 1,700 or 1,800 prisoners aboard. The vast majority of them would be Jews. He cringed as he watched hundreds of soldiers beating the new arrivals. Leading the way was the most repulsive human being Jacob had ever laid eyes on, more beast than man. "Who's that?" he asked Max.

"The head guard? That's Fat Louie. He's a real gem."

Fat Louie's uniform seemed a size too small for him, making his sleeves and pant legs a bit too short. This, in turn, made his tree-trunk arms seem even longer than they were.

The sadistic guard was squarely in his element now. He was shouting and cursing, forcing women and men out of the cars, though he tended to focus more on the women. He ordered them to leave all their belongings behind and pushed them into the courtyard, where he divided the men from the women and got both groups into single-file lines. Jacob helplessly watched the bewildered faces frozen with fear.

He watched one particularly beautiful girl, probably about his own age, tremble as Fat Louie ogled her. The girl burst into tears when he groped her while the other guards laughed and encouraged more. When she tried to pull away, her blouse tore, and then Jacob stared in horror as Fat Louie smashed this sweet, defenseless girl in the face repeatedly with the butt of his rifle until she was bloodied and unrecognizable.

Jacob wasn't the only one looking on without knowing what to do. Mothers and grandmothers had to keep moving forward in their single-file line, each of them fearing that they could be next.

Just as painful for Jacob was seeing the looks in the eyes of the husbands and fathers and grandfathers as they inched forward in their own single-file line. He could see many of them balling up their fists, ready to lash out, ready to fight to protect this young woman and the others, and he could see them being told by friends and relatives to cool it, not to do anything rash.

Suddenly and uncharacteristically, Jacob, who never liked to talk more than he had to, wanted to yell out to the men and urge them to join him in seizing Fat Louie and crushing his skull. Yes, they all would die, but wouldn't it be worth it to at least take out one of these monsters?

Then again, he thought, maybe it was better to warn them of what was coming. Maybe he should tell them it was better to die here and now standing up for the ones they loved than to watch them walk into the gas chambers and the ovens and then, perhaps, even follow them in there.

He didn't, of course. And he felt deeply ashamed. He hadn't fought when he'd arrived. Nor was he about to fight now. He wanted to, for the moment, but the moment would pass, and he would do nothing. Why? Because he didn't want to die. All he wanted to do was to escape, to run as far away from here as he possibly could. Did that make him a coward? He feared it did, and his guilt made the darkness around him seem to grow ever darker.

Once the guards had cleared the trains, Max and Jacob and a dozen other men from Canada moved in quickly. Car by car, they removed the luggage and trunks and other personal effects. They loaded everything on wooden carts and dragged it all back to a large processing area behind the Canada warehouse, always under the wary gaze of men with guns. Then they raced back to the train with shovels and brushes and hoses and bleach and thoroughly cleaned out each car. When that was finished, they laid fresh hay on the floor of each car and reported to the security foreman that their task was complete.

The foreman checked their work. Guards with German shepherds made sure none of the prisoners were trying to stow away in, under, or on top of the cars. And when that process was finished, the foreman gave the all-clear signal to the engineer, the whistle blew several times, and the train pulled out of the station.

At no time did Jacob, Max, or the other prisoners talk to one another. Conversation at such a time might not be expressly forbidden, but no one wanted to do anything that could make the Nazis think they were conspiring with one another for any reason. The only voice heard during those hours belonged to Hoess, shouting, "Right" or "Left." Listening, Jacob understood what the sifting process really meant, and it haunted him. For some morbid reason he couldn't explain, he wanted to follow the people sent to the left. He wanted to see where they went. He wanted to hear what they were told. He wanted to see if what Leszek had said was really true. He knew it was. But how could it be?

Following this group of doomed souls was not possible, of course, and even if it had been, it would have been exceedingly dangerous. So Jacob followed Max back to the sorting area behind Canada, just as he was supposed to do, and together they began to open the trunks and the luggage. Here they were allowed to talk, and Max didn't miss a beat. He went straight to work, giving Jacob a cursory explanation of what he was doing, and Jacob tried to absorb it all and follow Max's instructions.

Men's suits had to be put on a certain pile. Men's slacks were to be put on another. Dress shirts on still another. Men's shoes of all kinds had a separate pile. Ties and belts and other accessories still another. The women's clothing had to be separated out and sorted differently.

Jacob didn't laugh or smile. There were times he wished he could. But the gloom over the deaths of his family members and the cruelty of this place permeated every crevice of his being. He didn't see how Max could be so relaxed, so cavalier. Didn't he care? Didn't he see what was happening? Didn't he know as well as Leszek what was happening to these people—and what could happen to them if they didn't watch their step?

40

In the distance, Jacob heard another train whistle blow.

He glanced over at Max, who was admiring an old violin he had pulled out of one of the trunks. When Max saw him staring, he tossed it without warning over to Jacob. Startled, Jacob reached out for it and barely caught it.

"What'd you do that for?" he asked, annoyed.

"You looked like you wanted it," Max laughed as he continued to sort women's hosiery from a mound of scarves and hats.

"That's not why I was looking."

"Then what?"

"The train," Jacob said, carefully setting the violin in a large nearby crate of musical instruments and then getting back to stacking several hundred books they'd pulled out of the cattle cars. "Please tell me it's not coming here."

"Where else?" Max asked.

"Carrying more Jews?"

"Of course—and maybe a few Gypsies and political convicts thrown in for good measure."

"How many trains come every day?"

"It varies. Seems to be increasing of late—two, three a day. One time we had five."

"Five?"

"That was a special occasion, I guess," Max said. "Kill three Jews, get two free."

"That's not funny," Jacob said.

"I thought it was," Max replied. "You play?"

"What?"

"Violin?" Max pressed. "Do you play?"

"I used to."

"Maybe you should be in the orchestra."

"No thanks," Jacob said. "Actually, come to think of it, no one is playing today. Why not?"

"Their conductor was shot last night."

"For what?"

"For trying to steal bread from the kitchen. Two of his friends—a trumpet player and some guy who plays the clarinet—came down with dysentery. They asked him to go to the kitchen and bring them something half-decent to eat. Unfortunately, Fat Louie caught him. Shot him in the back of the head. Anyway, there's an opening for a conductor. Does that sound appealing?"

"Not anymore."

"Well, you could still play the violin," Max said. "Just don't steal any bread."

"I think I'll pass."

"Why? Aren't you any good?"

Jacob shrugged.

"I bet you are."

"I'm not," Jacob insisted, seeing the mischief in Max's eyes.

"You're just shy."

They went back to their work, Max folding and sorting like a department clerk in women's wear, Jacob sorting and stacking books like a librarian.

"Now you're handling the biggest temptation I've faced since coming here."

"What?"

"Stealing a book and taking it back to my block to read it through the night."

"Why don't you?"

"The same reason you don't want to play that violin—I want to live," Max said. "And besides, Leszek searches me each night to make sure I haven't gone rogue and stolen something despite all his warnings."

"What does he care?" Jacob asked.

Max didn't answer, which was odd. But it was the way he didn't answer that made Jacob feel like he'd stumbled onto something important. But Max quickly changed the topic.

"We need to hurry," he said. "Got to be ready when the next train arrives."

As they sped up their sorting and began to put their piles into crates and take their crates into the warehouse to be cataloged and shelved, Max asked a question. "Jacob, does May 10, 1933, mean anything to you?"

"Not specifically, why?"

"The great book burning—you don't remember it?"

"You mean the one in Berlin?"

"Not just Berlin," Max said. "It happened at every university in the country."

"I was very young," Jacob said.

"So was I," Max said. "But your father was a professor, right?"

"Right."

"Didn't he tell you about such terrible things?"

Jacob shrugged. "Maybe he was trying to protect me from them."

"Not my father," Max said. "I told you he was a rabbi. Actually, he was a great rabbi. Everyone in the town loved him. Well, the Jews, anyway. But he was a great lover of the written word, starting with the Torah and the Mishnah, but anything, really. He loved books. Absolutely adored them. He devoured them, sometimes several a week, eighty or ninety or more a year. He was insatiable in that way. And when the Nazis had those big book burnings, he was appalled—absolutely livid. That May we were in Berlin; my father was meeting with some of the top rabbis in Germany. That night, without telling my mother, he got me out of bed and took me up to the roof of the medical building on the University of Berlin campus, and we stood there together and we watched them do it."

Jacob forced himself to keep working, but he found himself drawn into Max's story.

"Students came from all over to burn books. They came by the hundreds. And they brought thousands of books. I was just a kid, of course, but I'd never seen so many books, even at the library. And then they built this enormous bonfire. The flames had to be leaping twenty, thirty, forty feet into the air. It was spellbinding. But they started throwing the books into the fire, and they'd shout the names of the authors and cheer. There were books by all kinds of writers—H. G. Wells, Albert Einstein, Sigmund Freud, all the greats. They were all thrown into the fire. Anything the Nazis called 'heretical' or 'un-German,' their ideas went up in flames. My father was beside himself. He was filled with grief and immense anger. For weeks and months after it happened, he fumed about it with anyone who would listen. But no one wanted to talk about it, and everyone was worried my father was going to give himself a heart attack by getting so worked up over it. Worse, they were sure he was going to get himself arrested by the Gestapo for speaking out publicly. Anyway, one day my father said he'd heard that Freud had quipped, 'What, only our books? In earlier times, they would have burned us.' It seemed to my father such a clever line and perhaps a better perspective. Yes, he told me, it was terrible what the Nazis had done. But Freud was right; it could have been worse. So much worse. So he tried to relax, tried not to let the whole thing destroy him. And then he and my mother and I were rounded up one night and thrown onto a train and taken through the darkness until we woke up here. And they sent me to the right. And they sent him and my mother to the left. And I never saw them again."

Jacob stopped working. He could hear the whistle again. The train was pulling into the station. They had to finish. They had to move. "I'm sorry," he said.

Now it was Max who shrugged and wiped tears from his eyes. "What are you going to do?"

"I guess Heine was right."

"Who?"

"Heinrich Heine."

"The poet?"

"Yes."

"He was one of my father's favorites," Max said.

"My father's, too," Jacob said.

"So what did Heine say?"

"'Where books are burned, they will, in the end, burn people, too.'"

Now Max stopped working.

"He really wrote that?" he asked.

"He did," Jacob said.

"When?"

"I don't know—1821, '22, something like that."

"Maybe he was a prophet," Max sighed.

Jacob nodded. "Maybe he was."

41

The next morning, Jacob arrived in Leszek's office right after roll call.

Max was already there, and together the three of them quickly swallowed several pieces of Swiss cheese, a banana, and a slice of bread, this time with a thin spread of apricot jam. These they all washed down with small metal cups of black coffee. Then they wiped the grounds out of the cups and hid them behind a file cabinet. Jacob wished he could have eaten and drunk more slowly, savored every morsel. After all, under such conditions, this was practically a gourmet feast. Men in the camp would kill for such food—literally. But when he saw how quickly the other two ate and drank and cleaned up and were ready for work, Jacob did his best to follow their lead. They had more freedom than most, but they had to be constantly on their guard.

Leszek then sent Max and Jacob out to clear and process two more trains, and fueled by the desperately needed calories, Jacob was ready to go.

The work was exhausting but not noteworthy. Far more interesting to Jacob was the discussion he and Max had when they got back to Canada and were free once again to converse without fear of reprisal by the guards. Here in Canada the guards' task wasn't to prohibit conversation but to prevent theft. Jacob wondered whether they knew Leszek was stealing bread and cheese and juice and jam. Maybe they had a deal. Maybe Leszek did it when their backs were turned. Maybe Max actually lifted the items or pocketed them in the train cars when no one was looking. Then again, Jacob thought, perhaps it was better he didn't know. He certainly wasn't going to ask. The less he knew, the better—especially if the food kept coming.

The conversation between Jacob and Max was really more of a soliloquy by Max, but Jacob found it all fascinating, and it made the time go by faster. Max talked about growing up in Bucharest and the girls who had caught his eye and the pranks he used to play on the girls he liked when they were going through their bat mitzvah preparations. He talked about the raging debates he and his friends used to have over whether Jews should emigrate to Palestine and lay the groundwork for the rebirth of the state of Israel. One of Max's friends had become obsessed with Zionism and the belief that Jews must move to Jerusalem and prepare the way for the coming Messiah. Max declared himself to be "one thousand percent" opposed to Zionism because, according to his father, only the Messiah could reestablish the Jewish state and bring all the Jews back to the Promised Land and establish peace on earth. Any human efforts to accomplish the Messiah's work were blasphemy. But Max's friend's family could not be dissuaded, and finally they sold everything they had and headed for the port of Jaffa, and six months later to the day, Max's family—and all the Jews in his section of Bucharest—had been rounded up and sent to the camps.

Jacob had never encountered debates like these, much less engaged in any. He'd heard of people moving to Palestine, of course. But he'd never heard of debates over whether Israel had to be rebuilt for the Messiah to come, or whether the Messiah had to come first and rebuild the nation of Israel. He'd never studied the prophecies from the Tanakh about the future of the Jews. No one he knew talked about such things—not even his own rabbi—and now Jacob wondered why.

While the cleaning and processing of the first train was uneventful and almost routine, if such a term could be used for something Jacob had done so few times, the handling of the second train was devastating. This time, for the first time since he had arrived, Jacob saw dozens of children step out of the cars, some of them no more than five or six or seven years old. The children weren't there by themselves, of course. They were holding the hands of their mothers and fathers, their sisters and brothers, their grandparents. But their presence caught Jacob off guard.

The little girls caught his eye first, in their ponytails and print dresses with little yellow Stars of David on them, holding dolls and clinging to the skirts of their mothers, some of whom were holding real babies in their hands.

Children? Babies? Had the Nazis really brought them to Auschwitz? Why? Jacob wondered. Since arriving, he hadn't seen any children wandering the streets or working the fields. Indeed, he couldn't remember seeing anyone under the age of sixteen or seventeen in the camp. He certainly hadn't seen any babies or toddlers. Where would they go?

With Fat Louie shouting obscenities at them, Jacob watched the newcomers form into the single-file lines. One by one the girls were sent to the left, sometimes with their mothers, sometimes without. The little boys were sent to the left as well. All of them. Every single one. Without exception.

Some of these precious children were brave little soldiers. Their fathers or mothers would tell them to follow the "nice men," and they would "see them real soon," and the kids would grimace but nod and shuffle off around the corner as though they were going to the first day of kindergarten.

Others had to be torn away from their parents, especially from their mothers, screaming and crying. More often than not, the mothers would break down weeping and plead with Hoess to let them stay with their children. And time after time, Jacob watched him say yes and send the mothers to the left as well.

Did these parents have any idea what was happening? Trembling with anger and unspeakable grief, Jacob stared at them. Some of them knew, he decided. He could see it in their eyes, in their body language that bespoke great fear and resignation and defeat. But most of them were like he had been when he arrived a few days before. They had no idea what was coming. They knew they were entering a terrible place, but they didn't know just how terrible. How could they?

Once again, Jacob wanted to warn them all. He wanted to shout it at the top of his lungs. But whom would it save? Anyone? Would anyone live if he told them the truth? The bitter reality was no. First of all, they would likely not even hear him before the guards shot him. Second, even if they heard him, they wouldn't have time to process what he was saying. Third, even if they did, they wouldn't believe him. Who *could* believe it? His words would sound like the ravings of a madman. Fourth, of course, even if they did hear him and believe him, there was nothing they could do now. They, like him, were trapped.

As Max moved into the first cattle car, Jacob had no choice but to follow. They had a job to do, and there was no margin for error or delay. But Jacob recoiled at what he found, for there in the corner lay a dead man. His skin was a grayish green. His body had stiffened from rigor mortis.

"Come on," Max whispered. "I'll grab his feet. You get his hands."

Jacob didn't move.

"Let's go; let's go," Max pushed, trying to keep his voice low. "Before we get in trouble."

Still Jacob couldn't do it. He had never been this close to a corpse, with the exception of his own sister, though he pushed the images of her out of his mind. This was far more grisly. This man had been dead for several days. The people on the train had apparently pushed him into the corner, covered him with hay, and sprayed him with perfumes, anything to keep away the smell. It hadn't done much good, and Jacob fought back the urge to retch.

Now seeing in Max's eyes the genuine fear of being caught doing nothing, Jacob finally grabbed the man's arms. Careful to take hold of the cloth of the man's sweater rather than the skin of his hands, Jacob helped drag the body out of the car and up onto a wooden cart. When two other prisoners from Canada wheeled the corpse away, Jacob promptly vomited all over the platform. Every extra morsel of food and every ounce of half-decent coffee Leszek was secretly giving him out of view of the guards was now out of Jacob's system. That was bad enough, but he now had to clean that mess up too.

42

At noon a gong sounded, marking the afternoon break.

Though they had barely begun to sort and process all the luggage, everything had at least been cleared away from the train, and all the cars had been thoroughly scrubbed, disinfected, and repacked with hay. Thus, as soon as the engine was loaded with enough coal again, it would be leaving for points unknown to pick up another shipment of Jews.

"Come on," Max said. "The guards will keep an eye on all this stuff. Let's get some lunch."

"I can't," Jacob said.

"What do you mean you can't?"

"I'm not hungry."

"Then you haven't been here long enough."

"Those children," Jacob said, but Max put up his hands.

"Don't."

"What do you mean?"

"I mean, don't."

"Don't what?"

"Don't talk about it."

"Why not?"

"Because you can't think about it," Max said.

"How can I not think about it? They're murdering—"

But Max was more emphatic now. *"I said stop."*

"I can't stop. I have to think about it," Jacob said.

"You don't have to," Max shot back. "Are terrible things done here?

Yes. Do I care? Of course I do. I'm the son of a rabbi, a child of the Book. In the middle of the night, when no one's looking, I grieve over it all just like you do. But there's nothing I can do about it. You can't do anything either. So why dwell on it? Why try to make sense of it? It doesn't make sense. It's horrible, filthy, ugly, evil. The only way to survive is to think about something else, anything else. Don't live in the present. Don't dwell in the past. Dream about the future. Keep a picture of that in your head. Lock on it and never let go."

That was it. That was the end of the conversation. Max had said all he wanted to say.

They entered the dining hall. Each was given a metal bowl filled with soup, if you could call it that. It was less than a liter of lukewarm water, some boiled cabbage, a piece of carrot, and if you were lucky, a small piece of potato. That, and a small hunk of bread and a tiny bit of margarine, was all they got.

Max ate his immediately and slurped down the "tea" they served as well.

Jacob looked at the slop, unappetizing to the point of being revolting. He looked around the room and saw the newcomers pushing it away. He also watched as any man who had been there more than a week or so not only drank his soup quickly but also gulped down any that was left behind by fools who clearly didn't know any better.

Jacob gnawed on the bread, trying not to think about the sawdust grating his throat. He was about to push the soup away and get up when Leszek entered the hall. The kapo walked over to Jacob and, without saying a word, pointed to the soup, raised his eyebrows, and then walked away.

Jacob got the message. Leszek was saying the only people who survived were those who stayed strong, and the only ones who stayed strong were those who ate what was given to them. It wasn't an option. It was the law of the jungle. It was an ironclad rule he must obey if he wanted to stay on the Canada detail.

So Jacob obeyed. He held his breath, drank the soup, and finished his last morsel of bread in the hopes of neutralizing the soup's wicked aftertaste.

It didn't work.

The moment they were finished, Max headed for the door.

Jacob moved to catch up with him, careful not to run or make any wild, sudden movements that might unnerve the guards.

"Where are you going?" he asked when he caught up with Max a moment later.

"For a walk."

"A walk?"

"Yes, a walk," Max said.

"Why?"

"It's safer than a run," Max quipped.

"But, I mean, they let you just walk around by yourself?"

"Until the gong sounds at one o'clock, yes," Max said.

"Why?"

"Why what?"

"What's the point of giving us time to walk?"

Max didn't respond. He just shook his head as though the answer were perfectly obvious.

It wasn't. Not to Jacob. He didn't press it any further, however, but rather changed the subject. "Leszek," he said. "Where is he from?"

"A name like Leszek and you don't know?" Max asked.

"Poland, I guess, but where?" Jacob pressed. "What city?"

"I wouldn't ask any questions about Leszek—some things are better left alone," Max said somewhat cryptically.

This confused Jacob too. For such a talker, why was Max so reserved when it came to anything related to Leszek? *So much for showing any initiative,* Jacob thought. Perhaps it was better just to keep his mouth shut. Anything he needed to know, Max would surely tell him in due time. So they kept walking for a bit, and sure enough Max soon started talking again.

"You need to be serious, Jacob," he began.

"What's that supposed to mean?" Jacob asked.

"It means you need to be serious about surviving this place," Max continued.

"I am serious."

"No, you're not."

"Yes, I am."

"No, Jacob, you're not," Max repeated. "If you were serious, you would eat everything you see. You would drink everything except water from the showers. You eat what you can, every time, whatever they give you. Got it?"

Jacob nodded.

"I'm serious," Max continued. "Leszek sees potential in you. I don't know why. I ask him, 'Why do you like Weisz so much? What's so special about him?' He won't tell me. He won't say anything about you, and he knows you won't tell me because you don't talk about anything. But I know he knows something about you. That's why he chose you, and believe me, he's very choosy. He's building something, Jacob, something very interesting. I can't say anything yet. He swore me to secrecy. And that's not easy for me, as you know, because I'm the son of a rabbi. I'm a talker. But I gave Leszek my word, and that's sacred to me. Anyway, if you keep doing your work and stay out of trouble, he will let you in on it all. I can see that. He has plans for you—for the both of us, I think. That's why he's paired us up. So we need to watch each other's back. We need to take care of each other. I've only been here four months. But I've seen almost everyone in my block die. Some of dysentery. Some of starvation. Others, well, you know. They couldn't take it anymore and ran for the fences. But for some reason Leszek spotted me, and he saw me working hard, and he saw me surviving, and he thought I had street smarts, which he said seemed surprising for a rabbi's son. He thinks most of us yeshiva boys are too soft, and maybe he's right. But he said he saw something in me. So in January he pulled me off the construction detail that I was on, working my tail off during the dead of winter, the most miserable conditions you can imagine. We were building a new crematorium in the blowing and drifting snow, and it was bitter cold—I mean, *bitter*. Only two men on my detail didn't die. They kept replacing them, and the new guys kept dying too. But then, out of nowhere, Leszek pulled me out of there. He got me reassigned to Canada. He started to feed me, and I, well . . . I survived."

Max suddenly became quiet. Jacob processed what his friend had said as they kept walking for a bit, past the main entrance of the camp. For the first time Jacob noticed the wrought-iron sign over the gate blocking the road coming into the camp. It read, *Arbeit Macht Frei*: "Work makes you free." In a labor camp with a life expectancy between eight minutes and eight weeks, Jacob thought, the Nazi slogan wasn't ironic; it was cruel.

"Anyway, just don't do anything to mess this up, Jacob," Max said, his voice more quiet and resigned than normal. "Don't do anything stupid, and who knows? Maybe you'll survive this place after all. Maybe we both will."

43

It bothered Max enormously to have to work on Saturday.

Actually, *bothered* didn't adequately describe it. The whole notion of working on the Sabbath enraged Max, who otherwise struck Jacob as unenrageable. For Maximilian Cohen, Nazis forcing Jews to work on Shabbat was a terrible indignity, and he fumed and cursed and grumbled all day about it. Jacob certainly got the principle behind the outrage, but he failed to see its practicality. Why did it still bother Max after being in Auschwitz for so long? How could he get so vexed about this and not about the children? There were so many other humiliations and indignities to suffer through. Was this one really so bad?

As Jacob put his head down and closed his eyes on Saturday night—in a bed he now had to share with just one other guy—he thought about how grateful he was to have met Max. It seemed this might be the start of a very interesting friendship. Yet they were so different. He doubted they would ever have been friends out in the "real world." Of course, in the real world they never even would have met. Jacob was German; Max was Romanian. Jacob's family was traditional but secular; Max hailed from fiercely religious Orthodox stock.

Jacob had been taught enough Hebrew to read his Torah portion at his bar mitzvah, but his rabbi had only taught him how to pronounce the funny-looking letters, not how to understand what he was reading. Max, on the other hand, knew ancient Hebrew fluently. Beyond a few passages here and a few there, Jacob had never read the Torah or the Mishnah. But Max said he and his father used to sit around their home on Shabbat reading from the Law and the commentaries, dissecting and discussing and often debating the meaning of the holy text.

Max seemed to truly love studying Torah and observing Shabbat and celebrating the high holidays and embracing the community of the *shul*. It was everything to him. It was not only who Max was; it was who he *wanted* to be. Jacob, by contrast, was certainly proud to be a Jew, but he'd never fallen in love with all things Jewish. Maybe that was because his family wasn't really religious at all. They kept kosher and went to *shul* and lit the candles on Shabbat, but these were traditions, not anything spiritual.

As Jacob lay awake in the darkness and stared up at the ceiling, he wondered if the evil he was now experiencing was punishment for his family's abandoning God. Jacob could barely remember either of his parents talking about God or the Torah or the importance of prayer.

Max believed that the Jews were being punished for forgetting the God of Abraham, Isaac, and Jacob. He was certain that the Nazis had risen to power as a way to punish the Jewish community for abandoning the Torah and forsaking the Sabbath. Was that true? Jacob wondered. Maybe it was, but what of Max's family? They hadn't abandoned the Torah or forsaken Shabbat. Why were they being punished? And there were many observant Jews here in Auschwitz. Why? It didn't make sense. Didn't the very presence of so many religious Jews negate the validity of Max's argument? Why would the God of Abraham be punishing faithful, religious Orthodox Jews? What in the world could they have done wrong?

Such things were beyond his province, Jacob decided. He was reminded of something his mother used to say: "My heart is not proud, nor my eyes haughty; nor do I involve myself in great matters, or in things too difficult for me." It was a simple little proverb, but it had helped her through many challenging times. Now Jacob hoped it would help him, too.

His eyes began to fill with tears as he thought of the woman who had loved him so much and had given her own life that he might live. He struggled to see her face in his mind's eye. It was already beginning to fade, and it grieved him greatly that hers was a face he would never see again.

44

APRIL 24, 1943
WASHINGTON, D.C.

Cordell Hull had never even dreamed of being secretary of state.

Born into a farming family in a log cabin in Pickett County, Tennessee, Hull was just glad to get a solid education. He became a lawyer, then a judge, and then—prodded by family friends—ran for the Tennessee House of Representatives in 1893. A friendly man with a quick mind and natural talent, he was encouraged to run for Congress in 1907, and he won. For the next twenty-four years, he represented the Fourth District, even serving a stint as the chairman of the Democratic National Committee, before running for the U.S. Senate in the fall of 1930 and taking office the following January. His Senate career was short-lived, however, for in March of 1933, President Franklin Delano Roosevelt tapped Hull to run the State Department.

What few knew was that Hull's wife, Rose, was part Jewish. It was not a fact Hull wanted publicized. Indeed, he went to some lengths to keep it quiet. But as one of Hull's closest advisors, William Barrett knew, which was why he pulled Hull aside this particular afternoon with news.

"Mr. Secretary, we have a new development you need to be aware of," Barrett explained when they were behind the closed doors of the small conference room off of the secretary's main office.

"What is it, Bill?"

"We're hearing reports of an uprising in Warsaw, sir. It started a few days ago."

"What kind of uprising?"

"Apparently the Jewish resistance movement inside the Warsaw ghetto have gotten their hands on some light arms and Molotov cocktails. We're hearing reports that they've launched attacks against German soldiers."

"How many people are we talking about?" the secretary asked.

"We're not certain, sir. It's not clear exactly how many Jews are left in the ghetto. Originally there were over 400,000, but most of them have died either due to the appalling conditions or else been shipped to concentration camps. There may be as few as 60,000 there now. We don't know how many of those who are left are involved in the uprising, but the Germans are moving hard and fast to crush them. We're hearing reports of many casualties. One of the Jewish leaders there has committed suicide. There's a news report of the suicide note he left. I thought you'd want to see it."

Barrett handed a cable to the secretary, who read it aloud.

"'I cannot continue to live and to be silent while the remnants of Polish Jewry, whose representative I am, are being murdered. My comrades in the Warsaw ghetto fell with arms in their hands in the last heroic battle. I was not permitted to fall like them, together with them, but I belong with them, to their mass grave. By my death, I wish to give expression to my most profound protest against the inaction in which the world watches and permits the destruction of the Jewish people.'"

Hull handed back the cable. "So? What am I supposed to do with this?"

"With Passover beginning this week, a number of Jewish leaders want to meet with you."

"What for?"

"They want you to let more European Jews come here for asylum," Barrett said. "They say we haven't allowed enough Jews to enter the U.S. since Hitler invaded Poland. They say we've admitted less than 10 percent of the quota allowed by law. They want us to do more."

"Fine, set up the meeting," Hull said. "But make it clear to them: I cannot set policy. We're doing all we can."

45

APRIL 25, 1943
AUSCHWITZ-BIRKENAU CONCENTRATION CAMP

Growing up in Berlin, Jacob had never needed an alarm clock.

Not to get up and off to school on weekdays. Not to get up and off to the synagogue on Saturdays. In the mountains at Uncle Avi's cabin, if he was told they needed to be out of bed by five or five thirty to go hunting, Jacob had the uncanny ability to wake up exactly on time. He couldn't explain how he did it. He just could.

On this particular day, Jacob awoke precisely at four thirty, as he had for the past several days, by force of a newly acquired habit. Yet for some reason, on this day the gong did not sound. No one else in his room or anywhere on the block stirred. Most of the men around him, his bunkmate included, were still snoring. It was still pitch-black outside, and Jacob didn't hear any movement. Gerhard Gruder, their block senior, was nowhere to be found. Nor did Jacob hear the guards in jackboots patrolling the streets around them.

Lying perfectly still, he listened for any sound at all that might give him a clue as to what was happening. But the camp seemed strangely devoid of human activity. An unusually strong wind was bearing down from the north, rattling windows and doors and howling as it found cracks and fissures throughout the building. Thunder, too, rumbled in the distance, but that was all.

A few minutes later his bunkmate sat bolt upright, a look of fear on his face. He scanned the room and saw everyone else sleeping, then turned and saw that Jacob was awake.

"What's happening?" the young man whispered. "Isn't it time to get up?"

"Yes, it is," Jacob said, also keeping his voice low.

"Didn't the gong go off?"

"No."

"You're sure?"

"Positive."

"I just had a dream that I was back at university," said the young man, who had broken out in a cold sweat. "I was late for class, and they hanged me."

"It was just a dream," Jacob said. "I think we're okay."

"You *think*?"

"Believe me," Jacob said, "no one's up—the camp's not moving."

"Something's wrong," the young man said. "Maybe we should get up."

"Are you crazy?"

"What if we're wrong? What if we're all late? They'll kill us all."

"I'm not getting up," Jacob said.

"We have to," his bunkmate replied.

"Maybe you have to," Jacob said. "But I don't have to. I'm going to stay here until Gruder shows up."

"What if Gruder is dead?"

"Then there really is a God in heaven."

"Don't be funny."

"You think I'm being funny?"

"Just get up and check things out."

Jacob shook his head. "I'm not getting up. You get up."

"You have friends here. They won't shoot you."

"What are you talking about?" Jacob asked, taken aback.

"I know you're getting extra food," the young man said. "I don't know where or how, but you've obviously made friends somewhere."

Jacob grew nervous. How did this kid know about his business? Was he spying on him? How else could he know?

"I don't know what you're talking about," he lied. "But I'm not going out there."

Both were quiet for a few moments, and then the young man leaned toward Jacob and whispered again.

"My name's Josef," he said. "Josef Starwolski."

"I'm Leonard Eliezer," Jacob lied, not daring to lower his guard to anyone outside of Canada. "You can call me Len."

"Sorry I didn't introduce myself before now," Josef said. "I was too scared to talk to anyone."

"Me, too. Where are you from?"

"Kraków. And you?"

"Brussels," Jacob lied again.

"I work in the records office," Josef said. "They needed someone who could type and file and translate from Polish to German. Somehow they found me."

"And how is it?"

"Could be worse. I work right down the hall from Hoess and Von Strassen, so I think I'm developing an ulcer already. But there are some pretty girls in the office. Actually, everyone there besides me is a girl, so that's not terrible. How about you?"

"I work in Canada."

"The warehouse?"

Jacob nodded.

"What do you do?" Josef asked.

"Nothing important," Jacob said, not wanting to talk about himself. "It's pretty boring. But at least it's inside."

"Yeah, that's good," Josef agreed. "So how old are you?"

"Twenty-one. And you?"

"I turn twenty today," Josef whispered back.

"Oh . . . well . . . congratulations," Jacob said, not sure what else to say. "Happy birthday, I guess."

"What's happy about it?" Josef asked.

46

When the sun finally came up, Jacob learned why Sunday was different.

Apparently, even Nazi murderers needed a day off.

To his astonishment, Jacob learned that meant most prisoners had the day off too, except for those baking bread and those performing a handful of other jobs deemed essential by Hoess for the "good order" of the camp. The ovens in the crematorium never seemed to stop, for instance, so the *Sonderkommandos* kept working in twelve-hour shifts around the clock. Most of the rest of the prisoners, however, could roam about freely, talk to whomever they wanted, write letters, play cards, or just sleep in. Certainly there were enough guards to prevent a riot or a breakout. But Jacob noticed that many of the guards and camp officers got rip-roaring drunk, mostly on cases of vodka that Leszek happily provided them from the storehouses of Canada.

This particular Sunday—April 25, 1943—was no ordinary Sunday. It was Easter, and to Jacob's astonishment, he watched as no small number of guards and officers and block seniors went to church. In fact, at just before ten that morning, while he and Max were out for a long walk, Jacob was flabbergasted to see Gerhard Gruder, Fat Louie, and several others heading to the camp chapel, dressed in their Sunday finest. Soon he could actually hear an organ playing and their torturers singing hymns and reading Scriptures and then ringing the bells when the service was over.

Who were these people? What God were they praying to? How could they beat and slaughter and burn human beings six days a week and then read the Bible and pray on Sundays? Though Jacob hadn't been raised religious, he certainly hadn't been raised to hate religious people either. He'd always thought of himself as tolerant not only of Orthodox Jews but also of Catholic and Protestant Christians. He'd been taught to respect every man and every faith, but how could he do so now? If this was what it meant to be a Christian, Jacob hoped all Christians would rot in hell, and the sooner the better.

"Come on," Max said. "Let's go see my sister."

Jacob did a double take. "Your sister?"

"Yeah."

"You have a sister?"

"Of course."

"I didn't know you had a sister."

"Well, I do."

"And she's here?"

"No, she's having tea with the king of England," Max retorted. "Of course she's here. She works at the medical clinic."

"How come you never mentioned her?"

"Haven't I?" Max asked, now walking more briskly. "I thought I had."

"No, not once," Jacob said, picking up his pace to keep up with his new friend.

"I must have," Max said.

"You didn't," Jacob said. "You talk about everything. You never shut up. And now it turns out you have family here, and you never said a thing."

Max shrugged. "What can I say? I have a sister. Her name is Abigail. We call her Abby."

Two minutes later they were just about to enter the clinic when Leszek came up from behind them and grabbed them both by the arm.

"Come with me," he said under his breath.

"Why—what's the matter?" Max asked, startled but compliant.

"Just keep your mouths shut and come with me."

Jacob and Max did as they were told, and soon they were entering the timber yard and zigzagging their way through huge piles of wood until they came upon two men who were smoking cigarettes.

"Otto, Abe, meet Max and Jacob," Leszek said.

Jacob and Max shook hands with the men, both of whom appeared to be in their early twenties. As they did, Leszek began talking very quickly and quietly.

He explained that Max and Jacob were his assistants in Canada and told what they did and where they were from. He gave a brief background on Jacob's uncle and his prominent role in the Resistance. He explained the circumstances by which Jacob had arrived in Auschwitz. Then he explained why it was best to call Jacob by the name Leonard Eliezer in public.

Leszek then told Jacob and Max that Otto's last name was Steinberger and that he was a Czechoslovakian Jew. Abe's full name was Abraham Irving Frenkel; he, too, was from Czechoslovakia. Leszek said Otto had for a long time worked in the Canada command but now was a registrar for Block 14.

"His job is to record the daily roll call, keep careful statistics on which prisoners have died and what their numbers are, keep detailed notes and records for his block senior on the activities of each man, and basically run errands for the senior, as needed. As long as he keeps his ledger under his arm and a worried frown on his face, he's free to go anywhere in the camp he needs or wants to go. That's critical for us."

Abe was a registrar as well, but he was about to be moved to Camp D in Birkenau, the vastly larger Auschwitz expansion camp a few kilometers away. There, Leszek said, the Nazis were building much larger barracks but also much larger gas chambers and crematoriums.

"Hoess is planning something," Leszek said. "Abe here is going to help us figure out what."

As Leszek spoke, Jacob found himself sizing up these two men. Otto Steinberger was ruggedly good-looking with intense but friendly dark-brown eyes and a strong jaw. He looked to be healthy and in better physical shape than most, suggesting he had probably arrived fairly recently. In some initial and superficial ways, Otto reminded Jacob of Uncle Avi. There was something about him that suggested he loved the outdoors and was a man with street smarts and a penchant for action.

Abe Frenkel, meanwhile, bore an uncanny resemblance to a professor at Frederick William University in Berlin who was a dear friend of Jacob's father. The man hadn't said a word yet, but he looked like a lover of words and ideas. He had an angular nose and bright, gentle brown eyes. Jacob could picture him wearing a tweed suit and smoking a pipe with cherry tobacco while sitting in his office at some European college of philosophy, holding office hours and discussing the finer points of Kant and Hegel. He, too, seemed surprisingly healthy, and Jacob surmised he was a relatively recent arrival as well.

That Otto Steinberger and Abe Frenkel were Jews hardly needed to be stated. It was apparent by the yellow triangles on their striped uniforms. Yet Jacob sensed that Leszek was trying to say as concisely as possible that the four of them were on the same team, of the same heritage—that they could trust each other, and that perhaps they would need to. What was not immediately apparent was *why* exactly Leszek was implying any of this. Why had they been brought together in such a rushed and unplanned manner? This was another matter altogether. Jacob assumed that he would learn the answer soon enough.

"When did you two get here?" Otto asked in a whisper.

Max took several minutes to tell his story.

When he was finished, Jacob simply said, "Thursday."

"You just got here on Thursday?" Otto asked.

"Yes, sir," Jacob replied.

"How about you both?" Max asked.

Jacob was stunned when Otto said he had been there since the summer of 1942.

"And I arrived on April 13, 1942," Frenkel whispered. "I was part of a group of a thousand Jews. We were all from Slovakia. I'm one of the few still around."

Frenkel finished one cigarette and lit up another. "There were only fifteen thousand prisoners when I got here," he said, looking off into the distance. "Now look at the place. They just keep coming."

"And dying," Steinberger said.

It was an odd meeting. Jacob had no idea why they were talking.

And then it was over.

47

"What was that all about?" Jacob asked Max at lunch.

"I have no idea," Max said, staring into his soup but hardly touching it.

"Have you ever seen those two before?"

"Never."

"Then what was the point?"

"Your guess is as good as mine."

"You've known Leszek a lot longer than me."

"He's still a mystery to me."

"Well, what did he mean when he said things like Otto's job is 'critical for us'?" Jacob pressed. "What did he mean when he said that when Abe is transferred to Birkenau, he is going to 'help us' figure out what the Nazis are doing with such a huge expansion? Who is 'us'? What's he talking about?"

"I don't know," Max said.

"You must," Jacob said, not buying his obfuscation for a second.

"Well, I don't," Max shot back, careful to keep his voice down. "I have a guess, but I don't really know."

"What's your guess?"

"We can't talk about it here."

"Then finish your soup," Jacob said, "and let's go someplace where you can tell me what you know."

Thunder boomed overhead, and soon the skies opened and it was pouring.

"Follow me," Max said, and he set off sprinting once again toward the medical clinic.

At first Jacob was hesitant to run. He'd seen what happened to prisoners who made the guards think they were trying to escape. But as the rain intensified, everyone began running for cover, guards and prisoners alike.

Through the muddy streets, Jacob sprinted to catch up with Max, and before long they were in the vestibule of the clinic. Jacob saw Max's look of surprise and concern as he stared at a blond-haired, blue-eyed, bespectacled gentleman sitting behind the desk. Roughly thirty years of age, Jacob guessed, the man was obviously a prisoner. He wore the requisite zebra-striped uniform and had bluish-green numbers tattooed on his left arm, though from this distance Jacob couldn't read the numbers. Still, this was clearly not someone Max expected or wanted to see.

"May I help you?" the man behind the counter asked.

"Where's my sister?"

"You mean Abigail? She's your sister?"

"Yes, but who are you?"

The gentleman stood and extended his hand. "You must be Max. I've heard a lot about you."

"I've heard nothing of you," Max replied, ignoring the man's hand.

"I'm new. Just arrived a few days ago. They assigned me here. The name is Leclerc—Jean-Luc Leclerc—but everyone calls me Luc. It's an honor to meet you."

"You know Abby?" Max asked warily.

"Of course," Luc said. "She's been teaching me—not just about the clinic but about her friends in the camp. She told me I was likely to meet you this morning. She said you usually come around ten o'clock on Sunday mornings. We were sorry when you did not arrive."

"Where is she now?"

"Dr. Mengele needed some supplies, scalpels and things," Luc explained. "Abby volunteered to make the delivery. I offered to do it myself. I didn't want her to be out in the rain. But she said no. She said I was new, and she was afraid I might get lost. She told me to wait here, so that's what I'm doing."

"How long has she been gone?" Max asked.

"Ten minutes, maybe fifteen," Luc said. "I suspect she'll be back at any moment."

Max mumbled something, then grabbed Jacob by the arm and began leading him toward the back of the clinic. "Are the doctors in?"

Luc shook his head. "They're at lunch. May I help you?"

"No," Max said. "We'll wait for Abby back here. Make certain we are not disturbed. We have important business to discuss."

When they got to the last exam room, Max shut the door. "Sit down," he ordered, and when Jacob complied, Max started pacing the room. "First, do not ever get sick. Do you understand me? *Ever.*"

"Why not?"

"Good, then we're clear on that," Max said. "Second, don't ever come into this clinic unless you're with me. *Ever.* Not if you have a cold. Not if you have the flu. Not if you've got dysentery. Not if you've got bedbugs or lice. Not if you've broken your arm or lost an eye in a fight. Do . . . not . . . ever . . . come . . . here . . . without me. Got it?"

"No, I don't," Jacob replied. "What in the world are you—?"

"Good, then we're clear on that, too," Max said, cutting Jacob off in midsentence. "Third, whatever friends you make—real friends, people you care about—warn them not to ever come here either. I mean, if they get assigned here to work, that's fine. But under no circumstances must you let a true friend come here to be treated. Enemies? Sure. Mere acquaintances? Fine. But not friends."

Jacob still had no idea was Max was talking about. The place looked clean and orderly enough. There were dozens of nicely made beds, with clean sheets and fresh pillows. There were locked cabinets filled with pharmaceuticals of all kinds. There were various pieces of medical equipment and a friendly-enough man at the front desk. What exactly was the problem? He tried to ask again, but Max refused to elaborate, except to say that Jacob should never accept an invitation to meet with Dr. Mengele under any circumstances.

"Why not?" Jacob asked.

But Max merely replied, "If you're ordered to see Mengele, run for the fences."

And that was that. Then Max leaned forward, lowered his voice, and turned to their real business at hand.

"Jacob, can you keep a secret?" Max asked, his eyes searching Jacob's for any sign of hesitancy or deceit.

Jacob nodded and leaned forward a bit as well.

"Things are about to change around here," Max said.

"How so?"

"Leszek is leaving tonight."

"Leaving?" Jacob asked. "What do you mean, leaving?"

"Escaping," Max said in a voice barely above a whisper.

Jacob stiffened, unable to believe what he was hearing. "How? When?" he asked.

"I don't know the details," Max said in a way that made Jacob believe him. "I just know it's going to happen, and it's going to affect us."

"How?"

"Von Strassen and his men are going to come after us and everyone in the Canada command," Max said. "They're going to assume we're in on it. We'll definitely be interrogated. We might even be tortured."

Jacob tensed as a new wave of fear crept over him.

"But you and I must be strong," Max continued. "We must not talk no matter what. You see, Leszek is a captain in the Polish army. He works for Polish intelligence. He actually volunteered to get arrested and sent here so he could report on what was happening. For the last two and a half years, he's been sending coded messages out through letters to various people. But now it's time for him to leave."

"Can we go too?" Jacob asked.

"I wish," Max said. "No, we can't go. I'm helping him pull some supplies together for his trip, but that's it. But here's the thing. If he gets out successfully, and if he can link back up with the Polish underground, then he's going to tell them about everything that's happening here in detail. He's going to persuade the Polish Resistance and the Allies to mount an operation and come liberate us. If all goes well, we could be out of here by summer."

Jacob was stunned by what he had just heard. Could it really be true?

Unfortunately, just at that moment, one of the doctors came back from lunch and found them chatting in the exam room. He blew a gasket. His face and ears turned beet red, and a vein in his left temple looked like it was about to explode. The doctor yelled at the both of them and ordered them to leave or face punishment. It did not seem to matter that Max was waiting for his sister. They were clearly persona non grata, and though Max was indignant, Jacob pulled him out of there for fear the doctor would call a guard and really get them in trouble.

Life was difficult enough. They didn't need anything else, especially not today.

48

Roll call began precisely at seven o'clock that night, just as it did every night.

The storm was now directly over them. Claps of thunder rattled windows and bones. The evening air flashed and crackled with bolts of lightning. The bitterly cold spring rains did not let up but were coming down as relentlessly as anything Jacob had ever experienced. Still, every man was ordered to stand at attention, waiting for his number to be called and the signal given that they could go back to their blocks, away from the elements.

Jacob's heart raced. At any moment, the sirens would go off as someone discovered Poczciwinski was missing. The manhunt would begin, and Poczciwinski would be on the run. Would he make it out? Could he? It was electrifying to think that Leszek was part of the Resistance, that he had been part of the underground long before coming to Auschwitz, and that he had apparently operated as such ever since arriving. That was why he had heard of Avi. That was why he had been so interested in their operation to liberate the prisoners of train 801. And that was why he had moved quickly to recruit Jacob into the Canada command. As frightened as Jacob was of the interrogation and torture that was sure to come, there was one thing he felt good about tonight. His instincts hadn't failed him. He had thought Poczciwinski was part of the Resistance—or hoped, anyway. And it turned out he was.

Indeed, Leszek Poczciwinski wasn't simply part of the underground. According to Max, he was a professional intelligence operative. He'd been recruiting people throughout the camp—people like Max, Otto, Abe, and surely others—to gather critical information about the evil that was being done in Auschwitz-Birkenau and its forty-plus satellite camps. To get word to the Allies. To persuade them to come here and crush the Nazis and liberate the prisoners. For the first time in a long time, Jacob felt hope. He didn't have to figure out a way to escape. All he had to do was stay alive. That's what Leszek and Max were trying to tell him. He only had to make it a little bit further, and then everything would be all right.

Roll call finished without incident. Much to Jacob's shock, there were no sirens. There was no manhunt. Jacob ran back to his block with the others, in the vain hope of drying off before bed. He listened to Josef tell him stories about all the beautiful girls he worked with in the records office, but the whole time he was wondering what Leszek was up to and when everything would be revealed. The tension was unbearable. Jacob was desperate to get an update. Several times he considered going to Max's block to see if he had an update, but he knew that would be unwise and could draw unneeded suspicions. So he tried to pay closer attention to what Josef was saying and not look as anxious as he felt.

Eventually Jacob excused himself to go to the latrine.

But the line ahead of him stretched on forever. More and more of the men in his bunk room were becoming ill. Over the past few days, many of them had gone to the medical clinic, and they hadn't come back. Jacob remembered what Max had told him about staying away from that place, and he felt a chill.

At least half of Jacob's afflicted bunkmates were vomiting and suffering from extreme diarrhea, some of it bloody, and all of it quite painful. For the past several nights Jacob could hear them groaning in the lavatory, some of them throughout the night. In the last few hours, the guy in the bunk below him had begun complaining of terrible abdominal pain. He was writhing and moaning nonstop. Others had high fevers and chills. Many of them were rapidly losing weight.

Jacob was no doctor, but he had no doubt they had contracted dysentery. Once again he was thankful he had not drunk the water from the showers on the first day. However they had gotten it, he was growing terrified of catching it himself and dying a slow, miserable death like they were. He hardly wanted to enter the latrine when it was his time. The smell alone was horrific, and since the place was rarely cleaned, much less disinfected, the chance of catching something fatal was high and growing higher.

As he wiped his hands and face, he found himself obsessed with trying to figure out how Leszek Poczciwinski was going to break free. It didn't seem possible. How was he going to move about the camp without attracting the attention of the guards? How was he going to get to the first fence without being shot? And even when he got there, how was he going to keep from being electrocuted? And even if he could manage that, what about the German shepherds patrolling the no-man's-land between the first and second fences? And even if he got through all those—which wasn't humanly possible—how then would he get past the second fence, not to mention the land mines beyond? Was someone on the outside helping him? If so, who? Did he really have a realistic chance of making it? On the face of it, Jacob certainly didn't think so.

It was Leszek, after all, who had told him that close to eight hundred prisoners had tried to escape from Auschwitz and that not a single one of them had succeeded. Why was he so sure he would be different?

The questions kept coming. Jacob desperately wanted to join his Polish friend, to at least try to break free from this terrible nightmare.

It was a selfish thought, he told himself. He knew that's what Avi would say. It was selfish to be consumed every moment of every day with how to slip away and go live his own life in obscurity someplace where the Nazis could not find him, somewhere he could marry and have a family and settle down and have his own cabin in the woods. It was selfish to want to escape from this nightmare and leave everyone else behind.

Avi had always been thinking about others, how to help them find a job or a house or a way to escape from the Third Reich or from a train to Auschwitz. That's who Avi was. That's how he thought. Jacob admired him for it, but unfortunately he was cut from different cloth. He wasn't thinking about how to help others here in the camp. He wasn't thinking about helping anyone else escape. He was just thinking about himself. Then again, was that wrong? In circumstances such as these, was that really so terrible?

When Jacob returned to the bunk room, he was surprised to find that some of the men had received letters from spouses, family members, or friends. Some even had received small packages with food and sometimes money with which to buy cigarettes. He couldn't help but feel a sharp pang of jealousy. He hadn't known there was a system here for incoming mail. He hadn't imagined that it was possible for prisoners to have any contact from the outside world. But then again, even if he had known, what would it have mattered? Who was going to write to him? Nearly everyone he knew was dead. Micah, Henri, and Jacques were—at best—on the run across Europe, fleeing the Gestapo. They weren't going to be writing to him. No one was. Seeing other men light up at the words and small gifts sent by their loved ones made him feel worse.

At nine o'clock, another gong sounded. It was time for lights-out and utter silence. Just then, Block Senior Gruder came into their room. To Jacob's surprise, he informed them that the next day, Monday, would be treated like a partial holiday. Morning roll call would not be until eleven o'clock, after which they would report to their regular jobs. The men knew better than to show any emotion for fear of setting Gruder off. They simply nodded and waited for the man to leave for his own private quarters.

Yet as he sat on his top bunk, Jacob's heart leaped. Leszek Poczciwinski knew what he was doing after all. Leszek had been here long enough to know the routine and rhythms of camp life on Easter weekend and the following morning. He had to know the guards drank heavily every year on Easter and that most if not all of them would be hungover in the morning. Everyone who wasn't drunk or hungover would be sleeping in. If Leszek had left immediately after the evening roll call was completed, he'd have at least fifteen full hours before the next roll call was taken. If his plan was solid and he had the tools he needed, this would give Leszek the time to create maximum distance between himself and the camp before anyone even noticed he was gone.

Jacob could barely sleep that night. On the one hand, he was so excited by what was happening. As he tossed and turned in the wee hours, he wondered how much more Max really knew. If he knew the whole plan or even a significant part of it, and if the plan worked and Leszek wasn't captured and hanged on the gallows in the camp's main square, then maybe Max would share the plan with Jacob. Maybe they could escape together.

Max had said he was helping Leszek gather supplies. Those had to be from the Canada warehouse. So he must know at least some of the plan. Jacob figured Leszek had probably acquired a backpack, foodstuffs, a flashlight and batteries, good boots and extra pairs of socks, and civilian clothes to change into before or immediately after clearing the fences. The civilian clothes were especially important. Jacob thought he might even need two sets. He wouldn't get far in the outside world wearing zebra stripes.

On the other hand, Jacob was scared. For Leszek, for Max, and most of all for himself. The moment the guards discovered Leszek was gone, Max had said they would come after the two of them and everyone in the Canada command. Jacob had never been interrogated. He wondered how long he could last. Suddenly he wished Max hadn't told him anything about Leszek's connection to Polish intelligence. He wished Leszek hadn't introduced him to Otto and Abe.

Wasn't simply knowing such things an automatic death sentence?

49

By Monday morning, April 26, the storm had passed.

As he finished a late breakfast and arrived for roll call at eleven, Jacob was amazed by how beautiful the weather was. The sun was shining. The skies were mostly blue with white wisps of clouds here and there. For the first time he noticed how green the grass was. He even commented to Josef how flowers were beginning to bloom and the trees were beginning to bud.

Yet again roll call came and went without incident. Jacob wasn't sure whether to be confused or worried.

When he arrived at the Canada command, Jacob was flabbergasted to see Leszek, who greeted him as usual. What in the world was happening? Jacob had no idea. He wondered whether he should say anything, but when Max arrived a moment later, he shot Jacob a look that told him to keep his mouth shut. Together, they quickly scarfed down some oranges and bread without saying anything of substance. Then Leszek sent them down to the main floor to catalog and store a large stack of fur coats, jackets, and stoles that they had not gotten to on Saturday.

To Jacob it seemed there were extra guards roaming the warehouse. All of them had bloodshot eyes and reeked of vodka. They barely seemed to be paying attention, but not once during the day—as relatively relaxed as it was compared to the previous week—did Jacob sense an opportunity to talk to Max about Leszek. Rather, he just listened as Max rattled on and on about some obscure passage in the Hebrew Scriptures that Jacob had never even heard of nor cared anything about.

For at least an hour, Max talked about the prophet Nahum preaching a message of judgment against the people of Nineveh, which much to Jacob's ignorance was apparently "the wicked capital of the wicked Assyrian Empire." Then Max droned on and on about how the prophecies of the judgment actually came to pass in 612 B.C. when Nineveh was completely and utterly destroyed. Jacob had little interest in any of it, but he assumed it was Max's way of sounding normal to the guards. It also helped keep Jacob's attention on the work in front of him and not drifting into unwise conversations.

– – –

And then it happened.

At precisely 6:30 that Monday evening, the sirens began to sound. Jacob was completely baffled now and more terrified than ever. He thought he heard gunshots, though in the commotion and confusion he couldn't be sure.

Not knowing what was done at a moment like this, he followed the crowd back to their barracks and soon spotted Gerhard shouting for everyone to line up to be counted. Evening roll call was not for another half hour, so clearly something out of the ordinary was happening. Jacob just hoped it was the thing for which he had been so nervously waiting for the past twenty-four hours. He hoped against hope that his friend Leszek Poczciwinski was now on the move. For the life of him, he couldn't understand why Leszek hadn't left the day before, but if he was on the run now, Jacob wished him all the best.

A buzz moved through the camp as people began to realize that someone was missing and began speculating that perhaps that person had actually tried to escape.

As Jacob stood at attention with the rest of his block, he watched with great interest to see how the camp reacted to an escape attempt. He watched as hundreds upon hundreds of heavily armed troops rushed from their barracks to take up predetermined positions around the camp while hundreds of other elite troops flooded out of the gates to search for the escapee. He could hear the barking of the German shepherds being loosed for the hunt. He watched as searchlights warmed up to full strength in all of the guard towers and scanned the camp perimeter.

Jacob's stomach was in knots. He had prepared himself for standing out in the chilly evening air for a few extra hours. He was stronger and healthier than most of the men in Block 18. What he had not anticipated was the word that Commandant Hoess was refusing to allow the prisoners to go back to their barracks or even sit down, much less lie down, or move at all until the escapees were captured or confirmed dead.

Again a buzz rippled through the camp. Had Hoess just used the word *escapees*? Plural? Jacob's pulse quickened. That meant it wasn't just a lone renegade. There were at least two men on the run, possibly more. Every prisoner was now not only wondering who they were and how they'd done it but was also rooting them on. Their escape was an escape for all of them. Their victory would give desperately needed encouragement to all the rest. Jacob wondered whether the men on the move with Leszek were Otto Steinberger and Abe Frenkel.

It seemed unlikely that Leszek would introduce him and Max to two men who might soon be gone for good—or dead. What would be the point? Still, whomever Leszek had taken with him, they had not been shot yet, nor electrocuted on the fence. They had clearly made it past the electric fences and outside the camp. That's why all the troops were being deployed beyond the fences.

Another thought hit Jacob. Could Max be one of the escapees? Could Max's sister, Abby?

Two hours passed—then three and four and five. In a way, this was good news. The manhunt was still on. No bodies had been dragged back to the camp. This meant Leszek Poczciwinski and whomever he'd chosen to go with him were still free. But the toll on the rest of them was rising fast. The prisoners around Jacob were increasingly cold and exhausted and growing faint. Those suffering diarrhea had no choice but to defecate where they were standing. Yet those who fell down were beaten. Fellow prisoners did their best to hold each other up.

They quietly pleaded with their comrades to be strong and not buckle under the pressure or the fatigue factor. Many simply couldn't make it, however, and the beatings were as savage as anything Jacob had seen since arriving. The guards seemed to be taking out their seething anger against the prisoners who had escaped on the prisoners who had grown too weak to remain standing and were too exhausted to get back on their feet.

By one in the morning, Jacob found himself swaying, barely able to keep his knees locked. He was drifting in and out of consciousness. At one point, he drifted to sleep long enough to have a dream. In it, Leszek was sipping tea in London with Prime Minister Winston Churchill, explaining what he had seen and heard and bravely endured and mapping out a plan to send in a rescue force to set the captives free. Then Jacob snapped awake and found himself wobbling to and fro, on the brink of collapse. He was about to drift away again when suddenly a pistol went off right next to him, nearly deafening him. Jacob's eyes shot wide open just in time to see an older man collapse to the ground with a gaping hole in his head. It was the man who slept on the bunk below Jacob and Josef, the man with the abdominal cramps. Blood and brain matter flew everywhere. Jacob was paralyzed with fear but fully awake again and standing erect. The guard who had pulled the trigger ordered Gerhard and another block senior to drag away the body, and as they did, word spread through the camp that Von Strassen had given the guards permission to shoot any prisoner deemed too weak to remain on his feet. Gunshots began echoing up and down the street.

Finally, as the sun began to rise, Von Strassen ordered all the men back to their barracks until a special morning roll call in an hour and a half. By now, Jacob was too delirious with fatigue to worry about only having ninety minutes to sleep before having to stand at attention once again. Following Josef, he limped back into the barracks and climbed up into the top bunk.

Just before he slipped into unconsciousness, he thought again of

Poczciwinski. Had he made it? Was he really out? Had he really slipped through the gates of hell?

He must have, Jacob thought. There was no other reason to let the men go back to bed. And for the first time since arriving at Auschwitz, he fell asleep with the trace of a smile on his face.

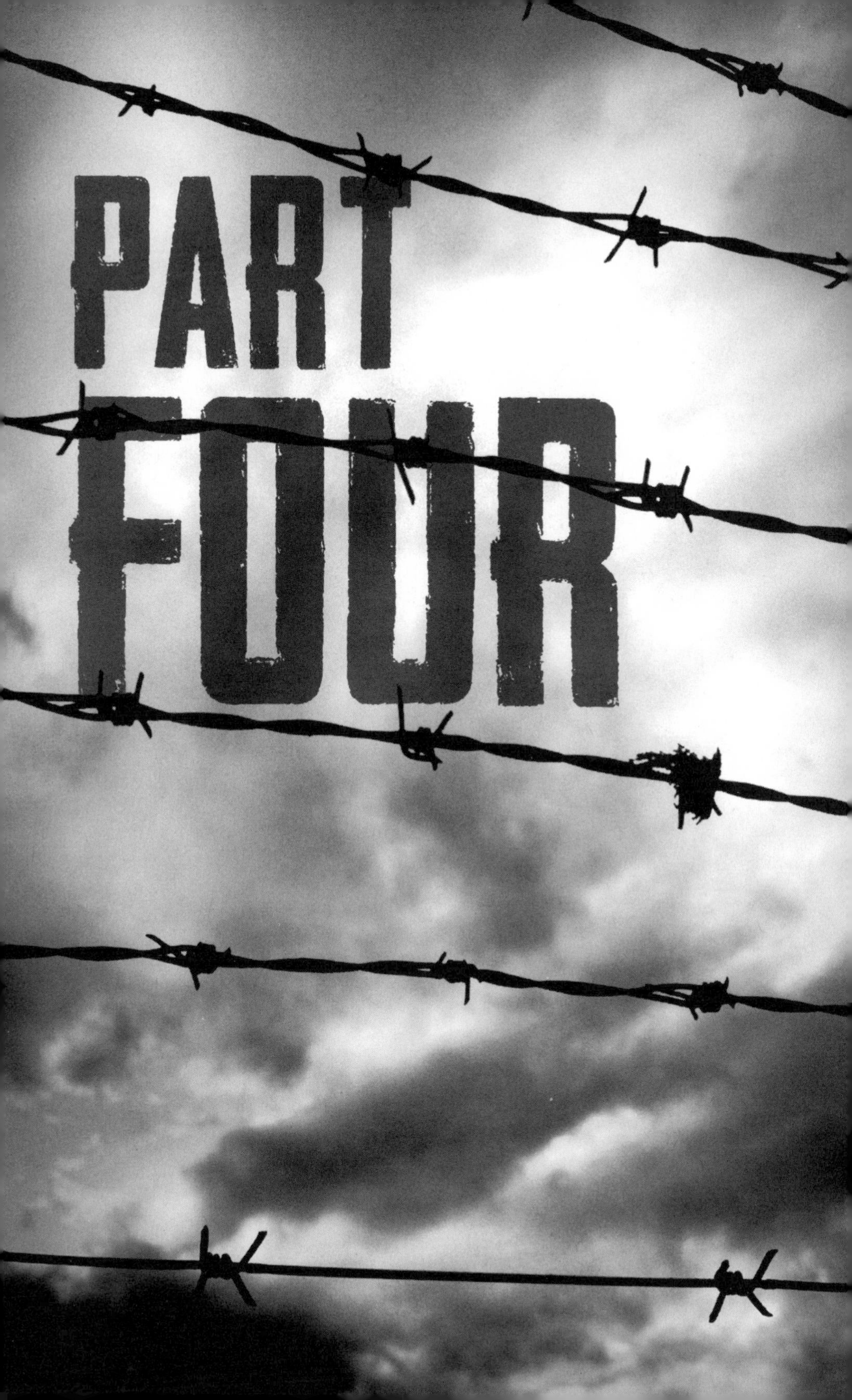
PART
FOUR

50

Everything changed that week in April, yet nothing changed at all.

For three days and three nights, Colonel Von Strassen and several thousand troops and dozens of dogs conducted the most intensive manhunt in the history of the Auschwitz-Birkenau camps. Yet in the end, Leszek Poczciwinski was neither captured nor killed in the daring escape. Neither were his two comrades—both of whom turned out to be Polish friends of his. For this, Jacob was overjoyed.

To his terror, Jacob was dragged in for questioning by Von Strassen and his men, but to his surprise, the interrogation lasted only for a few hours. Jacob played dumb, and it seemed to work. He kept saying he didn't know anything about Leszek Poczciwinski's activities. He repeated over and over again that he had just arrived. He kept pointing out that he spent most of his time working, not hanging out with the kapo of the Canada command. He and Leszek Poczciwinski had only had a few brief conversations, he insisted.

In the end, Von Strassen let him go. The whole episode left Jacob deeply rattled, but he was also proud of himself for keeping his cool and sticking to his story and not letting Von Strassen's threats wear him down. It was, he felt, sort of a rite of passage, a test of manhood, and somehow he had passed. Uncle Avi, he felt sure, would be proud. He hoped his father and mother would be too.

Maximilian Cohen, however, disappeared. Jacob looked desperately for his friend every day in the Canada command and throughout the camp, but he did not find him. Eventually, he heard a rumor that

Von Strassen had turned Max over to Dr. Mengele to be interrogated. The very thought made Jacob shudder. Since Max's warning to stay away from the medical clinic, Jacob had heard stories of the sadistic experiments Mengele performed on living human beings, all of them without anesthesia, and he feared greatly for his friend.

Finally, at 6:30 on Monday evening—precisely one week after the sirens had sounded—every man in the camp was lined up in the courtyard in front of the gallows. As every prisoner stood at attention to watch, Max, shackled and led by two armed guards, emerged from the basement of the building where Von Strassen had his office.

Jacob gasped. He watched as the guards led Max up onto the wooden platform and put the noose around his neck. His friend's face was white as a sheet. His lips were trembling. But when he briefly caught sight of Jacob in the crowd, no more than ten meters away, Max stiffened and lifted his chin. Then, before the guard could pull the lever, Max shouted at the top of his lungs, *"Long live the Jews of Romania!"* Then his body suddenly dropped. The rope tightened. His feet kicked wildly. His eyes bulged. Then he stopped struggling and grew still, and it was all over.

Jacob watched in horror. He did not cry. He did not make a sound. He just stared at his friend, swaying in the cool spring breeze.

As the life drained out of Max, the will to escape drained out of Jacob. He was not just watching the death of his only friend in the world. He was watching the death of the only person who knew how Leszek Poczciwinski had gotten out.

But that was not all. On Tuesday morning, the situation went from bad to worse. Von Strassen ordered Jacob removed from the Canada command and assigned him to a construction detail. Now Jacob was to help build a factory at one of Auschwitz's subcamps known formally as Monowitz-Buna, but known to the prisoners simply as Buna. No longer did Jacob have a protector. No longer did he have a friend. No longer was he working indoors. No longer did he have access to fruits and vegetables and half-decent cups of coffee.

Every day after roll call, a slew of kapos rounded up Jacob and several hundred other men, and they headed off, surrounded by armed guards. Buna was located quite some distance outside the double electrified fences of the main camp, and Jacob could have looked for any possible flaws in the security, but frankly he didn't see the point. He no longer had the stomach for trying to escape or helping anyone else get free. His only hope, he decided, was for Leszek Poczciwinski to mount a rescue operation.

If he could merely survive for another few weeks, he might actually be able to walk out of this death camp alive. Otherwise he was doomed. It was a painful, bitter truth, but to Jacob it was truth nonetheless.

The only question now was how to survive another month in the out-of-doors, with minimal rations, working far harder than he ever had in his life.

51

Jacob lost six pounds in just the first week.

After a month, he had lost nearly twenty, none of which he could spare. He hadn't had much body fat to begin with. Now he was a walking skeleton. His rib cage stuck out. He could see the bones in his arms. He had dark circles under his eyes, and his skin was a sickly gray. He had also developed a hacking cough, undoubtedly due to all the dust generated at the work site.

Jacob and his work detail were mixing and pouring concrete and laying a foundation at one end of an enormous complex of buildings being erected by the slaves of Auschwitz. For Jacob, it was as if he had been transported back to ancient Egypt. Even he, who had never cared much for the Bible or for the history of Judaism, knew how the Jews had been forced in ancient times to engage in huge construction projects for the pharaoh. But where was Moses this time? More importantly, where was God? Who was going to lead them out of Egypt and on to the Promised Land? They weren't going to be able to hold up too much longer.

One day, during a rare break, another man on Jacob's work detail told him he'd heard they were building a factory for a privately owned German industrial conglomerate known as I. G. Farben. Rumor had it that the Buna Works, once completed, would produce synthetic rubber for the Nazi war effort. Jacob didn't know if it was true. Nor did he care. The only thing that kept him going was the hope that he would see Leszek soon.

But a month passed, and then a second month and a third, and nothing changed, except that now Jacob had lost even more weight. No Leszek came to get him. No Allied troops came. There was no liberation. Just more grueling work and more dead and dying as far as the eye could see.

By the middle of July, Jacob's cough was worsening. He had not only lost all hope of escaping; he had lost all hope of surviving, too. Every day men dropped dead of exhaustion or starvation. Every day he and his comrades picked up the corpses, put them on wooden carts, walked them back to camp, and delivered them to the crematorium, where the ovens never stopped working and the chimney never stopped belching out its black, putrid smoke along with the ashes of human bodies that fell from the sky like snowflakes morning, noon, and night.

Over time, through short, furtive conversations with other prisoners, Jacob slowly pieced together a bit of the story of Leszek Poczciwinski. Occasionally Jacob ran across people who had known Leszek, and he kept his ears tuned to the camp gossip. After Von Strassen and his men had given up looking for the escapee, rumors swept through camp about who Leszek really was and who was working with him. Jacob dismissed most of what he heard as fantastic myths spooled up by people who had never met the man. He had become a superhero in their eyes, and the stories just became more and more far-fetched with each telling. But every now and then, Jacob heard a tidbit that sounded credible, and he tucked it away in his memory banks, though for what he could not say.

One day, for example, Jacob was working alongside a prisoner who had only recently been captured and delivered to Auschwitz. He told Jacob that he was a Polish army officer and that he knew Leszek Poczciwinski well. He also said that Leszek Poczciwinski wasn't Jacob's friend's real name. His real name was Piotr Kubiak. The man said he had been to boot camp with Kubiak years before and they had briefly served together after the Nazi invasion. He confirmed that Kubiak was a captain in Polish intelligence and a dedicated member of the Resistance. What's more, he confirmed what Max had told Jacob—that Kubiak had actually volunteered to be sent to Auschwitz. Once his plan had been approved, he had simply walked down a street in Warsaw when he knew there would be Nazi roundups that day and gotten himself arrested.

Jacob still struggled to believe this was true. "Why would anyone volunteer to come to a death camp?" he asked.

"Piotr didn't know what was really happening here," the man replied. "None of us did. Who could have imagined such monstrosities? I mean, if Piotr had known this was really a death factory and what that really meant and the scale it was really operating on, I don't think he would have come. His wife never would have let him do it. Nor would his commanders. He thought what we all thought: that this was just a labor camp. We thought they were building things and making things for the Nazi war effort, like this factory. That's why he wanted to come here. To figure out what was happening and get the facts back to his comrades. It was supposed to be a brief operation. In the end, it was more than he bargained for. I just hope to God that he's safe now and back with his family."

Jacob hoped so too. And he desperately hoped that Leszek Poczciwinski—aka Piotr Kubiak—hadn't forgotten all of them.

In time, Jacob also learned a few details about the two men who had escaped with Captain Kubiak. One of the men was James Mihilov. He was prisoner number 5340. The other, he learned, was Jahn Letski. He was prisoner number 12969.

One night after hearing these details, Jacob found himself curious. Were these things true? Could such information be verified? He asked his bunkmate, Josef, to look up the names in the records office. Two days later Josef got back to him. He confirmed the names Mihilov and Letski and their numbers. And there was more. Josef had come across information about the escape in the records as well.

These two men had worked in the camp bakery. Apparently Kubiak had met them there, and together they had broken through a back door when the guards weren't looking. They had cut the phone lines coming in and out of the bakery so that when the guards did find the men missing, they were delayed in relaying the news to Von Strassen's office.

These were interesting tidbits but hardly useful, actionable intelligence. None of it gave Jacob any kind of road map to follow to help him escape.

As the weeks passed, Jacob increasingly resigned himself to dying in Auschwitz. Probably soon.

52

AUGUST 1943

August was a brutal month.

For several weeks in a row the temperatures around Auschwitz consistently topped 40 degrees Celsius, or 104 Fahrenheit—far above normal, Josef said. There was no wind. Not even a light breeze. The mosquitoes were out in full force, as were the flies.

The stifling, suffocating nights in Block 18 were almost as unbearable as working in the blazing sun twelve hours a day. Jacob never had enough water to drink or food to eat. Slowly dehydrating and starving to death, he was getting intense headaches and rarely had to urinate. When he did, it hurt and what little was produced had an odd amber color.

Jacob was finding it increasingly difficult to get out of bed in the morning, despite Gerhard's incessant shouting and cursing. Josef said he was looking for openings in the records office that he could recommend Jacob for, but so far nothing had come up. And try as Josef might, he couldn't find any kapos willing to pull Jacob off the Buna detail and put him back in an indoor job.

It got so bad that Josef began giving Jacob his own cup of tea at breakfast every morning and half of his already-meager ration of soup at dinner each night. Jacob strenuously protested at first, but as he grew weaker, he reluctantly accepted both, though he was embarrassed that he could think of no way to return the favor.

Then, one evening, Jacob spotted a vaguely familiar face in the dining hall.

For the life of him, however, he couldn't remember the name of the man ladling the ever-so-small portions of soup out of a huge metal pot to the prisoners waiting in line. As the line inched forward, Jacob stared at the man and tried to place his name and where he knew him from. Was he from Siegen? Jacob didn't think so. He felt fairly certain he would remember anyone he had known well in Siegen. Was it one of the men who had worked in Uncle Avi's factories? Or someone from Brussels? From the Resistance? Or from one of the towns they had passed through? Did he live in one of the homes Jacob and his friends had stayed at?

When Jacob reached the front of the line, the man nodded politely but didn't say hello or give any other indication that they knew each other.

He did, however, ladle far too much soup into Jacob's bowl. Rather than filling it halfway, as he was supposed to, the man filled Jacob's bowl nearly to the brim. Jacob stopped in his tracks and stared at the overly generous portion and then back at the man. But now the man refused to make eye contact and seemed anxious for Jacob to move along. So he did.

Upon sitting down at a nearby table, Jacob stared at the bowl. Not only was it full to the top with broth, but it was chock-full of carrots, potatoes, and even pieces of cabbage. Jacob dug in immediately. It was lukewarm, as always, but he had to admit it was better than any soup he had tasted since arriving. He ate it all and pondered his good fortune.

The next morning, the same man was there. This time he was in charge of serving portions of bread to the prisoners coming through the line. When Jacob got there, the man nodded again but then looked away quickly. Then he tore off a somewhat-larger piece of bread than he was giving to the other men, though not so large that anyone else might have noticed. But Jacob noticed, and as he sat down and ate, he again wondered who this man was and why he was being shown such kindness.

The mystery continued on and off for a full week. The man wasn't always there, but most days he was. Jacob still didn't have the nerve to say anything to him. He didn't want to draw undue attention to himself or to the man, and he certainly didn't want the generous portions to stop. The man didn't seem to be upset that Jacob wasn't thanking him. Indeed, Jacob sensed he was nervous that Jacob might do or say something unwise. So Jacob just nodded his thanks and ate everything he was given.

Then one evening Josef came back to the bunk room after dinner, having smuggled out an apple. When he handed it over, Jacob couldn't believe his eyes.

"Where? How . . . ?" Jacob stammered.

But Josef didn't say. He just gestured for Jacob to eat it and do so quickly before someone else in the room spotted it and attacked him for it. They had seen worse things happen. The previous week, an older man had been attacked by two younger men who saw that he had an extra piece of bread that he had brought back to the barracks. They beat him until he was unconscious, then fought each other for the booty until Gerhard came along with several guards to break it up. The two younger men were sent away for punishment and had not returned. Jacob did not expect to ever see them again. The older man had been taken to the medical clinic. He had not returned either.

Jacob shut his mouth and devoured the apple.

Between Josef and the mysterious man in the dining hall, Jacob figured he was picking up a couple hundred extra calories a day. Given the intensity of the workload at Buna, he certainly wasn't gaining any weight, but at least he wasn't losing any more either.

But why? Jacob was deeply grateful, to be sure. But it was his nature to be skeptical, and he had to know who this man was and why he was showing him such favor.

August faded to September, and finally the heat wave broke.

The days became less infernal, and mercifully the breezes were picking up too. Soon most of the mosquitoes and flies had disappeared and it was becoming bearable once again—at least with regard to the weather.

The cooler temperatures did not stop men from dying all around Jacob out at the Buna camp, however. Indeed, it seemed as though he and his fellow prisoners were spending as much time handling corpses as they were pouring concrete and sawing wood and building door-frames and window frames and the like.

Then one night as Jacob was going through the line for dinner, the man ladling out the soup gave him only a regular portion. Surprised, Jacob looked down at the bowl, then back at the man.

"You need to go to the medical clinic," the man said.

53

Jacob tensed.

No one had ever said that to him before. But there was no way he was going to the clinic. Max had warned him in no uncertain terms never to do so. People who were sent there were never heard from again. Jacob himself knew of dozens of cases in recent months that had proved Max's counsel was accurate. Why was this man who had been so kind to him now giving him a death sentence?

"Keep moving," the man said. "Don't hold up the line."

Jacob was deeply bothered by the interaction, however brief. It didn't make any sense. At least not until he sat down at a table across from Josef and looked in his bowl. Floating on top of the soup was a small scrap of paper. Jacob glanced around to make sure no one was watching. Then he stared into his soup and saw that on the scrap of paper was written a single word: *Abby*. Startled, Jacob plunged his spoon into the bowl and scooped up some broth and the now-soaked piece of paper and swallowed them before anyone, including Josef, could see what had just happened.

As soon as he could, Jacob excused himself. He told Josef he would see him back at Block 18 later that night, then disappeared as the rest of the crowd exited the dining hall.

He forced himself to walk, not run, to the medical clinic. On the way it dawned on him that the man who had been so kind to him—the one who had been giving him extra soup—was the blond-haired man who had been sitting behind the desk at the medical clinic the day he and Max had gone to visit Max's sister.

Frustrated with himself for not having made the connection sooner, Jacob picked up his pace. As he did, he also realized that he had never gone back to meet Abigail and introduce himself before Max's death. Nor had he ever gone to express his condolences after Max was executed. He had been too consumed by his own grief. Then he had been transferred from the Canada command to the Buna work detail. How selfish could he have been? All this time he had only been thinking of himself. What was wrong with him? It was one thing to be shy, but hadn't he at least been raised to be polite? Yet to his shame, he realized he had never once remembered that Max had one sole living sibling and that she had to be grieving far more than he was.

Jacob was so embarrassed and upset that he was literally muttering to himself as he approached the front door of the clinic. At the last moment, he stopped himself, caught his breath, and tried to calm down. Then he opened the door.

The person who greeted him took him completely by surprise.

"*You're* Max's sister?" Jacob asked, hardly believing his eyes.

Sitting behind the desk in a crisp white nurse's uniform, albeit with a yellow triangle pinned on her chest, was the young woman who had caught his attention in the processing line the first day he had arrived at Auschwitz. While Jacob had wasted away over the past few months and now looked as emaciated as any of the other men who had not yet died but were well on their way, Abigail seemed just as attractive as he remembered her, with warm, gentle brown eyes and a shy smile.

"I am," she said softly. "Are you Jac—I mean, are you Leonard Eliezer?"

"I am," Jacob replied sheepishly.

"It's an honor to finally meet you, Mr. Eliezer," she said, standing. "Or more precisely, to meet you again. I think I handled some of your paperwork the day you arrived. Do you remember?"

"I do," Jacob said, embarrassed at his blushing and thus blushing all the more.

"Well, it's nice to see you again, Leonard," she said, coming around the desk to shake his hand. "I'm Abigail Cohen. But please call me Abby. All my friends do."

As they shook hands, Jacob realized this was the first time he had touched a woman since hugging his mother the day of her death.

Putting a finger over her lips to keep him quiet, she motioned for him to follow her down a hallway. Not sure what was happening, he reluctantly complied. She ended up leading him into the very same examination room that Max had taken him to so many months before. Jacob was suddenly seized by a terrible coughing fit, so Abby closed the door, covered the small window in the door with paper, and asked him to sit down. Then she poured him a glass of milk, which he hesitantly but gratefully accepted.

"Thank you for being such a good friend to Max, Jacob," she began as he drank the milk. "May I call you Jacob behind closed doors?"

"Yes, of course," he replied. "Thanks for the milk."

She smiled. "Max spoke often of you, and highly—so highly, in fact, that several times I asked him to introduce us. He said he tried but it never worked out. Something always prevented us from meeting. That's what he said, anyway. I guess it wasn't meant to be, until now. But I have to say, I was beginning to think that maybe you didn't exist, that maybe Max had invented a friend to help him cope with all the stress of trying to survive in this place."

Jacob blushed again. "It's nice to finally meet you," he mumbled.

Abby's smile widened. She didn't seem uncomfortable. Rather, she seemed to be waiting for him to say something, anything.

"Yes, well, um, I guess Max really wanted me to meet you too," Jacob finally sputtered. "He, uh, he even brought me to this very room and we waited for you, but you . . . well . . . you never came. A doctor yelled at us. We had to leave."

"So I heard," Abby said. "Sorry I was delayed."

"No, please, you have nothing to apologize for," Jacob said. "It is I—it's me—who's sorry."

"For what?" Abby asked.

Jacob looked down at his feet. "For not coming to see you after Max . . ." Jacob's voice caught, and he could not finish the sentence. "It was very selfish and rude of me," he eventually continued, trying to regain his composure. "I should have come to meet you before Max died. And when he passed, I should have come to see you, to tell you how sorry I am for your loss, to see if there was anything I could do for you. I'm very sorry. Really I am. My parents did not raise me to be so rude. Would you forgive me?"

"There is nothing to forgive," she replied, now acting like a nurse and preparing to take his temperature. "You had your way to grieve; I had mine. You hadn't met me. You didn't owe me anything. And like Solomon once said, there is a time for every activity under the sun, and everything is beautiful in its time. God must have had his reasons."

Jacob looked at her quizzically for a few moments.

"Is something wrong?" she asked.

"No, it's just that . . ."

"Just that what?" she pressed.

"Well, it's just that . . . I'm sorry, but I . . ."

"It's okay, Jacob," Abby whispered gently. "You can say whatever is on your mind. Any friend of Max's is a friend of mine."

"Thanks," he said, flustered by being so close to such an attractive woman. He forced himself to look away from her and to remember what he wanted to say. "I'm just surprised," he said at last.

"At what?"

"That you still believe in God," Jacob said.

She slipped the thermometer into his mouth. "Of course I do," she said. "Why wouldn't I?" She waited a minute or so, then removed the thermometer.

"Why wouldn't you?" Jacob repeated when he could speak again. "What are you talking about? I mean, look around you. If God exists—and that's a big *if* for me at the moment—it's pretty clear that he has long since abandoned us Jews. If he's even up there, he obviously doesn't care about us. He might even hate us. But to be honest, I'm not sure he's even there."

"Oh, Jacob, you must not say such a thing," Abby insisted, genuine hurt in her eyes. She rolled up his left sleeve, swabbed his arm with alcohol and began to give him a series of shots. "Wasn't God with the children of Israel when we were slaves in Egypt? Wasn't God there when the Hebrews were being tossed into the fiery furnaces in Babylon during the times of Nebuchadnezzar? Didn't he help us then? Didn't he save us from great evil? Yes, and he will help us now. He set us free back in ancient times, and soon I know he will set us free again. Don't give up hope, Jacob. Of all people, with your name, please do not give up hope."

"I'm afraid it's too late for that," Jacob sighed, surprised but also intrigued by the resilience of her faith, unwarranted though it seemed. Then inspiration struck. "'No man is an island,'" he quoted, "'entire of itself; every man is a piece of the continent, a part of the main. . . . Any man's death diminishes me, because I am involved in mankind; and therefore never send to know for whom the bell tolls; it tolls for thee.'"

"That's pretty," she said, looking genuinely surprised as she unlocked a glass cabinet, removed a bottle of pills, and gave him several to take with what was left of the milk. "What is it?"

"John Donne," he replied, washing down the pills without hesitation. "It somehow seems appropriate."

Jacob couldn't believe what he was doing. He was actually having a conversation with a girl, and a pretty girl at that. He was quoting poetry. He was talking about theology. He had no idea where this was all coming from, but somehow he felt comfortable with Abigail Cohen. Well, *comfortable* might be overstating it a bit. At least he didn't feel as uncomfortable with her as he'd have expected.

"Do you really believe that?" Abby asked him. "Do you really believe that the bell is about to toll for all of us?"

"What else am I to think? You and I are Jews. There is no future for us. All our hope has perished. It's just a matter of time before they exterminate us all, isn't it? What happened to Max is going to happen to all of us soon. And the worst thing is, there's nothing we can do about it."

"Well, I'm sorry, Jacob; you seem like a nice boy, but I have to be honest with you. I don't believe that."

"Even after they murdered Max?"

"Especially after they murdered Max."

"I don't understand."

She donned a stethoscope. "Jacob, surely you know that Max made it possible for Leszek and his friends to escape, right? The help he gave them was critical. They could never have escaped without him. That's why Von Strassen did what he did. Because Max did his job—and did it well."

54

Jacob was stunned.

Max had played a critical role in Leszek's escape? And his sister knew about it? He had no idea how to respond to that. Then he realized Abby was still talking.

"Did I grieve Max's loss? Of course I did. I still do. But don't you see? He gave up his life so the rest of us could keep living. Isn't that the mark of true love? Isn't that a supreme act of faith in a God who loves us and cares for us, even though the world is trying to destroy us?"

Jacob wasn't sure, but he was intrigued by how certain Abby was.

"Did you know his real name?" Jacob finally replied, deftly changing the subject.

"Who, Max's?"

"No, Leszek's."

"Of course I did—Piotr Kubiak," Abby replied. "I'm part of *Kampfgruppe Auschwitz* too, just like he was, and just like Max was."

"Part of what?" Jacob asked.

"You know, *Kampfgruppe Auschwitz*," she repeated. "Come on, Jacob, you don't have to play dumb. Not with me. We don't have time, and there is so much I need to tell you."

Jacob assured her that he had never heard the term before. At first she found it hard to believe Jacob didn't know what she was talking about, but he reminded her that he hadn't actually been in the camp that long before Leszek escaped and Max died. He further reminded her that both men were clearly trying to protect themselves and him by not telling him too much too soon. With Leszek's departure and Max's death, Jacob had lost all links to the underground movement within the camp.

Abby explained that the Auschwitz Combat Group was the underground Resistance movement throughout the camp, which Kubiak and several others had formed. Their goal was to gather and then send back to the Resistance leaders on the outside as much information as possible regarding what was happening inside Auschwitz for the purpose of mobilizing a rescue.

"So now you know," she said as she checked his pupils and took his pulse. "Now listen carefully. We know Piotr and his friends got out. We know that Von Strassen and his men didn't catch them. If they had, they would have brought back the bodies and put them on display. Or they would have brought them back alive and hanged them in the square, like Max. The problem is, we haven't heard whether Piotr and the others were ever able to link up with the Polish Resistance on the outside. Maybe they did. I pray to God they did. But they could have been caught by German troops elsewhere or been tricked by Polish double agents. Maybe they caught pneumonia and died on the journey. Who knows? All we can say for sure is that it's the middle of September and no rescue has come."

"Forgive me," Jacob said, "but isn't that another reason to give up hope?"

"No, it isn't," Abby insisted. "The fact is, we need to try again. You've met Otto and Abe?"

"Yes."

"They're next in the queue. We had developed an elaborate plan for them to escape, but both were transferred to Birkenau. That changed everything. They didn't know anyone over there. It took them time to get the lay of the land. Now they're reporting that the conditions there are even worse than here. Commandant Hoess has embarked on a non-stop building spree over there. More gas chambers. More ovens. More chimneys. More of everything. It's like the Nazis are getting ready for something. Otto and Abe don't know what it is, but they do think they may have found a new way to escape. They want to leave soon, but they need help. And they've requested you."

"Me—but why?" Jacob asked.

"You'll have to ask them when you get there," Abby said. "It's not like we have a detailed correspondence. Every now and then we're able to pass very brief coded messages through prisoners who have to do business in one camp or the other. One of them is Jean-Luc Leclerc. You've met him, right?"

"The blond guy who used to work here and now works at the cafeteria?"

"That's him."

"Yes, we've met, sort of."

"Good. I've asked him to keep an eye out for you and make sure you were getting enough to eat."

"That was you?"

Abby nodded.

"Thank you."

"You're welcome."

Jacob held her gaze for a moment but then felt himself reddening again and looked away as she continued talking.

"Anyway, Leszek recruited Luc to be part of our team."

"Is he also a Pole?" Jacob asked.

"No. He's French," Abby replied. "Interesting guy. Turns out he's a pastor."

"A pastor?" Jacob whispered. "You mean a priest?"

"No, he's not Catholic. He's Protestant."

"Then what in the world is he doing here? Shouldn't he be goose-stepping through Berlin or leading the Easter services for Fat Louie and his friends?"

"No, no, he's different. You'll like him."

"Different? You mean he got caught stealing money from his church?"

"No, of course not—he's not like that," Abby said. "He's *different* different. Good different. Leszek told me Luc was arrested by the Gestapo for helping rescue Jews out of Nazi-controlled areas. Something like five thousand Jews, or close to that, if I'm not mistaken."

Jacob was incredulous. "Five thousand?"

"Well, not all by himself. Apparently the other pastors in his church and most of the people in their town were helping."

Jacob shook his head in disbelief. "What town?"

"I don't remember exactly. Somewhere in the south of France."

"You're saying that guy, Jean-Claude . . ."

"Jean-Luc," Abby corrected. "But everyone just calls him Luc."

"Whatever. You're saying this Luc guy and his town helped rescue five thousand Jews escaping from Germany or wherever else when the Nazis rose to power?"

Abby nodded.

"I don't understand," Jacob said. "That doesn't make sense. Why would he do such a thing?"

"I told you; he's different." Abby smiled. "Anyway, I don't have time to tell you the whole story. I don't even know the whole story. You should ask him yourself. He's being transferred to Birkenau in the next few days. Somehow he and Otto and Abe will link up with you. They'll brief you on the plan and then tell you what they need you to do. Now, as for why you? I really can't say. You'll have to ask Otto. If I had to guess, I'd say you must have proven yourself a faithful assistant to Piotr, and now they need someone they can trust. Max is gone, so they're reaching out to you. Regardless, you're being transferred to Birkenau tomorrow. They'll make sure you get the food and drink you need to get your health back. But they will need you to take enormous risks on their behalf. Are you willing?"

"Are they going to take me with them?"

"When they escape?"

"Of course."

"I have no idea. You'd have to discuss that with them."

"And what about you?" Jacob asked. "Are you going to transfer too?"

"They need me here," she replied. She put the stethoscope in her ears, unfastened the top few buttons of his zebra-striped uniform, and listened to his heart.

When Jacob realized his heart rate had shot up and that she could hear it happening, he was mortified.

She just laughed.

55

The next day Jacob was put on a bus and transferred to Birkenau.

He had no idea what to expect, and he had tossed and turned much of the night worrying about the million different things that could go wrong.

For all his fears, however, Jacob was fixated on one central truth: he was about to meet Otto and Abe again, two men who, according to Abby, had a solid, realistic escape plan. They were specifically and personally requesting his help. Maybe they were going to invite him to escape with them. But even if not, he hoped to learn invaluable lessons he could use to escape soon himself.

Jacob's first impression on arriving at Birkenau was amazement at the sheer size of the sprawling complex. There were enormous sections for men, other sections for women, and one section exclusively for Gypsies. Abby had told him that Birkenau was one of the original Auschwitz expansion camps. It was built in 1941 to ease overcrowding since the gas chambers and crematorium at Auschwitz simply could not handle the volume of people being shipped in by train day after day. That might have been true, but Hoess and the other Nazis clearly weren't satisfied with how big Birkenau currently was. They were feverishly expanding the camp to accommodate more trains, more people. They were building more and larger gas chambers capable of killing far more Jews in a single moment, in a single fake shower room. There were also enormous crematorium facilities being built by the very prisoners who would eventually be burned in them.

Already four crematoriums were operational and working around the clock. Thus, in addition to the single crematorium and its infamous chimney operating in Auschwitz-I, there now were a total of five such facilities between Auschwitz-I and Auschwitz-II. Jacob did the math, and it was staggering. With ten furnaces per building, that meant that there were fifty or more furnaces in operation, each of which could completely burn a human body into mere ashes in a matter of only twenty minutes, and all of which could hold many bodies at a time.

"Hoess is obsessed with German precision engineering," Abby had told him before he left the clinic. "He doesn't want to just kill people with beatings and firing squads and starvation. That's not good enough for him. He's supposed to move faster. He's supposed to kill more people more efficiently. I hear he's getting pressure from the top, from Hitler and Himmler. They want him to create a 'death factory'—an assembly line that literally kills Jews by the hundreds of thousands and then disposes of the evidence of the crime into the sky. This is why we must not give up."

She had implored Jacob to help Otto and Abe get out and spread the message of what was happening here among the Jewish communities who hadn't arrived at Auschwitz-Birkenau yet.

"Please, Jacob," she had pleaded. "We need to stop Hoess. We cannot let him win."

As Jacob arrived and was processed, Abby's words echoed in his heart. She was right. As terrible as Hoess's orgy of murder had been to date, it might pale in comparison to what was coming. The evidence suggested Hoess and his minions were gearing up for something much larger and much worse. They were creating a capacity that suggested a surge of prisoners would be coming through here, and soon. That was bad enough, but as Jacob thought about it, he realized the situation was much worse even than it looked at first glance. After all, no one seemed to be building more or bigger kitchens to feed this surge of prisoners. No one seemed to be building more or bigger dining halls. No one was building enough barracks for all these new people to sleep in. An awful lot of construction was going on, but none of it was designed to let people live here. All of it was designed to bring people here to die, and no longer by the thousands but by the hundreds of thousands.

Jacob felt sickened by the new reality that was dawning on him. At the same time, though, he felt energized by the prospect of helping the two men who had arranged for him to come. Yes, it was dangerous. But as Leszek had once said to him, if he was going to get caught and killed, he wanted it to be for doing something useful. He was honored to help these men escape, and whether they asked him to join them or not, Jacob decided there and then that as soon as possible after they were gone, he would make his own escape as well.

56

Over the next few days, Jacob tried to adjust to a new routine.

He saw no evidence of Otto or Abe. But he did find new people, new rules, less food, and new guards with different idiosyncrasies who could erupt without notice. The most immediate problem, however, wasn't the guards. It was the lice.

Almost from the moment he arrived, Jacob found himself battling an outbreak of lice in the barracks that was driving him and the other men crazy. The tiny creatures were everywhere. They had infested the blankets and the mattresses and now their clothing. Every night, Jacob would take off his boots, put them on his hands, and use them to crush hundreds of the beady little insects. But to no avail. He woke repeatedly in the night feeling them crawling in his ears and on his arms and hands and face, biting and leaving little red spots all over him.

Abby had warned him that the conditions at Birkenau would be bad, but he hadn't been able to imagine how things could be worse than what he was already enduring. Now he knew.

If the lice were unbearable, the rats made things even worse. They were everywhere. It seemed not a night would go by without Jacob waking up in the wee hours to the screaming of some man in his barracks who had just been bitten by one of the verminous creatures. It seemed hard to fathom, but Jacob actually found himself wishing he were back in Block 18.

Making things even more awful, if that were possible, was the fact that the barracks to which Jacob was assigned did not have a lavatory or wash facility connected. When he and the other prisoners in his barracks wanted to bathe, they were required to strip naked first and then walk several hundred yards to a public facility, regardless of the weather. Jacob was humiliated. But he reminded himself that at least it was only September. The air was dry and not too cold, except in the evenings. What would he do when winter came?

Jacob was eager to link up with Steinberger and Frenkel, but they never showed. He had met them only that one time, so though he constantly kept an eye out for them, he had to strain to remember what they looked like. He wondered whether he could have forgotten any of Abby's instructions. Was he supposed to have met them, even one of them, at a certain place at a certain time on a specific day? He didn't think so, but now he was worried. He didn't dare ask anyone about them. Abby had warned him to trust no one. There were informants everywhere.

Soon after his arrival, Jacob was assigned to another grueling work detail. As September wore on, he was occupied building wooden huts for guards to sit in out in the vegetable fields while they were overseeing all their forced labor. They were not large huts. They could only fit four or five men at a time. But it kept them cooler on the sunny days and drier on the rainy days, and Jacob could often hear the Nazis laughing and drinking and playing cards inside.

Jacob resented every moment. It was dusty, dirty, exhausting work. He and his mates labored for twelve interminable hours a day in the sun. And it wasn't as if he were doing something for his fellow prisoners. All he was doing was making life easier for the enemy. Once again Jacob began to lose weight—and with it, his hope.

Where were Steinberger and Frenkel? They were supposed to take care of him, weren't they? They had promised to feed him and get him inside work, hadn't they? But September passed, and they never showed.

As October began, Jacob was transferred to yet another work detail. He had no idea why. Maybe he had angered someone. Maybe too many people had dropped dead and they needed new slaves to replace the others. Whatever the reason, he spent that month harvesting and washing potatoes and carrots out in the fields. During that time, he developed a sinking feeling that the plan Steinberger and Frenkel had concocted had already been smoked out by Von Strassen. He had to assume that the two men had either abandoned their plan or been arrested.

There was another possibility, Jacob realized. The two men might already be dead. Perhaps he needed to stop waiting and start coming up with an escape plan of his own.

The only shred of good news was that being on this new agricultural detail allowed Jacob to steal and eat a few carrots and even a few potatoes here and there. He had to be careful, of course. He could never let one of the kapos see him eating, much less the guards. He was even careful not to let any of the comrades he was working with see him. Instead he kept his head down, worked his fingers to the bone, and impressed his supervisor with his daily quota of vegetables. Otherwise he tried not to attract any attention whatsoever.

When the harvest ended, Jacob received a different assignment. He and three of the men on his detail who were still reasonably healthy—or at least not dead yet—learned that they had just been transferred to work in the bakery. Upon hearing the news, Jacob breathed a sigh of relief. Finally he would be working indoors. The change came not a moment too soon, for in November and December the leaves would have fallen, and the temperatures would follow. Soon the rains would come and then the snow.

When Jacob showed up at the bakery for his first day of work, he wondered for the first time in a month whether perhaps all hope was not lost after all.

The kapo who greeted him was none other than Jean-Luc Leclerc.

57

Jacob didn't know whether to be elated or concerned.

After all, this was the man he had first met at the medical clinic, the man who later had provided him additional soup and bread in the cafeteria. This was the man of whom Abby spoke so highly. Was he for real, or was he fooling them all?

Luc made no attempt to personally connect with Jacob that day. Indeed, for the first few days, Jacob's new kapo rarely even made eye contact with him. He did not say anything particularly friendly or personal or act like they had even met before. He simply showed Jacob and the new men assigned to him what their jobs were and put them to work.

One of the men was responsible for mixing enormous batches of dough. Two more helped Luc roll the dough and shape it into hundreds upon hundreds of loaves of bread. Jacob was assigned to the gigantic, industrial-size ovens. He was responsible for cleaning them at night and doing basic maintenance on them to keep them in working order. Throughout the day, Jacob's task was to put the large baking sheets of bread into the ovens and ensure the temperatures and timers were set properly. When the timers went off and the loaves were fully baked, he removed the sheets from the ovens and put them on cooling racks. In the meantime, he was supposed to wipe down counters, mop floors, and keep the entire bakery clean and orderly.

Luc was by no means rude or impolite during this time. He simply seemed indifferent, and this surprised and disappointed Jacob. Wasn't it Luc who had directed him to meet with Abby? Wasn't it Abby who'd directed him to meet with Steinberger and Frenkel? For Jean-Luc Leclerc to show up in Jacob's life now and say nothing about Steinberger or Frenkel nor bring him any message from Abby—nor say anything personal at all—seemed odd, to say the least. Indeed, there were times in those first few days when Jacob felt angry, even betrayed. And he wasn't exactly free to initiate a conversation with Luc on his own. Every day there was an enormous amount of work to be done. The conditions were hot, sweaty, and noisy. Armed soldiers came in often to demand bread for themselves and their friends. There was rarely a moment of privacy or solace.

Luc was not without some sense of compassion, however. Every few days he would let a large piece of bread drop to the floor near Jacob, and when the coast was clear, Jacob would reach down, scoop it up, and eat it as quickly as possible. Sometimes it was a chunk of warm, soft bread fresh out of the oven. Sometimes it was a piece of dry crust that otherwise might be thrown away. Either way, each morsel was a godsend. Eventually Jacob noticed that Luc was doing this for the other men, too, as well as making sure all of them had buckets of fresh, clean water that they could partake of whenever they wanted. The combination did wonders for the morale of their little team, and in time their estimation of their kapo grew steadily.

After a few weeks in the bakery, Jacob got up the nerve to ask his fellow workers their names and where they were from, something he had never done before in any of his other jobs.

It was already clear to Jacob that his fellow workers were not Jewish. They didn't wear yellow triangles on their uniforms. Rather they wore red ones, indicating they were political prisoners, just like Luc. Unlike Luc, however, who was—according to Abby—a Protestant minister, these three men were Catholics. Jacob learned that they all hailed from a little town in Czechoslovakia called Žilina. Stefan, it turned out, was twenty-five, a mathematics teacher and the son of a medical doctor. Andrej was twenty-six, a mechanic whose father had also been a mechanic before he was killed in the war. Janko was almost twenty-seven, a farmer. He was married and had three little girls. Remarkably, Jacob learned, they had all been arrested and sent to Auschwitz-Birkenau separately. That they had wound up together in the same camp, and working in the same place, they considered a miracle from God, and even Jacob had a hard time discounting the possibility that they were right.

It took some time, but eventually it dawned on Jacob that Luc had orchestrated all this. Yes, it had taken longer than Jacob had wanted. Perhaps longer than Luc wanted too. But even though Jacob and Luc had not had a serious conversation of any length yet, it was increasingly obvious to Jacob that it was Luc who had rescued him from the fields and brought him inside the bakery. It had to have been. Likewise, it was Luc who had rescued the Czechs and Luc who was making sure they were all being fed as well as possible under the circumstances.

The man wasn't moving precipitously. He wasn't doing anything that would attract the attention of the camp guards or the other kapos. But he seemed to have a plan. He seemed to know what he was doing. And it seemed to be working.

58

JANUARY 1, 1944
AUSCHWITZ-BIRKENAU CONCENTRATION CAMP

It was snowing furiously as the year 1944 began.

But Jacob refused to be disheartened. On the Saturday morning of New Year's Day, he made a resolution but told no one of it. This was the year he was going to escape from Auschwitz. Or die trying.

Defying his instincts toward introversion and reclusion, Jacob was slowly and haltingly but definitely reaching out to the three Czechs. He talked to them, engaged them with questions, tried to build friendships. Meanwhile, he had been waiting for Jean-Luc Leclerc to approach him. Thus far it had not happened. But again, Jacob refused to let the apparent lack of progress discourage him. He felt sure Luc would make contact in due time. When he did, Jacob hoped the conversation would lead him to Otto and Abe and out of this factory of death.

After roll call and breakfast, Jacob arrived at work before the bakery got busy for the day and was told by Luc to take two dozen stacks of empty wooden crates to the loading dock behind the main kitchen facility. Jacob grumbled at the assignment. Everyone he knew was envious of his job working in the warmth of the bakery during such a miserable storm. Now, however, he was having to trudge back and forth, back and forth, hauling crates through the drifting snow and bitter winds.

Around eleven that morning, after dropping off a load, Jacob stopped for a moment and stepped in the back door of the kitchen, hoping to take the chill off. His heart nearly stopped as he heard two guards walking down the hall. They weren't sneaking up on him. They were laughing and slapping each other on the back, making a terrible racket. Jacob quickly ducked into a broom closet and closed the door, praying to a God he wasn't sure he really believed in that neither guard had seen him. For whatever reason, they stopped in the hallway, not far from the closet door.

"Don't worry, Jürgen," one of the men boomed. "Soon we're going to have plenty of Hungarian salami to eat. It won't be long now!"

"*Ja,*" the other replied. "I've heard stories about those Hungarian women. They're so beautiful in those skirts. And I hear they are very, well, you know . . ."

"You're a pig, Jürgen; you know that? A real swine. They're all going to be kikes. You really want to get caught with a kike?"

"But I just thought—"

"You're an idiot. If Von Strassen catches you with a Jew girl, they will ship you to the front. Is that what you want?"

"Of course not."

"Then knock it off about the women. I'm talking about the food, you fool! They'll be bringing us trainloads of fresh food, straight from Budapest. Meats and cheeses and chocolates and all kinds of delectables. My mouth is watering just thinking about it!"

"Mine, too!" Jürgen said. "I can't wait. How soon can they get here?"

They walked off, laughing and talking and speculating about that last question. Jacob just stood in the closet, motionless, holding his breath. Finally he exhaled. After a few minutes had passed, hearing no one else around, he cracked open the door, saw that the coast was clear, and raced back to the bakery.

All the way he found himself mulling over what the Nazi guards had said to each other. Their vulgarity he discounted. He had become used to that by now. But these comments about trainloads of Hungarian salami arriving soon bothered him deeply. When he got back, he pulled Stefan aside near the back door.

"Have you heard anything about large groups of Hungarians coming here soon?"

"No," Stefan said. "Why?"

"No reason," Jacob said.

Later he asked the other Czechs. They hadn't heard anything either. But Jacob couldn't shake the feeling that he had stumbled onto something big. The more he thought about it, it occurred to him that he had not met a single Hungarian prisoner at Auschwitz or Birkenau since he had arrived. He had met Poles and Frenchmen and Russians and Romanians and Belgians and plenty of Germans, of course, and people from all over Europe, but not a single Hungarian.

Jacob decided he could not wait any longer. He had to speak to Luc. No soldiers had come into the bakery for most of the morning. Jacob had expected the place to be packed with soldiers trying to stay out of the miserable weather. But apparently there had been an all-night New Year's Eve party, and many of the men had gotten rip-roaring drunk. Most were sleeping in or finding a reason to stay back in their barracks. Perhaps the situation would change as the day went by, but for now, work was slowing a bit and the bakery was empty of all but the team.

"Herr Kapo, do you have a moment?" Jacob asked as politely as he could.

"Please, Jacob, call me Luc."

"Very well," Jacob said. "Could we step into the back room? I'd be grateful for a private word with you."

"Of course," Luc said, glancing around to make sure they were alone and then leading the way to the back room and closing the door behind them. "Actually, I've been hoping to find time to talk with you too. It's always so busy and so noisy in here, and there are so many soldiers. But today I was thinking this might be a good day. I guess you were thinking the same thing."

Jacob quickly tried to organize his thoughts. There was so much he wanted to talk about, and he couldn't be sure how much time he would have. A few seconds? A few minutes, maybe? What he needed was a few hours. Jean-Luc Leclerc was a mystery. He'd obviously been handpicked and trained by Leszek. He was close to Abby. He was linked to Otto and Abe. And Jacob sensed he might, in fact, be the key to his freedom.

"Do you know anything about trains full of Hungarian Jews headed our way?" he asked.

"I don't think so," Luc replied. "Why do you ask?"

Jacob briefly recounted the comments he had just overheard from the two guards. "Could that be why Hoess and Liebehenschel have embarked on such a building spree—because the next wave of Jews is on the way, coming from Hungary?" Jacob asked.

In November, Rudolf Hoess had been replaced by Arthur Liebehenschel as commandant of the Auschwitz-Birkenau camps. Jacob didn't know why, nor did he care. But lately he'd heard rumors that Hoess might be coming back, tasked with overseeing the massive building projects under way at Auschwitz-II. Now Jacob wondered whether the imminent arrival of thousands of Jews from Hungary had something to do with Hoess's return.

Luc said he didn't know, and Jacob could see that he didn't yet understand the implications of such a notion.

"Look—thus far, the Hungarian Jewish community has been spared being rounded up and shipped to the Nazi death camps," Jacob explained. "Why? Because the regime in Budapest is made up of fascists. They're part of the Axis powers. Their forces helped invade Yugoslavia. They helped the Nazis invade Russia. But what if Berlin's calculus is changing? What if Hitler is about to round up and kill every Jew in Europe, regardless of where they live? What if the Jews of Hungary are next?"

Luc now realized the stakes, and he looked stricken.

"I'll start asking around," he promised.

"Discreetly," Jacob insisted.

"Of course."

Jacob shifted gears. "I need to make contact with Otto and Abe," he said bluntly. "Abby told me they would contact me as soon as I got here. I came here to help them. But it's been months, and they've made no contact. They've been captured, or they've died, or they've got cold feet, or they've abandoned me. I just need to know which. You know full well what they were intending. Now I'm intending the same thing, and I can't wait any longer. I know you know them. Abby connected you. So talk to me."

Jacob was surprised by the directness in his own voice. He had intended to ask a series of questions, but they had all come out as declarative statements.

Rather than seeming put off by Jacob's sudden and unexpected show of assertiveness, Luc seemed to warm to it. "I'm sorry," he replied. "That was my fault."

"What do you mean?"

"I was supposed to tell you what was happening much earlier," Luc explained. "I wanted to. But there were complications."

"What kind of complications?"

Luc paused for a moment and listened for the sound of anyone approaching. Convinced they had a bit more time alone, he lowered his voice and began to talk.

"We have a man who works in Hoess's office," he explained. "He told us you were being watched."

"Me?" Jacob asked with surprise. "Whatever for?"

"Apparently Hoess and Von Strassen were convinced you were in league with Leszek and Abby's brother, Max. They've been monitoring you closely for months. They've been hoping you would mess up, drop your guard, and lead them to another operative in the underground. That's why Otto and Abe haven't been able to make contact. That's why I've been so distant for so many weeks. I was supposed to whisper something to you or slip you a note—something to let you know you hadn't been forgotten. But the truth is . . ."

"What?"

"The truth is I got nervous," Luc confessed. "I could see you growing more and more discouraged. But I was scared that if I said something to you, I might get caught as well. Max's death . . . it had an effect on me. It shouldn't have, I know. I'm ashamed of myself. You deserved better. But anyway, that's the truth. I'm deeply sorry. You deserved more from me."

Jacob didn't know what to say. He was stunned by the confession. Yet rather than be angry, he found himself grateful at the man's candor. Jacob, too, knew what it meant to be frightened. How could they not be frightened in this place? At least this Leclerc guy was honest, and Jacob respected him for that.

"Abby told me much about your heroism in the Resistance in Belgium," Luc continued.

"How?" Jacob replied. "I never said anything to her."

"Leszek told her and Max, and she told me," Luc said. "Actually, you've made quite an impression on Miss Abby there. She brightens at the very mention of your name."

"My name?" Jacob said.

"Abby is a member of the Resistance too, you know," Luc said. "She may turn out to be one of the most effective operatives Leszek ever recruited. She's a true believer in God's plan. That's where she gets her passion. And I think that's why she's so interested in you. You're a true believer too."

"In freedom, maybe," Jacob said. "Not in God."

"That's unfortunate," Luc said. "We should talk about that sometime. But, okay, you're a true believer in freedom. You've taken great risks to set people free. Abby sees it. So does the leadership of the underground. That's why they're drawn to you. That's why they think you can help them. Honestly, they're worried Hoess and Von Strassen will discover who you really are. They got close after Leszek escaped. But they fumbled their investigation. They got distracted by Max, and Max tried to steer them away from you. That's why they've been watching you so closely, Von Strassen especially. That's the bad news."

"So is there any good news?"

"Actually, there is. Our source in Hoess's office contacted us two days after Christmas. He said they arrested three people in the Canada command back in Auschwitz whom they claim were members of the underground, recruited by Leszek."

"Were they?"

"No. But they were hanged two nights ago. And now our source says they've given up on you. They concluded you were telling the truth during your interrogation last year, that you were too new and hadn't been involved. The written report indicates that you probably would have been recruited into the underground if there had been more time before Leszek escaped, but that neither he nor Max knew you well enough to trust you. The bottom line is that Hoess and Von Strassen think you don't know anything. They've watched you for months. You haven't led them anywhere. No one has made contact with you. And they don't suspect me. So they've closed the file."

Jacob took a deep breath. "That is good news."

"Yes, I thought you'd like that."

"So when do I see Otto and Abe?" Jacob asked.

"Actually, I just received a coded message from Otto this morning," Luc replied. "He and Abe want to wait a few more weeks, just to make 100 percent sure that you're not being watched and that we're not being fed disinformation. When they're convinced everything is okay, they'll make contact. But don't worry. They're not going to make their break until winter is over anyway."

"And what am I supposed to do in the meantime?" Jacob pressed.

"The same thing as me—work hard, keep your head down, and don't do anything stupid, like get caught."

59

JANUARY 15, 1944
WASHINGTON, D.C.

"Did you see the memo?" Barrett asked Secretary Hull.

"What memo?"

The two men were flying back to Washington from London. Hull had a fever. His doctors had told him he needed to sleep. But Barrett insisted it was urgent.

"The memo from Treasury," Barrett replied.

"I have no idea what you're talking about."

"It's a scorcher."

"What does it say?"

"It blasts the State Department for not doing enough to rescue European Jews."

"You're joking."

"I'm not. Morgenthau wants the president to set up a government commission to rescue Jews from Hitler," Barrett said. Treasury Secretary Henry Morgenthau was the only Jewish man in the cabinet.

"By doing what?"

"Evacuating Jews from Europe, establishing safe havens, providing humanitarian relief supplies to Jews in the concentration camps . . . There's a whole list of recommendations."

"It'll never happen," the secretary of state said. "The president has more important things to do."

But Hull was wrong. On January 22, 1944, President Roosevelt signed Executive Order 9417, establishing the War Refugee Board. Secretary Hull was required to cable all U.S. diplomats throughout Europe, instructing them to comply with the order's guidelines. Hull, in turn, directed Barrett to make it happen.

"How high a priority is this, boss?" Barrett asked.

Hull rolled his eyes. "Just make the president happy, and then get back to work."

60

JANUARY 25, 1944
AUSCHWITZ-BIRKENAU CONCENTRATION CAMP

Luc motioned for Jacob to step into the back.

The workday had ended. The Czechs had left the bakery to return to their barracks. The gong for roll call would sound at any moment. But obliging his kapo, Jacob waited in the storage area where they kept many of their supplies and began stacking new sacks of flour that had just been delivered. When Luc stepped in, he closed the door and rolled a small orange across the worktable in the center of the room.

Jacob caught it, stared at it for a few seconds, savoring its smell, and then slipped it into his jacket pocket. "What's this for?" he asked, genuinely perplexed.

"You and I are going to be working very closely together in the months ahead. We should get to know each other."

"So you're an orange farmer?" Jacob said with raised eyebrows and a bit more of a sarcastic edge than he had actually intended.

"Hardly," Luc replied. "Actually, I'm a carpenter by training."

Jacob wondered if he looked as surprised as he felt. "I thought you were a pastor," he said.

Now Luc looked surprised. "Who told you that?"

"Abby. She speaks very highly of you, as well."

"Does she now?"

"Should I be worried?" Jacob asked.

"Hardly," Luc said. "I'm happily married. I've got two daughters. And I'm not Jewish. Abby's all yours."

Jacob liked the sound of that, though he wasn't ready to admit it.

Luc joined Jacob stacking sacks of flour so they would both look busy if someone came upon them.

"Anyway, yes, you're right. My father, who was a farmer—though not an orange farmer—wanted me to be a carpenter, and since one of my uncles was a carpenter, he undertook to make me his apprentice. But I guess God had other plans. He called me to be a pastor—an *assistant* pastor, really. Actually a very poorly paid assistant pastor, if the truth be told."

"Where?" Jacob asked, picking up a sack of flour and placing it on top of the neat stack Luc was building.

"A little town in the south of France, Le Chambon. Have you heard of it?"

"Sorry, I have not."

"It's a beautiful place," Luc said. "You should come and visit us there sometime—you and Abby, maybe." He smiled.

Jacob changed the subject. "You sound like a good Christian."

Luc shrugged. "I've tried to be."

Jacob stopped his work and looked Luc in the eyes. "Then what are you doing here?"

"What do you mean?"

"I mean Abby says you've been rescuing Jews, giving them a place to stay, feeding them, putting their kids in your schools, giving the men jobs. What for? Why take such risks?"

"How could we not?" Luc asked. "My Savior tells me to love my neighbors. The Jews are my neighbors. It's not complicated."

"Did you really help five thousand Jews escape the Nazis?"

"I'm not sure it's that many," Luc said, not taking a break.

"But it's true that's what you've been doing?"

"Not just me," Luc demurred. "It's a whole town."

"A whole town in France is rescuing Jews?"

"We did what we could."

"But you're the leader?"

"No, I serve under two other pastors."

"But you're the one they arrested," Jacob pressed.

"The Gestapo arrested them, too."

"Are they here?" Jacob asked. "Can I meet them?"

"Well, no," Luc said. "By God's grace, they were released."

"But not you?"

"No."

"Why not?"

"You'd have to ask the Gestapo."

"But I'm asking you."

"I don't know."

"Because you're the leader," Jacob said. "You're the point man. That's why you're here."

"Maybe."

"So really, why did you do it?"

"I told you—I'm a Christian, a pastor. I'm a shepherd. My job is to lay my life down for my flock."

"But the Jews aren't your flock."

"They are God's chosen people. So are you. God loves you, and so do I."

"But you're a Gentile," Jacob said. "Look at you. You're blond-haired, blue-eyed. You could pass for an Aryan, for crying out loud. Why not just blend in? Why not pretend you're one of them, at least until the war is over?"

"Who, the Nazis?"

"Of course."

"I could never be a Nazi."

"Why not?"

"Because they hate the Jews," Luc said. "And I could never hate a Jew."

"Why not?"

Luc stopped working, straightened up, and looked Jacob square in the eye. "Because, Jacob, my Savior is a Jew," he replied. "A Jewish carpenter, come to think of it. The Bible teaches me to love the Jews. To bless the Jews. Haven't you ever read the Abrahamic covenant? Didn't God say that those who blessed the Jewish people he would bless, and those who cursed you he would curse?"

"Of course I've read it," Jacob said. "I just didn't think the goyim did."

"Well, we do," Luc said. "Some of us, at least. And anyway, if you ask me, the question shouldn't be 'Why are you, a Christian, here in a death camp, condemned for trying to save Jews?' The real question is 'Why aren't all the Christians here?'"

61

On a blustery, cold day in early February, Jacob spotted a familiar face.

The morning roll call in the Birkenau camp had just finished, and he was walking to the bakery when he saw someone who looked a bit like Josef Starwolski.

Jacob told himself it couldn't possibly be. Whoever it was appeared so emaciated and so sad, a mere shell of his former self. Yet still he resembled Jacob's old bunkmate from Auschwitz. He even walked like Josef. Could it be? There was a time not so long ago when Jacob would have merely wondered and not shown the initiative to find out the answer. But that was changing. Everything was changing.

Jacob decided to go find out.

"Josef, is that you?" he shouted, going over to get a closer look.

Sure enough, it was him. When Josef turned, his sunken eyes lit up, and he gave Jacob a feeble hug. "How are you, my friend? I never thought I'd see you again."

"I'm fine, Josef," Jacob replied. "But how are you? You've lost so much weight."

"I'm afraid I have," Josef said. "I'm dying here, and I'm scared. I don't think I can make it much longer."

"Don't worry," Jacob replied. "I will help you."

He discreetly pulled a piece of day-old bread from his pocket and quickly slipped it to Josef, who took it and devoured it greedily.

"Where did you get this?" Josef asked.

"From the bakery," Jacob said. "I work there. I can get all the bread I want. Fresh, too. Come with me. I'll give you more."

Jacob knew he could get in enormous trouble for doing such a thing, or even saying it, especially out in the open. But this was Josef. This was his friend.

"I can't, not now," Josef replied. "I have to get to my job. But I will come when I can."

"How long have you been here?" Jacob asked. "I had no idea you were here."

"Two months. They've been hellish."

"What happened? Why aren't you still in the records office? I thought that was good work."

"It was, but Von Strassen started sleeping with one of the new girls. He sleeps with all the girls in that office, you know, but unfortunately he found a new one, and he gave her my job."

"I'm sorry."

"So then Abby and Jean-Luc—you know, Leclerc—got me transferred here. Abby said it would be better for me here, that Luc would take care of me. But I haven't seen him. Have you?"

"Seen him?" Jacob said. "I work with him. He's my kapo at the bakery."

"You're not serious."

"Yes, yes, I'm heading there now. Come with me."

"I can't today," Josef said. "In fact, I have to go quickly now. I'm on a work detail. An outside detail. We're shoveling the parking lots behind the administration building. We're shoveling the walks and the driveways and—"

Josef stopped midsentence. Two guards were approaching. They had to keep moving.

"The bakery," Jacob whispered as Josef began walking away. "Come as quickly as you can."

Two days later, Josef finally came into the bakery.

It was a Sunday. He had the day off. Jacob, the Czechs, and Luc did not. As food service workers, they labored seven days a week, but they were eating fine and weren't complaining.

In his arms Josef carried a big box. The moment Jacob saw him, he knew it was only for show. Josef couldn't be seen coming into the bakery to get food for himself. He had to pretend he was making a delivery. Jacob played right along.

"Yes, yes, come in; come to the back, and we'll get all that unloaded," Jacob said, glancing over at Luc to see if he would give a nod of approval. He did.

Jacob took Josef to the workroom in the back, sat him down, and then brought him several slices of fresh, warm bread from a special batch they had made without wood shavings, dust, or other fillers. Jacob also made him a piping-hot cup of tea.

"Are we safe here?" Josef asked, hungrily eyeing the feast before him.

"Yes," Jacob assured him. "We have about fifteen minutes. Eat up."

Josef didn't need to be asked twice.

While Josef ate, Jacob told his friend about getting transferred to Birkenau and about the work he'd had to do on the construction detail and in the fields before being moved to the bakery.

Then he shifted gears. "By the way, Josef, I'm curious about something," he said while Josef slurped his tea. "Have you heard anything about Hungarians coming, a lot of them?"

Josef suddenly stopped drinking the tea. He looked up and straightened, catching Jacob off guard with such a reaction.

"Why do you ask?"

"I don't know; just been hearing some rumors. Thought you might have too."

"I might have," Josef said.

"Well, don't be shy," Jacob said. "We don't have all day."

"It's just . . ."

"Just what?"

"It's very sensitive."

"Why?"

"It's all Hoess and Von Strassen talk about," Josef said, lowering his voice to a whisper now. "But everyone's under strict orders not to say anything."

"Why? What have you heard?"

"Nothing while I was in the records office. Well, not nothing. There were whispers that a whole lot of Hungarians were coming, but that's all they were—whispers. No paperwork. Nothing on the record. But a few days ago—just before I saw you, actually—I met a guy whose sister worked with me. He hates Von Strassen. Wants to kill the man for how horribly he's treating his sister. But anyway, he said he was on an errand back at the main camp. He got a chance to see his sister. Said she looks terrible. Sad, lost, hollow. It's so bad that he's afraid she might harm herself. Anyway, she told him that she overheard a couple of Von Strassen's deputies talking. They were griping about how Hoess was so obsessed with speeding up construction that he's driving everyone crazy. When one of them asked why Hoess was making such a fuss and working them so hard, the other said they had to be ready to absorb half a million Hungarian Jews by sometime this spring."

"Half a million?" Jacob could hardly believe what he had just heard.

"That's why Hoess has been spending so much money expanding everything."

"You're saying they're getting ready to bring five hundred thousand Jews from Hungary here to Auschwitz?" Jacob asked.

"Well, to Birkenau, to be precise," Josef said. "And it may not be half a million. It may actually be more. That's why everything is supposed to be ready, and soon."

"Ready for what?"

"Ready to kill them—all at once."

The hair on the back of Jacob's neck stood on end. He suddenly found it hard to breathe, as though someone were pressing against his chest.

"You're sure about this?" Jacob asked.

"I'd trust this guy with my life," Josef said.

"Have you told anyone else?"

"No, you're the first."

"You're certain?"

"Who would I tell?" Josef asked. "I don't know anyone else here. I kept expecting Luc to find me, but no one ever made contact until I saw you the other day."

"Okay," Jacob said. "Look, we need to get you out of here. Put this extra bread in your pocket, and this orange, and then head out the back door. I'll give you more food every morning after roll call. But for now, don't tell anyone you know me. And don't come back here. It's too dangerous. Got it?"

"Okay, my friend, whatever you say," Josef said. "What are you going to do?"

"I don't know," Jacob said. "But just leave that to me."

Josef stood, gave Jacob another hug, and fled out the back door.

Jacob just sat in the back room for a moment. He had to inform Otto and Abe, and they had to get word to the chief rabbi of Budapest. They had to warn him and all the Jews of Hungary what Hitler was planning. He had to make sure the Jews never set foot on those trains.

Jacob pulled Luc into the back room.

"How's Josef?" Luc asked when he had shut the door behind him.

"Not good," Jacob said, then quickly changed the subject. "Look, have you picked up any intel on the Hungarians yet?"

"No, I'm sorry," Luc replied. "I've asked a number of sources, but no one's heard a thing. Why? Have you heard something?"

Jacob quickly told him what Josef had passed along. "I can't wait any longer. I need to meet with Otto and Abe—tonight. It's urgent. If not them, then someone else who's running the show. We need to take this information and pass it up the line to whoever is in charge of the underground. Someone has to warn the Hungarian Jews not to get on those trains. I can't do it. I know that. But someone has to, Luc, and fast."

Luc promised to take the information and get it into the right hands. For this Jacob was grateful, but he could hardly rest peacefully. So many

Jews had perished at the hands of the Nazis. But now half a million or more could soon be on their way to this death camp. He couldn't bear the thought. They had to get word to the leaders of the Jewish community in Hungary and to the Allies. And Jacob couldn't rest until they all were safe.

That night the barracks where Jacob normally slept were being disinfected, deloused, and scrubbed down from top to bottom. So were about a dozen other barracks. So Jacob and several hundred other men had to sleep on the floor in the dining hall.

Jacob tossed and turned. He tuned out the cacophony of men talking and groaning and snoring and even dying. His thoughts were elsewhere. They were all about escape.

If Steinberger and Frenkel were still alive and ready to go, Jacob would do everything in his power, take any risk, to help them. But he would not just help them get their freedom. They would have to have a plan to get to the Jewish leaders in Hungary and tell them what was happening in Auschwitz, what their people were facing. They had to persuade the Jews of Hungary to revolt. What would the Nazis do if half a million Jews rose up and attacked them? Would the Nazis kill them all? Maybe they would. But they would pay a high price. They would have to kill the Jews in the open, with the whole world watching, and then the world would know who Hitler really was. Churchill and Roosevelt and the rest of the leaders of the free world would no longer be ignorant of the evil being done in the darkness. It would all come to light.

Then they would come and liberate the camps. Not just Auschwitz-Birkenau. But all the camps.

They would have to. What other choice would they have?

62

The meeting didn't happen that night or the next.

But three days later, just as the gong signifying the end of the workday was being sounded and they had just stepped out of the bakery, Luc passed a note to Jacob.

Jacob looked down and unrolled the little piece of paper. It read simply, *Table nine.* Jacob looked up again, but Luc was gone. So were the Czechs. But wasting no time, Jacob walked quickly for the dining hall.

Upon arriving, he scanned the hundreds of faces but saw no evidence of Steinberger or Frenkel. He waited in line, got his half bowl of soup and piece of bread, and found table nine. There was no one there he knew, but he began to eat slowly and forced himself not to look around, not to look anxious, not to do anything that would draw attention. He stalled as long as he could, but more and more prisoners were coming into the hall. He couldn't hold the seat much longer. The soup was stone cold, but he finally took the last spoonful. When he put the final scrap of bread in his mouth, he decided to give up and go back to his barracks. But just then someone came up behind him and whispered, "Follow me."

Startled, he turned and watched the figure move away from him, through the crowd. Afraid of losing him, Jacob jumped from his seat and tried to catch up. When he finally made it out of the hall, he saw the man going west along a row of barracks and then around a corner. Jacob moved quickly to follow him but didn't dare break out running.

As he rounded the corner, the man grabbed him by the arm and pulled him into a doorway. Whispering, the man told him to exit through the other side of the barracks.

Jacob did as he was told, and six minutes later he was in Camp D and entering another barracks.

The building was empty, save two men.

"Master Weisz, so good to see you again," Otto Steinberger said, vigorously shaking Jacob's hand. "I hope you remember me. I'm Otto, and this is Abe Frenkel."

"Yes, of course, I remember you both," Jacob said a bit warily. "But I thought you had forgotten about me."

"Forgotten? Not at all," Otto assured him. "Come, sit down and have tea with us. And apples and honey. Please sit."

"Apples and honey?" Jacob asked. "Is it Rosh Hashanah?"

"Not for everybody," Abe replied. "But for us, yes. It's the start of an entirely new year, and it's time to make you an active part of it."

Jacob sat down. Otto handed him a slice of apple. Abe offered him a small bowl of honey. Jacob dipped his apple, as did they all, and they ate them together.

"Shana tova!" Otto said.

"Shana tova," Jacob said less enthusiastically, not sure how it could possibly be a good year with the lives of half a million or more Jews hanging by a thread.

Jacob was having mixed emotions being with these two. On the one hand, he was eager to get down to business and tell them what he knew and find out their plans and how he could help. But seeing them so happy and so healthy annoyed him. Where had they been? And why had they seemingly cut him loose?

"I was told I was coming here to help you," he said cautiously. "Why haven't you contacted me before now?"

"We were testing you," Otto said. "We needed to see what you were made of."

"Leszek trusted me," Jacob said.

"Piotr liked you, yes, but he didn't trust you," Otto replied. "There's a difference."

"What do you mean?" Jacob asked, growing defensive.

"If he'd trusted you, you would have been part of the team that helped him escape," Abe noted. "Don't get us wrong. Piotr did like you very much, and he thought you might prove useful in a larger way. But he wasn't entirely sure. You were too new. So he eased you into the mix, just enough to let Max assess you, and Abby and us. We all liked what we saw. We just needed to see more."

"But that wasn't all," Otto said.

"What else?"

"As Luc no doubt told you, you were being watched," Otto said, sipping his tea. "Because you'd worked for Piotr, Von Strassen and his men suspected you might know as much as Max. They took it easy on you at first. But they were watching you like a hawk. They hoped you would lead them to others in the Resistance. But you didn't."

"Because I couldn't," Jacob said.

"Precisely." Otto dipped another slice of apple in the honey. "And now they've arrested and executed three petty criminals back at Auschwitz. They think they've rolled up a good chunk of the conspiracy. Which is good for us. Throws them off the trail. So we waited a little longer, just to be absolutely certain it wasn't a trick. And in the meantime we told Luc to make sure you had plenty to eat in the bakery."

"To fatten me up for the slaughter?"

"To get you ready to escape."

The words hung in the air. Jacob could hardly believe he'd heard them. They nearly sucked the breath right out of his lungs. "Pardon?" he stammered. "Would you repeat that?"

"You heard him," Abe said. "Otto and I are going to go very soon. But we learned a lesson from what happened with Piotr and his team. We can't just help one group get out. We need to prepare several teams at once. That way if a month goes by and nothing changes, if no one comes to liberate the camp, then the next team is fully ready to go. And if the camp isn't liberated in another month, the next team leaves. We want you on one of those teams."

Jacob felt his spirits suddenly lifting.

"You've proven a very hardworking and faithful young man," Otto said. "Sharp. Clever. Resourceful. And quiet. And we had the highest respect for your uncle."

"Thank you. That's very kind."

"Kindness has nothing to do with it," Abe said. "This is based on merit. Everyone in this camp would love to escape. Obviously. But not everyone can pull it off."

"I understand."

"Do you?"

Jacob nodded. "I think so."

"You'd better think again. We give ourselves no better than a one in four chance of making it out and to the Allies alive. We think your chances are even lower. Maybe one in five or one in six."

"That low?"

"That high!" Otto said. "Most men in this camp wouldn't have as much as a one in twenty chance of survival."

"Five percent?"

"If that," Otto insisted. "In the grand scheme of things, we think you and your team have a half-decent shot."

"How many on each team?" Jacob asked.

"We think two is best," Abe said. "Three can be unwieldy."

"Can I choose my own partner?"

"No, we'll assign you someone."

"Why?"

"Because we know what we're doing, and you don't," Otto said frankly. "We'll get you ready. We'll help you develop a plan and teach you everything we've learned and tell you whom to contact when you get out—if you get out—and what to tell them. But you'll have to pull together all the supplies. And you'll need to agree to do exactly what we say, no questions asked."

What? They had to be joking, Jacob thought. "I can't agree to that," he said bluntly. "Not yet. I have questions first. Then I'll give you my answer."

"There's only so much we can tell you before you say yes," Abe warned.

"Nevertheless," Jacob insisted.

Otto and Abe looked at each other, said nothing, then turned back to Jacob. So far, Jacob had not touched his tea. But he did now, sweetening it with a few drops of honey and savoring every ounce. He was battling conflicting emotions and trying to keep his thoughts in order. Coming into the meeting, he had been ready to pounce on these two. He'd been angry that they had left him out to dry and run the very real risk that he could have dropped dead from starvation or exposure or exhaustion or been randomly beaten or shot by one of the crazed guards who ran this insane asylum. Now, however, he could see their rationale. If he was being watched, they obviously needed to wait. He was new. They needed to see him be tested through many trials and find the will and wisdom and craftiness necessary to survive. Now they had brought him in because he had passed all their tests. He just wished someone could have bothered to tell him any of this ahead of time so he could have known what was happening.

"Okay, I guess I have just one question for now," Jacob said at last.

"What is it?" Otto asked.

"Did Luc tell you what I've learned about the Hungarians, and have you heard the same things, and is it all true, and what can we do about it?"

Abe laughed. "That's four questions."

"Consider them one," Jacob said with a newfound assertiveness that sounded more like his uncle Avi than like him or his father.

"Fair enough," Abe replied. "Yes, we'd heard some vague rumors about the Hungarians. We've been hearing them for several months, but we're impressed you picked up on it as well and that you were able to get us such specific information. That was good work, and that's why we've got to move now. Piotr and his team got out. But we don't know what happened to them. Ever since they left, we haven't heard anything from the Resistance on the outside. We have no idea why. Maybe Piotr and his men were eventually captured and killed. Maybe they're still in hiding and never reconnected to the Resistance. Maybe they told the Resistance and the leadership doesn't believe them or didn't have the resources to come liberate us. Or maybe it's something different altogether. We don't know. But we can't wait around any longer."

"I couldn't agree more," Jacob said.

"Good, but that's not all."

At this point, Otto picked up the story. "As best we can tell, the Hungarian Jews will be rounded up in June or July and shipped here. There won't be a selection process when they get here—'You go left; you go right.' They'll get off the trains and be marched straight into the gas chambers. So as you've been saying to Luc, this is why we absolutely have to go now. We have to warn the Jewish council in Budapest to keep their people off the trains. But time is running out. We have to get to them soon. And here I must make a personal confession, Jacob."

"What is it?" Jacob asked.

"For almost two years, from the moment I set foot in this wretched place, I have thought of nothing but escaping," Otto said. "At first, it was just selfish. I wanted my freedom. Over time, though, that changed. The more I saw here, the more I developed an objective reason. I wanted to escape to tell the world what was happening at Auschwitz. But now I have an urgent, imperative reason. It's no longer a question of reporting a crime. Now it's a matter of preventing a crime. A terrible crime. The act of genocide. We must warn the Hungarians. We must rouse them. We cannot change the evil that has been done so far. But I will never be able to live with myself if I don't do everything possible to stop the genocide yet to come."

63

For the next two nights, the three men again gathered secretly after dinner.

Otto and Abe laid out their plans for Jacob. They walked through their carefully developed checklist of what they needed to do—day by day, step by step—and what supplies they needed to gather.

They had not committed any of this to writing, of course. Even if they'd had access to paper, pens, or pencils, to do so was far too dangerous. But they methodically walked Jacob through the reasoning behind each step and the lessons they had learned in developing the plan over several years. And one of the things they made clear right up front was their deep trust in Jean-Luc Leclerc.

"Work closely with Luc," Abe told Jacob. "Get his input. Listen to his advice. Use the bakery as a staging area to store all the supplies you'll be gathering. Luc's a good man. He's going to be an invaluable asset for you."

Jacob readily agreed. He had no problem with Luc. The man wasn't Jewish, but then again, Leszek hadn't been Jewish either. And Luc clearly was a useful ally. He seemed a sober, focused, and trustworthy man. In a place like this, that was an incredible thing.

The entire process that unfolded from this point forward was electrifying for Jacob. He had dreamed of a time like this for so long and then given up on it, then gotten excited again, only to see his hopes fade. But now, finally, the moment of truth had come. Maybe Abby was right. Maybe it was all a matter of divine timing.

One of the most interesting things Jacob learned was that while there had indeed been close to eight hundred escape attempts from Auschwitz since the camp opened in May of 1940, not all of them had been unsuccessful. In fact, there had been a number of successful escapes. Not all of the stories were applicable to the present circumstances, of course. After all, each time someone had gotten out, Hoess and his men had figured out the holes the escapees had exploited and made sure to plug them. Steinberger and Frenkel weren't going to be able to copy precisely what had worked in the past. But each of the successful getaways—including Leszek's—had provided proof that it was possible to get out of this hellhole, and that was the most important thing. Auschwitz-Birkenau was not impenetrable. When it came to foiling the camp's defenses, Jacob now knew it could be done, and as he listened to the stories—each as exciting as it was harrowing—he grew increasingly confident it could be done again.

The first successful escape occurred in the summer of 1940 when a Polish shoemaker named Tadeusz Wiejowski broke free with the help of five Polish citizens who lived near the camp. They helped Wiejowski cut through the fence wires and then provided him normal clothes and shoes, food to eat, water for his trip, and money to take a train far away. Otto noted that the local Polish population hated the Nazis who had invaded and raped their country. They didn't know all that was happening in the camp, but at the very least they could see men were starving to death behind the fences.

Then Abe noted that while Hoess's men never caught Wiejowski, they did eventually hunt down and capture the five Poles who had assisted his escape. Four of the five later died in Auschwitz. After that, the Nazis forcibly removed every Pole from every house in a forty-kilometer radius around the camps. Some houses remained empty. Others now housed Nazi officials or families of Nazi guards.

This intelligence was critical, Jacob saw. It meant that even if a man could slip through all of Von Strassen's security measures, he still was in grave danger far beyond the guard towers and searchlights, and he could never trust help from any civilian he met.

The most dramatic escape, to Jacob at least, was the one that had occurred on June 20, 1942. That was the day that four men—three Poles and a Ukrainian—brazenly stole Nazi uniforms from a storage closet. They suited up as SS officers, walked into the motor pool—miraculously without setting off any alarm bells—and got into Rudolf Hoess's personal staff car, a Steyr 200. To their astonishment, the keys were in the ignition. They started the car and drove out of the garage and on toward the main gate. As they approached, the guards were startled to see Hoess's car. They hadn't been notified about his departure. But the driver started shouting at them to wake up and open the gate.

"What happened?" Jacob asked.

"What do you think?" said Otto, who was telling the story. "They opened the gate."

"And the men just drove away?"

"They just drove away."

"What happened to them after they got out?"

"We have no idea. But you'll like this. They were carrying a report written by Leszek explaining what was happening here."

"And they really made it?" Jacob asked.

"So far as we know," Abe said.

"Unbelievable."

"I know." Otto began to chuckle. "Can you imagine? I mean, wouldn't you have loved to have seen the look on Hoess's face when he came down for a drive the next morning and found his precious car missing, along with four prisoners?"

They were all smiling now.

This is really happening, Jacob thought to himself. *I'm not just going to escape from Auschwitz. I'm being trained for it by people who really know what they're doing.*

But then came the countervailing thoughts: *Why me? Am I really ready for this? What if I fail? I will never forgive myself.*

64

The next day at work, Jacob said nothing to Luc.

He wanted to, but he had been given strict orders not to say anything to anyone—including Luc—at least for now.

And then, two days later, Jacob was transferred out of the bakery. This was Otto and Abe's doing. Luc was part of their plan. Indeed, they needed Luc and Jacob to be allies, Abe said. But for operational security, they didn't want the two men to be physically in such proximity. Plus, they had a new mission for Jacob now, and that required him to have new responsibilities and new freedoms.

Jacob was now to be a registrar. Like Otto and Abe, both of whom were also registrars, Jacob would keep careful statistics on all the goings-on of the prisoners in the block to which he was assigned and run errands for his block senior.

Otto's advice echoed what Leszek had said months before. "As long as you keep your ledger under your arm and you walk around looking annoyed and worried and in a hurry, you're basically free to go anywhere in the camp you want to. No one's going to stop you. No one's going to ask you pesky questions. Just constantly mutter to yourself and look harried, and you'll hardly be noticed."

This was a significant development, for now Jacob had not only the cover he needed to make critical preparations for Otto and Abe to escape, but also the access he needed to key people and key buildings. Within a few days he had begun to acquire the supplies they had assigned him, and inwardly he smiled, noting that their list was for the most part the same one he had compiled for himself months ago. They wanted a backpack, a sweater, a jacket, two civilian shirts, a pair of trousers, sturdy walking shoes, a half-dozen pairs of clean wool socks, a flashlight, a Swiss Army knife, a wristwatch, a small pot for making coffee, and a box of matches.

Then they asked for something Jacob would never have imagined: large amounts of Russian tobacco, soaked in petrol. That part seemed odd. They didn't say why they needed it, and Jacob did not ask. He had to get moving.

It was dangerous to be *looking* for such things. It was even more dangerous to be *gathering* such items and stashing them away. But Jacob wasn't supposed to merely take the risks necessary to get enough supplies for Otto and Abe. He was supposed to get a second complete set of supplies for a backup team and a third set for himself and whoever was eventually recruited to escape with him. The entire concept was terrifying. It would call on him to remember every detail of every lesson he had learned since arriving at the death camp and would require him to use every trusted relationship he had developed thus far.

Everything began with storage, he decided. Even if he could gather the needed items, if he didn't have a safe and secure place to hide them, what was the point? This, in turn, led him back to Luc and the bakery. Abe had told him to use the bakery as a staging area, and Jacob had to agree that it was perfect. While cleaning every nook and cranny of that place day after day, Jacob had found plenty of places to hide bits of bread that fell to the floor that he couldn't eat fast enough or the extra apples Luc might toss his way.

There were loose floorboards in the workroom in the back. Jacob could hide the clothing beneath them. There was a narrow crawl space behind the ovens. He might be able to hide the backpacks there. Or better still, he had once helped Luc hide a whole box of carrots by pushing up some ceiling tiles and storing the box in the rafters.

There was, of course, always the risk the Czechs could stumble upon the contraband. Jacob liked the Czechs, but he was not entirely certain he could trust them on something like this. When he discussed the matter with Luc, the Frenchman said he was certain they could trust the Czechs. He didn't think they should tell them specifically what they were doing or show them the supplies they were hiding. But Luc was confident that if the Czechs stumbled upon the hidden goods, they wouldn't steal them or squeal.

It was settled, Jacob decided. The bakery was ground zero.

In their planning, Jacob realized that Abby was also going to be critical because she still worked at the medical clinic and because the clinic was in the main camp, Auschwitz-I. After all, most of the things that Otto and Abe and the rest of them needed could only be gotten from inside the Canada warehouse, which of course was at the original camp. But as Jacob noted, they could not simply carry their stolen supplies over to Birkenau in a single shipment, or even several shipments. Even after acquiring what they needed from Canada, it would likely take several weeks to hide the items in otherwise-legitimate boxes of medical supplies moving between the two camps. Where was Jacob going to keep the rest in the meantime? The medical clinic seemed best.

It would create an enormous risk for Abby, and he worried about that. But then an idea occurred to him. When it was time for him to make his break, why not take Abby with him? She was young and healthy and smart, and she had been a loyal member of Leszek's team, had she not? With the death of Max, hadn't she suffered faithfully for the cause of the Resistance? Otto and Abe said they wanted a team of two. Why not Abby? For now, however, Jacob kept this thought to himself.

As February unfolded, Jacob focused his mind solely on the highest priorities: safely gathering three full sets of the necessary supplies and getting them into position at the bakery without being caught. He would approach Otto and Abe with the "Abby question" once he had proven himself faithful in these central things.

Jacob's original plan was to gather the three backpacks first, then the six sets of civilian clothing, then the six sets of shoes, and so forth.

But Otto demurred. He and Abe were analyzing several different escape routes and also monitoring the weather. When conditions were perfect, Otto said, they would have to move quickly. He and Abe insisted, therefore, that Jacob compile one full set of supplies immediately, and only then gather a full second set, and then the third. Jacob argued that this was more dangerous, as it required him to go back to each source three times. But Otto refused to budge. They had to have one full set ready by April 1, he said. The second set could be ready by May 1, the third by June 1.

Jacob pushed back one last time. "Once you two escape, assuming they don't catch you, Von Strassen and his thugs are going to crack down hard," Jacob argued. "You said it yourselves. They're going to look for the holes, and they're going to plug them. That means the rules for the guards will be changed. That means our methods of operating will have to change. Searches of prisoners going back and forth from Auschwitz to Birkenau will be intensified. Boxes of medical supplies will be scrutinized more carefully. Anyone connected with you two will be interrogated thoroughly. It'll be ugly."

"What's your point?" Otto asked.

"My point is that once you guys go, the next two teams need to be ready to roll," Jacob insisted. "When one of them sees an opportunity to move, they need to be just as ready then as you want to be by April 1."

Otto and Abe listened carefully to the argument. Jacob was certain they were going to say no. To his surprise, however, they ended up agreeing with his logic.

"Okay, everything needs to be ready for all three escapes by April 1," Otto said. "That's going to put a lot of pressure on you, Jacob. It's going to be a lot more dangerous. But let's make one thing clear."

"What?"

"You still have to assemble the supplies team by team, starting with Abe and me."

Jacob reluctantly agreed.

"Good," Abe said. "Any more questions?"

"Yes," Jacob said bluntly. "I have two. First of all, who is on the second team?"

Otto looked uncomfortable. "Why do you want to know?" he asked.

"I need their sizes to get the right shoes and clothes for them."

Otto and Abe stepped away for a moment to confer. When they came back, they conceded that Jacob was right. They had been holding the names tightly for obvious reasons, to reduce the risk of their leaking out. But they agreed to tell Jacob the names to allow him to make his final preparations.

"The men on the second team are Judah Fischer and Milos Kopecký," Abe explained. "Do you know either of them?"

Jacob shook his head.

"That's probably better for now," Abe said. "Kopecký is a Slovak Jew. Fischer is Polish. Kopecký has been here a couple of years. He was originally assigned to be a *Sonderkommando*, but he managed to get out of it by bribing somebody and got himself transferred. Eventually he became a block senior. He's over in Barrack 24. Fischer got here in December of '42. His mother and sister were killed in the gas chambers. All he had was his father. When his father died too, he got sent to a work detail in Buna. It nearly killed him. One of our men got him transferred back to an inside job, a registrar in Barrack 18. We fed him, watched out for him, helped him get his strength back. Both are good men. And they've been very resourceful, to say the least. I'll tell you more later. Now, what's your second question?"

Jacob wasn't finished with the first, but when Abe jotted down the measurements he needed for both men and slid it over to him, he decided not to ask any more about the second team. Instead he turned to the "Abby question"—could she be the second member of his team? But no sooner was the first sentence out of his mouth than both men said an emphatic no.

"Absolutely not," Otto said.

"Out of the question," Abe agreed.

"Now, look," Jacob said. "I really—"

"No," Otto interjected forcefully. "No, period. End of sentence. Look, we can see that you like her—"

"No, no, that's not it," Jacob insisted, shaking his head, but Otto would have none of it.

"Jacob, we're not fools. We get it—you like her. And believe me, we're sympathetic. But Abby would be a distraction and thus a serious liability. She would slow you down. At best, you'd spend more time thinking about how to protect her than how to reach your objective. At worst, you'd spend all your time thinking about how to get her to marry you, and you wouldn't be concentrating effectively on not getting caught and reaching your goal."

"Which is this, and only this: warning the Jewish leaders in Hungary," Abe chimed in.

"Besides, we've already chosen someone for you," Otto said matter-of-factly.

"Who?"

Otto leaned forward and whispered in Jacob's ear. "Jean-Luc Leclerc."

"No way," Jacob shot back.

"What do you have against Luc?" Otto asked.

"Nothing," Jacob insisted. "He's a fine man, but I want a Jew, not some goy pastor."

"Well, it's not your call," Otto said firmly. "It's ours."

"It's my life," Jacob said.

"It's our mission," Abe replied. "If you don't want in, we'll find someone else. But we're not having a debate. You're escaping with Luc, or you're not going at all."

65

For most of March, Jacob strained to gather all three sets of supplies.

He focused on completing the list of items for the first escape kit, as ordered, though he took advantage of opportunities to collect supplies for the next two kits as well. He worked without complaining. And also without talking to Jean-Luc Leclerc about the mission. Otto and Abe didn't want to argue with Jacob over his teammate. They had made the choice, and it was final. But they also didn't want Jacob arguing with Jean-Luc Leclerc or urging him to drop out. They didn't even want him brainstorming about the mission. They just wanted Jacob to focus on his job of gathering everything that was needed in the very short time frame they had. Everything else was off-limits.

On the evening of March 25, the three gathered again after supper in an empty bunk room in Camp D. Jacob explained that he wasn't sure he would have everything together in one week's time, but he was still trying. At the moment, they had no backpacks and no shoes that would fit Otto. It was taxing his patience, but Jacob insisted that he was doing everything he could to finish on time. He simply couldn't be certain. Otto assured him he was doing fine.

"It'll all work out," Abe added calmly.

"How?" Jacob said, his nerves growing raw.

"I have no idea," Abe conceded. "It just will. We've survived this far. I think God is letting us live for a reason: so we can escape and warn our brothers."

Jacob wasn't sure about that, but this was no time to argue. Not about theology, anyway. But there was another issue he needed to bring up.

"I need to talk to you about Luc—" he began, but Abe cut him off.

"I know, I know—you think we need to let Luc know he's going to be on your team," Abe said. "But it's still too soon. Luc has enough on his plate at the moment. He doesn't have the same freedom of time or movement we do. He can't gather supplies, scout out possible escape points, or meet together like this and refine plans. Let Luc do his work, and let us do ours. He's a good man. He's been very willing to do everything we've asked him thus far, and he hasn't asked for anything in return. Not for special privileges or food. Not to join us in getting out. Not for anything. You can't ask for more."

"I wish we had a thousand Lucs," Otto said.

Jacob explained that he had no dispute with anything they had said thus far. It was all true. Luc was hardworking and loyal and never complained. He had saved Jacob's life several times and had introduced him to Abby. And his record of saving Jews in France was beyond compare. Jacob would be forever grateful. There was just one problem.

"He's not Jewish," Jacob said.

"So what?" Abe asked.

"Yeah, so what?" Otto echoed. "What's your point?"

"My point is that we're Jews," Jacob said. "The people the Nazis are trying to kill most are Jews. The Hungarians we're trying to warn are Jews. We need a Jew to talk to Jews."

"You're wrong," Abe said.

"I'm not," Jacob said. "At least Abby is Jewish. This guy is blond, blue-eyed—for crying out loud, he looks like an Aryan. How in the world are we going to get the Jewish council in Hungary to trust him?"

"That's not why we chose him," Otto said.

"Then why?" Jacob pressed.

Otto looked at Abe. There was a long pause.

"I guess it's time we tell you," he said.

"Tell me what?" Jacob asked.

"Luc is a man of connections."

"Connections?" Jacob asked, the cynicism in his voice barely concealed. "He's a pastor—an assistant pastor. He doesn't have any connections. He's told me that himself."

"He's just being modest," Otto said. "He actually couldn't be more highly connected."

"How?"

"His grandfather used to be the French ambassador in Washington."

"Ambassador?" Jacob said, incredulous.

"Right."

"So just to be clear," Jacob said, "you think the chief rabbi of Budapest is going to listen to this man—this goy, this pastor—just because he's the grandson of a French diplomat?"

"No," Otto replied calmly. "I think the chief rabbi of Budapest is going to listen to Abe and me. If we get caught or killed, I hope he'll listen to Judah and Milos. And if they get caught or killed, then I hope he'll listen to you."

"Then why bring Luc?" Jacob asked. "Why not Abby—or Josef, for that matter?"

"Because the goal here isn't simply getting to the chief rabbi of Budapest," Otto said. "Look, Jacob. We've thought a lot about this. And we've concluded that if we get out—if any of us get out, and hopefully if *all* of us get out—we cannot simply talk to our fellow Jews. Yes, that's critically important. We have to warn them not to get on the trains. But that's not enough. We cannot just talk to Jewish leaders. Because what, in the end, can they really do? We need to get to decision makers. We need to get to the Allies. At the highest possible levels. We need to convince Churchill and Roosevelt and their closest advisors to take action. Decisive action. Action the Jewish communities cannot take for themselves."

"Like liberating Auschwitz?" Jacob asked.

"Sure, if they can," Abe said.

Jacob was confused. "And if they can't?"

"Then bomb the railroad tracks leading here," Abe said.

Then Otto added, "And if that's not enough . . ." His words trailed off mysteriously.

"And if that's not enough, then what?" Jacob asked.

There was a long pause. Neither Otto nor Abe would look him in the eye.

"Then what?" Jacob pressed again.

"Then we want them to bomb Auschwitz," Otto said at last.

Jacob was stunned. "What did you just say?"

"You heard him," Abe said.

"Bomb Auschwitz?" Jacob asked.

"And Birkenau," Abe said. "The gas chambers and the ovens."

Jacob was incredulous.

"But . . . but . . . so many people . . . so many would die," he stammered.

"They're dying already," Otto said. "Think of how many more would be saved."

Jacob shook his head, pushed away from the table, and stood. "No," he said. "That's not right. We want them to liberate us, not bomb us."

"Of course we want them to liberate us," Abe said. "But what if that's not possible? What if they can't spare the troops? Think about it, Jacob. We're deep in enemy territory. It might be impossible to get to us unless or until the Allies win the war. But even if that happens—and I pray to God every night that it does—it could take years. Look how long we've already been here. Look how many have died. Hitler's clearly trying to liquidate the entire Jewish race. Give him a few more years, and he just might do it. No, we can't wait that long. If the Allies can't liberate the camps, then they need to destroy them."

Jacob was pacing now, trying to make sense of all this. Otto stood, walked over to him, and put his hand on his shoulder.

"We've thought through every possible scenario," he said calmly. "Believe me, if there were another way, we'd be all for it. But each of us has to know—beyond the shadow of a doubt—what we're going to say to any government official we get the chance to talk to when we get out of here. And we all have to be singing from the same song sheet. We all need the same message. And when we're free, and when God opens the door for us to meet with world leaders—and I know he will—then we need to repeat our message again and again and again until they listen and until they act."

Abe now stood as well and walked over to them.

"That's why we need Luc on this team. The people making the decisions in London and Washington, do you think they're Jewish? They're not. They're Christians. Oh, they're not all as devout and religious as Jean-Luc, but believe me, he speaks their language. The fact that he's a Gentile—a goy, as you put it—that helps us. The fact that he's blond and blue-eyed, even better. He's one of them. But he's also one of us. He's seen what we've seen. He can speak to them. He can convince them of what's happening here and of the need to take strong, fast, decisive action. And we think the fact that Luc will be able to reconnect with his grandfather will come in very handy in opening doors to the decision makers at the White House and in Congress and in the State Department and the War Department. If anyone can convince them to do something serious before it's too late, it's him."

"Don't fight us on this, Jacob," Otto said. "It's a decision we've come to in close consultation with the leadership of the underground throughout the camps. Believe me, we've all agonized over this, but this is where we've come out. What we're asking you to do is to carry out orders, not give new ones. Can we count on you for that? Can we trust you to execute our plan, no matter what the cost?"

Jacob looked both men in the eye and sighed. He didn't agree. He didn't want to escape with a Protestant minister at his side, even someone like Jean-Luc Leclerc. But Steinberger and Frenkel were in charge.

Jacob knew that if he refused to submit, they might very well give the chance to escape to someone else, and he could not let that happen under any circumstances. He was torn. Already he had almost completed his immediate task. He had gathered nearly all the supplies

Steinberger and Frenkel needed and most of two other full sets as well. But he was rattled by the decisions his superiors were making and asking him to make. Actually, *rattled* didn't even capture it.

Jacob remained silent as he stewed over the things his overseers had said. It was bad enough that they wouldn't let him choose the person he would risk his life with to escape. But did they really have the gall to suggest that they were going to ask Churchill and Roosevelt to bomb Auschwitz-Birkenau?

Here he was, taking enormous risks to help them escape, only to have them say they would recommend that the British and the Americans bomb concentration camps filled with Jews? It was ludicrous. It was beyond ludicrous. It was madness. The point was to stop the Nazis from killing Jews, not to persuade FDR and Churchill to do it for the Nazis. What was wrong with these men? How could they be so cold?

He tried to consider the other side. Was it really fair to think so poorly of Steinberger and Frenkel? They weren't idiots. They weren't fools. And they certainly weren't cowards. They had more than proven their courage to save Jewish lives at grave risk to their own. What's more, they had pinned a lot of hopes on the notion that if Leszek Poczciwinski—aka Piotr Kubiak—could escape, then the liberation of the camps would happen soon. But it hadn't happened as they had hoped. There were any number of possible reasons for that. Maybe Leszek never made it safely back to the Polish Resistance. But maybe it was because though he did, no one had the time or the resources or perhaps the interest to wage a brutal military campaign to liberate one camp, much less dozens. They were deep behind enemy lines. They were far from any Allied strongholds. Maybe the operation would end up like the one to liberate train 801—a well-meaning, good-hearted effort and a partial success, but in the end a failure. Maybe Steinberger and Frenkel knew something he didn't. And Jacob had to admit that there wasn't time for any more well-meaning, good-hearted failures.

One thing was certain: the Nazi death machine had to be stopped once and for all. That would necessitate dramatic, decisive action. If the death camps were obliterated by Allied air strikes, then many Jews would die. That was the hard truth, and Steinberger and Frenkel knew it all too well. But then what would happen? The killings would stop, would they not? Then the Nazis would have no way to systematically annihilate the rest of the Jews of Europe. Would Hitler have the time or the money or the manpower to rebuild the death camps amid the rest of his all-consuming war operations? Maybe not, even if he retained the motive. And Jacob began to wonder if perhaps Steinberger and Frenkel were right after all.

"Okay," he said finally, resigning himself to their authority. "I'm in."

66

APRIL 5, 1944

Two weeks later the team met again.

This time, however, Steinberger and Frenkel decided to invite Luc to attend as well.

Jacob privately resented the notion that these men would include Luc without discussing it with him first. After all, any meeting significantly increased the risk of all four of them being discovered and arrested. Jacob felt that was a decision they should evaluate carefully and in consultation. What's more, Jacob secretly wanted to limit the amount of specific information Luc had about the escape plan. The less Luc knew in terms of operational details, the easier it could be for Jacob to replace him with a different partner after Steinberger and Frenkel had escaped. They couldn't well stop him from making his own decisions once they were gone. Yet it was becoming clear that neither Steinberger nor Frenkel was prepared to surrender leadership to Jacob before their departure. They had been insistent on Jean-Luc Leclerc's being Jacob's partner, and they weren't about to change their minds now.

"Mr. Leclerc, so good that you could join us," Otto said, giving the Frenchman a warm embrace and directing him to take a seat in the cramped bunkhouse quarters.

"I'm honored to be here," Luc replied. "I was surprised to be invited."

Jacob said nothing.

"The three of us have been deeply impressed by your character, your hard work, your team spirit, and your bravery," Abe said. "We know the history of your work back home in France, that you've risked your life to rescue innocent Jews from Hitler's clutches, and we are all grateful for this."

"How could I do any less?" Luc said quietly.

"Many in your position have done far, far less," Abe said.

Steinberger and Frenkel then looked to Jacob. It took a moment to realize what his comrades were doing, but Jacob quickly cleared his throat and picked up where they left off.

"We've discussed it thoroughly, and we've considered a number of candidates, but at my request, Otto and Abe have agreed with me that we should invite you to be on my escape team," Jacob said, looking Luc square in the eye. "It will be an enormous risk, and I cannot guarantee your safety. To the contrary, the likelihood is high of being shot to death or hanged. But the mission is important. We have to get word of what is happening here to the Jewish council in Budapest and then to the Allies in London and Washington. And I think you'd be a great asset. I'd be honored to have you as my partner. What do you say?"

It wasn't an entirely truthful statement, of course. But it made no sense to communicate his doubts. After all, it wasn't that Jacob had something personal against Luc. He had simply wanted a fellow Jew, pure and simple. But he had been overruled. Pure and simple. Now it was time to unify and focus intently on the mission ahead.

Jacob was grateful to Steinberger and Frenkel for giving him the opportunity to make the invitation directly to Luc. It allowed Jacob to set the tone for the relationship, to assert himself as the team leader even though he was the younger partner, and to signal his confidence in Luc, something that would be absolutely vital for success if they were really going to put their lives in each other's hands.

Luc was visibly taken aback by the question. "I—I'm not sure what to say," he stammered.

It was clear Luc had not come to the meeting expecting to be invited on such an assignment, and Jacob found himself encouraged by that. It was a good sign, he thought, that Luc didn't feel entitled to be on one of the escape teams but simply wanted to help his fellow prisoners. It spoke volumes about his motives, and thus his character.

"You have an asset that tipped the balance for us," Jacob said.

"What's that?" Luc asked.

"Your grandfather."

"My grandfather?"

"We understand he served as the French ambassador to Washington until Prime Minister Reynaud was forced from office and the Vichy government took over. Is that correct?"

"Well, yes, it is," Luc said. "But how did you know my connection to him? I haven't told anyone."

"The underground is fairly resourceful," Jacob replied. "It's critical once we escape that we be able to take the intelligence about what's really happening here to a trusted source, particularly in Washington. We need to be able to secure a private meeting with President Roosevelt, inform him of the situation, and insist that he take action. We believe you could play a vital role in this. If you can get us to your grandfather, then hopefully he can get us that meeting with the president. Will you help us?"

"Absolutely," Luc said. "Whatever I can do, I am ready."

"Good, then it's settled." Jacob smiled and shook Luc's hand vigorously. "Welcome aboard."

67

Jacob had thought that would be the high point of the meeting.

But he was wrong. Steinberger and Frenkel weren't merely bringing Luc onto the team. They were also ready to explain their own specific plan to escape.

"We've found our route," Otto said. "It's time to go."

Jacob's pulse quickened. He and Luc listened carefully as their team leaders laid out the specifics of their plan.

"You know the big construction site they're calling Birkenau-III?" Abe asked.

"You mean in the outer camp?" Jacob asked.

"Right."

"The one where they're pre-positioning all that lumber for the new barracks?" Luc clarified.

"Exactly," Abe said. "We were watching them out there a few days ago, and we suddenly got an idea. We bribed some kapos to stack one of the lumber piles in such a way that there's a cavity in the middle. From the outside, it looks like a solid stack of wood. But actually it's got room inside for two grown men to hide, with all of our provisions."

"The entrance is on the top," Otto said. "There's no other way in or out. What we'll need one of you to do when we give you the signal is to remove a few planks off the top of the pile. We'll be able to lower ourselves down into the hollowed-out area. Then you'll put the planks back, and everything will look normal."

"Once we're in, you need to sprinkle a bunch of the Russian tobacco on the top of the woodpile and around the sides," Abe explained.

"The stuff we soaked in petrol?" Jacob asked.

"Yes," Otto said. "Is it all dry now?"

"Dried and stored in bags and hidden at the bakery," Jacob said.

"Excellent."

"I don't understand," Jacob said. "What does that do?"

"It throws off the dogs," Abe responded. "They can't stand the stuff. They hate the smell of tobacco—the Russian kind, anyway—and the stench of petrol makes it even worse."

"You're sure about that?" Luc asked.

"No," Otto conceded. "But that's what we've been told, and we're going with it."

"Told by whom?" Jacob asked. "Leszek? He didn't even smoke."

"No, by a Russian sergeant we met a few months ago," Abe explained. "The guy escaped from a German POW camp by using this trick. Unfortunately, he got so excited after he got out of the camp that he was laughing and singing as he ran through the woods on the other side of the river. Poor fool. He stumbled over a German colonel who was making out with his girlfriend in the tall grass. Anyway, he said the Russian tobacco and petrol worked just fine. Dancing through the woods? Not so much."

"Okay, fine," Jacob said. "But I still don't understand how this is going to work. How are you going to get through the electric fences? And even if you do, why hide in the woodpile? Why not just double-time it to the Soła River, and then to the train tracks, and ride the rails south to the Czech border?"

"It's simple," Otto said. "The only way to get beyond the electrified fences is during the day when the guards are out there with all the men who are working, building those new barracks, right?"

Jacob and Luc nodded.

"But here's the thing. At night, that outer camp and all those half-finished barracks are unguarded. Why should they be? All the prisoners are back in the main camp behind the electric fences. So here's our plan. We hide in the lumber pile during the day."

"While there are guards patrolling all over?"

"Unfortunately, yes," Abe said. "But if we can pull that off, then at five o'clock the guards will take all the men back into the main camp for roll call."

"And you'll already be hiding?" Jacob asked.

"Right. Then they'll figure out we're missing and the sirens will go off. At that point, the troops will start moving. The dogs will start running. But what are they expecting? They're expecting two men on the run. So that's where they go. They'll scour the camp for sure. But they'll also scour the surrounding countryside. For exactly three days and three nights—that's what the regulations say, seventy-two hours, no more, no less—they will search every field and river and house and barn, convinced that we're running. But they won't find us heading to the Soła River or near the train tracks or hiding in a barn or under a bridge. They won't find us at all."

"Because you'll still be hiding in the woodpile," Jacob said.

"You got it," Otto said. "We'll be hiding right under their noses."

"And then what?"

"When the seventy-two hours are up, Von Strassen will call off the men and dogs. They'll stand down like they did after Leszek broke free. That's when Abe and I will make our move. That should be around dinnertime of the third day. We'll wait a few more hours for darkness, of course, but then it should be relatively easy."

"Easy?" Jacob asked, far from convinced.

"Well, we'll already be out beyond the two fences, and no one will be chasing us," Otto explained. "The manhunt will be over. We'll have a good eight or nine hours of darkness ahead of us. We'll head south with our backpack of provisions. After a week or so, we should reach the Czech border. We'll head for Žilina. We've got good sources there. We'll link up with the Jewish council, then head to Budapest. We'll tell them of everything that's happening here—all of it. We'll warn them not to get on the trains, no matter what they're told. We'll convince them to start a rebellion if they have to but not to get on those trains under any circumstances. After that, if God is with us, we'll head to London and then to Washington to make our case to Churchill and Roosevelt to liberate Auschwitz-Birkenau and every other camp before it's too late."

"And if you don't make it?" Luc asked, breaking his silence.

"Then you two and the other team will."

For nearly a minute, Jacob and Luc sat in silence. It was an audacious plan, Jacob thought, but the more he pondered it, the more impressed he was. Rather than try to outrun the Nazis and their dogs, Steinberger and Frenkel would hide nearly in plain sight. If they survived the first seventy-two hours without being caught, and if Von Strassen really did call off the manhunt after three days, according to the regulations, then maybe they were right. Maybe they'd have a real shot at freedom.

The four men spent most of the next hour going over the plan in even more specificity. As Otto and Abe answered every one of Jacob's and Luc's questions, the initial elation of hearing a credible escape plan began to morph into a weight on Jacob's shoulders. This was it. This was really happening. Steinberger and Frenkel would soon be gone. Very soon they'd either be free or dead. Either way, Jacob and Luc would be on their own. Jacob hoped they were ready. In the meantime, he knew that he and Luc had to understand the plan in all its nuances and be ready to adapt it at a moment's notice.

Steinberger and Frenkel explained that Fischer and Kopecký had developed an entirely different escape strategy and planned to make their attempt a few weeks later, though they didn't go into the details. Indeed, for operational security, they didn't want Jacob or Luc even to meet the other men, much less know their plans. Instead Steinberger and Frenkel went over the last-minute preparations they needed help with, and then they dropped their bombshell. They announced they were leaving Friday night.

Jacob tensed. That was just two days hence. The clock was ticking. But the two men stressed that by all indications, the Nazis were going to start rounding up the Hungarian Jews in just two months. They could wait no longer. They had to move now if they were going to get to Budapest in time.

"So what do you think?" Luc asked when Steinberger and Frenkel had gone back to their barracks and he and Jacob were alone for the first time.

"It's risky, but I like it," Jacob said. "What about you?"

"I like it well enough, but there does seem to be a major problem," Luc said.

"What's that?" Jacob asked.

"If it doesn't work—if Otto and Abe are captured and killed—they haven't come up with a plan B for us to escape," Luc noted. "I mean, they just said that they've helped Fischer and Kopecký come up with an entirely different escape plan from their own, right? But they haven't told us what it is. So if I'm hearing them correctly, they want us to escape using their plan as our blueprint. That's fine, if it works. I mean, if they get out safe and sound, that's fantastic. We can follow their plan as well. But what if it doesn't work? What if the Russian tobacco doesn't work like they hope? What if the dogs find them in the woodpile? What if something else goes sideways? What do we do then?"

68

Jacob tossed and turned all night.

Finally, unable to sleep, he just got up. It was Friday, April 7. This was it. This was the day Otto and Abe had decided to go for it.

Jacob could hardly believe it. His palms were sweaty. His stomach was in knots. On the one hand, he was very excited for them. On the other hand, Luc's questions weighed heavily on him. What if it didn't work? What if Steinberger and Frenkel were caught? Luc was right. They didn't have a plan B.

It didn't matter, he told himself. There was no time to come up with one today. To the contrary, he knew he had to stay focused on the task at hand and not let himself get bogged down by a bunch of what-ifs and if-onlys.

Something else Luc had said just before they parted paths on Wednesday night now rang in his ears as well. "There's no point worrying about tomorrow," Luc had concluded. "Today has enough trouble of its own."

Luc was right, Jacob decided. There were very real and enormous problems facing them in the days ahead if this operation failed. But they would have to deal with those in due course. For now, they had to do their jobs and do them with great care and precision.

Jacob knew the biggest challenge he would face that day was going through the usual motions of his normal routine while not giving anyone the impression that this day was different from any other. There were a hundred things that could go wrong, but most of them were out of his control. Steinberger and Frenkel had repeatedly stressed—much as Avi had done in the past—the importance of going over the plan again and again and staying focused on the objective. Don't get flustered. Don't get rattled. Don't worry about the things that are beyond anyone's control. Just stay calm, keep moving, and pay attention to the littlest details. That was the recipe for success, they argued, and Jacob tried his best to be faithful to the task they had entrusted to him.

Morning went fine. He did some errands and took care of some paperwork. He made sure he was out and about the camp, chatting with prisoners and politely acknowledging guards who knew his face and saw him all the time. The goal was to be visible, to be building an alibi that he had been doing his job all day, doing what he was supposed to do when he was supposed to do it. Dozens of people would be able to vouch for that. A lot of time had passed since Leszek and his team had escaped. Thus, so far as Jacob knew, the guards weren't seriously anticipating more escapes. They were just looking for things that were out of the ordinary, little things that didn't seem right. That's why Jacob had to be so careful about even seemingly insignificant details. Those were the things that could give the whole operation away.

Jacob made it a point to have lunch with Josef, something they tried to do at least once a week. Josef, who had somehow managed to get himself taken off outdoor work duty and assigned to the Canada warehouse, had known for weeks that something was up. Indeed, he was the one who had found the Russian tobacco for Jacob and gotten him access to a barrel of petrol. Still, Josef didn't know what was actually happening, and he certainly didn't know when.

Today Josef was distraught.

"What is it?" Jacob asked. "What happened?"

Josef leaned in and whispered over his bowl of soup. "It's Von Strassen. He's gone berserk."

"What do you mean?"

"I talked to a friend who's been assigned to the records office. Von

Strassen is convinced all the women in the office are talking about him behind his back."

"The ones he's sleeping with?" Jacob asked.

"Right," Josef said.

"So what?"

"So apparently two days ago he had his men round up all the women in the office at gunpoint and lead them to one of the gas chambers, where they were forced to strip naked. Then they were herded inside, the doors were locked, and they were just screaming and crying in there for nearly an hour. Finally the pipes started creaking and suddenly water started coming out of the showerheads."

"Not gas?"

"No. Water. Warm water, even."

"So what happened?"

"The doors opened a few minutes later, and the guards gave the women towels to dry off, and then they were sent back to the office, where Von Strassen and his deputies were laughing and carrying on and having a birthday party for one of Hoess's kids, complete with cake and ice cream."

"That was it?" Jacob asked. "Von Strassen didn't say anything?"

"What does he have to say?" Josef asked. "He'd made his point. But he's an animal, I tell you. A man with no soul. He should burn in hell. Someday I hope to send him there myself. In the meantime, he's on edge—worried. I think he's afraid another escape is coming. He's afraid Hoess will fire him, or worse. So he's got all his men on high alert, and he's driving everyone crazy with his constant talk about keeping the camps as tight as a drum."

Jacob hoped his face didn't betray him. He'd been operating on the assumption that the guards were not on heightened alert. Now Josef was telling him the opposite was true. Still, there was nothing he could do about it. The day had come. There was no turning back.

69

At precisely one o'clock, Jacob began to move into position.

An afternoon spring rain began to fall, and he was soon soaked to the bone, but he refused to let anything dissuade or distract him now. He carried two large jugs of fresh cold water and several sets of clean socks wrapped in newspaper to keep them dry. The first set was for the guards manning the gate out of the main Birkenau camp en route to the construction site at Birkenau-III. The second set was for the guards overseeing the prisoners slaving away on the new barracks. They were bribes, pure and simple. Jacob had experimented with such things in the past, and they worked. This time was no different. The gate guards waved him through without incident.

Out on the work site, the guards were huddled in a small wooden hut, smoking cigarettes and playing cards. The harder the rains fell, the less time they spent standing outside. They would poke their heads out for a moment and make sure the prisoners weren't starting a riot, but they certainly were not giving them their full attention. Luc would say that was the hand of Providence, Jacob thought. Abby would too. Maybe it was. Or maybe it was just good luck.

Next he handed out small bags of Swiss chocolates to some of the kapos on the work details and made small talk with them about the weather and the new group of Frenchwomen that had just arrived in the main camp. Jacob wasn't doing much of the talking, of course. By this point he had learned to ask a few provocative questions to get a conversation started. Once the men started talking, it was hard to stop them.

So far, his plan was working like a charm.

Just before two o'clock, Jacob spotted Steinberger and Frenkel heading from different directions toward the pile of lumber.

This was it. Moving sure and fast, he met the men and scrambled to the top of the pile. The wood was wet and quite slippery. He glanced around to make sure no guards were watching, then quickly moved the top planks, revealing the hole and the cavity below. He grabbed Otto's hand and pulled him to the top. Two seconds later, Otto dropped into the hole and disappeared from view.

Next was Abe's turn, and moments later he was in and safe as well. They had already pre-positioned their backpack of supplies in the small space, and they now had everything they needed.

"Good luck, boys," Jacob whispered.

Five seconds later he was gone. He was halfway back to the guard hut when his heart nearly stopped. He had been so nervous and so wet and so focused on getting the men into the woodpile that he had completely forgotten to sprinkle the Russian tobacco. Cursing himself for making such a foolish mistake, he turned around and raced back to the pile. When he got there, he said nothing to the men but rather pulled out the small burlap satchel of tobacco and did what he had promised to do in the first place.

When he was done, he left in a different direction, his heart racing, terrified he would be spotted and captured and that everything would be for naught.

Then another fear came to mind: would the rain wash away the tobacco scent, allowing the dogs to find Steinberger and Frenkel after all?

The hours could not pass by fast enough.

Jacob got back to his barracks and continued to carry out his normal routine.

He learned from a kapo that a forty-five-year-old French Jew had just dropped dead on a work detail at the Buna camp. He also learned that a thirty-eight-year-old Polish political prisoner had been beaten to death by two guards.

Jacob wasn't sure how much more he could handle. In March, twenty-nine prisoners in his barracks had died. In February, thirty-six had died, adding to the fifty-one who had died in January. Typhus. Dysentery. Starvation. The elements. Beatings. Exhaustion. The Nazis didn't even need Zyklon B. They had no shortage of methods to kill a man.

Jacob finished his daily reports and filed the paperwork with the records office. Then, in his only departure from his regular schedule, he made a brief stop at the bakery to assure Luc that all was well. All the while he felt like a time bomb was about to go off.

And then it did. Jacob was dutifully standing at attention with all the other men from his barracks at the seven o'clock roll call when the sirens went off and sent a shudder down his spine. Von Strassen had run a few drills in recent months to make sure the new emergency response procedures for escape attempts were being followed precisely, and most of the men around him assumed this was another test. Jacob, however, knew differently, though he did not tip his hand even as he marveled at the sight of literally thousands of heavily armed troops pouring out of their bunkers and taking up their preplanned positions or forming into their squads and moving outside the camp to begin their search.

The hunt was on. The clock was ticking. Jacob just hoped he could endure the suspense.

Due to his indoor work at the bakery and all the food he had eaten there and now his job as a registrar and the generous extra rations of food that Steinberger and Frenkel had made sure he received every day, Jacob was physically stronger and much healthier than he had been during his months at Buna or out in the vegetable fields. He was therefore much better prepared this time for the nine hours of standing outside in the rain that all the prisoners had to endure. Still, he knew the men around him were weaker than they had been a few weeks or months earlier, and it grieved him to see them drop one by one throughout the evening.

He told himself over and over again that this was a cost that could not be avoided. If they were going to save the many, they had to be prepared to lose a few. He had told himself that numerous times before this night, but as he watched grown men weeping and collapsing and being beaten and shot, Jacob could hardly bear it.

The men were released just before sunrise, but the manhunt continued. For three days and three nights it continued, just as Jacob expected. But on the evening of April 9 something happened that he did not expect.

Jacob was walking back to his barracks after supper when he heard a low but distinctive rumbling to the west. It was a sound he had heard before, though never here. It sounded like a plane. Actually, it sounded like several planes.

Jacob turned and searched the sky. Just then, the clouds parted for a moment. To his astonishment he could see a squadron of Allied planes dropping dozens of bombs.

The planes were not immediately overhead but were several kilometers to the southwest, so the bombs weren't coming straight down on top of them, and Jacob wasn't in immediate danger.

But it didn't matter where the bombs were falling. Fear was the furthest thing from what he was experiencing at that moment. Rather, he felt a combination of shock and sheer joy. It had happened! They had waited for month after month, but it had finally happened! Leszek and his team had broken through enemy lines after all! Their friend had told the Allied generals what crimes the Nazis were committing at Auschwitz, and the Americans and the Brits had finally come to make it stop.

Soon prisoners of all ages were pouring out of the dining hall and out of their barracks and out of the washrooms, yelling and cheering as the bombs hit their marks. The ground shook as massive fireballs could be seen in the distance and thick black smoke rushed into the dusky sky.

But then, even before the camp guards began blowing their whistles and the men in the towers began firing their machine guns into the air and additional soldiers ran to their artillery batteries and began unleashing triple-A fire into the sky, the Allied planes were suddenly gone. The ordnance stopped falling. The ground stopped shaking, and soon all was silent save the roaring of the fires at the I. G. Farben factory.

A second roll call was taken, and only when Von Strassen and his men were certain that only Steinberger and Frenkel were missing—that no one else had escaped during the bombing raid—were the men ordered back to their barracks. It was not yet even eight o'clock. The night was still young, but the guards were taking no chances.

After seventy-two tense hours, the manhunt was finally called off.

Then the inevitable interrogations ensued. Men working directly for Otto and Abe were tortured and then hanged. But miraculously the trail never led to Jacob or Luc or Josef or Abby or anyone on their team. The system they had created was diffused enough that Von Strassen wasn't able to find a single loose thread to pull on, and within ten days or so, a sense of relative calm had returned to the camp, but for the daily systematic murder of thousands of Jews.

When the coast seemed clear, Jacob and Luc huddled in the back room of the bakery one morning, hardly able to believe their good fortune. They were still alive. Steinberger and Frenkel were safely out of the camp, en route to Czechoslovakia and then Hungary. Fischer and Kopecký had their own plans and were ready to move whenever the proper moment presented itself.

The only immediate disappointment—and indeed, source of tremendous confusion—was trying to understand why the Allied bombing run had been directed only at the synthetic rubber plant and not at the railroad tracks or at Auschwitz or Birkenau or any of the subcamps. Why had the Allies chosen to penetrate so deep into enemy airspace only to hit a not-yet-fully-completed rubber factory rather than a death factory? Hadn't Leszek explained everything to them?

Something was terribly wrong.

Maybe this was just a test run, Jacob told Luc one night. Maybe the bombers were coming back. After all, even though the Germans had positioned antiaircraft batteries in the area, the Allies could see that the men using them weren't really well-trained. The Allied bombers hadn't encountered any serious resistance, so far as Jacob or Luc or any of their sources throughout the camps could determine. There was no reason, therefore, for London and Washington or even Moscow not to order further air strikes, so every prisoner fully expected more to come.

Yet another week went by and nothing happened.

Two more weeks went by and no more bombers.

Then it was May, and there were still no follow-up bombing runs. Not even the sound of planes in the air.

70

MAY 14, 1944

"What if we're wrong?" Jacob asked.

He and Luc rarely spent significant amounts of time together anymore. They didn't want to run the risk of being seen together. Thus, their meetings were usually quick and to the point and all about business. They gave each other brief updates and scraps of intelligence they had picked up and made plans for their next meeting.

But today was different. It was a Sunday, and it was quiet, and the weather was beautiful, and thousands of prisoners were outside. Some were walking. Some were playing checkers in the dust with rocks. Others were reading alone or flirting with the women or taking a nap. Sundays were a surreal break from the grisly routine of the death camp, and each man savored them in his own way.

So today Jacob and Luc went for a walk amid the other prisoners.

"We've been assuming that Leszek finally made it to the Resistance alive and in one piece and that the bombing was a response to his report," Jacob noted as they strolled.

"So?" Luc asked.

"So what if we're wrong about that? What if Leszek is dead? What if the Allies have no idea what's happening here and it was—I don't know—just a fluke that they hit a target so close to us?"

"A fluke?" Luc asked. "You think Eisenhower would send bombers deep behind enemy lines for fun?"

"No, no, that's not what I'm saying at all," Jacob said. "Obviously it was a specific target. Obviously there was a plan. I'm just saying we've been assuming it was a trial run for a larger bombing campaign either against the rail lines into Auschwitz, to cut off the trains bringing more people here, or a test run for actually bombing the main camps and especially the gas chambers and the crematoriums. But what if it wasn't? What if the target was the factory, and they got it, or thought they did, and that's that?"

"It certainly looks like that's the case, doesn't it?" Luc said. "It's been more than a month since Otto and Abe escaped, and there's still no rescue. I think we need to get word to Judah and Milos. It's time for them to move."

Jacob agreed. They discussed how best to contact the men, who lived in a different section of the camp. They deemed it best to send a message through Abby, via Josef. It was important that Jacob and Luc keep their distance, lest both teams be identified and rounded up by Von Strassen before either team could make their move.

Two days later, however, events took another turn for the worse. Luc received a coded message from Abby, which he immediately showed to Jacob. She said she had learned the Nazis were beginning the deportation of Hungarian Jews to Auschwitz. Hundreds of thousands were coming, and coming soon.

Jacob couldn't believe it. Until now, his and Luc's intelligence had said that the Hungarian Jews would start being moved in the summer—June at the earliest but more likely July. Now, however, if Abby's intel was correct, the calculus had drastically changed. It was only May. The Jews of Hungary were about to be shipped to their deaths earlier than anyone in the underground had expected.

Jacob and Luc sent another message to Fischer and Kopecký, informing them of the news and urging them to leave immediately.

Within days the trains from Hungary, filled with Jewish families, began arriving. They did not go to the original Auschwitz camp. They went straight into Birkenau, and day after day, Jacob and Luc watched thousands of men, women, and children step off the trains, leaving their luggage and personal possessions behind, and march straight into the gas chambers. There was no longer a selection process. No one went to the right. Everyone went to the left. Everyone was being exterminated.

Jacob was distraught. What had happened to Leszek? And what had happened to Steinberger and Frenkel? Had they, too, been captured and killed? If so, why hadn't word gotten back to them? Why weren't Hoess and Von Strassen flaunting the news in front of their prisoners? Yet if their two friends had truly escaped successfully, hadn't they gotten back to their homeland of Czechoslovakia? Hadn't they warned the Jewish council? Hadn't word been sent to the chief rabbi in Budapest? If so, why were all these Jews coming so silently and compliantly, like sheep to the slaughter?

Then, on May 27, the sirens went off again. The troops and dogs were deployed again. The manhunt began all over again. Judah Fischer and Milos Kopecký were finally on the run.

On June 1, when the manhunt was over, Jacob gambled with his own life and with Luc's. Rather than avoid contact like they had agreed, Jacob decided he absolutely had to see Luc. So he ducked into the bakery that afternoon and pulled Luc into the back room.

"You shouldn't be here," Luc said, his face pale. "We agreed not to see each other for ten days. It's only been five. It's too soon. If they catch us, they'll kill us."

"We cannot wait any longer," Jacob replied. "We need to move now."

"That's crazy," Luc said. "We need to stick to our plan, and you need to get out of here immediately."

Jacob glanced over his shoulder to make sure the workroom door was still closed and that the Czechs in the kitchen couldn't hear them. Then he turned back to the French pastor and pressed his case.

"Listen to me, Luc," he whispered. "We're out of time. Every day more and more Jews arrive from Hungary. Every day more and more of them are gassed and thrown into the ovens. What are we going to do? Wait another month? Hope against hope that Otto and Abe are still alive and the Allies are coming? Hope against hope that Judah and Milos won't be caught and will be able to do what Leszek couldn't do, what no one seems to have done yet—actually get word to the Hungarian Jews and convince them not to get on those trains? We can't wait. We need to get out now, while Von Strassen and his men are still trying to figure out what's just happened and before they do something to change their security procedures and make it impossible for us to escape."

"No, Jacob—we have a plan, and now we have to follow it," Luc said. "We are not free agents. We are men under orders. Our commanders have a plan. It's our job to follow it to the letter, not second-guess them."

But Jacob adamantly disagreed. "History will never forgive us if we don't move now." Jacob was scarcely able to believe how much he had changed in recent months, how full of conviction he had become and how willing to argue his case so forcefully. "I, for one, will never forgive myself. I'm not saying we'll get out alive. And even if we do, I'm not saying we'll make it to Žilina, much less to London or Washington. I'm not saying if we do get there, we'll succeed in persuading anyone as to the atrocities that are really happening here. Maybe the Jewish council in Hungary will listen; maybe they won't. Maybe your grandfather will believe us and help us persuade Roosevelt; maybe he won't. But we have to try. We can't just sit on our hands and be passive. We have to move. We have to act. We have to do whatever we can to save these Jews. Events have been set into motion that cannot be undone. The liquidation of Hungarian Jews is happening as we speak. A month from now, it could all be over. That's half a million Jews or more. And then what will we say? What will we say if Hitler kills another half-million Jews and you and I just sat here saying, 'We have a plan; we have to stick to it'?"

Luc stood and began pacing the room. "I need more time," he said. "I need to pray about it. Give me another few days."

"No," Jacob said emphatically. "You must give me an answer now. Or tomorrow I leave alone."

"You can't do that," Luc said, showing a flash of anger for the first time since Jacob had met him. "We have a deal."

"The deal has changed. If you don't come, I'll bring Josef or Abby."

"You can't wait another two or three days?"

"That's another four or five thousand dead Jews, minimum," Jacob said. "Besides, I just heard something very disturbing from Josef."

"What?"

"The workers have almost finished another row of barracks in Birkenau-III. By the end of the week, they'll be starting the last row, which means they'll start using the lumber pile where our hideout is. If we don't go tomorrow, we may not have a way out."

The two men stared at each other for several tense moments before Luc finally conceded that his younger partner was right. They had no choice.

"Okay, I'm with you," he said at last. "You're right. We can leave tomorrow. I'll be ready if you are. Can you put the backpack in the woodpile this afternoon?"

Jacob considered that. "I don't know. There are a lot of guards out there now. But I'll try. Either way, I'll see you tomorrow at two o'clock sharp. Don't be late."

71

JUNE 1, 1944

Jacob stood outside the medical clinic.

He was too nervous to enter. He had come to say thank you and good-bye to Abigail Cohen. In his heart, he wanted to say more than that, but he didn't see how. Though he was still loath to admit it to anyone, he had developed feelings for her, feelings deeper than those he'd secretly harbored for Naomi Silver back in Siegen for so many years. That was merely a schoolboy crush, he knew. This was something else. But there was nothing he could do about such feelings. He didn't really understand them. The fact was, he was embarrassed to have them.

In twenty-four hours he would be gone—or dead. He couldn't take Abby with him. Likely he would never see her again, even if the Allies did come to liberate the camps rather than bomb them.

Jacob could read the handwriting on the wall. He knew the liberation of Auschwitz-Birkenau was a long shot at best. It was possible, therefore—indeed, perhaps even likely—that Abigail Cohen would not live to see the end of 1944.

The more such thoughts rushed through his mind, the more uncomfortable he felt about going inside. But he couldn't simply stand outside, staring at the front door. It wasn't safe, and he still had so much else to do.

The moment he entered, he knew it had been a mistake to come. His mouth went dry. His face and neck started to turn red, like they had the first day he had met her. His palms began to perspire and he could barely make eye contact with her, but before he knew it, she was calling him over to her.

"Oh yes, Mr. Eliezer, I have the medicines you requested," she said, a bit louder than she had to, as she motioned him to come around the counter and into a supply room behind the main desk.

Jacob followed and saw a large box of supplies waiting for him. He was perplexed. He hadn't told her he was coming. He certainly had not requested any supplies. Yet there they were. Why?

Suddenly the door closed behind him. As he turned to face her, Abby moved close to him and hugged him tightly. The warmth of her body against his was intoxicating, as was the softness of her cheek against the scratchy stubble of his unshaven face. After a moment, she leaned back a bit, still holding him around the waist but now looking deeply into his eyes. He was surprised to find her eyes filling with tears.

"Good-bye, Jacob," she whispered in a voice at once intimate and pained.

Jacob was caught off guard. "How did you know?" he asked.

"Josef told me it would be soon," she replied. "He could see it coming. Honestly, I didn't really think you'd come to see me again. I'm glad you did. I wanted to see you."

"You did?" A thousand different thoughts swirled through his head, yet he was hard-pressed to understand a single one of them, much less articulate any of them to her.

"Here," she said. "I have something for you."

She pulled a small package from the pocket of her crisp, white nurse's uniform. It was wrapped in brown paper and tied with a piece of string.

"What's this?" he asked as she handed it to him.

"Just a little going-away present," Abby said. "Promise me you'll open it the first night you're really free, okay?"

"Of course," he said, deeply moved by her gesture of kindness. "What is it?"

"That will be the fun part," she whispered. "Something to look forward to. Something just between you and me. But don't open it until you're free, okay?"

"I promise."

"Good."

"Thank you, Abby," Jacob replied. "Whatever it is, I'll treasure it and the memory of your kindness to me."

Now it was Abigail's turn to blush.

"You probably think I didn't bring you anything," he said. But to her visible surprise, he reached into his pocket and pulled out a small, brown leather diary.

"I'm sorry I didn't wrap it. I didn't think of that part."

"That's okay," Abby said, taking the journal in her hands and smelling the leather. "Oh, goodness—it's real."

"Yes."

"Where did you get it?"

"I lifted it from Canada soon after I started working there," he said. "It was going to be a diary of everything that happened here, but I just couldn't."

"Couldn't what?"

"I couldn't write any of it down. I didn't want to remember anything. So I started to write poems."

"Poems? Really?"

Jacob shrugged. "I loved reading poetry growing up. My mom got me started. And after I met you, well, I started writing some of my own. They're not very good. And no one's ever read them. But—I don't know—I just, well, thought I'd give them to you. Feel free to throw them away if you don't like them. I—I'm sorry. I know it sounds kind of foolish. But . . ."

His voice trailed off. He had already said too much.

"No, it's not foolish," she said, looking back into his eyes. "It's sweet, just like you." She leaned forward and kissed him gently on the lips. "Thank you, Jacob."

For a moment, Jacob stared at the floor, unable to hold her gaze. But then, with an uncharacteristic flash of confidence, he looked up and half smiled. "Thank you, Abby. I'll never forget you."

His voice caught. He was overcome with embarrassment. He hugged her once more, then fled the room, his heart racing.

72

That night, Jacob lay in bed and stared at the ceiling.

Unable to sleep, he wanted to just think about Abby and replay their last conversation in his head again and again. But he wouldn't let himself. Not now. He had to stay focused.

Jacob carefully reviewed his mental checklist. Had he done everything he was supposed to? Had he paid attention to every tiny detail? Had he dotted every i and crossed every t? The backpack was now in place—that was the most important thing. It was filled not only with all the supplies he had gathered but with bread and carrots and apples and even several hunks of cheese that Luc had been able to obtain over the past several days.

Most important of all, the backpack contained a metal box that was filled with all manner of details about Auschwitz-Birkenau. It contained precise maps of the camps, detailing exactly what each building was and how it was used. It contained schematic plans of the gas chambers themselves. Also in there were handwritten copies of critical documents from the records office listing all the trains that had ever arrived, where they had originated from, how many prisoners were on each train, and how many of the prisoners were sent to the left and how many to the right. There were carefully copied pages from the official ledgers detailing how many Jews had been killed and in what manner, as well as how many political prisoners had been killed and the nature of their deaths. There were three actual labels from canisters of Zyklon B gas. There was even an empty canister with its label still attached.

It had taken more than two months to collect all these materials. It had been Jacob's idea, and he had gathered much of it himself, using Luc and Josef and Abby and their various contacts throughout the camps. They had begged, bribed, and cajoled to get every item. They hadn't been able to pull everything together in time for Steinberger and Frenkel. But the package was ready now. The problem was they had only one. They didn't have packages to send out with future teams of escapees. That put even more pressure on Jacob and Luc not only to get out of the camp safely but to get all the way to London and Washington. So much was riding on their escape. It absolutely had to work.

Jacob was now more certain than ever that the only way to convince the leaders of the Jewish councils in Czechoslovakia and Hungary and ultimately the Allies of what was really happening inside Auschwitz-Birkenau was to have hard evidence of genocide, not simply eyewitness accounts, as compelling as those were. Luc had been stunned when he first laid eyes on the strongbox and the complete set of treasures it contained. This was exactly what they needed, he told Jacob. Luc said he was humbled and honored to be entrusted with the task of getting this evidence to the proper authorities on the outside. It was, Luc agreed, vital that they have rock-solid proof of the terrible crimes that Hoess and Von Strassen and the others were committing—proof he could give to his grandfather, proof his grandfather could give to President Roosevelt.

They were ready. They had everything they needed. And now the day of reckoning had arrived.

As the sun began to rise and the barracks began to stir, Jacob realized he had not slept a wink. He knew he should have, and he had genuinely tried. It simply was not possible.

One way or the other, he and Jean-Luc Leclerc were leaving Auschwitz-Birkenau today.

And not by the chimneys.

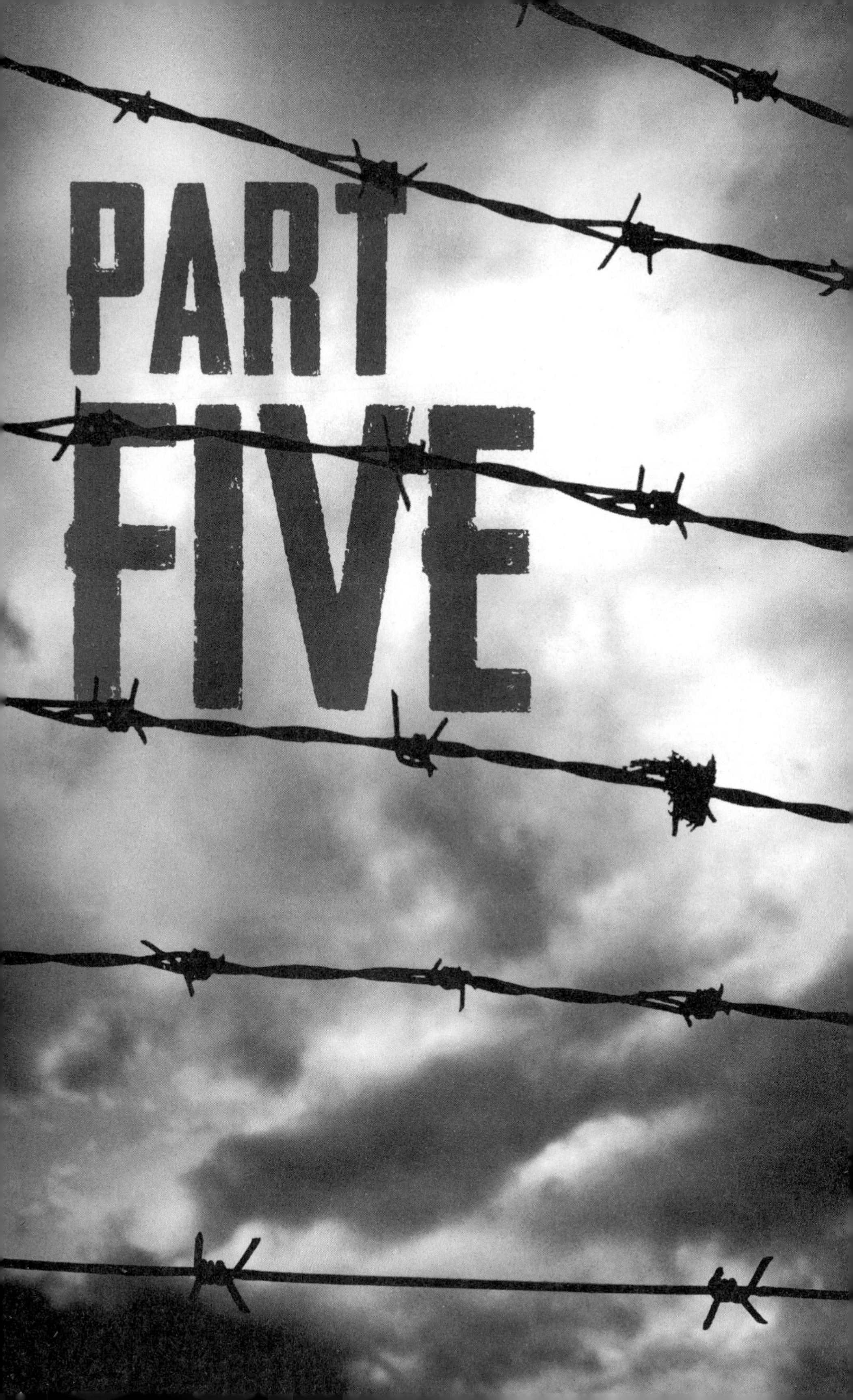
PART
FIVE

73

JUNE 2, 1944

It was already six minutes after two o'clock.

Jacob was late. He was caught in a ridiculous conversation with his block senior about some paperwork the records office said was not filled out correctly, and he could not seem to get out of it. He promised his block senior he would correct the paperwork later that day. But he simultaneously insisted that he had some supplies he was supposed to deliver to some guards out on one of the construction sites on behalf of the men in their block, and he really needed to get that taken care of before they got angry.

"Supplies?" his senior asked. "What kind of supplies?"

"Gloves," Jacob said. "Brown leather gloves. They're very particular. So may I go now?"

"Why don't they get their own gloves?" the senior asked skeptically.

"They're lazy bums; what can I say?" Jacob said. "But when I took water out to the men yesterday, the guards insisted I bring them more gloves. I was supposed to take them before lunch, but I ran out of time. I really need to go."

"Let me see them," the senior demanded, grabbing for the package under Jacob's arm.

Jacob froze. What was this all about? Why all the questions? Why the suspicion? And why today?

Fortunately, the package under his arm really was filled with brown leather gloves. Josef had smuggled them out of Canada for him. Actually, Josef had been willing to smuggle out items far more valuable than gloves. After all, these guards had to be mollified at any cost, especially today. But all that these Nazi thugs had wanted were brown leather gloves, so brown leather gloves it was.

Jacob tried not to imagine what would have happened if his block senior had been this nosy about the large crate he had "taken to the men" the day before. That crate had actually contained the backpack with all of their supplies. Had his block senior inquired about the contents of the crate instead of these gloves, Jacob would now be swinging from a beam with a rope around his neck. Maybe there really was a God.

"Very well, carry on," the block senior said at last, satisfied that Jacob was telling the truth. "But get me some too."

"Uh . . . sure . . . of course. What color?" Jacob stammered.

"Black, like the commandant wears," the senior said. "Can you get me a pair like that?"

"I don't know, but I can try," Jacob lied. "Might take a few days. Is that okay?"

"Fine, just do it," the senior ordered, then waved him off.

Jacob turned and moved quickly out the door of the barracks without pause and without looking back. Only when he was several hundred yards away from the barracks did he begin to relax. Still, he was late, and he knew Luc and Josef must be nearing panic.

Clipboard under his arm, and making sure he had the requisite countenance of a registrar—busy and bothered and harried, as usual—Jacob finally reached the checkpoint and waited for the guards to let him pass. But they, too, began to harass him. They asked at least a dozen questions about why he kept going out to the construction site when he wasn't on a construction detail. When he said he was keeping an eye on the men in his block, on the direct orders of his block senior, they demanded to know the name of his senior and why the kapo in charge of the detail wasn't supervision enough. They searched his package, of course, coveted the gloves, and confiscated two pairs for themselves.

There was nothing Jacob could do. There was no point in protesting, certainly not today. So he tried to be patient even though he could see the watch on one of the guards' wrists.

It now was nearly two thirty.

Minutes went by, and the guards seemed in no mind to let him pass. Then, all of a sudden, they let him go. He hadn't done or said anything differently. Nothing else had happened out of the ordinary. It was simply as though someone had thrown a switch and changed their minds. It was a curious moment. And then another curious thought crossed his mind. Luc was praying for him. Maybe Abby was too.

Jacob shook off the thought and told himself to stay focused. He didn't need his head filled with all kinds of hocus-pocus today of all days. He needed to do his job and be careful about every little detail.

He passed out of the main Birkenau camp, through the double electrified fences, and onto the path to Birkenau-III. Once through, he walked as rapidly as he could for the guard hut. Though he wanted to run, he knew full well it was *verboten* to run outside the fences. It was an automatic death sentence, no questions asked. A few brown leather gloves would be no help in such a scenario. The best he could do now was walk briskly, so that's what he did.

Five minutes later he arrived at the hut, knowing he was going to get an earful from the four guards who expected a pair of gloves each. Sure enough, they exploded. Two of them, anyway. The first two grabbed their gloves and put them on. The other two were livid. Jacob tried to explain what had happened, that the guards at the gate had taken some of them, but they wouldn't listen. They ranted and raved and spewed obscenities at him, and one of them grabbed him and slammed him against the wall of the hut.

For a moment Jacob forgot about the escape mission. He began to fear for his life. He knew fellow prisoners who had been beaten by guards for far less serious infractions than this. He apologized profusely.

He pleaded with the men to let him go. He promised on his mother's grave that he would get more gloves and bring them first thing in the morning, as soon as roll call was finished. Finally this seemed to mollify them, if only temporarily.

"You will be here with the gloves first thing tomorrow, and no excuses," one said, spitting as he fumed. "Otherwise I will smash your skull with my boot. And if you don't show, I will hunt you down and kill you in your sleep. Don't think I won't. You hear me?"

Jacob nodded.

"Do . . . you . . . hear . . . me?" the guard shouted in his face.

"Yes, sir. Absolutely, sir," Jacob replied, nodding and trembling and not entirely sure they were really going to let him go.

But they did, and he bolted out of the hut. He didn't dare go straight to the woodpile, even though it was now almost 2:45 p.m. He was terrified that he was being watched, so he started walking along the path back to the main gate, back to the main camp. Then, glancing over his shoulder and convinced the guards weren't watching—at least not at that split second—he ducked inside one of the newly built barracks, came out the other side, and doubled back around to the lumber pile where his friends were waiting.

He could see the intense anxiety etched on the faces of Luc and Josef. He knew they could see the fear on his face as well. There was no time to ask questions about their day, and there was no point in their asking about his. They were behind schedule and scared, and they had to get moving. So with a quick glance around, Josef scrambled to the top of the pile, just as Jacob had done for Steinberger and Frenkel. Once up there, Josef pushed aside the top few boards that created the roof of the hideout and pulled Luc up with him. They glanced around again and saw that the coast was clear, and Luc dropped into the hole and out of sight. Then Josef helped Jacob up, and he dropped into position too.

"Thank you, Josef," Jacob said as his friend replaced the boards over their heads. "Now, remember all I told you. Take your first chance to get out too."

"Thank you. I will—you can count on it," Josef replied as he sprinkled dried tobacco over the top of the lumber and then jumped down to sprinkle more around the base. "Godspeed, boys. We're counting on you."

The words echoed in Jacob's ears and in his heart. His dearest friends in the world were counting on them to succeed. Indeed, the entire camp was. Though almost none of the thousands upon thousands of prisoners around them knew it, their very lives depended in no small measure on what Jacob Weisz and Jean-Luc Leclerc did next.

It was a tremendous honor, yet a daunting responsibility, and Jacob didn't dare let them down.

74

It was an odd hiding place.

It was not simply a normal pile of lumber. Yes, there were several layers of two-by-fours on top, but underneath those was a stack of six prefabricated hut sections. There were six frames, six sets of doors, and six sets of wall panels. Normally they would have been positioned in such a way that there was very little space between the various pieces. In this case, they had been arranged to allow for two average-size men to lie down side by side or to stand nearly erect in the space between the hut sections. Before arriving, Jacob had assumed it would be sufficient. But now he found it more cramped than he had expected. It was also almost pitch-black, for the only sources of light were the tiny slivers coming through a few of the narrow crevices between the boards.

Jacob and Luc had decided ahead of time that they would not say a single word to one another from the time Josef closed them inside till the moment they could be certain the manhunt had been called off. Theoretically, Von Strassen and his team could keep hunting for longer than the seventy-two hours mandated by the camp regulations, but being Germans, they went by the rule book. If the field manual said seventy-two hours, then they would conduct their manhunt for seventy-two hours and not a minute more.

That said, the next roll call would begin at seven. It would probably be around seven thirty before they were discovered missing. They figured, therefore, that the manhunt would begin at or around 8 p.m. It would continue until 8 p.m. on Monday, June 5. But though the hunt would officially be over at that point, there would still be plenty of daylight, especially with summer approaching and the days growing longer. That's why Steinberger and Frenkel had added another few hours to their time in the hole, deciding not to leave their hiding spot until two in the morning.

Personally, Jacob felt comfortable leaving the hideout at midnight. That would be well after everyone in the camp except for just a few night watchmen would be fast asleep. But Luc was insistent that they stick with Steinberger and Frenkel's approach. All told, it added up to about eighty-four hours.

They would endeavor not to talk or make any sound during all that time. After all, they couldn't really see who, if anyone, might be walking near the lumber pile at any given moment, and they didn't dare take the risk of being overheard. So they went into silent mode.

Still, there were things they needed to do quickly, before the evening roll call began. The first task was to change clothes. Jacob had noticed the two sets of camp uniforms lying on the ground when he dropped into the hole—mementos of Otto and Abe's stay almost two months earlier. He was glad the two had left their uniforms behind, for it gave him and Luc something relatively clean and dry to lie down on. Unfortunately, it did little to insulate the men from the ground, which was colder than Jacob had anticipated.

It was challenging to change clothes in the dark. Jacob went first. As quietly as possible, he opened the backpack and felt around for his clothes. He had positioned his set on top to minimize confusion. First, however, he pulled two watches out of the side pocket of the backpack, gave one to Luc, and put the other on his own wrist. The phosphorescent dials allowed them to see the time at any moment, day or night, and they made sure both were in sync. It was precisely 3:07. They were in business.

Next Jacob stripped off his zebra-striped uniform and removed his cap and wooden clogs and set them aside. Then he put on a black undershirt, a dark-blue button-down work shirt, and khaki trousers with a leather belt already threaded through the belt loops. Over the shirt he pulled on a thick black knit sweater and a black knit cap. Then he located the jacket Josef had found for him at Canada and put that on as well. Last of all he donned a fresh pair of clean black socks and brown leather walking shoes.

He couldn't believe how good it felt to be wearing fresh, clean clothes, and the sweater and jacket over the top felt wonderful as well. He could not remember when he had last felt so insulated from the cold and so comfortable in his own skin. Already he could feel his psychology changing ever so slightly. He couldn't wait for the hours to pass and for the two of them to finally be free. What would that feel like? Jacob wondered. What would it really feel like to be breathing free air?

When he was finished changing, Jacob lay down on his stomach on one of the uniforms that had been left behind and tried to stay quiet and motionless while Luc went through the same process. Again, it was challenging to maneuver in such tight quarters and to do so quietly, but Luc finished quickly.

Then they rooted around for the bag of petrol-soaked Russian tobacco that Josef had pre-positioned for them and found it lying in the corner. They sprinkled the nasty-smelling concoction all around the base of their little fort and in all the crevices they could find. Now they were covered inside and outside of their hideout. Jacob silently prayed this really would throw off the dogs, who were sure to come in full force in just a few short hours.

When this was done, there were two more things for them to do. The first was to take a few hunks of bread out of the backpack along with two small metal canteens of water and set the provisions between the two of them. The second was for each of them to take a few necessary precautions against sneezing and coughing. Jacob went first, tying a strip of cloth around his head, just over his nose. The way he fixed it around the back of his head gave him the ability to tighten or loosen the cloth without much trouble. If he had the sudden urge to sneeze over the next three days, he was to tighten the cloth in an attempt to prevent the sneeze from happening. For the rest of the time, however, he could keep it loose.

He also took a fresh, clean handkerchief out of the backpack and held it in his left hand, where it would stay. If he needed to cough, he was first to take a small sip of water from his canteen and then stuff the handkerchief in his mouth in the hopes of stifling it or at least muffling the sound. It might have looked ridiculous, but fortunately he couldn't see himself or Luc. And who knew—it might just save their lives.

Finally Jacob fished through the nearly empty backpack for the Swiss Army knife. Before he found it, he felt wrapping paper and a string tied in a bow around a small package. Abby's gift to him was safe, and he couldn't wait to open it. He wondered if she had already begun to read his poems.

A moment later, he found the knife and slipped it into his jacket pocket. He, for one, was not going to be taken alive. If he was found by the Nazis, he was never going to give them the satisfaction of torturing him or hanging him. He was going to slash his wrists and then plunge the knife into his heart. He didn't want to die. The truth was he was very scared of dying. But he wasn't going to let the Nazis win.

That was the one argument he'd had with Luc after inviting the French pastor to be his partner in this escape mission. They had discussed worst-case scenarios, and Jacob had explained his position—the same all the men who had gone before them had taken. Luc, however, had said he refused to commit suicide. It was against God's way, he said, and it was nonnegotiable.

Jacob had agreed; it *was* nonnegotiable. If Luc didn't promise to commit suicide if caught and thus prevent the naming of other Resistance members throughout the camp, then he couldn't be part of the mission.

"So be it," Luc had said, unwilling to compromise his core religious convictions.

But Steinberger and Frenkel had overruled Jacob, telling him he could not make willingness to commit suicide if caught a precondition of Luc's participation in this mission. In the end Jacob had backed down to Luc's convictions, and that was that.

Now, as Luc completed his own preparations, he lay down on his stomach as well. Using his watch dial for a bit of light, Luc motioned to their canteens and pantomimed removing the metal tops and then leaning the canteens against the side of the enclosure. They didn't make much noise unscrewing them, but they made a little. Better to make that noise now than later, when the manhunt would be in full swing. Just that little bit could mean all the difference between getting caught and breaking free.

Then, to Jacob's surprise, they were done with all their preparations. All was quiet. Jacob glanced at his watch. It was only 3:23. They had just over three and a half hours before roll call, and then the real mayhem would begin.

Jacob told himself he should close his eyes and get some sleep, but that was impossible. He was already terrified that a Nazi patrol would be able to hear his heart pounding in his chest. And despite the coolness, he was sweating profusely. What was worse, he was beginning to feel claustrophobic.

He looked at his watch again. It was 3:24.

How in the world was he going to make it for eighty-three and a half more hours?

75

For the first time in forever, Jacob had too much time on his hands.

He couldn't remember the last time he had hours with nothing to do but think, but whenever it was, it not only predated his arrival at Auschwitz, it predated his time in Belgium, too. Indeed, lying on the cold, hard ground on his stomach like this made him think back to days long ago when his uncle was trying to teach him to hunt.

How he wished he now held the walnut-wood stock of a Mauser carbine rifle in his hands. Jacob no longer feared such power—the power to shatter, to wound, to take a man's life. Now he understood what Avi had been trying to teach him. The Jews of Europe had been foolish to entrust their safety and security to anyone but themselves. What if they had been organized? What if they had been armed and trained and mobilized? No one could have sent them to concentration camps to perish by the hundreds of thousands. Perhaps they would have died defending themselves, but wouldn't that have been better than this?

At the time, Jacob had not understood. That, however, was no longer true. What Avi had told him about King Solomon had been right. There *was* a time for every activity under the sun. A time to give birth and a time to die. A time to kill and a time to heal. A time for war and a time for peace. It was not for a man to choose his times, but he had to be ready when they came. Jacob had not been ready before. Now he was.

Jacob could feel his heart beating wildly in his chest. Try as he might, he could not entirely control his breathing. But this wasn't fear any longer. Not entirely. It was mostly anticipation. He desperately wanted to be free, and not just for his own sake. He couldn't wait to reach the Jewish leaders in Czechoslovakia and Hungary. He couldn't wait to meet with the Allied leaders in London and Washington. Jacob had spent all his life too timid to speak. But now he had something to say, and he was determined to say it.

As Jacob thought about the trajectory of all that he had seen and heard and witnessed and experienced over the past six years or so, he was struck by the counterintuitive manner of his response. The worse things got, the stronger he had become. Back when times were relatively good, he had been so shy he could hardly speak. But now, trapped in hell, he had come to life and found his voice. He wasn't entirely sure how that had happened, but he wished his parents had been around to see it, and Ruthie, and Avi most of all. He wondered if they would be proud of him. He hoped so.

Where were they now?

He lay there quiet and still, mulling that thought. It was a painful question to ask. Almost physically painful. Because he had no answers.

Josef was certainly sure he had all the answers. He didn't believe in an afterlife. He said he was a man of science and an atheist. He claimed that no right-thinking scholar could believe in fanciful notions of heaven or hell. According to Josef, life was like a candle. When the flame was blown out, that was it. You ceased to exist. There was no more.

Max, by contrast, had been a deeply religious man. He had no doubt there was a God who had created the heavens and the earth and all the people therein. As he prattled on and on during their workdays in the Canada command, it was clear Max had no flicker of doubt whatsoever as to whether there was an afterlife or not. Of course there was.

These were the only two people Jacob had ever discussed such matters with, he realized as he lay there. He certainly had never discussed religion with Steinberger or Frenkel. There had been too much else to cover when they were together. Nor had he talked about life and death and the mysteries of the universe with the guys in Belgium or the Czechs in the bakery or even with Luc, who by all accounts was very religious.

He wished he could have discussed religion with Abby. Other than her few fleeting comments in the exam room, they had never had the time or opportunity, but he was certain he would have liked those conversations. To Jacob, Abby was not just a stunning beauty. She was a thoughtful, insightful, intuitive person. She had depth and purpose. He could see it in her eyes; they were full of life and hope, and the more he thought about it, the more he realized that was why he was so drawn to her.

Jacob thought about the gift she had given him, and his anticipation to open it surged. He was honored that she had wanted to give him anything at all. They had barely spent time together, and yet somehow they had made a connection that Jacob savored and found himself pondering. He wondered what she was doing at that moment. Whatever it was, he knew she was thinking about him, and that quickened something deep inside him. Of all the people in the world, he was the one person in Abby Cohen's thoughts right now—and in her prayers, too. Like her brother, Max, Abby believed in stuff like that. And in the stillness of the moment, Jacob found himself hoping she was right. He wanted there to be a God who was loving and kind and whom you could talk to and who would answer you. He wanted there to be a God to whom he could pray for Abby to be safe and protected from all harms. He wanted to believe. He just didn't know if he could.

Jacob closed his eyes and reimagined the kiss she had given him to say good-bye. He relished the things she had whispered in his ear and the way she had held him. He hadn't expected any of that. He would have been happy just to have had the chance to lay eyes on her one more time, to tell her thank you, maybe shake her hand. He still couldn't quite believe how happy she had been to see him.

Life had a funny way of surprising him. Just when he thought good things were coming, the opposite came true. And just when he thought bad things were coming, something good happened instead. It made him not want to think too much about the future. Or maybe he should always just expect the worst. Most often he would be right, and the few times he was not, at least he would be pleasantly surprised.

The more he thought about Abby, the quieter his pounding heart became. The heavier his eyelids grew.

And before he knew it, he had fallen asleep.

76

JUNE 2, 1944

The screaming of the sirens shocked Jacob awake.

Pure adrenaline rushed through his system. All his senses were on full alert. Luc put a hand on his back as if to say everything was going to be okay. Jacob hoped he was right.

Jacob checked his watch. It was 7:29, a little earlier than he would have predicted. More than fifty-five thousand Birkenau prisoners were all assembled for the evening roll call, and Jacob could picture the scene. He envisioned Josef standing at attention with his block, holding his breath, hoping the trail would not lead back to him, hoping no one had seen him spending so much time with the fugitives. Jacob could see soldiers mobilizing, running with machine guns, shouting orders, cursing, deployed for the hunt. He could hear hundreds of dogs barking, running, sniffing, searching in every nook and cranny of the camp, though most of them would now be deployed to the enormous manhunt outside the camp.

For the first twenty or thirty minutes, the drama seemed quite a ways away. But now Jacob could hear soldiers approaching, running and shouting commands. The dogs were getting closer. Lorries were driving by, filled, he could only assume, with men and weapons. Von Strassen's theory, so the rumor went, was that he and his men had spent too much time checking hiding places inside the camp on previous manhunts. The new goal was to deploy forces a good forty kilometers out and then work backward toward the Auschwitz-Birkenau perimeter. It might take a little longer, but it meant escapees wouldn't have as clear a path to freedom as they had had in the past.

Now Jacob could hear several units of soldiers flooding the Birkenau-III camp along with their dogs. He felt a tickle in his throat. All the commotion around them was kicking up an awful lot of dust, and the dust was pouring into their hideaway. He began to panic, terrified that he was about to sneeze. He took a quick sip of water, tightened the cloth around his nose, and put the handkerchief in his mouth. But now the dogs were right on top of them. They were growling and barking as they sniffed the lumber pile. A moment later, someone was scrambling on top of the pile. Before Jacob knew it, someone began taking a piece of lumber off the top.

Jacob pulled the Swiss Army knife from his pocket and opened the blade.

Just then shots were fired close to the main camp. There was a commotion and lots of shouting, and suddenly all the troops and dogs that had been right on top of them and about to find them were gone. Jacob could still hear all kinds of activity out there, but the center of the hunt was quickly shifting to the east, and Jacob and Luc began to breathe again.

As the hours passed, more gunfire could be heard, but not from outside the camp. It came from behind them, inside the camp, and Jacob knew exactly what was happening. Men dropping from exhaustion were being shot in the head.

Jacob felt overwhelmed by guilt, and he was sure Luc was feeling the same thing. It was hard not to think of it as their fault. Innocent men were suffering—dying—just to give them the chance to go free.

Jacob tried not to count the shots, but he couldn't help it. It was up to twenty-three. And now twenty-four.

77

Von Strassen could hear his superior screaming obscenities all the way across the courtyard.

Suddenly a lamp came flying through one of Hoess's office windows, smashing on the ground right in front of Von Strassen, along with a shower of shattered glass. When he raced up the stairs and finally reached the anteroom outside of Hoess's office, the typically unflappable Nazi officer felt physically ill as he listened to the full-throated tirade under way behind the door.

Hoess had become completely unhinged. Though no longer the camp commandant—that post now belonged to Arthur Liebehenschel—Hoess had been brought back to Auschwitz specifically to oversee the Hungarian operation, which was proceeding smoothly except for these recent unaccountable escapes. As chief security officer, it was Von Strassen's job to keep the prisoners under control, and he was failing miserably.

Hoess was screaming at someone and threatening to have heads removed from shoulders by sunup. Von Strassen wondered who was taking the man's wrath, but he found out soon enough. Suddenly the door opened and two of the young women who worked under Von Strassen came out, sobbing uncontrollably. They rushed past their boss without even acknowledging his presence.

"You!" Hoess fumed when he saw Von Strassen. "Get in this room!"

The colonel obeyed, then shut the door behind him and stood at attention to take his dressing-down like a man.

"How could you have let this happen?" Hoess raged, his face turning ever-darker shades of red, curses spewing out of his mouth in every other sentence. "Four prisoners in a week? Six prisoners in two months? Shall we just open the gates and let them all walk out? Is that your plan, Colonel Von Strassen?"

"Sir, I realize—"

"Shut up!" Hoess screamed. "How dare you open your mouth to me! Do you know how enraged *der Führer* is? He wants my head on a platter. But if you think I will go down for this, think again. You will find these men. You will capture them alive. You will personally escort them into this office and then you will watch me execute them—or it will be your head on a platter I send to Berlin."

78

Thunder rumbled overhead.

The winds picked up, and soon it was raining. It was a light rain at first, but it intensified in the wee hours of the morning. And it was cold.

The gunshots continued, accelerated even, punctuating the night with guilt and shame. Fifty-six so far. Fifty-seven.

Jacob tried to imagine the look on his block senior's face when Jacob's number had come up as one of the missing. He must have told the guards that Jacob had spent much of the day in Birkenau-III. Had they believed him? Or had they thought he was part of the conspiracy? For the first time Jacob wondered if perhaps they had tortured him. Maybe they had even shot him already.

Then he thought of the Czechs who worked at the bakery. Certainly Von Strassen and his men were tearing the bakery apart. So far as Jacob knew, he and Luc had left no clues. The Czechs had never had an inkling of what was going on. They were good men, and Luc had been insistent that they be insulated from any retaliation. But at this point, who knew what was happening? With so many escapes in just a matter of days, Jacob realized that Von Strassen's own job could be in jeopardy. Perhaps even his life.

Jacob hoped that as the hours passed, a buzz would sweep through the camp, a wave of hope that two more of their comrades had escaped and not yet been caught. He knew Josef was rooting for them, and Abby, of course. He hoped others were too, wondering, *Could they really make it? Might they tell the world our story and come back to set us free?*

That's how he had felt when Leszek and the others escaped and again when Steinberger and Frenkel broke away. It had given him hope, and even a shred of hope, he had discovered, was a powerful force.

A watched pot never boils.

It was something his mother used to say. Now, as Jacob stared at his watch, he could hear her whispering to him that time would never pass this way. *Go to sleep,* she told him. *You have a very hard journey ahead of you. You need your rest.*

Luc began to snore. Startled that his partner could fall asleep at such a time as this, but even more frightened that someone might hear him, Jacob poked him in the ribs—not enough to wake him, just enough to get him to shift from sleeping on his back. The snoring stopped, and Jacob's pulse began to normalize. As for him, he simply could not sleep while fifty-five thousand other souls were standing and groaning in the wind and the rain.

Somewhere out there, he knew Abby was praying for everyone to be brave and strong and make it until the dawn. But where was God in all of this? Why didn't he just rain fire down from heaven on these wicked troops and consume them once and for all? Why didn't he shake the Third Reich with a devastating earthquake? Why didn't he just open up the earth and let Berlin fall into the fiery cauldrons below? How much longer must the innocent suffer? If God had really chosen the Jews as his special people, where was he now?

As day one turned into day two, the driving rains continued.

Water was seeping in through various crevices, and Jacob again worried the smell of the Russian tobacco was being washed away. The ground was cold and damp, and even with all their extra clothing and the uniforms of Steinberger and Frenkel beneath them like sheets and their own uniforms on top of them like blankets, they were still cold and cramped.

On the second night, the foot patrols seemed to increase. There were more dogs in the area. More lorries drove past. It seemed to Jacob that the Nazis were carrying out a renewed and much more intense search of the Birkenau-III area.

A cramp was developing in both of Jacob's legs. He could hardly feel his toes. They were so cold they had become numb. He was desperate to stand, to stretch, to get the blood moving through his legs and feet and toes again, but that was impossible. With all the guards combing the area, he and Luc dared not move. But the pain was becoming unbearable.

Somehow, Jacob knew Luc was praying. There were moments when Jacob wished he, too, could believe in an all-knowing, all-loving God who was with them in that hideout, helping them, sustaining them in their darkest hour. But he couldn't. Try as he might, he just could not believe. Not with all that he had seen and experienced.

Instead of praying, he tried to keep his mind sharp by thinking about what they needed to do once these eighty hours were done, reviewing the things Steinberger and Frenkel had taught him before they left.

"Lesson one: trust nobody," Steinberger had insisted.

"Lesson two: don't be afraid of the Germans. There are many of them, but they can die just as quickly as anybody else.

"Lesson three: once you're out, don't trust your legs; a bullet can always run faster. Don't give them a chance to shoot. Rest by day; move by night.

"Lesson four: carry no money. If you're starving, you'll be tempted to buy food. If you've got no money, you can't. Live off the land. Keep away from people.

"Lesson five: travel light. You'll need a knife for hunting or for defending yourself or in case you're about to be captured. Don't let them take you alive. You'll need matches because you'll have to cook what you steal. You'll need salt because with salt and potatoes you can keep going for months. You'll need a watch so that you can time your journeys and make sure you're never caught in the open by day. You can use it as a compass, too."

Steinberger had learned these five lessons from Dmitri Volkov, the same Russian prisoner of war who taught him and Frenkel to throw off the tracker dogs using the dried tobacco soaked in petrol. "But only the Russian tobacco, remember," he had warned them. "I'm not being patriotic. It's the only stuff that works."

Volkov had also told them never to carry meat because it would draw the attention of the dogs. And he warned them never to let down their guard.

"Never forget," he said, "that the real fight only begins when you're away from the camp. Never relax so long as you're in enemy territory. Never get drunk with freedom, like I did outside Kiev, for you never know who is lying in the bushes."

79

JUNE 5, 1944

"Tell me what I want to hear," Hoess said.

Breathless, Von Strassen stepped into his commander's office and saluted with a *"Heil Hitler!"*

He took a deep breath, then admitted, "I'm afraid I cannot yet do that, sir." Von Strassen's breathing was rapid, and his voice trembled ever so slightly. "We have not found these two yet—Leonard Eliezer or Jean-Luc Leclerc—but we've completed our preliminary investigation. We know much more about who they are. Eliezer was a registrar. Leclerc ran the bakery. We've identified their workmates and associates. We're in the process of interrogating each of them as we speak. I am confident, sir, that we'll break them and find out what we need to know. Once we do, we'll have a better idea of where they are likely headed—probably eventually toward France, since that is where Leclerc is from—and we can radio ahead to units in that area to capture them and bring them back alive to be hanged in the courtyard."

"Hanged?" Hoess fumed. "You think I'm going to hang them? Never. I'm going to make an example of these two. We'll tie them up alive and put them into the ovens with the rest of the camp watching."

"Yes, sir," Von Strassen said. "Very good, sir. That will send a powerful message to all the prisoners."

Von Strassen then handed Hoess the file he was building on the investigation. Hoess opened it and quickly leafed through the typed reports and the handwritten notes. Von Strassen didn't wait. He explained to Hoess that "Leonard Eliezer, age twenty-two," was likely not the real identity of the escapee.

"In the course of the last three days, sir, we have come to believe that this Eliezer figure is actually a young man by the name of Jacob Weisz," Von Strassen explained. "A man named Avraham Weisz was a German Jew who was a leader in the underground movement, in Germany initially but then more extensively in Belgium. We believe Jacob Weisz is his nephew. Weisz's parents were shot by the Gestapo in the town of Siegen almost five years ago. Afterward, he was recruited by his uncle to join the underground. He was well trained in Belgium and was involved in the raid on train 801 last year near Brussels. During that raid, Avraham was shot and killed, and as best we can piece together, Jacob Weisz was accidentally caught in one of the cattle cars while trying to help prisoners escape. It was then, on the way here to Auschwitz, that Weisz assumed a new identity, that of Leonard Eliezer."

"You're saying we've had a trained member of the Resistance in our midst for over a year and we didn't know it?" Hoess asked, visibly incredulous.

"It would appear that way," Von Strassen admitted. "But I'm afraid it gets worse. Almost as soon as he arrived, Jacob Weisz linked up with Leszek Poczciwinski in the Canada command."

"You mean the Poczciwinski who escaped last year?"

"Yes, sir."

"Go on."

"Well, sir, you may recall that at the time, we arrested and interrogated several men who worked under Poczciwinski in Canada," Von Strassen continued. "Among them was a young man named Maximilian Cohen. Another was Leonard Eliezer, aka Jacob Weisz."

"We hanged Cohen."

"Yes, sir, we did. He never confessed to involvement in the plot, but it was clear he was lying. Unfortunately, I let Jacob Weisz go. He was new in the camp. He claimed he didn't know anything. I believed him.

I was wrong. Now we think it was Poczciwinski who was the head of the underground movement in the camp. One of the top leaders, at least. I now believe that Cohen, Weisz, Steinberger, and Frenkel were all associates of his. I have not yet ascertained whether they were all directly recruited by him or not. But given that they all were plotting to escape—and have done so successfully—I think we can safely assume they were conspiring together."

"And this Jean-Luc Leclerc," Hoess said, reading the name from a file. "What do we know about him?"

"At the moment, he's a mystery, sir. We don't know anything about him except his name, serial number, and country of origin."

"Why not?"

"Well, sir, his file is missing from our records. Actually, the files on all these men—except for Max Cohen—have disappeared. We seem to have, or have had, a mole in the records office. But my men have just pulled in for interrogation two prisoners who seem to have been connected to all of the men I just mentioned."

"Who are they?"

"One is a young woman, Abigail Cohen," Von Strassen said, pulling another file out of his briefcase and handing it over to his superior. "She's a nurse in the medical unit and the sister of Max Cohen."

Hoess looked through her file. "And the other?"

"His name is Josef Starwolski. He's a Polish Jew. Used to work in the records office. Was transferred a few months ago but still has close connections there."

"Where are they now?" Hoess asked, standing.

"They're in the pit, sir," Von Strassen replied. "I have not had the chance to personally interrogate them yet. My men have questioned them, but only briefly. But as you know, I just got back from leading the search effort. I am heading over there now."

"Your search is over?"

"It's about to end, sir. We are at the end of seventy-two hours. With your permission, I will bring the troops back. But this is by no means over, sir. I am convinced we can get information out of Cohen and Starwolski that will lead us to Weisz and Leclerc. I just need a little more time."

"Time?" Hoess asked. "You want more time? *Der Führer* is waiting personally for a call from me. Do you understand how little time we have to make this right?"

"Please, sir," Von Strassen begged. "I give you my word that I will catch these two."

"Your word means nothing to me, Colonel. Find them. Now."

80

JUNE 5, 1944

"Cordon down!"

Jacob could hear the soldiers shouting in the distance. The word was spreading. The manhunt was over. Jacob could hardly believe it. Somehow, seventy-two hours had actually passed. And they weren't dead yet.

Jacob rubbed his painful legs vigorously, trying again to get the blood moving. He shook his feet and bent his knees. But for now, it only seemed to make the pain increase, so he stopped. He looked at his watch. It was seven thirty in the evening of day three. As was their standard, the Nazis were right on time. They had searched for exactly three full days. They had come up empty. Now they were done.

He glanced over at Luc. The Frenchman nodded acknowledgment of the time and the circumstances. But it was clear from Luc's face that he, too, was in severe pain. Worse, his face was pale, and he was perspiring profusely.

Jacob felt his forehead. The man was burning up. He desperately needed cold water, which they did not have. He needed medicines, and they did not have any of those either.

They needed to get moving. In just the first full day of their intense anxiety and mind-numbing boredom, they had finished much of their limited supply of food and all of their water. Now they hadn't had anything to eat or drink in nearly two full days. They needed supplies, but they both knew they couldn't leave their hideout yet. They still had a few more hours to wait.

As the next few hours passed, Jacob could hear the lorries bringing troops back from the field and the dogs barking and the men chatting with one another. Then two men stopped directly beside their position. They lit up cigarettes and complained about how furious Von Strassen was about another two Jews escaping. Their German shepherd urinated on the woodpile, and soon they were gone.

Jacob smiled. He couldn't help himself. Von Strassen had no idea who Jean-Luc Leclerc was, not if he thought the man was Jewish.

Jacob was glad for the final favor he had asked of Josef. He had asked his Polish friend to sneak back into the records office, pull his file and Luc's—their official files with all their personal information—and destroy them. With everything else going on and the stress of those last few days, he had forgotten to follow up with Josef to see if he had been able to do it. It was risky, to be sure. But if it could be done, it would mean that all Von Strassen had right now were Jacob's and Luc's serial numbers, the ones tattooed on their forearms. If Josef had been successful, that meant Von Strassen did not have their names or their photographs or their personal histories or the names of their relatives or any description of their physical characteristics, except for whatever details they could force out of their block seniors and the men in their barracks.

Maybe Josef had done it. Maybe he hadn't. But if Von Strassen thought he was hunting for two Jews, perhaps that was a sign Josef had actually pulled off the minor coup. If so, Von Strassen was at a disadvantage. Then again, maybe he knew exactly who Jacob and Luc were and had just described them both as Jews to get the troops whipped up into a frenzied bloodlust.

There was no way to know for sure. The one thing Jacob was certain of was that with Luc becoming so ill, there was no way they were waiting until two in the morning to make their move. They needed as much darkness as possible to get as far away from this place as they could.

That meant only one thing: they were leaving at midnight, two hours earlier than planned.

Someone was poking him.

Jacob rubbed his eyes and tried to sit up but found himself dizzy and disoriented in the pitch-dark.

His shirt was drenched with sweat. He felt his forehead and realized he was feverish. Whatever bug Luc had picked up, now Jacob had it too, and the timing could not have been worse.

"Jacob, we need to go," Luc whispered.

"What time is it?" Jacob whispered back.

"It's almost three," Luc replied.

"What?"

"Three in the morning," Luc repeated. "We fell asleep. Both of us. It must be the fevers. We have to move now, or we're going to run out of darkness."

Jacob began to panic. How was this possible? How could they have let themselves waste three precious hours? The sun would be rising in less time than that.

"Should we wait another night?" Jacob asked, mopping the perspiration off his face.

"No, we cannot take such a risk," Luc said. "Remember, they're going to start using this lumber soon. We need to go now."

Jacob's legs ached terribly. Plus he was hungry and thirsty and growing sicker by the hour.

Standing up had never been so difficult. Jacob had to brace himself against the side of the lumber pile not to lose his balance. Luc, who was doing a bit better, but not much, grabbed the backpack and suggested Jacob climb out first.

But now they had a new problem. As Jacob tried to push away the boards above them, he could not do it. He pushed harder, straining against the wood, but he simply did not have the strength to budge the lumber even a little.

"Come on; let's go," Luc urged.

"I'm trying," Jacob said, the anxiety in his voice clearly audible.

He pushed again, to no avail. "You've got to be kidding me," he muttered to himself under his breath. He tried still again, but with little effect.

Exasperated, he turned to Luc and said, "You try it."

Without saying a word, Luc set down the backpack and made the attempt. He was able to move the boards up a few inches but could not push them over to the side.

"What are we going to do?" Jacob asked. "We're trapped in. This isn't a hideout. It's a tomb."

"Shhh, Jacob, don't worry," Luc said in a whisper.

"What do you mean, don't worry?" Jacob shot back. "Don't you see what's happening here?"

"It's going to be okay, Jacob. The Lord is with us. He brought us to this point. He's not going to let us die here. I promise you that."

"How do you know?" Jacob asked. "How can you say that? There's no other way out. We can't dig our way out. And we ought to be on the run by now. This is unbelievable. Absolutely unbelievable."

Had there been room to pace, Jacob would have been pacing. As it was, he just dropped to the ground and put his face in his hands, muttering and cursing.

Luc, however, said nothing. Rather, he reached into the backpack and pulled out their two flashlights. Putting one in his pocket, he put the other under his chin. Then he reached up and pushed again on the boards above them. They rose not more than three inches, but that was just enough. Without turning the flashlight on, Luc took the one from under his chin and wedged it into the three-inch space between the planks and the side panels. It wasn't much, but it was a start.

"Get up," Luc whispered. "Give me a hand."

Though nearly beside himself with panic now, Jacob stood. "And do what?" he asked.

"Give me a boost," Luc said.

So Jacob did. He bent down and linked his fingers together, and Luc put one foot into Jacob's hands.

"One, two, three, go," he said.

Jacob lifted him upward as far as he could, but it wasn't enough, and the flashlight fell down.

The sound terrified them. What if someone heard?

"Come on," Luc said, more urgency in his voice. "Try it again."

Jacob's back was aching. The muscles in his legs were screaming. His heart was racing, but he tried again. And again.

The fourth time was the charm. The very real and growing fear that they might be trapped in a wood coffin of their own design gave both of them a burst of adrenaline. With the last of his strength, Jacob heaved Luc upward, and Luc thrust the boards up and to the side. Suddenly they could see the stars and the moon. They grabbed the backpack again and helped each other out of the hole and off the lumber pile.

They were out!

Jacob could hardly believe it. His fever was spiking. He now had splinters in his hands. But he was out. They both were. They were out of Auschwitz-Birkenau. They were past not just one twenty-foot-high electrified fence but two. There were no soldiers to be seen. Even the guard towers, which were rarely manned at night, appeared empty.

Jacob gave Luc a hug but resisted the temptation, as strong as it was, to cheer at the top of his lungs. And then they just stood there for a moment, drinking in the fresh air and staring up at the night sky. It was a beautiful sight to behold.

But Jacob's attention was drawn back to the towering chimney in the distance with its hissing blue flames and belching black smoke, and a sadness settled right back down on him. All the elation he had felt just moments before was gone. He couldn't believe how fast it was replaced by a heaviness he knew he would never be able to adequately describe to those who had not been to Auschwitz. Jacob remembered what Gerhard Gruder had said when he had first arrived: the only way out of this hell was through the chimney. Jacob had believed him at the time. But now here he and Luc were. They were out. Maybe they would make it all the way to true freedom. Maybe not. But already they had accomplished what he had once been sure was utterly impossible.

Yet Jacob knew that Gruder wasn't really wrong. How many Jews and Poles and Gypsies and others had departed this place only through the chimney? More than he could bear.

Jacob looked back over the camp that had been his home. With its twinkling lights, it seemed so still, almost peaceful. A stranger, he thought, might pass by at this hour and not think twice about the place. It didn't seem so dark and menacing in the night.

But Jacob knew he could never make such a mistake. He had seen too much. He knew all too painfully well what was happening behind those walls. He knew those flames were being fueled by the bodies of his fellow prisoners.

Jacob was reminded afresh that he and Luc were not escaping to save themselves. They were, they hoped, witnesses rising as if from the grave to tell the world and make the atrocities stop.

And then Jacob realized that what Leszek Poczciwinski once told him had been right. The reason for all the security measures Hoess and Von Strassen had put into place was not simply to keep the prisoners in. It was to keep the story in. It was to make sure no one ever learned of the Nazi killing machine.

81

JUNE 6, 1944

They put the planks back where they had been.

Though they thought it unlikely, there was a slim chance the barracks would not be built this week after all, and they wanted Josef to have an escape option of his own if he opted for it.

The temptation then was to run for their lives. But they could not. Not yet. Rather, they got on their bellies and began to crawl.

Jacob led as inch by inch they made their way across several hundred yards of no-man's-land, heading toward a forest of birch trees. Jacob feared he might set off a land mine at any moment, blowing himself to bits, but he was following the precise plan Steinberger and Frenkel had given them. They hadn't been killed by mines. Neither, apparently, had Fischer and Kopecký. So maybe his heart was palpitating for no reason. Then again, maybe Von Strassen had made changes Jacob knew nothing about.

Jacob realized such thoughts were dangerous. They ramped up his anxieties, slowed down his movements, and distracted him when he needed to concentrate. He tried to stay focused on the task at hand. He wanted to believe God was with him, as the man who was crawling behind him did. He would have given anything to have Luc's preternatural calm. Even in sickness, Luc had a peace about him.

Finally they reached the forest. Jacob was now on his hands and knees. As much as he wanted to run, he didn't think it was safe yet, but at least they were no longer out in the open. They were in the shadows now. They were making progress.

But then something happened Jacob had not counted on. He felt sand in his hands. Looking ahead and to the right and the left, he could see a river of sand several meters wide stretching out in both directions. *Is this where the mines are?* he wondered. Maybe so, but he couldn't jump it. They would have to walk straight through.

He got to his feet and scanned the forest around him in every direction, fearing the random patrol, fearing a couple of policemen hiding in the dark. Yet he put one foot in front of the other. He had no other choice.

He didn't die. He and Luc crossed the sand river in two separate places, making sure to smooth out the sand behind them to cover their tracks. And then they had had it.

It was time to run, they agreed, and they bolted. They were a good kilometer away from the main perimeter of the camp now, not completely free and clear but far enough away—and deep enough in the forest—that they couldn't be spotted by anyone in the towers.

At one point they came to a clearing and stopped to catch their breath. There they found a wooden signpost. The sign read, *Attention! This is the Auschwitz concentration camp. Any unauthorized persons will be shot without warning!* It was hardly news to either of them, but it was jarring. They looked around, watched and listened to see if anyone was near them, decided they were okay, and started running again.

To Jacob's relief, his legs were thawing out. The combination of the adrenaline coursing through his system, the thrill of being out, and the dread terror of getting caught had helped his muscles adjust. His lungs, however, were another matter. He was impressed by how well Luc was doing. The man seemed built like a runner. Jacob was not. He hadn't had this much exercise since his days in the Resistance in Belgium, and his chest burned. But as much as he wanted to stop and rest, he wouldn't let himself. If his lungs exploded and he died as a result, he would gladly accept his fate. On the other hand, if he stopped and lounged around for a while and got caught doing it—and was returned to the camp to be hanged—he would never forgive himself.

Using the fading North Star as their guide, they continued in a steady run for another half hour or so until Jacob came to a stop.

"Why did you stop?" Luc asked, winded but doing better than his comrade. "We need to keep moving."

"No, look at the sky," Jacob said. "It's getting light. We need to find a place to hide to ride out the day."

They could see that they were approaching the outskirts of a village. Though they had no idea which one it was, they had to assume that everyone in it was hostile. Jacob spotted a small farm about a kilometer to their right. There were no lights on in the main house or smoke coming from their chimney. There was, however, a large barn in the back.

"How about that?" he asked, and Luc readily agreed.

They made their way across a field of corn, disappointed it was too early in the season to find any ears they could actually eat, and reached the barn just as reddish-orange streaks of daylight began to break forth in the east. Slowly, carefully, they entered the barn from the far side, away from the house, and learned—first by the odor, and then by all the cows—that this was a dairy farm.

That was a risk. It likely meant a farmer would be coming out at any moment to milk these cows. Then again, given the time, they might have already been milked. But neither Jacob nor Luc wanted to find out the hard way. So, spotting a loft with a wooden ladder leaning against it, they stealthily moved inside and climbed to the top.

Just then someone entered the barn from the other side. The fugitives froze dead in their tracks as they heard not just one but two people whistling. Looking down through two slats, they soon saw a pair of teenage girls emerge. The girls, probably sisters, each grabbed a wooden stool and set about milking their father's cows.

Step by cautious step, Jacob and Luc moved to the back of the loft. Easing into the shadows, they covered themselves with hay and tried to remember to actually breathe in and out every few moments. They didn't dare cough or sneeze or make any sound at all. But Jacob, for one, found his mouth watering. He hadn't tasted milk since the glass Abby had given him in the clinic. It seemed like ages ago. Dare he try to get some today?

"Hit him again," Von Strassen said.

Fat Louie didn't have to be told twice. He hit Josef Starwolski in the stomach so hard, blood spurted out of his mouth.

The twenty-one-year-old Polish Jew, his hands and feet locked in chains attached to a cement wall, was already a mess. His face and eyes and nose were so bruised and swollen and bloody he would have been unrecognizable even to his own mother. But despite hours of brutal interrogation by Von Strassen, Starwolski had not yet broken.

"Do you really think I'm going to kill you?" Von Strassen asked him now. "You don't know me at all, do you, Josef? You would love that. You would actually love it if I would simply put you out of your misery, wouldn't you? But what would be the fun in that? No, no, I'm not going to kill you, Josef. I'm just going to keep asking you questions until you tell us what we need to know. And if you don't answer me, I'll have my friend here begin cutting off your fingers, one by one. Does that sound better? Now, tell me what I want to hear. Where are your friends Jacob and Luc heading?"

The answer was no.

The girls were very efficient at their work. They filled their pails, poured the milk into a larger vessel of some kind, then filled them up again and again, and when they were all done, they struggled mightily to carry the vessel back into the house. When they were gone, there was no more milk to be had. What's more, it turned out they had little brothers and sisters who soon were up and awake and running about, darting in and out of the barn all day. They were leaping and laughing and carrying on as though they had not a care in the world. Jacob had forgotten that there were children in the world who felt like that.

The father also came in and out of the barn at various times during the day. One time he came for a pitchfork. Another time he came for an ax. Soon Jacob could hear him chopping wood in the backyard of the house amid the squeals of delight coming from the children. It made him think of Ruthie. In two weeks, she would have turned fifteen. It had been five and a half long years since he had looked into his sister's eyes.

The gnawing hunger and constant fear that they would be discovered made it hard to keep to the plan their mentors had laid out for them: sleep all day, run all night. It was not until around three in the afternoon that Luc finally fell asleep, and Jacob didn't succumb for probably another hour.

Just a few hours later, they woke to the smell of smoke from a brick fireplace wafting through the air and detected something wonderful cooking in the kitchen. Jacob's mouth was watering, and it was all he could do not to sneak down from the loft and steal the first thing he saw that was edible.

Soon a bell rang. The children came running from everywhere, and then all was quiet.

Jacob imagined all the different things that might be on the dinner table, trying to match the aromas to the foods, but often just salivating over what he wanted to be eating. An hour later, the girls were back, milking again, and laughing and complaining about the terrible roast their mother had made for dinner, oblivious to the fact that two starving fugitives were listening to their every word just a few meters above their heads.

Von Strassen was livid.

Josef Starwolski still wasn't talking. So Von Strassen nodded, and Fat Louie raised his ax and chopped off Josef's right thumb.

Josef did not start talking, however. He screamed and then slipped into unconsciousness.

This infuriated Auschwitz's chief of security all the more.

This wasn't working. Either Starwolski really didn't know anything, or he was exceedingly loyal to these two men. Either way, the effect was the same. Hour after hour was going by, and Von Strassen was no closer to catching these escapees, much less to forestalling his own increasingly imminent execution. Worse, the three Czechs who had worked in the bakery with both Jacob Weisz and Jean-Luc Leclerc weren't talking either. They, too, had been tortured to the limits of any normal human being's capacity to endure. But they knew nothing.

It was time for Von Strassen to shift his attention to Abigail Cohen.

82

"Did you know Jacob before arriving at Auschwitz?" Von Strassen asked.

"Who?"

"Do not take me for a fool, Miss Cohen," the colonel shot back as he paced around the room, circling the wooden chair she was chained to in the dank and cold, foul-smelling basement known among most prisoners as the pit. "Did you know Jacob Weisz before you came here?"

"I'm sorry, but I don't know who you're talking about," Abby replied.

"Jacob Weisz," Von Strassen said again. "Are you actually going to sit here and lie to my face that you don't know who I'm talking about?"

"I'm sorry, but I've never heard that name before."

"Liar!" Von Strassen shouted, leaning down inches from her face. "You are a liar, Miss Cohen, and if you don't start giving me the answers I want to hear, I will have no choice but to turn you over to savagery you cannot imagine."

Behind him, Fat Louie stood in the shadows, fiddling with a blood-stained wooden club and staring at Abigail with a half-crazed look in his eyes. Von Strassen watched as she glanced to the corner and then back at him. She had a steely resolve in her own eyes, but he perceived it was beginning to falter. Von Strassen had not given permission to lay a hand on this girl—not yet—but he had no doubt the man was itching to be unleashed, and his time would come soon enough.

"Really, I've never heard that name before," Abby insisted.

"*Rubbish!* We know you met repeatedly with Mr. Weisz. We know your brother, Max, was his best friend in the camp. We know the two of them were caught sneaking into the medical clinic, where you work. And we know more. We know that you introduced Mr. Weisz to Jean-Luc Leclerc. And that Mr. Weisz gave you a gift before he escaped. And that you gave Mr. Weisz a gift before he escaped. And that you and Josef Starwolski were the last Jews to speak to Mr. Weisz before he escaped. So I'm thinking it's likely that you gave him instructions on how to escape and instructions on where to go and instructions on whom to meet on the outside and what to tell them. Are you really going to deny all this when we have proof, when we have eyewitnesses, when we even have the journal Mr. Weisz gave you, which my men are analyzing right now for hidden codes and messages?"

"Wait a minute, wait, wait—are you talking about Leonard?" Abigail asked, looking as perplexed as she was frightened. "Leonard Eliezer? Yes, I know Leonard. And yes, we were friends. But I've never heard this name, Jacob . . . What did you call him?"

"*Weisz,* Miss Cohen," Von Strassen said. "Yes, Jacob Weisz, aka Leonard Eliezer. Jacob is his real name. That was his given name when he was born in Berlin on February 2, 1921, to Dr. Reuben Weisz and Sarah Schmidt Weisz. He was never really Leonard Eliezer. That was a fiction, an alias. That was the name he lifted from a dead man on the train ride from Brussels. But his real name was Jacob Weisz, and I'm asking if you ever met before you got to Auschwitz."

"Herr Colonel, please, I have never heard the name Jacob Weisz before today," Abigail said. "If you say that was Leonard's real name, then maybe it was, but I never heard it. He never said it to me. Nor did Max."

"What about Poczciwinski?"

"No."

"Leszek Poczciwinski never used the name Jacob Weisz?"

"No, never—not that I ever heard."

"But he talked to you about Leonard Eliezer?"

"Once, I think—but really I met Leonard through Max."

Von Strassen circled the chair several more times, trying to decide whether he believed her.

"I will ask the question one final time. Did you meet Leonard Eliezer before you arrived here in Auschwitz?"

"No, Herr Colonel. I had never met Leonard before we got here. I wish I had. I think of him as my friend. I wish I'd had more time to get to know him."

"Where is he going?"

"I have no idea."

"I think you do."

"But I do not."

"Then what did you give him just before he escaped?"

"Nothing."

"Do not test me, Miss Cohen. We have eyewitnesses. We know Mr. Weisz left the hospital carrying a small package. Now, what was in it? What exactly did you give him?"

83

Luc still had a fever.

So did Jacob, but Luc looked far worse. His temperature seemed higher. His face and hands were cold and clammy, and he could not stop shivering. For the moment, however, he was actually sound asleep under the hay and under Jacob's own coat, which he had put over him when Luc first began shivering uncontrollably. For now Jacob decided to let him keep sleeping. The sun was just beginning to sink in the west, but he could hear some of the children still playing in the fields. It would still be several hours until they were all in bed and he would feel safe enough to get moving again.

Without anything else to do, Jacob considered that perhaps it was finally time to open Abby's gift. He had wanted to open it the moment she had given it to him, and he had thought about it constantly ever since. Indeed, its very presence in his backpack was one of the things that had kept him moving forward through so many trials in the past few days. And now, at last, he could see what she had given him.

As quietly as he could, he reached into the backpack, down to the bottom.

First he came across the padlocked steel box containing all the precious documents, photographs, ledgers, and other materials he and his colleagues had stolen from the Nazis. This was the elixir, the prize they had smuggled out of the camp—the materials that bore irrefutable proof of the specific nature and magnitude of the Nazi atrocities taking place inside the Auschwitz-Birkenau camps. It was this, even more than their own testimonies, Jacob was certain, that would convince the Hungarian Jews and the Allied leaders of what *der Führer* was really doing behind closed doors. It was this that would move them to take decisive action to save the Jewish people and forever alter the destiny of Europe.

Instinctively Jacob felt for the thin leather strap around his neck, at the end of which dangled the brass key that could open the box. It was still there, still safe. It was not the only key they had. Luc had one as well, wrapped around his left ankle, hidden by a sock and a boot. If something happened to one of them, whoever had the backpack could break away from the other and never look back, knowing he could open the strongbox to the right people at the right time.

Jacob put his hand on the box and felt the coolness of the steel. Then he patted it and kept digging.

A moment later, he fished out Abby's package. When he held it in his hands, he stared at it for a while, hardly believing it was real, wanting to simply savor this curious moment. How could he have imagined when he had first arrived at the death camp that someone would give him a gift? How could he have imagined that that someone would be a girl who had such a profound effect on him? Was it only because he hadn't really met any other girls in the camp? Jacob didn't think so. There was something about Abby that was special.

He had not anticipated receiving a gift from her. It was an unexpected act of kindness in a place that engendered very few. And yet as he reflected on the horror of his time behind the barbed wire, he couldn't help but be struck by how many small yet significant acts of kindness he had experienced. He had done nothing to deserve any expressions of kindness or favor from Leszek or from Max. He certainly hadn't done anything to merit them from Josef or Steinberger or Frenkel, much less Abby. Or Luc, for that matter. Why had they all been so kind? Why had they chosen him and helped him to escape? It was almost as though someone were looking out for him, as though someone were watching his back and leading him out.

The package was wrapped in brown paper and bound with a string that Abby had tied in a little bow. On the front, in the top right-hand corner, she had written his alias, *Leonard J. Eliezer*. Her handwriting was lovely, but it was strange to see the name written out.

He smiled at the middle initial, *J.* It was Abby's way of winking at him, of using his real name, Jacob, without risking getting caught for it, and he adored her all the more for this little act of remembrance. His name was important to him. Yet the Nazis had tried to strip him of it. To the officials in the camp, he wasn't even a name. He was known only by the number on his arm, 202502. It had all been part of the Nazis' process of dehumanization. He wasn't a person, just a head of cattle. He didn't have a soul, just a number.

Jacob cocked his head and listened intently for no less than a full minute. When he sensed no one in the barn below or near enough to the barn to potentially overhear him or accidentally stumble upon him and Luc, he decided to proceed. Carefully removing the string, he set it aside, then slowly unwrapped the package and set aside the paper. In his hands now lay a cardboard box, similar to the kind a new pair of shoes might come in, though maybe half that size. Again he paused and listened for anything that could suggest he was in danger, but there was still no evidence of anyone close by.

With his heart pounding, he removed the top of the box.

Inside, Jacob saw not just one gift but two, each the size of a small book. Both were wrapped in white tissue paper. He was terrified by the prospect that removing the tissue might be overheard by someone walking past. But then he remonstrated with himself. It was one thing to be cautious; it was another thing to be paranoid. He had come this far and survived. He had to be willing to trust his judgment. So he unwrapped the first gift and was stunned by what he found.

In his hands now lay a small copy of the book of Psalms. It was a beautiful edition with a brown leather cover that was well-worn but still bore the faintest evidence of a Star of David on the front that looked as if it had once been embossed with gold leaf. He stroked the leather in his hands, and it felt wonderful. He closed his eyes and smelled the leather. The fragrance was heavenly. He opened the book and turned through the pages to a random spot in the middle, and a verse caught his eye. He read it to himself, mouthing the words but making no sound.

> I will not die, but live, and tell of the works of the Lord.

He flipped back a few pages, toward the front, and another passage seemed to jump out at him.

> I waited patiently for the Lord; and He inclined to me and heard my cry. He brought me up out of the pit of destruction, out of the miry clay, and He set my feet upon a rock making my footsteps firm.

Jacob realized his hands were trembling. He was not a religious man. He was not from a religious family. He had never owned his own copy of the Torah or the Tanakh. He had never read the Scriptures, except a brief passage during his bar mitzvah that he couldn't even remember any longer. Nor could he remember his parents ever reading from the Psalms or any other portion of the Scriptures, except on Passover, and only briefly at that. He couldn't even remember ever wanting to read such things. But now as he held this copy of the book of Psalms in his gaunt, bony fingers, knowing the last person to have touched this book was Abby Cohen, he was surprised at how moved he felt. Turning to the front of the book, curious to see where it had been printed and when, he came upon a brief inscription, written in Abby's distinctly feminine penmanship.

> *May this book be a lamp unto your feet and a light unto your path, a very present help to you in times of trouble. Oh, how I would love it if you would read a psalm every morning when you*

wake up. And not just to yourself—read it aloud. And when you do, would you say a prayer for me, and for all of us here, until you come back to set us free?

Love, Abby

(P.S.—My favorite is Psalm 23. When I see you again, please tell me yours!)

Jacob felt a lump forming in his throat. He swallowed hard and glanced over at Luc, relieved that he was still fast asleep. Then he flipped through the pages until he came upon the Twenty-Third Psalm, which he noted was described as a psalm of David.

The Lord is my shepherd, I shall not want. He makes me lie down in green pastures; He leads me beside quiet waters. . . . He guides me in the paths of righteousness for His name's sake.

He was struck by the beauty of the words. He had never read them before. He didn't recall ever even hearing them before. But they captivated him in a way that surprised him. *Why?* he wondered.

He read the entire psalm again and then a third time. What was it that touched him? He wasn't sure. He felt a range of conflicting thoughts and emotions he couldn't quite sift through and categorize at the moment. But one question did echo in his heart. Who was this "shepherd" David knew so intimately?

Uncomfortable with the question, Jacob shifted gears.

He set down the book of Psalms and turned to the other gift in the box. Again he carefully removed the tissue paper, and again he was stunned by what he found.

This gift, too, was from the Bible, but not the Jewish Bible. It was not a book of Psalms. It was, instead, a small German New Testament.

Suddenly all of Jacob's warm feelings toward Abby evaporated like the morning dew under the heat of the sun. He felt a surge of anger like he had not experienced in quite some time. A New Testament? The book of the Christians? How could Abby have possibly thought he would want or appreciate such a thing? His deeply offended heart raced as a wave of powerful emotions came rushing over him.

Luc shifted in his sleep, startling Jacob. He did not awaken, however, and when he had settled and it was quiet once more, a thought came to Jacob that embarrassed him with its simplicity and its obviousness. The second gift wasn't for him. Abby had sent it for Luc.

He quickly opened the leather-bound book and, sure enough, found an inscription on the inside cover, written again in Abby's now-unmistakable style.

To Luc—

Thank you for your kindness and all the ways you helped me in the brief time I knew you. I had no idea how to thank you properly, but perhaps this Bible will comfort you on your journey. I know you cherish your faith, and I can see it has made you different. I have just one request. Would you read a passage from your Bible to your companion each day you're together and let him read to you some of his? And when you do, would you both say a prayer for me, and for all of us here, until you come back to set us free?

Gratefully, Abigail Cohen

As Abby's words entered Jacob's head and heart, all the anger and bitterness he had just felt drained away. She wasn't trying to provoke him. To the contrary, she had simply sought to show some kindness to Luc. Everything suddenly made sense again, and the relief he felt was palpable. Abby was a good soul. The very thought made him miss her all the more.

Looking across to the facing page, Jacob saw another inscription, one not in Abby's hand.

To Yens, on the occasion of your tenth birthday.

May you remember the words of Jesus all the days of your life, dear Son. "If you continue in My word, then you are truly disciples of Mine; and you will know the truth, and the truth will make you free" (John 8:31-32). Go with God.

Love, Papa and Mama
May 9, 1904

Jacob had no idea who Yens was. Clearly he was no longer a child; he was a full-grown man and evidently a Christian who for some reason had wound up in Auschwitz. Judging by the date of the inscription, he had recently turned fifty—that is, if he was still alive. Was he? Jacob wondered. It wasn't easy for men that age to endure the hardships of the camps. Indeed, it was very likely that he was dead. But either way, for whatever reason he had been condemned to Auschwitz, this man apparently had clung to his faith strongly enough to have brought his childhood Bible with him.

Jacob mulled this as he flipped through the pages of the New Testament, as well-worn as those of the book of Psalms, if not more so. He was quickly struck by how many verses were underlined in pencil and how many notes were in the margins. Whoever this Yens was, he had obviously cherished this book dearly and studied it extensively. It must have been stripped from him upon arrival at Auschwitz, Jacob realized, as everything else of value was taken and cataloged and categorized and stored in the giant warehouse of the Canada command.

How hard it must have been to part with something so precious to him. Yet the very thought led to a separate question: why in the world would a Gentile—a Christian—wind up in Auschwitz? It made no sense. And yet here was Luc, too. Jacob had never imagined meeting a Christian in a concentration camp. But he had, and apparently there were others.

84

"I'm not going to ask you again, Miss Cohen."

What little patience Colonel Von Strassen possessed was quickly fading.

"I don't know what else you want me to say," Abby replied. "I keep telling you, they were Bibles, just Bibles—a book of Psalms for Leonard and a New Testament for Luc. I didn't give them any maps. I didn't give them any contacts outside the camp. I don't have any contacts like that. I have no idea where they were going. Yes, I knew they were going to escape. And yes, I was happy for them, and a little scared. But I wasn't involved in the planning."

"You just keep saying the same thing over and over again," Von Strassen fumed.

"Because it's the truth."

"Because it's a *lie*! Because you've got your cover story, and you're sticking to it. But that's only because you think there aren't consequences. How long have you been here in Auschwitz, Miss Cohen? Do you really believe you can lie to *der Führer* and his representatives with impunity?"

Von Strassen motioned with his right hand, and Fat Louie opened the cell door. Two guards now dragged in the battered body of Josef Starwolski and dumped it in front of her. Abby gasped and looked away, but Von Strassen grabbed her head from behind and forcibly turned it toward the man lying in a heap before them.

Josef was still breathing.

Von Strassen nodded again, and one of the guards pulled Josef's head up so she could see his battered, bloodied, disfigured face.

"Last chance, Miss Cohen," Von Strassen said, whispering in her ear like a lover.

Abby began to cry. "I don't know what else to say," she said, unable to wipe away the tears streaming down her cheeks because of the chains on her hands. "I've told you the truth. Please . . ."

Von Strassen circled her twice more like a shark preparing to attack. Then he pulled out his Luger and pressed it to Josef's right temple. "You have five seconds, Miss Cohen. Tell me where your friends are going. Tell me who their contacts are. Tell me the truth, or I'm going to shoot your friend—your accomplice—and blow his brains out, right before your eyes. And then I'm going to bring in each nurse who works in the clinic and shoot them before you, and then each doctor and then everyone in the Canada command, until you tell me what I want to hear."

"Don't do it," Josef said in a barely audible voice. "Not for me. God will judge them. All of them."

"One . . ."

Abby broke down sobbing. "I can't," she cried. "I've told you all I know."

"Two . . ."

"Please, stop," she begged.

"Three . . ."

She pleaded with Von Strassen to have mercy. "Don't punish Josef, please. I can't tell you what I don't know. I can't help you. I—"

"Four . . ."

And with that, Abby Cohen did a one-eighty. "Okay, okay!" she cried. "Leszek. They are going to link up with Leszek."

"No!" Josef cried.

"Where?" Von Strassen demanded, lowering the pistol. "Where are they meeting?"

"Płońsk," she said.

"Near Warsaw?"

"Yes, yes, there is a farmhouse there, not far from the old monastery. I don't know the road. But that's where they're going. Leszek is running a cell group of the Resistance movement from there. They're gathering weapons to come here, to try to take this place. But please, Josef doesn't know anything about it. Please, let him go."

"You had better be telling me the truth, Miss Cohen," Von Strassen said.

"I am," she insisted. "Now, please, don't hurt Josef anymore. Let him go. He hasn't done anything wrong."

"We will know the truth soon enough," Von Strassen replied. "I will radio the Gestapo in Warsaw and have them investigate. And if you're lying, you will hang in front of the entire camp. Do you understand me?"

Abby was sobbing uncontrollably now, but she nodded.

"Good," Von Strassen said. "Now, just to be sure there are no misunderstandings . . ."

He raised the Luger again, pressed it against Josef's head, and pulled the trigger anyway.

85

Night fell, finally.

One by one the lights in the farmhouse went out. It was time to get moving again. Jacob gently woke Luc up around eleven o'clock. He gave his friend the last bit of bread they had with them, stale and hardened though it was. Luc protested, indicating that Jacob should really eat it, but Jacob would not take no for an answer. Luc finally ended his protest, expressed his thanks to Jacob, and hungrily devoured the few dry morsels.

When they were convinced the coast was clear, the two men slipped out of the barn and began running through fields. Unfortunately, it was a full moon, making it more possible for them to be seen. Yet they knew they could not stay still. They had to keep moving toward the Slovakian border and maintain a rigorous pace.

They would not be safe even there, they knew. The Nazis fully occupied all of Central Europe. But Steinberger and Frenkel had been clear that they must not stay in southern Poland a minute more than necessary. The Nazi presence was too strong, and the chances of their being discovered and rearrested were far too high.

They were desperate to find more food, but there were not many options. The farm they had just come from was a dairy farm, but there were acres upon acres of cornstalks stretching out as far as the eye could see. The problem was that it was June, and the corn would not be ready to eat until August, at the earliest. So they kept running. Eventually they passed through a potato farm and scooped up a handful of potatoes they hoped they could boil and eat very soon.

In terms of water, they were in much better shape. When they came, as expected, to the Soła River, they stopped for a few minutes to plunge their heads in the chilly waters and to soothe their parched tongues. When they had drunk their fill, topped off their canteens, and washed the sweat and stench off their arms and chests, they continued on their way.

They followed the river southward, upstream. They had learned from Steinberger and Frenkel that the Soła's origin was about ninety kilometers away, somewhere in the mountain range known as the Beskids, near the border. Under ideal conditions, they could have hugged the riverbank and let it guide them south toward Žilina. The problem was that there were towns and villages nestled along those banks, places where soldiers and policemen and ordinary townsfolk could spot them. And even when there were long stretches of unpopulated territory, there were still boats making their way up and down the river, some for pleasure and some carrying various types of cargo from town to town. So Jacob and Luc knew they needed to keep some distance between themselves and the gently flowing current while still using it as a road map and a source of water.

Given Luc's weakened condition, they were not moving as fast as Jacob would have liked, but it couldn't be helped. And so, as they settled on a manageable pace through the darkened forests, they actually began talking to each other for the first time since their escape.

Uncharacteristically, Jacob initiated the conversation. He began by giving Luc the New Testament from Abby and apologizing for opening it, saying he hadn't realized the gift was for Luc and not for him. Luc wasn't bothered in the slightest. To the contrary, he said he was touched by Abby's thoughtfulness.

"Luc, can I ask you a question?" Jacob said as they emerged from a forest and began to hike up the side of a large grassy hill.

"Of course," Luc replied, winded and weak but somehow hanging in there.

It took a moment for Jacob to figure out exactly how he wanted to put it, and he still wasn't sure he knew how to ask without offending Luc, so he finally just plunged in and asked what was on his mind. "Why didn't you ever tell me your grandfather was the French ambassador to the United States?"

"What do you mean?" Luc asked.

"It's sort of an important detail, don't you think?"

"Well, I wasn't trying to hide anything, if that's what you're implying," Luc responded. "It's just not the kind of thing that comes up in everyday conversation. I don't know anything about your parents or grandparents, do I?"

That was true but hardly relevant, Jacob thought. Still, Jean-Luc Leclerc struck Jacob as a man largely without guile. To be sure, he could deceive his Nazi captors, but he didn't seem to be trying to deceive the underground.

"What's he like?" Jacob asked.

"Who, my grandfather?"

"Yeah, have you ever met him? Do you know him?"

"Of course," Luc said. "He and my grandmother lived in Paris when I was growing up. We went to visit them every Christmas."

"But I thought you came from a family of farmers."

"That's my father's side, the Leclercs—all farmers," Luc explained. "But we're talking about my mother's side. She comes from a long line of intellectuals and academics and government officials. Her father—my maternal grandfather—is François d'Astier. He was originally from Cherbourg, on the northern coast of France, right across the channel from England. But he had a great passion for history and politics. So he went to university in Paris and became an officer in the navy and eventually went into politics. Fascinating man, actually. Erudite. Sophisticated. Seemed to know everything about everything. And what a storyteller! I could listen to him for hours. I remember how proud we all were when he was named ambassador. It was quite an honor."

"I'm sure," Jacob said, genuinely intrigued. "But how did your parents meet? They came from such different backgrounds."

"Oh, goodness, that's a long story," Luc said, laughing a little.

"Good," Jacob said. "We have time."

As they continued walking south, Luc began to tell the story, and Jacob was struck by how the conversation seemed to give Luc new energy. He still looked emaciated, haggard, and ill, even in the moonlight. But his thoughts were crisp, and his voice sounded surprisingly strong.

When Luc had finished telling about his own parents, he asked how Jacob's parents met and how they had handled the anti-Semitism in Berlin. He seemed intrigued by their move to Siegen and how they had tried to integrate into the Jewish community there, even though they knew practically no one. This, of course, led the conversation to Uncle Avi and the critical role he had played in Jacob's life.

At first Jacob hesitated to talk about his uncle. The loss was too great, the memories too painful. And yet the more Luc pressed—not prying, just interested—the more Jacob opened up. He'd had no one else to talk to about Avi. He found that he liked telling the stories and remembering this man who had loved him so much and whom he had loved so dearly.

Von Strassen finished his briefing.

"So the Gestapo in Warsaw is on it?" Hoess asked.

"They are, sir."

"Do you think she's telling the truth?"

"I cannot say," Von Strassen conceded. "But under the circumstances, I'd say it's likely."

"Why?"

"Because all the evidence we have gathered so far points to Leszek Poczciwinski as the head of the underground movement here at Auschwitz," the colonel explained. "He's the one who recruited Steinberger and Frenkel. He recruited Maximilian Cohen and through him Abigail Cohen. It's now clear that he recruited Jacob Weisz and probably Jean-Luc Leclerc, too. Her story fits with all that we've learned already."

"What about this Josef Starwolski?" Hoess asked, thumbing through the report in his hands.

"We cannot say for certain who recruited him into the movement, but all the evidence thus far indicates he was the mole in the records office. It is likely, therefore, that he intercepted the information I received about the raid on train 801 last year and passed the information on to Poczciwinski, who used it to recruit Weisz. But there's more."

"What's that?"

"When I spoke to the Gestapo station chief in Warsaw, he told me something curious about Leszek Poczciwinski."

"And?"

"Poczciwinski wasn't his real name," Von Strassen said. "It was Piotr Kubiak. And it turns out Kubiak is a captain in Polish intelligence. He wasn't just the head of the underground movement here in Auschwitz. The Gestapo believes he is now a senior commander in the national Resistance movement. And if our information leads to his arrest, they're hoping it will lead to the arrest of most if not all of the Resistance leaders in Poland."

"That would be a real development, Colonel."

"Indeed, sir."

"Perhaps something that will attract favorable attention in Berlin as well."

"Let us hope so, sir. Let us hope so."

86

"Jacob, I want you to know how sorry I am," Luc said.

"Sorry for what?" Jacob asked.

"That you didn't get your first choice for this mission."

"What do you mean? Of course I did."

"We both know that's not true, though I appreciate the sentiment," Luc said. "It was clear from the beginning that it was Otto and Abe who wanted me on this team, not you. And to be clear, I don't take it personally. You've been through so much already. You've suffered so much. I don't want to be the cause of any more hardship."

"Haven't you suffered too?" Jacob asked.

"Of course, but I don't mean just you and me, or even just you and your family," Luc said.

"What then?" Jacob pressed.

"The Jewish people," Luc replied as they hiked up a steep hill. "You've been through so much, and to be honest, I am deeply ashamed for what we have done to you, or let be done to you. We the Gentiles. We the Christians."

Jacob remained silent as they crested the hill and soon began to climb an even steeper one.

"You already know that I'm a Christian," Luc continued. "I love to read the Bible. It is my great joy in life. I believe Jesus is the Messiah, and I love him with all of my heart, soul, mind, and strength. I know that makes you uncomfortable, and I'm sorry about that. I don't want to make you uncomfortable."

Jacob felt a twinge of guilt. "Luc, it's not you," he replied. "I mean it's not you personally. It's just that—"

"You didn't want me to come, true?"

Jacob sighed. "Okay, yes, that's true; I didn't."

"You wanted Josef or Abby to come, right?"

Jacob winced. He did not like how it sounded, but it was the truth. "Look, it wasn't personal, Luc—really, it wasn't," he explained. "I mean, yes, I would have asked Josef or Abby to join me if it had been up to me. And yes, to be perfectly honest, I pushed back pretty hard with Otto and Abe over it. But it was never about you personally. You've always been very good to me, to all the Jews—to Abby, to Josef. Please don't think I have a personal disdain for you, because I don't. I have great respect for you."

"I understand, Jacob, and I appreciate that," Luc said. "I do, and I want you to know that I pushed back hard with Otto and Abe too."

"What do you mean?"

"I mean the day after you invited me, I went and found Otto and told him I couldn't accept the mission."

"You did?"

"Yes."

"But why?"

"Because it seemed ridiculous to choose me. I could see it wasn't your choice. You weren't part of the underground high command; they were. You weren't close to Leszek; they were. You weren't planning this mission; they were. I could see that. And that's why I told them they should have chosen Josef or Abby or anyone Jewish. Not a Gentile. Not a pastor. Not me."

Jacob was flabbergasted. "What did they say?"

"They wouldn't listen. They said we had to get to my grandfather and that if I really wanted to help the Jews, I would stop resisting them and just help them. So finally I gave up and said yes."

It was quiet between them for a few moments.

"Thank you," Jacob finally replied.

"Don't mention it."

"No, really. I mean it. Thank you for understanding where I was coming from, and thank you for saying something—to them and to me."

"It was nothing."

"Hardly. But what did you mean about being ashamed of the things Christians have done to Jews?" Jacob asked. "Were you talking about things like the Crusades, the Inquisition? The pogroms?"

Before Luc could answer, they heard a truck coming around a bend in the road they were crossing.

Diving into the tall grass, they pressed their bodies to the ground and waited. A few moments later, a lorry rumbled past on the otherwise-deserted mountain road. In short order all was quiet again. They waited for a few minutes more, but all they heard were the sounds of crickets and mosquitoes and the wind rustling through the trees. So they cautiously poked their heads up above the grass and scanned in every direction for signs of life. When they were confident they were alone, they got back up and started moving again, deeper into the tall grass, away from the road, heading for the ridgeline. And as they did, Luc began to answer Jacob's question.

"Many who have called themselves Christians have done terrible things to the Jewish people," Luc said. "Terrible things. But they did these things on their own. They didn't get those ideas from the Bible. They didn't get them from Jesus. You asked about the Crusades, the pogroms—those are the exact opposite of what the Bible teaches. Jesus commanded us, 'Love your neighbor as yourself.' He told us, 'Love your enemies and pray for those who persecute you.' He commanded us to turn the other cheek, not to rob, kill, or destroy. Those are the works of the devil."

"You said many who call themselves Christians have done terrible things, but what about people who really are Christians? What about Martin Luther? Didn't he write all sorts of things against the Jews? Didn't he say our prayer books should be burned and our houses destroyed and all kinds of other things?"

"I'm ashamed to say he did," Luc readily conceded. "Martin Luther was the leader of the Reformation movement and the founder of the Lutheran church. But he wasn't perfect. Far from it. And I won't defend him for writing those things. He was old and he was sick and he was probably losing his mind. That doesn't excuse what he wrote, but it helps explain it. After all, he'd been very loving and compassionate toward the Jews for most of his life. Anyway, all of us who truly love Jesus disavow what Luther wrote about the Jews in the last years of his life."

"How can you?" Jacob asked. "You're a pastor; you're a Protestant."

"When I was growing up, and even when I went into the ministry, I didn't know any of those things about Luther," Luc said. "I never heard any pastor talk about those things, positively or negatively. When I first heard Hitler and Goebbels quoting such awful sayings a couple of years ago, I didn't even believe Luther had really written those things at first."

"But he did," Jacob said.

"Yes," Luc said. "Luther wrote some terrible things about the Jews. There's nothing I can do about that. But they didn't come from Jesus. And those of us who follow Jesus put our hope and trust in what Jesus said, not in what others have said throughout history. I follow Christ, not Luther."

"But what about all the German pastors who preach against the Jews?" Jacob asked.

"Listen—what the Nazis are doing has nothing to do with Christianity. Hitler is just using Luther's anti-Semitic writings for his propaganda campaign. True, some pastors have caved to the Third Reich. But many others are as mortified by what's happening as we were in Le Chambon. Look, I have pastor friends in Germany. They've seen Hitler and the National Socialists trying to take over the church. They've seen the Nazis installing their own leaders to create a 'national church.' They've seen the Nazis banning them from preaching the Bible. They've seen Hitler trying to co-opt the church to turn against the Jews, and they hate it. They've resisted as best they can. They've created an underground church movement called the Confessing Church, made up of true followers of Jesus who refuse to obey Hitler."

"I've never heard any of this," Jacob said, deeply skeptical.

"Well, it's true. The Confessing Church has resisted Hitler. They've done whatever they can to protect Jews, to rescue them, to smuggle them out of Germany and get them to Switzerland or to France—even to our town, where we did the best we could to take care of them. Many of these pastors have been arrested. Quite a few went to prison. Some of them even wound up in Auschwitz. I actually met a few there."

"But I still don't understand," Jacob said. "Why would any of you Christians risk your lives to help Jews?"

"I can't explain the motive of every Christian," Luc said. "But for me and my wife, Claire, the answer was obvious. Our Savior was Jewish. His disciples were Jewish. They were born in Israel. They lived in the Promised Land. Jesus preached to 'the lost sheep of Israel.' He died on the cross in Jerusalem. He was raised from the dead in Jerusalem. And the Bible teaches that our Savior is coming back again to reign and rule from Jerusalem. Why shouldn't we love Jews, then? Jesus never taught us to hate anyone. He taught us to love, and he set the supreme example for us to follow. Jesus commanded us to love one another. He commanded us to love our neighbor as ourselves. You're my neighbor, Jacob. If not you, then who? You're from the same family and people as my Savior. How could I hate you or do you wrong?"

Jacob said nothing for several minutes as they descended a large hill and entered a new forest.

"I'm not saying we have done everything right," Luc said. "To the contrary, I'm afraid we have made many mistakes. My pastor friends in Germany readily admit it. They didn't grasp at first just how evil Hitler was. And some of them made compromises with his regime until they realized just how despotic and demonic he really is. But when they came to this understanding, they did not stay silent. You once asked me why a good Christian would be thrown into Auschwitz. Well, this is why. Good Christians—real Christians—do their best to love their neighbors and serve their Savior, even if that means being arrested. Even if that means being sent to a concentration camp. Even if it means death."

87

JUNE 6, 1944
OSWIECIM, POLAND

Before dawn, the girls were again helping their father milk the cows.

As the sun came up, they returned to the kitchen, where their mother had prepared a hearty breakfast for the entire family. When their father came in from trying to fix a broken tractor, they sat down, said grace, and dug into the meal.

Just then, a large black sedan could be seen coming up their driveway, kicking up a cloud of dust along the way.

"Why, that's the constable," the father said, wiping his mouth as he stared out the front window.

"Whatever for?" his wife asked.

"I have no idea. Wait here."

The farmer pushed away from the table, rose, and stepped into the front yard.

"Why would the constable come here, Mama?" one of the girls asked.

"Hush," her mother said. "That's none of your business."

Nevertheless, she allowed the children to get up and gather by the front window to see what was happening. They watched the car pull up to the front and come to a stop. They saw their father walk over to the car and converse with the constable, though they could not hear what was said. And then, as quickly as it had come, the car pulled away.

When the farmer returned to the kitchen, he found his family sitting around the table as before, eating quietly.

"There's news," he said.

"What is it?" his wife asked.

"Some men have escaped from a prison camp up north," the farmer said.

"Again?"

"Apparently."

"That's the third time in the last couple of months."

"That's what I said."

"What kind of men, Papa?" one of the girls asked.

"Dangerous men. The kind none of us wants around here."

"Why are they telling us?"

"They want us to take special care," the farmer said. "They want us to keep our eyes peeled for anything unusual."

"Would they really come here?" another daughter asked, trepidation thick in her voice.

"The constable said it was unlikely," the father replied.

"That's what they said last time," the mother said. "And the time before."

"I know," the father said. "I don't want you to worry. But let's all keep a sharp eye out, all of us. If you see something strange, come immediately to your mother and me and let us know. But I won't let anything happen to any of you. You have my word."

"Yes, Papa," they dutifully replied.

But he could see in their eyes that they were afraid.

He didn't dare tell them that he was afraid too. The war had been hard enough. But now, more and more, week after week, this Polish farmer was hearing dark rumors of terrible deeds being done in the north. The first few times he had dismissed such things as ghost stories and malicious gossip. But the rumors persisted. The tales were getting worse, the details more macabre.

Could any of it be true?

88

Before the sun came up, Jacob and Luc found a small cave in which to hide.

Out of loyalty to Abby, Jacob dutifully read Psalm 1 to Luc. In return, Luc read the first chapter of Matthew to Jacob. They didn't discuss either passage. They just read their texts.

Jacob then recited the one Hebrew prayer he knew. Luc, in turn, asked God to comfort Abby and Josef and the rest of their friends back at the camp. He prayed for each of the men who had escaped, that God would keep them alive and give them favor. Finally he prayed for the strength and the courage to complete the mission for which they had been chosen.

It was a longer prayer than Jacob's, and it was odd to Jacob because it was not a written or memorized prayer. It was as though Luc were having a conversation with someone. But Jacob didn't want to talk about it. His only thought was of Abby. If he ever saw her again—or rather, when he did—he wanted to be able to say he had honored her request.

With that, they both curled up and tried to sleep.

The cave provided some much-needed shade from the summer sun, but it certainly did not solve their problems. They had no bread or vegetables or food of any kind. Their stomachs were grumbling. They were losing more weight and growing weaker by the day. The only good news was that Jacob's fever had finally broken. But Luc's had not. And so much walking had created numerous blisters on their feet that were now oozing pus and blood and hurt something terrible. But as night fell, they knew they had to keep moving.

Jacob had been told the entire journey was roughly 135 kilometers. But walking or running through unfamiliar terrain—especially at night and especially hungry and ill—was slow going. Jacob figured they were making no more than ten or eleven kilometers a day. At that rate, he feared they might not reach Žilina until the eighteenth or nineteenth of June—if they were lucky.

This was not good enough, Jacob told himself. Every day trains of Hungarian Jews were pulling into the gates of Birkenau, and every day thousands of them were going straight to the gas chambers and the ovens. They couldn't afford to slow down. They had to pick up the pace. They had to warn the Jews of Hungary what the Nazis were really doing.

Jacob discussed this with Luc, and Luc readily agreed.

"We have no choice," Luc said, his hands and face and arms now blotchy from a strange rash. "We have to keep going."

They headed first toward the river. They desperately needed to wash and cool down and fill their canteens again. This stretch of the Soła River had no houses, no barns, no signs of civilization whatsoever, so they followed the riverbank for a time.

As they walked, they talked about what they were actually going to say when they met with the Jewish leaders of Hungary and what they would say if they had the opportunity to meet with Churchill and Roosevelt. They speculated about whether any of the others had reached such leaders already. Maybe they weren't needed. Maybe a rescue operation was already being set into motion.

Just then, however, they heard the rumble of several aircraft rapidly approaching from the west. The two men scrambled for cover under a grove of trees. Moments later, they saw two Luftwaffe fighter planes roar into view. It was unusual to see them flying at night. It was more unusual still to see them flying so low.

The planes' presence rattled Jacob. Were they running a surveillance mission? Were they flying cover for a ground unit? Were they here for them, or was it merely an unnerving coincidence?

89

When the planes were gone, the two men headed out again into the humid night air.

As they walked, Jacob did his best to recall what Steinberger and Frenkel had told him about the route they would be taking and the dangers they would face.

"If we're still on course," he said to Luc, "we should eventually reach a small dam. There's a train station there and a German military base, so we'll have to be careful. Otto said it's heavily guarded. Nazi troops everywhere and roving patrols every hour, all day and all night. We won't want to go anywhere near the dam or the base, but we'll keep moving south into the mountains."

Once they crossed the mountains, if they were still alive, they would reach Żywiec Lake. The plan called for them to stay on the west side of the river, in the forest, until they reached a place where the river forked. The smaller tributary to the right would lead them to Milówka, only about ten kilometers from the Slovakian border.

After they had hiked another several days, Jacob realized everything Steinberger and Frenkel had told them was proving accurate. By June 13 they had passed the dam and steered clear of the heavy concentrations of Nazi troops, grateful for the warnings. Now they were approaching the second large lake. They were making progress. They were nearing their objective, and they weren't dead yet.

But all was not well. Despite their spirited conversations, Luc's health was steadily worsening. Jacob was barely finding enough fruits or vegetables to keep them going. Their stomachs were in constant pain. Their feet were swollen and blistered. And Luc still had a serious fever. He was beginning to stumble as he walked. His breathing was becoming raspy and painful. He was increasingly too tired to talk.

Rather than accelerating, they were slowing down.

"Papa, Papa, come quickly!"

On the night of June 14, one of the teenage girls burst into the kitchen just as her mother was setting plates of roast pork and boiled potatoes and peas on the table and her father was washing his hands for a late dinner.

"What is it?" the farmer asked, alarmed at the panic in his daughter's voice.

"In the barn—quick!"

Without hesitation, the farmer bolted out the front door and raced for the barn, fearing the worst, his adrenaline surging. Was someone sick? Injured? Dead? Was one of the animals in distress? Was there a snake or a skunk or some other animal putting the children in jeopardy? A thousand fears crossed his mind, including the fresh warnings from the constable.

When the farmer reached the barn, he found his other teenage daughter and several of his younger sons up in the loft.

"What is it, children?" he asked, scrambling up the wooden ladder to join them.

When he reached the top, he found his children pointing into the hay in a corner of the loft. It was growing dark outside, and it was darker still in the barn. He called for a kerosene lamp, and when it was brought to him, he lit it and looked closer at what the children had discovered. But all he saw were a piece of string, several crumpled pieces of brown paper wrapping, and a few pieces of white tissue paper, equally crumpled and cast aside.

He began to relax and couldn't decide whether to laugh or scold them. Foolishness was bound up in the hearts of children, he reminded himself.

He took a deep breath and was about to ask the children where they had gotten these things and why they were bothering him with such trivialities when his little boy pointed to something sticking out of the hay.

When he looked closer, the farmer could see that it was a dark sock. Carefully he pulled at it and brought the lamp closer. It was a man's sock, and it was covered in blood.

His heart began to pound again.

Now, as he looked more closely at the hay in the corner, he saw drops of what appeared to be dried blood in several places and numerous footprints on the dusty floor.

Someone had been here, he realized, and not his own children. A man had been here. A wounded man. Possibly two of them.

He ordered his children into the house. It was time to call the constable.

90

"It's time," Jacob whispered as darkness fell upon the land.

Thunder rumbled over them. The wind had picked up. It was getting cold. A storm was moving in, and Jacob was concerned it might be a major one.

They had holed up for the day in an old, dilapidated loggers' shack they had stumbled upon in the middle of a forest. It had protected them from the sun and the heat, but Jacob didn't trust staying there any longer. He had found a yellowed newspaper on the floor dated just a few months before, and there were several empty beer bottles lying around. Clearly locals used this shack from time to time. They couldn't afford to be anywhere near here when the next person or group came around.

"Come on, Luc, on your feet," Jacob pressed.

But Luc would not budge. "I cannot."

"Of course you can," Jacob said, putting on the backpack and preparing for the all-night trek southward. "We're almost there. Just a few more days."

"Leave me here," Luc groaned.

"I'm not going to leave you anywhere," Jacob said. "Come on—you can do it."

Still Luc would not get up. His eyes were bloodshot. His skin was burning up.

Jacob poked him, tried to rouse him, but Luc wasn't moving, and Jacob suddenly grew scared. "Please, Luc, get up," Jacob pleaded.

"I'm sorry, my friend," Luc whispered. "But I cannot."

It dawned on Jacob that Luc wasn't complaining, and he wasn't being lazy. The man truly was in extreme distress. When he said he could not go another step, he was being utterly honest, and Jacob found himself facing a moral conundrum he had never contemplated. He couldn't imagine leaving the man, but they couldn't stay here either.

The crazy thing was that they were likely less than twenty kilometers from the border. They might be able to cross the border in one night, and they certainly could do it in two—if they were both healthy. But they were not.

Jacob stared down at Luc and for the first time considered the possibility that his friend might die from his illness, even that very night. He knew for certain now there was no point trying to push the man to get to his feet. It simply wasn't possible. Luc needed two things above all: food and medicine. Without both, he was not long for this world. Even with both, it might already be too late.

Some good it was doing them to read the Scriptures to each other or pray, Jacob decided. They had been doing both every day. Yet had it helped them in the slightest? Jacob could see no evidence of anything positive.

"Okay, listen; you stay here and rest," Jacob said, changing tactics. "I'm going to go find you food and medicine. I'll be back by morning. Don't go anywhere, all right?"

Luc smiled ever so faintly at the last comment and then closed his eyes, his breathing heavy and labored.

Jacob sprinted out of the old shack, fueled not by hope that he could save his friend but by fear that he could not. But he was determined to try.

For more than an hour he ran through the forest until he reached a ridge overlooking a quaint little hamlet several kilometers south of Żywiec Lake. Surveilling the sleepy village consisting of no more than two dozen homes at best, Jacob found himself drawn to a wooden house built on the outskirts of the tiny community. He noticed that while nearly all the other homes had laundry drying on clotheslines in the backyards, the clothesline behind this home was empty.

Jacob considered the options. Maybe these folks were tidier and more efficient than the rest of the hamlet. Or maybe they weren't at home. He didn't have time for an assessment more thorough than that. He was desperate for provisions he could take back to Luc, and it was already well after midnight. If he didn't move now, he was unlikely to make it back to the shack before the sun came up.

Almost forty minutes later, Jacob was down in the river valley, creeping alongside a small barn behind the house. Peeking through a dusty window, he confirmed that no car or truck was parked inside the barn, but he found tire tracks near the doors to the barn on the other side of the structure, suggesting that normally a vehicle was parked there. Moving from tree to tree, he made his way to the back door of the house and then stopped and crouched down to catch his breath and control his breathing.

Listening intently, he strained to pick up any sound that could be coming from inside the house. He heard nothing. He moved around the corner of the house and again stopped to listen. Again he heard nothing. It wasn't proof there wasn't someone—or an entire family—inside, of course. But at the very least, they were likely sound asleep.

As quietly as he could, Jacob continued moving around the side of the house until he came to a door. He tried the handle, but it was locked. He doubled back to the rear of the house to see if there was a door there he had missed. There wasn't, but he did find a door on the far side of the house. Unfortunately, this, too, was locked.

The only option left, aside from smashing through a window, was to try the front door. It seemed risky, but what choice did he have?

He carefully stepped onto the front porch and tiptoed toward the door. Wiping his hands on his pants to dry off the perspiration, he turned the doorknob.

To his shock, it kept turning, and before he knew it, the door was opening.

Jacob knew he was taking a terrible risk. Steinberger and Frenkel had warned him in no uncertain terms against making any contact with the "real world" until they were in Žilina. But the situation had changed, and in Jacob's judgment he didn't have a choice. He knew the stakes if he were found and caught. He would be hanged or shot by a firing squad if he didn't manage to kill himself first, and Luc would be left to die alone in the shack. But they desperately needed food—and medicine, if it could be found—and he was willing to take a chance to save his friend and, by extension, himself.

Without giving it another thought, Jacob entered the house. He did not see any dying embers in the fireplace. Nor did it seem as though the smell of a fire were lingering in the air. It was a simple home with simple wooden furniture. There was a wooden cross on the wall, and the floor creaked with every step. He noticed a cane by the front door and picked it up. Perhaps he could use it as a club if someone came upon him.

He moved through the front room, then stopped again and listened carefully. Hearing no one stirring, he kept moving forward, through the dining room with its table and six chairs, and down a hallway. He crept forward like a cat burglar, holding the cane so tightly his fingers were white. He tried to imagine what he would really do if the owners woke up and surprised him. Would he really hit them, here in their own home? It went against everything he was raised to be, and yet he could not allow himself to be captured and returned to Auschwitz.

Finally Jacob entered the kitchen. He just stood there for a few moments, taking in the sight in the moonlight coming through the windows. There were no dishes stacked in or around the sink, either clean or dirty. There were no crumbs on the counters, no food left out. The kitchen was clean and tidy.

But what made Jacob's eyes go wide were all the foodstuffs on the shelves and in the adjacent pantry. There were loaves of bread and jars of pickles and boxes of walnuts and almonds. There were bowls of fruit—apples and pears and even some grapes. There were baskets of freshly picked tomatoes and sacks of potatoes and bags of rice and flour. There were jars of sugar and salt and all manner of spices. There was even a plate of freshly baked cookies sitting on the counter alongside a basket of neatly folded laundry.

Jacob's mouth began to water. But as much as he wanted to, he didn't dare eat anything. Not here. Not yet.

The cookies and laundry scared him. They suggested to him that either the owners of the house were, in fact, upstairs sleeping or just away for a brief trip and would soon return.

He moved quickly to the laundry basket and found a freshly ironed pillowcase, one of at least a dozen. Using it as a sack, he loaded it with a little bit of everything except the flour and sugar and spices, which had no practical value for them since they could not bake or do anything but boil. As tempted as he was to clean out the kitchen completely, he tried to take only what he thought would not be noticeable. He even resisted taking a cookie, though that might have been the hardest decision of all. He couldn't afford to have the masters of the house think for one moment that they had been robbed. That would draw in the local constable and raise all kinds of questions that he did not want asked, much less answered.

Then, just as he was preparing to leave, he noticed a small bottle on the windowsill by the sink. Looking more closely, he realized it was filled with aspirin. He opened it quickly, poured out a dozen or so pills, and then replaced the cap and returned the bottle to its exact spot.

Would the pills actually help Luc? Of this Jacob was doubtful. What his friend needed was a hospital. He needed a team of trained medical professionals, not a couple of pills. But what else could he do? If he could get Luc to Žilina, he was sure the underground leaders there could put him under the care of good doctors and nurses. The question was how in the world Jacob was going to get Luc out of Poland before it was too late.

91

More than two dozen Gestapo agents took up their positions.

Acting on a tip from a suspicious neighbor, they moved toward the house under cover of darkness, guns drawn. Their orders were to capture this man alive, but they were taking no chances.

"No warnings," the officer whispered to his deputy. "We don't know who else is in there, and I don't want a hostage situation. Understood?"

The deputy nodded, and the Gestapo officer gave the signal.

Then agents stormed the house from every direction. They crashed through several windows and simultaneously kicked in the front and back doors. Gunfire soon rocked the night, and then, as quickly as it had begun, it was over.

"Colonel, you have a phone call."

Von Strassen was still in his office, as was his staff. Theirs were the only lights burning so late at night. Everyone else in Auschwitz had long since gone to sleep, save a few roving patrols of soldiers and the men who now manned the guard towers twenty-four hours a day, seven days a week, to prevent yet another escape.

He picked up the phone on his desk. "This is Colonel Von Strassen."

"Colonel, this is Commander Strauss," said the voice at the other end of the line. "I have news."

"Yes, Commander, what have you found?"

"Tonight my men and I stormed a farmhouse in Płońsk. Two men are dead. Six more are under arrest. But they were running a house of ill repute, not a safe house for the underground. I'm afraid your man Poczciwinski was not among them. I'm sorry. We'll keep looking. But we've been at this for several days, and I can't find any evidence that what your prisoner says is true. We've searched the monastery. We've searched more than two dozen houses in the area. If Poczciwinski and his men are operating here, we have not found them. But I must tell you that I highly doubt they are here. I think you have been sold a bill of goods, Herr Colonel. Sorry to be the bearer of such bad news."

Von Strassen cursed, but only under his breath. "I am in your debt, Commander," he replied. "Please thank your men for their hard work for *der Führer*. And I thank you for your call. Please let me know if there is anything I can do for you in the future."

Von Strassen hung up the phone and lit a cigarette, as angry as he had ever been.

Abigail Cohen had lied to him, and she was going to pay.

– – –

Jacob sprinted back through the forest, heading for the shack.

He had not eaten a bite of the food he had stolen. He had to get back before the sun came up, and he had to start feeding Luc as quickly as possible.

As he ran, trying desperately not to stumble in the darkness, he found himself overcome with anxiety that Luc might not live through the night. They were very different people, and they believed very different things. But Jacob knew he would have died inside Auschwitz if Luc had not shown him mercy again and again. What if Luc hadn't given him more soup in his bowl each night? What if he hadn't pulled him out of the elements to work in the bakery? What if he hadn't given him additional scraps of bread so often, without anyone else seeing? What if Luc hadn't been around to help prepare for this escape? Luc had never been acting on his own, of course. He'd had others helping him and watching his back. But the truth was he had proven himself a loyal and faithful friend, and Jacob was determined to nurse him back to health.

Finally he burst through the door of the shack. He found Luc curled up in a fetal position, barely conscious. Jacob quickly gave him some sips of water and two aspirin. Luc tried to swallow them but gagged, and they did not go down. A few minutes later, Jacob tried to give him a few small pieces of bread. Luc was almost too tired to chew and nearly too sick to swallow. Finally he choked it down, but not without an immense struggle, and Jacob realized this was going to take far longer than he'd thought.

If he couldn't take food, Luc had no hope of regaining his strength. If he didn't regain his strength, he wouldn't be able to run. If they didn't run, they would be caught and killed. And not just them. The lives of so many hung in the balance.

Discouraged, Jacob slumped down on the floor in the corner and bit into an apple he had taken from the pillowcase. Then, for the first time in his life, he got on his knees and said a prayer. Not a written, memorized prayer. Not any he had learned in the synagogue back in Siegen. But a conversational prayer. A prayer like the ones Luc always prayed. In this case, it was simple and direct. Jacob didn't have any fancy words or ornate verbiage.

He just pleaded with God to spare Luc's life.

92

Von Strassen was on his feet.

He buttoned his uniform and put on his hat and leather gloves and was about to march over to the detention cell where Abigail Cohen was being held.

But just as he was leaving the office, the phone rang.

His secretary, like the rest of the security chief's staff, looked haggard and was chain-smoking like there was no tomorrow. She had been up most of the night, and the work was far from over. But she took the call, listened for a moment, and then quickly flagged his attention before he could slip away. "Colonel, you have another phone call. I think you're going to want this one."

Von Strassen stopped in his tracks and muttered to himself. Then he turned and headed back into his office. He didn't acknowledge his secretary, much less thank her. He simply brushed past and asked the time. It was now just after six in the morning.

"Colonel Von Strassen?" asked the voice on the other end of the line when he picked up.

"Speaking."

"I am sorry to bother you so early in the morning, sir."

"To whom am I speaking?" Von Strassen demanded.

The man on the line explained that he was the chief of the local *Polizei* in a little town about five kilometers south of the Auschwitz-Birkenau camps. "I have a *konstabler* here who took an odd call last night," the man continued.

"How so?" Von Strassen asked.

"He was called to a farm by a resident," the police chief said. "He found evidence of at least one man, but probably two, who apparently were hiding out in the loft of the family's barn."

Von Strassen's attention was immediately piqued. "What kind of evidence?"

The police chief described the footprints, the bloody sock, the brown paper wrapping, and the dried drops of blood.

Von Strassen felt a rush of adrenaline. It was minimal evidence at best, but he knew instantly that Abigail Cohen had lied to him in more ways than one. Jacob Weisz and Jean-Luc Leclerc hadn't gone north to Warsaw. They were heading south. Where and to whom, he did not know. But he would find out, and he would hunt these men down if it was the last thing he did.

"Keep the evidence and the crime scene secure," Von Strassen ordered. "My men and I are coming to you."

He told the secretary to contact his deputy and order a half-dozen armed soldiers to meet him in the motor pool in fifteen minutes. He would deal with the traitor Cohen later. Right now he had a lead, and he was going to pursue it with all that he had. There were rumors that Heinrich Himmler, the Reich's interior minister, would soon be visiting Auschwitz, and Von Strassen did not want to be caught empty-handed.

If Himmler was coming, Von Strassen wanted to give him a gift, and two recaptured, terrified prisoners seemed as good a gift as any.

Jacob slept for a few hours.

When he awoke, he woke Luc up too and helped him take a few more sips of water. Then he unsuccessfully tried to get Luc to eat some apple slices. He offered him some grapes and finally a few small pieces of bread, but Luc simply closed his eyes and drifted back off to sleep.

It was growing clearer that solid food was not going to suffice. Jacob thought maybe some vegetable soup would be helpful, and if not the vegetables themselves, then perhaps some hot broth. They had brought a small metal pot. They had matches and salt, just as they had been instructed. They had a Swiss Army knife to cut up vegetables, and now they had a handful of potatoes, carrots, and onions. They had plenty of water. It was the makings of a feast.

But Jacob was nervous about preparing a fire, even a small one. What if someone saw the smoke rising through the forest? It was a risk he could not afford.

Rather than make a fire in the daytime, when the smoke would be so obvious, he decided to wait until nightfall. He could make a small fire with twigs and leaves and put it out as soon as the soup was done. He wasn't going anywhere tonight anyway. Until he helped Luc regain his strength, they were going to have to hole up in this shack and pray that no one saw or heard them.

In the meantime, Jacob munched on the bread and the fruit, savoring every morsel, and then he lay down and went back to sleep.

Von Strassen stepped out of his car and surveyed the farm.

He greeted the local police chief and told him he had no interest in meeting the family or the constable who had performed the initial investigation. His staff would interrogate them. All he wanted was to see the loft for himself.

"Take me there now," Von Strassen said, and the chief did as he was told.

The two men and Von Strassen's deputy entered the barn. But only Von Strassen and the deputy climbed the ladder, flashlights in hand. They crouched down and examined the evidence. All of it had been carefully preserved, as Von Strassen had ordered. Nothing had been disturbed or removed. The footprints were still there. So were the sock, the brown paper wrapping, and the rest.

"Clearly someone's been up here recently," the deputy said. "But it's not much to go on."

Von Strassen pulled out a pen and poked at the sock and then the wrapping paper but said nothing.

"Could've been anyone," the deputy added. "Certainly can't say who. Might be our guys. Might not be. Who's to say?"

But Von Strassen shook his head. "It's them," he said.

"Weisz and Leclerc?" the deputy asked.

Von Strassen nodded.

"How can you be sure?"

"See for yourself," Von Strassen said, pointing to the upper corner of the wrapping paper.

The deputy leaned in with his flashlight and immediately saw what his boss had seen—a single name written in a woman's handwriting: *Leonard J. Eliezer.*

Jacob finally awoke in the early evening.

He helped Luc take some more water, then drank some for himself and stepped outside. The summer sun was beginning to set, and the shadows in the forest were growing longer.

Neither seeing nor hearing evidence of anyone nearby, he went right to work. He gathered stones and created a small fire pit. Then he collected twigs and leaves and dry bark and even a few small, dead branches. After waiting another hour until it was completely dark, he lit a match and made the fire.

It didn't take long to boil the water. It had been a long time since he had cooked anything, and he found it almost fun slicing the vegetables and dropping them into the water one by one. He used a stick to stir the soup. He was sparing with the salt at first, not wanting to overdo it, but soon he had seasoned it perfectly, and he couldn't believe how good it tasted.

When he was finished, he kicked dirt on the fire and stomped on it until he was certain it was completely out. Then he took the small pot into the shack and sat down next to Luc.

"Hey, psst, sleepyhead."

Luc slowly opened his sullen, bloodshot eyes.

"Guess what? I made us some soup."

Luc's lips were chapped and blistered, but his eyes and mouth formed a slight smile, and Jacob proceeded to lift his head and help him take a spoonful of broth.

"Not bad," Luc whispered. "Who knew you could cook?"

Jacob smiled and gave him another spoonful, then regaled him with tales of cooking all manner of dishes for his parents and his uncle back in Siegen as he continued to feed him the warm, tasty broth.

When Luc had enough—not that much, really, but as much as his system could bear for now—Jacob hungrily wolfed down the rest. Rarely had something so simple tasted so good.

Luc quickly drifted back off to sleep, but Jacob wasn't tired. Achy? Yes, especially his back. Battling painful blisters on his feet? Absolutely. In desperate need of a hot shower? Without question. But Jacob was not tired. He had slept most of the day. He was young. He finally had real food in his system. And he was filled with anxieties. There was no way he was going to sleep tonight.

The fact was, he should be running. They both should be. Instead they were committing cardinal sins—everything Steinberger and Frenkel had warned them not to do. They had not effectively lived off the land. They had not made sure to have enough food every day. They had let themselves get too weak to continue. Jacob had entered a Polish village, running the risk of being spotted. What's more, he had actually broken into a private home and stolen food. He had tried to cover his tracks. He hoped the family wouldn't notice the missing items when they returned. But what if they did? What if they called the local constable? The amount of food he had taken and the effort he had expended to make it look inconspicuous would be giveaways. If common criminals had broken in, they would have taken valuables. Not potatoes. Not apples. Any half-competent investigator would know a fugitive was in the area. And if there was one, there could be two.

On top of all this, he and Luc were now staying in the same place two nights in a row. This was a fundamental error. Von Strassen and his men were cruel and soulless, but they were not idiots. They would not give up. Nor would they be allowed to. Not after three successive escape attempts in such a short time. Von Strassen was coming after them—that much was certain. And he had all the resources he needed to hunt them down and trap them like animals. What if a report from a local constable got back to him that a pair of fugitives might be lurking in the area? How long would it take to flood this area with soldiers and policemen and dogs? True, he and Luc were holed up a good hour away from the house he had broken into. They were in the mountains, far from civilization. Maybe Von Strassen wouldn't think to extend the search zone quite that far.

But what if he did?

Racked by fear, unable to sleep, and with a whole night ahead, Jacob had to find something to do. He wished he had stolen a good book from the house. Actually, any book would suffice. He had already gone so far as to take food for the body. Why not a little food for the mind?

Then Jacob remembered that he already had a book with him. Two, in fact. So he propped himself up against one wall of the shack, pulled from the backpack the book of Psalms that Abby had given him, and began to devour it as hungrily as he had devoured the soup.

93

The next day a major summer storm descended upon them.

Lightning flashed. Thunder boomed. Fierce winds howled through the forest, and against his will, Jacob had to remain hunkered in the shack. They were beginning to run low on provisions again, but there was nothing to be done. He certainly could not go out in this nightmare. Then again, Luc wasn't eating much anyway. He was sleeping almost around the clock, and Jacob didn't know what to do for him.

Still, one element had become a daily ritual. Each morning Jacob would read aloud another psalm to Luc, keeping his commitment to Abby. And each morning Jacob would also read a chapter from the Gospel of John, since Luc hadn't the energy to read aloud himself.

The truth was, reading from the New Testament was somewhat uncomfortable for Jacob. But he reminded himself he was doing it for Abby's sake. Yet Jacob also did it because it was becoming clear that the words of Jesus seemed to comfort and console Luc in a way that nothing else did.

This particular morning's first reading was Psalm 10.

Why do You stand afar off, O Lord?
Why do You hide Yourself in times of trouble? . . .
Arise, O Lord; O God, lift up Your hand.
Do not forget the afflicted. . . .
Break the arm of the wicked and the evildoer,

Seek out his wickedness until You find none. . . .
O Lord, You have heard the desire of the humble;
You will strengthen their heart, You will incline Your ear
To vindicate the orphan and the oppressed,
So that man who is of the earth will no longer cause terror.

Then Jacob picked up the New Testament and read John chapter 10, in which Jesus described himself as the "good shepherd." Reading it, Jacob thought of the Twenty-Third Psalm—Abby's favorite—the first full psalm he had read upon opening her gift.

When Jacob was finished, Luc motioned for him to come closer, and Jacob did.

"That's my favorite verse in the Bible," Luc whispered, his eyes still closed, his voice raspy and weak.

"Which one?" Jacob asked.

"Ten."

Jacob looked back at the text and reread John 10:10 aloud. "'The thief comes only to steal and kill and destroy; I came that they may have life, and have it abundantly.'"

Both men were silent for a little while, and Jacob felt helpless as he looked at his friend wasting away.

"What day is it?" Luc suddenly asked.

Jacob had to think about that. "I think it's June 17."

Luc sighed. "I wanted to make it to my . . ."

"To your what, Luc?"

". . . my birthday."

"When is that?"

"August."

"August what?"

"Eleventh."

"Don't worry, Luc. You'll make it," Jacob said. "And we'll have a big party with your grandfather in Washington, the grandest party you've ever seen."

Luc tried to smile. "No, I'm . . . I'm not going to make it to Washington, my friend."

"Of course you are," Jacob replied. "You just stick with me. I'll get you there."

"No, Jacob, I'm going home to be with my Lord," Luc said, weak and yet strangely calm.

"No. Don't say that."

"It's okay," Luc assured him. "I want to go. I can't wait to be with my Savior. To be with him in person? To see him face-to-face? I cannot think of anything better, though I will miss you. You have been a good friend."

Jacob wouldn't hear of it. He tried to encourage Luc to stay focused and stay positive, but though Luc's voice was faltering, his conviction was firm. He was leaving this world and heading to the next, but he promised to pray for Jacob before the very throne of Israel's King.

"You can't leave now," Jacob said, fighting to keep his emotions in check. "We're not finished with our mission."

"I am," Luc whispered. "And I'm holding you back from finishing yours."

"That's nonsense."

"No, it's true, and you know it," Luc said. "I've run my race. I've fought my fight. Now it's on you. Everybody's counting on you. So go, get that strongbox to the Jewish council. Then take it to my grandfather. Take out a piece of paper and a pencil. I will give you his address in Washington. And when they liberate the camps and the war is over, go find Abby. Marry her. Settle down someplace quiet and safe, and have lots of babies. Okay?"

Jacob's bottom lip began to quiver. He had to wipe away a tear, and then he turned away lest he embarrass himself any further. But he wouldn't give up. He knew Luc was in a weakened state, and he could hardly blame the man for thinking this way. But Jacob refused to accept the idea that their mission together was over.

There was a long silence, and then Luc finally spoke again in a whisper. "Did I ever tell you Claire and I were expecting another child when I was arrested?" he asked.

He never had. "Really?"

"I wonder if it was a boy or a girl," Luc said so softly that Jacob could barely hear him.

Then he closed his eyes.

Abby Cohen sat chained in a cell, all alone, no other prisoners in sight.

They had not tortured her yet. Not physically, at least. They had not yet beaten her or cut off her fingers or gouged out her eyes.

They had, of course, shot a friend of hers in the head right in front of her. They had put her in isolation, unable to walk, unable to move about, unable to see or converse with anyone. They had taken away Jacob's journal before she had had the chance to read his poems, let alone remember them or recite them.

Maybe Von Strassen knew her better than anyone else. Cutting off her contact with people was like cutting off her supply of oxygen. She wasn't suffering physically, but she was dying all the same. And for what? How much longer could it possibly take for the Gestapo to determine that she was lying? Then what was going to happen? Were they going to kill her, or were they going to make the suffering last forever?

She tried not to think about what Von Strassen and Hoess had done to Max. It was too much to bear. She tried instead to think of Jacob and Luc. Would she ever see them again? Would they really come back for her, for all of them?

That was too much to hope for, she decided. She recalibrated her thoughts, narrowed her focus a bit. Were Jacob and Luc free? Were they safe? If so, where were they now? How were they doing? Had they opened their gifts?

She would have given anything to see their faces.

94

As evening fell, Jacob went out into the woods to relieve himself.

When he had finished and was returning to the shack, he came back up the dirt trail, walked around a bend, and stopped dead in his tracks and gasped.

Standing on the trail ahead of him, not ten yards away, was a young boy.

"Who are *you*?" the boy asked, as startled as Jacob was.

It took Jacob a few seconds to recover. He stared at the boy, who was wearing muddy trousers, work boots, and a red flannel shirt over a gray T-shirt. He had a knapsack slung over his back and was carrying a fishing pole in one hand and a tackle box in the other. He wasn't carrying a rifle, thank goodness, but Jacob knew instantly the boy wasn't out in the wilderness alone.

"What are you doing here?" he replied, trying to give his voice a tone of authority that might scare the boy off.

"Just walking with my papa," the boy said.

"Where is he?" Jacob demanded.

"I'm sure he'll be along in a few minutes, mister, so please don't do anything to hurt me."

Jacob thought for a moment, and then, without saying another word, he began running. He ran right past the boy, no doubt giving him a terrible fright, and back to the cabin.

That was it. They'd been blown. They couldn't stay there another minute. A man with a rifle and no doubt a whole lot of ammunition was on his way.

Jacob burst into the shack. He grabbed the backpack, tossed everything they had into it, and put it on. Then he reached down, lifted Luc over his back, and began running down the trail, away from the boy and his father, toward the town with the house he had robbed.

Suddenly a gunshot rang out in the night. Then another. Jacob could feel the bullets whizzing by his head, but he didn't look back. He just kept running down the path, over rocks, around trees, careful not to get entangled in roots or branches.

Unfortunately, Luc was bigger and heavier than he'd realized, and the extra weight slowed Jacob down considerably. Indeed, the man was about six feet tall and had to weigh at least one hundred and thirty pounds, though he had, no doubt, been much heavier before being shipped to Auschwitz.

After less than twenty minutes, Jacob had to stop and take a break. He checked the trail behind them. No one. He set Luc down on the ground and fought to catch his breath.

So far there was no sign of the father or the boy. But that was the question haunting him. Did they know who he was, and if so, were they coming after him?

Von Strassen was back in his office at Auschwitz when he got the call.

It was from an SS officer in Żywiec, a city of close to thirty thousand. The officer told Von Strassen that the local police had just received a report of a father and son stumbling across two men who appeared to be fugitives hiding out in an old hunting cabin in the hills not far from the town of Cisiec. "The witnesses say one of them was carrying the other over his back," the SS officer reported. "They weren't sure if the man was wounded or just ill. But it was clear they were disreputable and up to no good. The father fired several shots at the men but missed."

"Why didn't he pursue them?" Von Strassen demanded.

"The man's son is only thirteen," the officer said. "To protect the boy, the father thought it wiser to retreat and call the police."

"How long ago was this?"

"Several hours."

"Why am I only finding out about it now?" Von Strassen pressed.

"I just learned of it myself no more than ten minutes ago," the officer said. "It took the two quite some time to hike back to civilization and longer still to find a phone. Once I got the news, I tracked you down immediately. What do you want us to do?"

"I want a full lockdown of the entire area for twenty-five kilometers in every direction," Von Strassen ordered. "Total military curfew. No one leaves their houses until we say they do. Mobilize every policeman and every soldier in the region. Put up roadblocks every two kilometers. All cars must get off the roads. Official vehicles only. Every car still on the road must be pulled over and searched thoroughly. Every house will be searched, door to door. Search every store, every shop, every barn, every petrol station, all of it. Get search planes in the air. Get the word to the radio stations. Have newscasters give out descriptions of Weisz and Leclerc. Put out the word that they are murderers, wanted for killing two little girls in a farmhouse near Oświęcim. Tell people these two are armed and dangerous, but we want them alive. I want radio updates posted every fifteen minutes. My men and I will be there soon."

"Yes, sir," the SS officer said. "We'll get right on it."

"You had better," Von Strassen warned. "You have six hours. If these two are not caught by then, I will hold you personally responsible."

Jacob knew exactly where he was taking Luc and why.

He had only one option, and there was no point agonizing over it. If it worked, they might be safe. If not, they'd be dead by sunup.

Jacob thought it would take about two hours to get there, but it took nearly four. He stopped to rest. He stopped to gulp down water. But panting and exhausted, he finally reached the ridge overlooking the tiny community and lay Luc down under a grove of trees.

"Okay, we're almost there," Jacob said. "Now listen, Luc. Remember that home I told you about—the one where I got the food?"

Luc nodded.

Jacob hadn't told his Christian friend that he had stolen the food. But that was the least of his worries just now.

"Well, they have a car they keep in their barn," Jacob whispered, not lying yet but about to. "I'm going to ask them to help us. They took pity on us before. I'm hoping they'll take pity on us now. Hopefully they can drive us close to the border and drop us off. Then I'll carry you across, and we'll make our way to Žilina. How's that sound?"

Luc nodded groggily, and Jacob knew he was really out of it. The plan, after all, would have been a terrible one if it were true. The problem was, the real plan wasn't much better.

"So you just wait here, and I'll be back for you soon," Jacob said.

"When?" Luc asked.

"As soon as the coast is clear and the family agrees to help us," Jacob replied. "Then I'll come back for you and get you in that car. Before you know it, you'll be with your grandfather in Washington. So you just rest here, and I won't be long. I promise."

No sooner had he said it than Jacob wanted to take that last sentence back. How could he promise that he would be back quickly? What if he were shot or captured? There was a very real possibility he wouldn't be back at all.

95

As the sun began to rise, Jacob heard two planes fly low overhead.

He quickly hid in some bushes and waited for the planes to pass. They were flying unusually low, and he couldn't help but wonder once again if these were search planes. He no longer had the cover of darkness, just when he needed it most. But there was nothing he could do about it. If he was going to move at all, now was the time.

Jacob dashed down the hill, zigzagging through the trees. When he got to the bottom, he saw no signs of anyone walking about the property. He did, however, see smoke rising from the chimney. Someone was home, and they likely were beginning to cook breakfast. The problem was that the kitchen looked out into the backyard and a grassy field that stretched beyond it. Yet there was no way to get to the barn other than through the field. Jacob considered crawling on his hands and knees, but the grass wasn't really tall enough to hide him. The only option, he decided, was to run for it. But first he had to pray.

"Dear God, uh, I don't really know if you're there," he said with his eyes closed and his head bowed. "But if you're real, please help me now—not for my sake, but to help my friend Luc. Okay, that's—that's all."

Feeling somewhat ridiculous, he opened his eyes again and scanned in both directions for any signs of people. Seeing none, Jacob broke into a mad dash across the field. Nine seconds later, he was hiding behind the barn, panting hard, trying to catch his breath, and waiting to hear sounds of anyone stirring or the cocking of a rifle.

After two or three minutes, hearing nothing and knowing there was no time to spare, he crept along the side of the barn farthest from the house and peeked through the dusty, smudgy window, just as he had done the first time he had come.

His instincts had been right. Not only was the family home, but they'd parked their car in the barn. Actually, it was a pickup. Now Jacob prayed they had left the keys in the ignition.

He carefully opened the side door of the barn and slipped inside. Then he headed straight to the cab of the pickup and opened the driver's-side door. But when he looked inside, he found no keys. He looked on the seat and under the floor mat but found nothing. He went around to the other side and opened the passenger door and looked all around, then opened the glove compartment but found no keys there either.

That was when he heard the pump action of a shotgun.

Jacob's heart sank, and fear began to envelop him like a thick, dark cloud.

"Hold it, right there!" ordered the voice behind him. *"Put your hands where I can see them. Do it!"*

What choice did he have? If he tried to flee, he'd be shot dead. That was fine, as far as he was concerned. There was no way he was going back to Auschwitz. But he couldn't leave Luc alone to die in the elements. So he raised his hands over his head, and when the man told him to turn around slowly, that's exactly what he did.

Now he was staring into a double-barreled shotgun. The Polish farmer who was holding it looked to be in his mid- to late sixties. He had a firm jaw and a weathered face, and what was left of his hair was all gray now. But it was the look in the man's eyes that struck Jacob most. The man looked as scared as Jacob was. His eyes were darting back and forth even as he kept the gun aimed straight for Jacob's head.

What's more, his terrified wife, a plump little lady with gray hair tied up in a bun, was standing not far behind him.

"Where's the other one?" the man demanded.

Jacob was startled. "What do you mean?"

"Don't toy with me, son. The man on the radio said there are two of you. Now where's the other one?"

The man on the radio? What in the world was he talking about?

"You've got three seconds, boy. If you don't tell me where he is, I'm going to blow your head off and then hunt him down too. So talk."

Jacob was dumbfounded by this sudden turn of events. But the calculation was obvious—talk or die. So he talked. In fact, he found himself pleading for mercy. He explained that his friend was dying and that he had left him lying under a grove of trees on the side of the mountain.

"What's wrong with him?" the man asked, his skepticism palpable.

Jacob wanted to lie but couldn't. He told the couple exactly what was wrong with Luc and how he was trying to save his life. He confessed to entering their house the other night and taking some of their food, and he didn't simply confess but apologized profusely and begged their forgiveness.

And then, before he fully realized what he was doing, he told the couple about their escape from Auschwitz. He didn't say he was Jewish, and he didn't describe the place as a death camp. He simply said he and Luc had been persecuted by the Nazis and thrown into a prison camp for crimes they didn't commit. He even told them of his friends in the Polish underground and how they helped each other escape, hoping to appeal to some shred of nationalism in the couple.

Jacob couldn't believe what was coming out of his mouth. Not because it wasn't true but because it was. Other than Luc and the boy in the woods, Jacob had not spoken to anyone outside of Auschwitz-Birkenau since Brussels. And now, in a moment of sheer madness, he had just confessed to a whole series of capital crimes, the most serious of which was escaping from a Nazi prison.

"The radio says you two are murderers," the wife said, more of an indictment than a question.

"Murderers?" Jacob said, a fresh wave of fear washing over him. "Who did they say we killed?"

"Two little girls."

Jacob gasped. "It's not true," he said. "Never would we do such a thing."

The man's hands were trembling so much Jacob was afraid he might accidentally pull the trigger at any moment.

"How do I know you'd never do such a thing?" the man asked. "You've just confessed to being in prison, escaping from prison, helping others escape from prison, breaking into our house, and stealing our food. You don't sound like a good person. Not to me."

"What he wants to know is, are you a God-fearing man? Were your folks God-fearing people?" the wife asked bluntly.

Jacob's stomach tightened. He didn't know what to say. He definitely didn't want to lie. Not to a question like that. Not just because it would be too easy to expose it as a lie—after all, he knew next to nothing about Christianity but what he had learned from Luc and read in the Gospels over the last few days. But he also felt a deep sense of conviction that it would be wrong to mislead this couple. He had told them the truth thus far. Why stop now?

"Speak up," the man demanded. "Are you a Christian or aren't you?"

Jacob paused. "No, sir," he said.

The man looked surprised. "You're not?"

"No, sir."

"Then what are you?"

Jacob took a deep breath. "I'm a Jew."

It was as if all the air had been sucked out of the room. The couple's eyes went wide, and both of them, independent of each other, literally took a step backward. It was suddenly clear to Jacob that they had never met a Jew before—had probably never even seen one. And they knew what the penalty was for harboring a Jewish fugitive.

"Where's your yellow star?" the wife asked, visibly trying to regain her composure.

"When I escaped, I refused to wear one again," Jacob said, trying to imagine what his fate would be now that he was cornered. "I didn't want to be arrested or sent back to Auschwitz."

Jacob closed his eyes and winced, bracing for the shot that would take his life.

The barn was quiet again.

Unlike Luc, Jacob was terrified of dying. He had no idea what would greet him on the other side. He had no idea whether he was going to heaven or to hell, and he suddenly realized he didn't want to find out. Not here. Not now. And the longer he waited for the man to fire, the more fearful he became. But nothing happened, and Jacob slowly opened his eyes.

To Jacob's shock, the man lowered the shotgun. His wife came to his side. They didn't look like they were going to kill him anymore. They were not smiling. But something in their bearing had changed. They seemed more peaceful and more trusting than they had just moments before.

"We believe you, son," the man said at long last.

"You do?" Jacob asked.

"Yes."

"All of it?"

"All of it."

"Why?"

"Well, the way I figure it, no one in his right mind would tell a man pointing a loaded shotgun at his face that he's a Jew unless that was God's honest truth. And if that's true, I figure it's all true."

"It *is* all true."

"I'm sure it is, son. What a terrible ordeal you and your friend have been through. What do you say we go get him and bring him to the house and see if we can't take care of him—or at least make him comfortable?"

Jacob didn't know what to say. He was in shock. So he just nodded.

"What about the military curfew?" the wife asked.

"Who's going to see us?" her husband replied. "We'll be there and back before anyone is the wiser. But we better get going. By the way, my name is Jedrick, and this is my wife, Brygita."

They reached out their hands and shook his warmly.

96

Cisiec was a sleepy little town.

It was nondescript, without major industries or attractions, home to only about three thousand people. It was located just south of the city of Żywiec, which had about ten times the population. But Cisiec had just become the center of one of the most extensive manhunts in the region's history.

Von Strassen and his men pulled onto the town's main street and drove immediately to the local police station, where the SS officer was directing all of the activities and tracking the progress of the air and ground units as well as those forces patrolling the Soła River and its banks. Von Strassen was given a briefing on what had happened thus far while his deputy reinterrogated the father and son who had reported seeing the fugitives several hours before.

"Your men are moving house to house, barn to barn, store to store, searching every possible hiding place?" Von Strassen pressed.

The SS officer assured him that every step was being taken and that his men were well-trained and well-briefed on what a high-priority operation this was.

"All nonessential vehicles are off the roads?" Von Strassen asked.

"They are now, Colonel. That took a while. But the roads are now clear."

"Very well. Any leads?"

"We've gotten a flood of calls from citizens who think they've seen something. Most of it is, as you might expect, not helpful. But we are treating every call with great seriousness, and we are continuing to put out radio bulletins every fifteen minutes asking for more citizen help, as you requested."

"Show me the grids of the areas you have completed searching so far," Von Strassen demanded.

"Absolutely, Colonel," the SS officer said. "We have the maps in the next room."

"What town is this?" Jacob asked as he and Jedrick moved out to get Luc.

"It's actually not a town at all," Jedrick explained. "It's too small to be a town."

"Well, what's the nearest town?" Jacob asked.

"Well, you've got Żywiec to the north; that's about twenty kilometers away. Between here and there is the town of Cisiec. To the south is Milówka and then Rajcza, then Ujsoły and Glinka, and then you're at the frontier with Slovakia."

There was a pause, and then the man said, "I assume that's where you're headed."

Jacob said nothing, but he figured his silence was confirmation. "Your wife said they've imposed a curfew," he said instead. "They're looking for the two of us?"

"They are," Jedrick said. "They've even given out detailed descriptions of what you look like, and they mentioned that you have numbers tattooed on your arms, which I see you do."

"Every prisoner at the Auschwitz camp is given one," Jacob explained as they kept moving up the hill toward Luc.

Jedrick nodded but quickly backed away from the subject.

Jacob used the moment. "May I ask you a question, sir?"

"Of course."

"Aren't you worried about taking us in?"

"Well, sure, a little."

"Why are you doing it?"

"Because the Bible teaches us to love the Jews," Jedrick said without hesitation. "God told Abraham that he would bless those who blessed him and curse those who cursed him. When we stand before our Savior, we want to be found faithful, plain and simple. That, and the fact that the Nazis killed both of our boys right after the war started. It's the least we can do to help you two survive this hell we're all in."

Jacob didn't know what to say, so he just said, "Thank you."

Together, Jacob and Jedrick walked over to Luc, who was still lying under the trees. Luc wasn't moving. He didn't even look like he was breathing.

Panicked, Jacob checked for Luc's pulse, but he could not find one. He began shaking Luc, willing him to wake up, but his friend didn't respond.

How was this possible—and now, when they finally had found people who could help them, who could feed them and keep them safe?

Jacob's eyes welled up with tears, and he had to fight to maintain his control. He couldn't lose it. Not now. Not out in the open. The longer they were out here, the more he was putting this man's life, his wife's life, his own life, and his entire mission in grave danger. And yet how could he not mourn? His friend was gone, and he hadn't even had the chance to say good-bye.

"Get down!" Jedrick shouted all of a sudden.

He pushed Jacob to the ground under the grove of trees and flattened himself to the ground as well just as a pair of Luftwaffe planes came roaring overhead. This time Jacob had no doubt they were looking for him.

"Do you think they saw us?" he asked when the planes had passed out of view.

"I don't know," Jedrick said. "Probably not. But we'd better get moving. I will help you bring your friend. For now we can hide his body, and then as soon as we can, I will help you give him a proper burial."

The two men struggled to carry Luc's body down to the house. For almost the entire way down the hill, they were out in the open, utterly exposed if the search planes made another pass. But finally, soaked with sweat in the rapidly rising morning temperatures, they made it to the back porch of the house.

"Did you find your friend? Is he okay?" Brygita asked as she came to the screen door.

"He's dead," Jacob said numbly.

The woman put her hand over her mouth.

"Where can we put him?" Jacob asked. "There's no time to bury him now."

"No, there surely isn't," she said. "The radio says the Gestapo and the army are going door to door to search everyone's house. The last report said they were just finishing Cisiec now. That means they should be here any minute."

Jedrick thought for a moment. "I was going to say the barn, up in the loft, but with the storms over and the sun out, it's going to be an inferno in there by lunchtime. The body will start to smell as it decomposes."

"Do you have a basement?" Jacob asked.

"We do," Jedrick replied.

"Is it cool?"

"Certainly cooler than the barn."

"What's down there?"

"It's where we stack all our firewood to keep it dry. I have my workshop down there and my gun cabinet."

"Is there a place to hide a body?" Jacob pressed.

"Yes," he said. "Actually there is, and a place to hide you, too."

"Then we'd better move fast."

They quickly carried Luc's body up the porch steps and into the kitchen while Brygita carried the shotgun and Jacob's backpack. But no sooner had they set him on the floor for a moment to catch their breath than someone began pounding on the front door.

Brygita gasped. "It's them," she whispered with terror in her eyes. "It's the Gestapo."

But Jedrick didn't flinch. "I'll answer the door, keep them occupied," he said. "Son, you take your friend downstairs. My wife will show you where to put him and where to hide yourself. Then, Brygita, you scramble right back up here and bring out cookies and milk or something, real hospitable. Got it?"

They both nodded even as the pounding grew louder.

Jacob lifted Luc into a fireman's carry and hustled down the basement steps. Brygita was right behind him. When he reached the bottom, he saw a massive woodpile lining the far wall. Taking Jacob around the side, Brygita showed him a crawl space behind it that looked just wide enough for him to squeeze into.

"I've got to get upstairs. Hide here and keep quiet. And know this: we're praying for you. God bless you."

Then she handed him his backpack, raced up the stairs, turned out the lights, and closed the door.

Jacob was speechless.

And now he was alone in the dark with Luc's body and no way to defend himself when the Nazis came down those steps.

97

Jedrick walked slowly, acting like a much older man, fumbling with his keys.

"Open this door!" someone shouted from outside.

Through the window Jedrick counted three heavily armed Nazis on his front porch and glimpsed at least three others bearing submachine guns fanning out over his property.

"Yes, yes, I'm coming; just a moment," he said, moving as if he were in his eighties or nineties rather than his sixties.

When he finally opened the door, he said, "What can I do for you, gentlemen?"

"Are you the only one in the county who doesn't know?" the lead soldier asked.

"I'm sorry," Jedrick said. "Know what?"

"Don't you listen to the radio?"

"Sometimes, but not today, I'm afraid. Why?"

"We are conducting a hunt for two dangerous fugitives."

"Fugitives? That does sound dangerous. What kind of fugitives?"

"Murderers. Two of them."

"Here, in the middle of nowhere?"

"We have reason to believe they may have come your way."

"Well, I haven't seen anybody out of the ordinary—except for you, of course."

"Of course."

"But if I do, should I call the constable?"

"Yes," the soldier said. "But first we will make a thorough search of your house, barn, and property."

"Oh, that won't be necessary," Jedrick said. "We will call if we see anything strange."

"Ah, but we insist." The soldier poked the muzzle of his submachine gun into Jedrick's chest and backed him away from the door. "These men are psychopaths. We wouldn't want you to be in any danger. Is the *Frau* of the house here too?"

"Yes, of course."

"Then all the more reason to be careful."

Two soldiers stepped into the house as Brygita came in with a tray of cookies, a small pitcher of cold milk, and several glasses.

"Welcome, gentlemen," she said, setting the tray on the coffee table in the living room. "What an honor to have you in our home. Can you stay for a while and tell us more about what is happening?"

"That won't be possible. We are here not on a social call but in the interest of public safety."

One of the soldiers headed upstairs, while another brushed past them and made for the kitchen. A third man stood calmly on the porch, neither entering nor leaving his post. He wore a long black leather coat and shiny black boots and displayed a classic officer's uniform and bearing. Jedrick assumed he must be SS.

"Sit here," the lead soldier said, gripping the submachine gun at his side. "You may not leave or move until I give you the all-clear signal. Have I made myself clear?"

The couple nodded and sat down on the couch, their hearts racing and mouths dry. Yet they dared not have a drink of milk. At this point, they dared not move at all.

98

Jacob heard the jackboots walking across the kitchen floor.

Then he heard the basement door handle turn, and someone flipped on the lights. Then, step by step, someone—a soldier, he had to presume—began moving down the stairs.

Jacob was not in the crawl space behind the woodpile, though his backpack was, along with the strongbox containing all the documents they had smuggled out of Auschwitz.

He had decided he would never be safe in a house crawling with Nazi soldiers, especially trapped in an enclosed space. A manhunt was under way. They were looking for him and Luc. A plane had just overflown them. How could he be sure they hadn't been seen? How could he be certain they wouldn't tear this house apart to find them? This was no time to hide. It was time to fight.

In a split second, Jacob had decided that his only hope was to turn the tables and go on offense. He had no idea if it would work, but he had made his choice, and now he would live or die by it.

So Jacob stood inside a storage closet with the door partially ajar. Now that the lights were on, his position gave him a rather commanding view of the main section of the basement. He watched the Nazi come down the last few steps and observed the soldier as he saw Luc's body lying facedown on the floor.

The soldier raised his weapon and demanded that the man stand up. When Luc didn't reply, the soldier kicked him, but again, of course, there was no movement. Now the soldier was poking and prodding him. When he was convinced the man was not a threat, he bent down to check his pulse.

That's when Jacob made his move. He burst out of the closet and smashed a piece of firewood across the back of the man's head as hard as he could. The soldier instantly collapsed to the floor on top of Luc, but Jacob didn't stop. He couldn't afford a fight with this man, a trained killer. So he smashed his head in until he was sure the Nazi was dead. Then he checked his pulse, just to be sure, rolled him off of Luc, and removed his submachine gun and his Luger.

Now Jacob had the initiative, and he used it to full advantage. Gauging the Nazi to be roughly his same height, Jacob quickly stripped him of his uniform and put it on himself. It wasn't going to be enough to come up from the basement with guns blazing. He realized he was going to need an additional element of surprise both in the next few minutes and for his escape into Slovakia, if he lived that long.

A few minutes later he was ready, and just in time. For now another soldier was calling down the stairs.

"Hans, are you down there?"

"*Ja,*" Jacob said.

"There's no one in the upstairs. Did you find something?"

"*Ja*, come," Jacob said, muffling his voice a bit in hopes of convincing the man to accept the bait.

It worked. As Jacob stood there in the Nazi uniform, looking over the two bodies facedown on the floor, he heard the other soldier coming down the stairs, gasping and laughing with joy.

"Hans, you did it! You found them! Were they dead already, or did you kill them yourself? I didn't even hear the shot."

Jacob did not answer. Instead he quickly pivoted around, faced the second Nazi, raised the silencer-equipped Luger, aimed it at the man's chest, and fired three shots in rapid succession. The stunned man died and collapsed to the floor before he even knew he was being ambushed.

Jacob's heart was racing, but he didn't dare let down his guard. He had no idea how many other soldiers were upstairs. For all he knew, there could be an entire battalion. But he had killed two, and if he were to die, he was determined to take more Nazis with him.

Taking the second man's Luger as well, he fit it also with the standard-issue silencer in the man's coat pocket. He also fished out of the man's pockets additional ammunition for the pistol and the submachine gun and reloaded.

With the submachine gun from the first soldier he'd killed strapped to his side, he moved carefully up the stairs and entered the kitchen as quietly as he could. At that moment another soldier was coming up the steps onto the back porch. He smiled as he opened the door to the kitchen, ready to see a familiar face. Instead he found Jacob aiming a pistol at his head and firing twice.

The man dropped instantly, but unlike the others, he made a lot of noise as he fell backward and crashed down the steps.

Jacob scanned the backyard, the field, and the barn. He didn't see anyone out there at the moment, but that didn't mean someone wasn't there. Also, he had not yet cleared the living room, and he was worried that someone could catch him off guard and shoot him in the back as easily as he had taken down these first three.

He turned quickly and moved back through the kitchen, then pressed himself against the wall between the kitchen and living room and tried to calm his breathing. That proved impossible, and he feared someone was going to hear him and ambush him at any moment.

The only chance he had was to seize the initiative. The uniform had clearly bought him precious time. Perhaps it would do so again.

Jacob took a deep breath and then marched into the living room as if he owned the place. Remarkably, Jedrick and Brygita didn't even recognize him at first. But he wasn't looking for them. He was looking for other soldiers.

There were none in the room. He saw one outside by the car, taking a swig of water from a canteen. He was dressed differently from the others—in a long leather coat—and Jacob assumed he was a Gestapo officer, though at the moment the man's back was to him, so he couldn't get a good look at the exact type of uniform he was wearing.

To Jacob's relief, there were no other soldiers in the front yard, so he headed upstairs. He went room by room, checking to see if anyone was up there. No one was, but through one of the bedroom windows he could see two soldiers in the barn, turning the place upside down in search of the two men from Auschwitz.

Jacob quickly looked out the other bedroom windows. There were no other soldiers to be seen. If he was right, then there were only two in the barn and the Gestapo agent out by the car.

This was his chance. But he had to move fast.

He raced down the stairs and blew past the Polish couple so fast they never had time to see his face. Then he rushed out the back door and ran across the backyard to the barn. Peeking through the window, he saw one soldier searching the loft and the other going through the pickup truck.

Gripping the Luger in his sweaty right palm, Jacob moved around to the door on the far side of the barn and entered quickly. The soldier looked up from his task of rummaging through the pickup. He saw Jacob and shouted to his partner. A split second later Jacob fired two bullets into his head. But the damage was done.

The soldier searching the loft swung around and opened fire with his submachine gun. Jacob dove behind the pickup truck, which was now being pelted with bullets. Shattered glass flew everywhere. Jacob suddenly found himself pinned down behind the truck, and his enemy had the high ground.

Another burst of submachine-gun fire ripped up the barn walls behind him, sending splinters of wood through the air like daggers. Jacob knew he desperately needed to regain the momentum. But he had to watch his back. All this gunfire was surely going to draw the Gestapo agent, and Jacob was going to find himself in a two-on-one gunfight with men who really knew what they were doing. Another burst of gunfire came his way. But when it stopped, Jacob could hear the soldier ejecting a spent magazine and loading a full one.

Releasing the safety on his own submachine gun, Jacob popped up from behind the pickup truck and fired his first burst, sending the Nazi diving for cover. He fired a second burst, too, then dropped back to his knees.

The soldier sensed his moment. He returned fire, taking out the barn window immediately over Jacob's head, raining shards of broken glass down on him.

This time Jacob didn't stand up. Instead he raised the submachine gun over his head, pointed into the far left corner of the barn, and unleashed two long bursts. Now his magazine was empty. It took him a moment to figure out how to eject it and several seconds more to figure out how to load a full magazine, and in this time the Nazi fired three more long bursts.

Suddenly Jacob shrieked in pain. He'd been hit by something in the left leg. For the moment, he couldn't tell if it was broken glass or a bullet that had ricocheted off the truck or the back wall, but it hurt like nothing Jacob had ever experienced before. It was a hot, searing pain that set his entire left leg on fire. But Jacob was determined not to die in a crouched position, defensive, taking fire. If this was really it, he was going down swinging.

When he heard the Nazi reloading a second time, he gritted his teeth and forced himself to his feet. Limping now toward the back of the barn, Jacob fired a long burst into the corner of the loft, forcing the soldier into a crouch. A moment later, Jacob was at the other end of the barn, under the loft and out of the view of the soldier above him. Now Jacob had the advantage, and he used it. He aimed straight up and pulled the trigger. In less than six seconds, he had completely emptied his last magazine. But he had also hit his target and could hear the Nazi screaming in agony until at last he was no more.

Just then the man in the leather coat ripped open the main barn doors and started firing his submachine gun.

Jacob instantly dropped to the ground and scrambled for cover against the front of the pickup truck. Then he tossed aside his empty submachine gun and pulled one of the pistols from his pocket. Looking underneath the carriage of the truck, Jacob could see the man moving to the left. So Jacob moved to the right. He thought about trying to shoot out the man's legs but knew he was not a good-enough shot. Plus, he had limited ammunition and no time to reload.

This was it. He had one chance to take this guy out, or he was a dead man. The problem was that Jacob's left leg was in the most excruciating pain he could possibly imagine. He was growing dizzy and feared he could soon go into shock and black out. He had to shoot first. He had to make something happen, and fast.

The first thing he did was change his mind. He fired two shots from underneath the truck. He wasn't expecting to hit the man, but he hoped it would throw him off-balance and confuse him, and that's exactly what it did. The officer went scrambling backward, and Jacob forced himself to his feet again. Even as he himself screamed in pain, he fired four rounds at the officer in rapid succession.

At least one of them hit its mark. The man reeled around and went flying back against the wall, hollering in pain.

Limping forward as rapidly as he could, Jacob kept firing until the pistol was out of bullets. His tactical goal wasn't to kill the man but to keep him from regaining his focus and firing back.

For the moment, at least, he had achieved his objective. The man was on the ground, wallowing in blood from a gaping wound to his left shoulder.

As Jacob came around the rear of the truck, he had a clear shot at the man's back. But as he pulled out the second Luger and squeezed the trigger, nothing happened. The gun didn't fire. Panicking, now fully exposed, Jacob quickly checked the safety, but it was off. He aimed and tried to fire again, but again the pistol would not fire, and then Jacob realized that he had no functioning weapon and no way to run for cover or back to the house, where he knew more weapons were.

With no other options, Jacob did the only thing he could. He lunged for the man and began beating him with his fists, beginning with the wound in his shoulder.

At first the officer was caught off guard, and then he was nearly incapacitated by the blows to his shoulder, but this trained killer quickly rediscovered his instincts and landed a crushing punch to Jacob's left leg.

Now the tables were reversed. The man's submachine gun had been inadvertently kicked out of reach, but he rolled Jacob over, grabbed him by the throat, and began to squeeze the life out of him. Jacob gasped for air and struggled to break free. But the man was taller and heavier and fitter.

And then, in the thick of the enraged battle, Jacob finally saw the man's face. It was Von Strassen.

As each man realized who the other was, they were both temporarily stunned. For a few split seconds, Von Strassen eased his grip. Jacob made the most of it. He brought up his knee hard and fast into the man's groin. Then he landed another blow on Von Strassen's profusely bleeding shoulder, instantly loosening the man's death grip. Jacob was able to scramble away, but because his own leg was in so much pain, he was moving too slowly.

He couldn't run. He couldn't flee. Then he heard Von Strassen shout at him to halt, and there was something in the way he said it that did, in fact, make Jacob stop in his tracks.

"Turn around," Von Strassen ordered.

Jacob slowly turned.

The man's head and face were covered in blood, but he was standing there—staggering, really—in the doorway of the barn, holding his pistol and pointing it at Jacob's chest.

"Did you really think you could get away with all this, you filthy swine?" Von Strassen bellowed. "Did you really think you could defeat the Aryan people? *Never.* You are not human. You are a cancer. You and all of the Jews. You must be exterminated once and for all. You must not be allowed to infect the Fatherland or any part of Europe or any part of the world. Exterminating vermin like you is my job. And how I love it."

Jacob could not see Von Strassen's face clearly. With the barn doors open and the morning light coming in from the back, the Nazi was mostly a silhouette. But his voice and his words were crystal clear, and every hair stood up on the back of Jacob's neck as he heard the man speak.

It was so sad, Jacob thought. He had come so far. He was almost free. And far more important, he was so close—just a few short kilometers—from being able to deliver the strongbox to the Jewish council, so close to saving so many Jewish souls otherwise destined to perish in the gas chambers and ovens of the death camps. How could he have gotten so far and still failed? Why? What was it all for?

"If you're going to kill me, do it now," Jacob told Von Strassen.

He was terrified of dying, but he was even more terrified of going back to Auschwitz.

But Von Strassen just cackled his sick, twisted, demonic laugh. "I have no intention of killing you now, Mr. Weisz. I want you to spend a little time with my friend Dr. Mengele first. And then I want you to watch as we flay Miss Cohen's lovely flesh from her bones before your eyes. And then, when I am good and ready, I will send you from one hell to another. Until then, however—"

But Von Strassen never finished his sentence. Instead a gun went off—not once but twice.

Jacob staggered back, sure that Von Strassen had been toying with him, certain that he had pulled the trigger and fired the Luger. But then blood started pouring out of Von Strassen's mouth. He dropped the pistol and fell forward, flat on his face.

Standing behind him was Jedrick, a smoking double-barreled shotgun in his hands.

PART
SIX

99

SIX WEEKS LATER
JULY 29, 1944
WASHINGTON, D.C.

"I don't understand," the old man said. "You just walked out?"

Ambassador François d'Astier, age eighty-four, shifted in his overstuffed chair in the parlor of the brownstone walk-up where he and his wife, Camille, lived in Georgetown, just over a mile from the White House. The couple had been listening intently for nearly two hours, but as the balding yet distinguished-looking man puffed on his cigar, Jacob could see that Luc's grandfather was struggling to make sense of all that he was hearing.

"Actually, we drove out," Jacob said simply.

"Drove out?"

"Yes, sir."

"Weren't there soldiers when you got to the frontier?"

"Yes, sir."

"Nazi soldiers or Poles?"

"Both," Jacob said. "Plus Slovak soldiers on the other side."

"And they just let you pass?" d'Astier asked again.

"Yes, sir."

"I'm sorry; I'm just not following," d'Astier said. "Why would they do that?"

Now Jacob shifted in his seat. He took a sip of tea and gathered his thoughts. He tried not to look it, but he felt deeply frustrated. Did they not believe him? Did they think he was making this all up? Why would he? How would he have known so many details about their grandson—indeed, about their entire family—if he hadn't met Jean-Luc Leclerc in Auschwitz, if they hadn't truly escaped together?

Jacob couldn't bear the thought of people not believing him. He didn't have time for such foolishness. People were dying. Day after day, thousands of Hungarian Jews—and so many others—were being sent to the ovens. How many more cups of tea was he going to have to drink with how many more people before someone not only believed him but did something real, something meaningful to save lives?

It had already been an unbearable six weeks since he had escaped Auschwitz and arrived in Žilina. Since then he had told the Jewish council in Czechoslovakia everything he knew about what was happening in the death camps. He had turned over the strongbox and all of its documents. He had helped draft the *Auschwitz Protocol*, a forty-page report documenting in great detail exactly what the Nazis were doing to the Jews in Auschwitz-Birkenau. But everything seemed to go so slowly. It was maddening beyond belief. He had told his story and explained the *Protocol* to more rabbis than he could count. He had detailed what he had seen and heard to untold representatives from the International Red Cross, British intelligence, even the Vatican.

Yet the Nazi trains were still running. Day and night the Jews of Hungary continued to be shoved into cattle cars and sent to the death camps to become ashes. Nothing Jacob had said had moved the Allies to mount a rescue operation. Nothing he had done had saved a single Jewish life.

Now he was finally in Washington, D.C., sitting in the home of Luc's grandfather. Yet he felt farther from his goal than ever before. Still, Jacob fought to push away the gloominess and despair that threatened to engulf him. He told himself he could not lose hope now, not after he had come so far. He reminded himself that Ambassador d'Astier was not the problem. He might still be the answer. If Luc was right, this crippled old man—confined to a wheelchair—might be the Jewish people's best hope. Yet he could only help if he understood and believed everything Jacob said. Otherwise it had all been for nothing.

Jacob took a deep breath and tried to figure out where he had gone wrong. He had carefully and patiently explained everything that had happened, from the raid on train 801, to meeting Luc inside the camp, to how they had survived, to their extensive planning and preparations and the details of their escape. So far the d'Astiers had seemed to track with all of it, even while mourning the loss of their grandson—news they had not heard until Jacob had shown up unannounced at their door just a few hours earlier. Now, however, the French couple seemed baffled, even somewhat skeptical.

It occurred to Jacob that in his fatigue and haste, he had left out some very significant details.

"Forgive me," he said, suddenly desperate to correct his mistake, "but I forgot to tell you something."

"Please go ahead; we're listening," the retired diplomat said, leaning forward in his chair.

"As I said a moment ago, after the gun battle in the barn, we couldn't stay in the house," Jacob explained. "We knew we had to flee, yet the roads were all shut down. Jedrick and Brygita begged me to take them with me. I was skeptical; this had not been part of my plan. But they had saved my life. And together we had buried Luc. I knew I couldn't just leave them there."

"So what did you do?" Camille d'Astier asked. The woman had the face and the bearing of a French aristocrat, though she was probably also in her eighties and seemed quite frail and a bit hard of hearing.

"I suggested Jedrick don a Nazi uniform, as I had done," Jacob said. "He was horrified at first but quickly realized it was the only way, so he agreed."

"What about you?" the ambassador asked. "Your leg was wounded."

"Brygita was a nurse," Jacob replied. "She bandaged me up as best she could. Gave me some painkillers, which I'm afraid didn't do much good. Then I stripped an undamaged uniform off one of the men I'd shot—in the face, not in the chest—and put it on."

"What about the wife?" Mrs. d'Astier asked. "She didn't dress up as a Nazi, did she?"

"No, ma'am," Jacob said.

"What did she do?"

"We put her in the trunk."

"The trunk of what?"

"Colonel Von Strassen's car."

The couple looked aghast.

"Then what did you do?" the ambassador asked.

"I rifled through Von Strassen's briefcase and found copies of his orders and a sheaf of other official papers. Then I told Jedrick to drive. I got in the passenger's side. And we raced for the Slovakian border like we were on a mission from Berlin."

"And they let you right through?" d'Astier asked, incredulous.

"Yes, sir," Jacob said.

"Why?"

"Well, sir, I think we just looked the part," Jacob said. "I spoke flawless German. We had official papers. They had no reason to doubt us."

"They never searched the car?"

"No, sir."

"So you just drove through the checkpoint?"

"It was the most terrifying moment of my life," Jacob confirmed.

"Even considering everything else you had been through?"

"Yes, I think so."

"And then?"

"Otto Steinberger and Abe Frenkel had given me precise instructions," Jacob said. "I knew exactly where I was supposed to link up with the underground. Unfortunately, I knew I would not be allowed to bring the couple with me. I apologized profusely, but they understood. Together we ditched the car in a river and made sure it sank to the bottom. We hid the Nazi uniforms so others could retrieve them later and put them to good use. Then we put on regular civilian clothes we had brought from the house, and we said our good-byes. They went their way, and I went mine."

"And now here you are," the ambassador said.

"Well, six frustrating weeks later, yes, here I am," Jacob said.

"Then I'm guessing you have it with you, no? This *Auschwitz Protocol*?"

"I do, sir, yes," Jacob said, patting the leather briefcase at his feet.

"And all the documentation that you and Luc smuggled out of the camp?"

"Yes, sir," Jacob said. "It's all here."

The ambassador nodded, and Jacob opened the satchel—a gift from a leader of the Jewish council in Czechoslovakia. He pulled out the forty-page document and handed it over.

The old man just sat there for a few moments, holding the report in his hands and staring at it.

"This tells the whole story?" he asked finally.

"Well, sir, it depends what you mean by 'the whole story,'" Jacob said. "It tells the factual details of what Hoess and his men are doing inside Auschwitz-Birkenau and the subcamps. It documents the systematic extermination that is under way. It provides detailed maps of the camps, schematics of the gas chambers, technical details of the ovens—including who built them and when—the schedule of all the trains that have come, how many people were on those trains, how many perished, and so forth. But no, it doesn't tell the story I just told you. It doesn't tell our personal stories in the camps or how we escaped. We just wanted to explain as carefully and precisely as we could what the Nazis are actually doing, what the 'final solution to the Jewish question' really means. We made it as clinical and dispassionate as we could. But I'll let you be the judge."

"And you wrote this?"

"I helped, sir," Jacob said. "But I was not the only one who survived to tell the story."

"Oh?"

"Steinberger and Frenkel also made it."

"Both of them?"

"Yes, sir," Jacob said. "And Fischer and Kopecký made it too."

The old man looked at his wife. They were both astonished.

"I couldn't believe it myself," Jacob said, seeing the look in their eyes. "But when I got to Žilina, there they were. I was stunned. I was so certain they had been captured or killed. But they told me of the miracles that had happened to get them all the way out. So I asked them, 'What went wrong? Why aren't the Hungarian Jews revolting? Why are they still getting on the trains?' They said it was complicated. Steinberger told me that for weeks after they reached the council, no one believed them. Everyone thought they were delusional or exaggerating or embellishing to get more sympathy."

"Even though they were eyewitnesses?"

"Apparently, yes," Jacob said. "Then Fischer and Kopecký arrived. They told the same story. Then I arrived, also with the same story, and documents—proof. And I sent them to get the Nazi uniforms. And I told them to go find the car. And I had Von Strassen's papers and other intelligence documents from Hoess and the Gestapo. And the mood began to change. The others—the four of them—they were already working on the *Protocol* before I arrived. But they asked me to help, and I did. We added material that I was able to bring out, and I helped them translate it into several other languages."

"And when the council read it?"

"They were finally convinced."

"And the Red Cross representatives?"

"They were convinced as well."

"But still nothing has been done to stop the killing."

"No."

"How many Hungarian Jews have died so far?" d'Astier asked.

"Last I heard, about 483,000," Jacob said, feeling sick at the thought. "But that number is going up every day. It could be over half a million at this point."

"Did the Jewish council in Czechoslovakia get the report to the Jewish leaders in Hungary?"

"So far as I know, but we didn't stay around long enough to find out for sure."

"Why not?"

"Because when the council could finally figure out a way to get us safely out of the country, including false papers and so forth, they immediately sent me to find you. The others went to London."

Jacob waited for the next question, but it did not come. Instead the octogenarian former diplomat sat back in his chair, puffed on his cigar, and silently flipped through the pages of the *Auschwitz Protocol.*

After a bit, his wife got up and padded into the kitchen, eventually bringing back a fresh pot of tea. She poured cups for them both, but to no effect. The old man didn't touch it. Jacob didn't reach for his either. He just kept still and tried to read the expression on the old man's face. He searched for any sign of acceptance or rejection of the message Jacob had come to deliver. Yet he simply could not read the man. His face was inscrutable.

After almost twenty minutes, d'Astier leaned forward and, without saying anything to Jacob, picked up the telephone receiver from the end table beside him. Then he dialed, leaned back, and waited.

"Helen, it's François. Is Jack there?" he finally said into the receiver. "Actually, it is quite urgent. . . . Well, I'm sitting with a man who just escaped out of Nazi-controlled Poland. He has vital information the president needs to see immediately."

Jacob's heart leaped. Was this for real? Was Ambassador d'Astier really requesting a meeting for him with the president of the United States?

"No, it cannot wait," the ambassador said after a brief pause. "Thank you."

There was a long pause. Jacob was dying to know what was happening, but the old man never looked at him. Rather, he kept leafing through the *Protocol.* Finally, whoever the ambassador was calling came on the line.

"Jack, thanks for taking my call. I need to bring someone to see the president right away," he began. "Yes, it is that urgent. . . . No, it's too sensitive to discuss over the phone. . . . Well, I've never needed a meeting on such short notice. . . . Of course. . . . That would be fine. Thank you. We'll see you then."

The old man hung up the phone. "They're sending a car," he said, snuffing out his cigar.

"Who?" Jacob asked.

"The White House."

Jacob gulped. "We're really meeting with President Roosevelt?"

"No. We're meeting with his military aide, a lieutenant colonel by the name of Jack Dancy. We have to convince him first, but if we do, we might be able to meet the president tomorrow."

"I don't know what to say," Jacob said, a lump forming in his throat. "But thank you."

"I'm not doing this for you, Mr. Weisz," d'Astier replied. "I'm doing it for my grandson—for Luc—and for every Frenchman held in those camps. If all you say is true—and I must tell you it is very difficult to accept at face value, but you certainly have an awful lot of documentation here—then we cannot be silent. We must take action. And I have no doubt that once Mr. Roosevelt and his staff know what is happening and can verify it, they will take decisive action."

100

But they did not.

To be sure, Jack Dancy was gracious with his time. He gave Jacob forty-five minutes in his spacious and well-appointed West Wing office to make his case. He skimmed through the *Auschwitz Protocol* while Jacob gave an abbreviated account of the narrative he had told the ambassador. And Dancy asked Jacob for additional copies of the documents to give to the president, the secretary of war, the secretary of state, and the director of the Office of Strategic Services.

Then the aide asked Jacob one simple, blunt question.

"What do you want?"

"I beg your pardon?" Jacob replied, caught off guard by the directness of the inquiry.

"You heard me," Dancy replied.

"Well, I . . . I just . . ."

"Surely you did not come all this way just to give me a long memo, Mr. Weisz," Dancy said with nary a hint of compassion. "You want something. What is it?"

Again Jacob fumbled for the words. He was disoriented and exhausted. He was in awe of being in the White House, just a few steps from the Oval Office. He was intimidated by the Marine guards and the beauty and the history, and he felt young and out of place.

"Liberation," he finally said.

Dancy did a double take. "Say again?"

"We want you to liberate the camp," Jacob repeated. "And not just Auschwitz-Birkenau, but all the others, too."

"You're kidding, right?" Dancy asked, visibly dumbfounded.

"No, sir."

"How many camps are there?"

"About 1,200."

Dancy laughed out loud.

"I'm afraid I fail to see the humor, Mr. Dancy," Jacob said, his anger suddenly rising, though he saw the look in the ambassador's eyes, imploring him to be diplomatic.

"So you just want the president to call up General Eisenhower and tell him to take all of the Allied forces who just stormed the beaches of Normandy and are finally moving across France and divert all their efforts from liberating Europe and focus on liberating 1,200 Nazi labor camps."

"They're not labor camps," Jacob said. "They're death camps."

"All of Europe is a death camp, son. In case you hadn't noticed, people are dying everywhere—including a lot of our own boys."

"Not like this," Jacob said defiantly. "Colonel Dancy, did you hear what I just told you? People are being put in gas chambers. Children are being tossed into ovens. Innocents are being mowed down by gunfire. The most gruesome experiments are being done on them—while they are alive. Were you listening to any of that?"

Dancy just stared at him, clearly not having expected such a forceful confrontation from a gaunt Jewish boy from Germany.

"Of course I was listening," Dancy finally replied. "But maybe you weren't listening. Ten thousand Allied soldiers, sailors, and airmen were killed or wounded on D-day alone, including almost seven thousand Americans. Don't make it sound like we're not doing everything we can to liberate Europe, to say nothing of the Pacific. We didn't get into this war right away. We didn't listen to Churchill when he begged us to help the Brits stop Hitler early. That was our mistake. But we're in it now. I'm sympathetic to you and the plight of your people. I'll take your report and run it up the chain of command. I'll make sure it gets a fair hearing. But I can guarantee you General Eisenhower is not going to change his war plan to liberate 1,200 Nazi camps."

At that point the ambassador stepped in. "Well, what about just one, Jack?" he asked.

"What do you mean?"

"Would the president consider ordering the liberation of just one camp?" d'Astier clarified.

"This Auschwitz place?"

"Yes."

"I'm afraid that's not possible," Dancy said.

"Of course it's possible," d'Astier returned, showing the first signs of emotional strain. "It's not a matter of capacity. It's a matter of will."

"Mr. Ambassador, with all due respect, it most certainly is a matter of capacity. To liberate a Nazi concentration camp means sending thousands of troops—probably tens of thousands—deep behind enemy lines. Plus providing air cover. And then we have to get all our boys out of there again, along with all the prisoners. That simply isn't possible under current conditions."

Jacob couldn't believe what he was hearing. But the old man did not give up. "Jack, you and I have known each other a long time, have we not?"

Dancy nodded.

"When Hitler rose to power, I came to you and told you what was happening in my country and what was going to happen, did I not?"

"You did."

"And when it began to happen, I fed you as much intelligence as I could get my hands on, and then I came to you to ask for political asylum, correct?"

Again Dancy nodded.

"I told you the man was a demon," d'Astier said. "But even I underestimated what he was capable of. I never could have seen this coming, this systematic extermination of the Jewish people. Millions are dead. And one of them is my grandson."

"Jean-Luc?"

"Yes."

"I had no idea," Dancy said, looking genuinely troubled. "What happened?"

D'Astier briefly recounted the story Jacob had told him just a few hours earlier.

"I was not going to bring it up," the ambassador said in conclusion. "I didn't want to make this personal. I didn't want to appeal to you as a friend. I wanted you to look at the evidence and decide on its merits. But I don't think you are hearing what this young man is saying, Jack. This is not normal warfare. This is not just a few more people dying. This is something else altogether. This deserves the president's most earnest consideration. And it deserves action. Before millions more die."

Suddenly Dancy's phone rang, and the meeting was over.

Jacob wheeled Ambassador d'Astier out of the White House, and they soon found themselves on Pennsylvania Avenue on a lovely July evening. The air was warm and humid, almost sultry. The trees swayed slightly in the breeze. The moon was full.

But as Jacob drank in the scene and stared at the president's beautiful, majestic home all bathed in spotlights shining from several directions, his heart sank. How could he have come all this way only to be told no? Was the world's most powerful country really not going to lift a finger to free Abby or Josef or the rest of the doomed souls back in Poland?

"Don't despair, Jacob," the ambassador said as Jacob pushed his wheelchair to the waiting car. "We made our case. Jack is a fair man. I'm sure he will do the right thing. But we won't wait. Tomorrow we'll talk to someone else. If Jack won't authorize decisive action, we'll keep talking to people of influence in this town until we find someone who will."

101

The next day they went to the State Department.

Secretary Hull was traveling, but William Barrett, the secretary's top aide, agreed to meet with them. They gave Barrett a copy of the *Auschwitz Protocol*, but he was extremely busy and gave them very little time to explain what was happening and what they wanted.

"Liberation?" Barrett asked as if he were amused. "You're not serious."

"I'm dead serious," Jacob said, speaking with a sense of conviction he was sure his uncle would never have imagined he was capable of.

"Well, I'm sorry, but that's out of the question," Barrett said. "D-day was less than two months ago. Eisenhower has his hands full, and frankly so do we. Besides, it's not me that you want. You should be talking to the War Refugee Board."

"We will," the ambassador said. "But you know as well as I do that they're a toothless tiger. The power rests here, Bill. If action is going to be taken, it's because you and the secretary make it happen."

"I'm sorry, but my cup runneth over, Mr. Ambassador. I took this meeting as a courtesy, but I really must go."

Jacob realized the meeting was about to come to a close. "What about air strikes?" he asked desperately.

"Air strikes?" Barrett asked.

"Right."

"What kind of air strikes?"

"Bombing the train tracks leading into Auschwitz."

"You're serious?"

"Yes."

"Well, theoretically that's possible, of course," Barrett replied. "But it would be a very dangerous mission. Remember, southern Poland is deep behind enemy lines."

"Yes, I realize that." Jacob was doing his best to restrain himself but feared he was about to come unglued.

"Well, then, you also know that the German Luftwaffe is formidable. It would be quite an undertaking to send bombers that far, and we would need fighters to protect them. There could be heavy losses."

"There are already heavy losses," Jacob said. "Inside the camp. That's our whole point. An entire race of people is being exterminated."

"Yes, but I'm speaking of our air assets," Barrett said. "Anyway, this is not a matter for State. It's a matter for the War Department."

"But you've done it before," Jacob said.

"Pardon?"

"You've bombed the Auschwitz camp before," Jacob repeated. "So it can be done."

"No, I don't believe we have," Barrett said.

"Yes, you have. I was there. A few months ago, I saw Allied bombers attack a factory on the edge of the Auschwitz complex. All the prisoners started cheering. We thought the liberation had begun. But then the bombers and their escorts disappeared, and we never saw them again."

"I wouldn't know anything about that."

"Could you check on it?" the ambassador asked.

"I really think you should talk to the War Department," Barrett said, standing and putting on his coat. "I'm late for a meeting at the White House. I hope you'll forgive me."

Jacob got to his feet as well, but the ambassador was not finished. "History will not, Bill," he said.

"Excuse me?"

"History will not forgive you if you do not seriously review this evidence, if you do not properly brief the secretary, and if you do nothing to stop this genocide," d'Astier said. "Have you forgotten the *St. Louis*?

Have you forgotten those 937 German Jews who were trying to flee from Hitler, trying to find a haven of refuge? You turned the ship away. You turned them away and forced them to go back to Europe. They're probably all dead, Bill. They may have been sent to Auschwitz, for all we know. Maybe five years ago you could say you didn't really know who Hitler was. Maybe you could say you didn't know he was capable of genocide. But what about now? Now you do know. It's all there. It's all detailed in the *Auschwitz Protocol.* The world is watching. What are you going to do?"

102

Day after day went by, and they made no headway whatsoever.

Jacob and d'Astier asked for and were granted dozens of meetings. They met with congressmen and senators. They met with officials at the War Department and the OSS. They met with members of the War Refugee Board, who were the most sympathetic, but the Refugee Board couldn't make policy. They tried repeatedly to meet with Secretary Hull, but he was growing ill and taking fewer meetings. They tried repeatedly to meet with the president, but to no avail.

At one point, Jacob reached Otto Steinberger by phone. He learned that the *Protocol* had been distributed to officials in Great Britain and at the World Jewish Congress and to Allen Dulles, head of U.S. intelligence in Switzerland. The team had met personally with several senior British officials, including Foreign Secretary Anthony Eden, and had given each a copy of the report. They, too, had urged the Allies to bomb the railways to Auschwitz-Birkenau, but they, too, had met the same resistance, told time and time again that it was too risky and that the Germans would simply rebuild the tracks. So Steinberger said they had gone a step further. They had asked the British to bomb and destroy Auschwitz entirely, despite the terrible loss of life that would ensue, on the basis that the Germans would have neither the time nor the resources to rebuild a death camp at this stage of the war, and that this would prevent millions of additional deaths. But their pleas seemed to fall on deaf ears.

Finally, in desperation, d'Astier suggested to Jacob that they leak copies of the *Protocol* to various influential American and British reporters in the hopes that the sensational headlines would spark public outrage and bring pressure to bear on the Allied leaders.

At first Jacob was hesitant. He had no experience in such things, and he was under strict orders from the Jewish council's leadership to give the document only to government officials who could effect change. But the ambassador's case was persuasive. Following the Jewish council's strategy was getting them nowhere. Perhaps this was the only way.

Jacob tried to track down Steinberger again but could not reach him. Then he tried to find Frenkel, Fischer, and Kopecký, but he couldn't locate them, either.

They were running out of time. So Jacob made a decision he hoped his colleagues would forgive him for. He and d'Astier met again with several sympathetic members of the U.S. Refugee Board and asked them to leak copies of the *Auschwitz Protocol* to select reporters.

To Jacob's astonishment, the effect was instantaneous and explosive. Unlike the diplomats, the reporters immediately understood the horror of the story. They could see the credibility of the evidence, and they felt the emotional impact of this heretofore largely unknown human drama.

The story created a media firestorm, making front-page headlines throughout the United States, and quickly became news around the world.

"Two Million Executed in Nazi Camps," read the *Washington Post* headline, with the subhead "Gassing, Cremation Assembly-Line Methods Told by War Refugee Board."

The *New York Times* headline read, "U.S. Board Bares Atrocity Details Told by Witnesses at Polish Camps."

"U.S. Charges Nazis Tortured Millions to Death in Europe," screamed the headline in the *New York Herald Tribune*.

And it wasn't simply the major newspapers that reported the story. Small and regional papers did too.

"The Inside Story of Mass Murdering by the Nazis," read a headline in the *Louisville Courier-Journal*. In just three weeks, 383 similar stories were published.

Not surprisingly, much of the public was outraged. Jewish and Christian leaders who hadn't known before what was happening in the camps now appealed to the Roosevelt administration to take action.

Yet nothing happened. Neither the U.S. nor the British bombed the rails. Nor did they bomb the camps. Auschwitz was not liberated. It was not put out of business. The Allies' fight against the Axis powers continued, of course, and day after day Jacob tracked its progress through the papers and on the radio.

During this time, the d'Astiers took Jacob into their home, and for this he was deeply grateful. He lived with them and took meals with them. He went shopping for them and cooked for them. He answered their many questions about Luc and about the camps and about his time in Belgium and his childhood in Germany. They answered his many questions too—about Luc's family and what he was like as a boy and about Luc's deep faith. Jacob appreciated their hospitality and their gentle manner. They respected him as a Jew. They did not pressure him or ever make him feel uncomfortable. To the contrary, they cared for him as if he were their own grandson.

Often he lay in bed at night on a comfortable mattress, in a sturdy bed, with clean sheets, in his own room, staring up at a freshly painted ceiling with a fan that kept him cool on these hot summer nights. He lay there and wondered how the world had become such an evil place. How could so many good people turn such a blind eye to the atrocities being done all around them? It was one thing if they didn't know that millions of lives were being extinguished. But now that people knew, how could they do nothing? How could they see such evil and take no action?

And why was the world so cold toward the Jews? Why did so many hate them? What had he and his people done to make the world so casually turn a blind eye to the extermination of the Jewish race?

Before long Jacob could no longer bear living a safe and peaceful life in Washington, D.C., while his friends were suffering and dying in Poland. So when he heard through the grapevine one day that

Otto Steinberger had actually returned to Czechoslovakia to join the Resistance and fight the Nazis on the front lines, Jacob decided to do the same.

Despite the Allied reluctance to take specific actions to liberate or even bomb the camps, Jacob could see that the tide of the war had shifted. The Allies were gaining ground. Hitler and the Nazi war machine were being systematically pushed back. Jacob believed the war was winnable. Indeed, he was beginning to believe he would live to see the day that Hitler was captured, tried, and hanged for crimes against humanity. But Jacob could not bear to think of Abby—if she was still alive—hearing that he had done nothing to save her, that he had sat around in a brownstone walk-up in Georgetown while she had suffered in Auschwitz.

So early one morning he packed his suitcase, thanked the d'Astiers for their kindness, and walked out the door to catch a cab to the airport.

– – –

Ninety-six hours later, he was back in Žilina, not far from the Polish border, meeting with the leaders of the Resistance, having a Mauser rifle placed in his hands.

He had escaped Auschwitz and told the world of its atrocities. But that was not enough for Jacob Weisz. The people he'd worked and suffered with in Auschwitz were still working and suffering there, if they still lived at all.

He would fight his way back to them or perish in the fight.

103

And then it happened.

As 1945 began, the Allied forces, under the leadership of General Eisenhower, won victory after victory over the Nazis and pushed deeper and deeper into enemy territory from the west. Meanwhile, the Soviet Red Army pressed Hitler from the east. Town after town, city after city, region after region was liberated. The Hitler war machine was on its heels, and the Allied noose was tightening.

Then one day Jacob and his friends in the Resistance came back from a mission and huddled around an old wireless set and heard the stunning news. The date was January 27, 1945.

"The Red Army has liberated the Nazis' biggest concentration camp at Auschwitz in southwestern Poland," the announcer said. "According to reports, hundreds of thousands of Polish people, as well as Jews from a number of other European countries, have been held prisoner there in appalling conditions, and many have been killed in the gas chambers. Few details have emerged of the capture of Auschwitz, which has gained a reputation as the most notorious of the Nazi death camps. Some reports say the German guards were given orders several days ago to destroy the crematoriums and gas chambers. Tens of thousands of prisoners—those who were able to walk—have been moved out of the prison and forced to march to other camps in Germany."

Jacob could not believe what he was hearing. This was the day he had longed for, fought for, and now it had come. It seemed unreal.

"Details of what went on at the camp have been released previously by the Polish government in exile in London and from prisoners who have escaped," the announcer continued. "Since its establishment in 1940, only a handful of prisoners have escaped to tell of the full horror of the camp. . . . When the Red Army arrived at the camp, they found only a few thousand prisoners remaining. They had been too sick to leave."

Jacob wanted to be elated. But he was horrified. Only a few thousand prisoners had been found alive out of the sixty thousand who were normally held at Auschwitz? It couldn't be. There had to be more.

But as the details kept coming and the reality of what had happened began to sink in, Jacob wept as he had never wept before.

He had no idea who, if any, of his friends had survived. But now he had a new mission: he would get to them. He would find them. Whatever it took.

EPILOGUE

JUNE 5, 2014
AUSCHWITZ-BIRKENAU CONCENTRATION CAMP

Four months after his ninety-third birthday, Jacob Weisz returned to Auschwitz.

He had long ago vowed never to return. He had no desire to revisit the places or the memories they invoked. He had a quiet, peaceful life now. He had a little four-bedroom house on Long Island, and it was all paid for. It was in the country—plenty of green grass and farms and sunshine. Yet it was still close to the city and the heart of the Jewish community there. Why would he ever want to return to the place of his nightmares?

Yet on the seventieth anniversary of his escape, he finally agreed to make the trip.

Nearly all the friends he had made in the camp were gone now. Leszek Poczciwinski had long since died. So had Otto Steinberger and Abe Frenkel. Judah Fischer had passed just a few years earlier, and Milos Kopecký had died six months before.

But Abby was still alive, and it was she who persuaded him to make the voyage, as hard as it was. She was, after all, his wife, and it was there, in Auschwitz, in the depths of hell, that they had met. And to his astonishment, she had been one of the 2,819 prisoners the Red Army had found still alive when they had liberated the camp in January 1945.

As guests of the Polish government, Jacob and Abby flew first class, something they had never done before, on Lufthansa flight 7636, departing New York City at 6:25 in the evening. After a brief layover the following day in Frankfurt, they proceeded on to Kraków, touching down just before ten o'clock in the morning. There, before a bank of television cameras and a gaggle of journalists from around the world, the elderly couple were helped down from the plane, set carefully in wheelchairs, and greeted by the prime minister of Poland, flanked by thousands of people cheering them—many of them Jews, but also many Christians—all of them with tears streaming down their faces.

Jacob had never seen anything like it. He squeezed Abby's hand.

This was her idea, not his. She had taken the calls from the Polish, Israeli, and American authorities asking them to come and offering to take care of all the arrangements. It was she who asked that their entire family be invited too—their six children and eighteen grandchildren and thirteen great-grandchildren. Abby had pored over the itineraries and the flight plans and all the logistics.

"Welcome back, Mr. and Mrs. Weisz," the Polish premier said as the cameras rolled and the world watched. "You are the heroes of the Polish people, and we welcome you here as two of our own."

Jacob was so overcome with emotion he could barely speak. "I never imagined," he said, his voice quavering.

"I suppose not," said the premier, the son of a famed leader of the Resistance. "But I hope you will believe me when I tell you that this is not the place you both left. You are welcome here today. Indeed, you are living testimonies to God's grace and mercy. One of you escaped. One of you was liberated. Yet both of you endured and have lived full and fruitful and wonderful lives. You have your family here today to bear witness that, in the end, evil did not triumph. It tried, but it did not succeed. Evil was defeated because good people rose to the challenge and refused to surrender. We endeavor with you today to live up to your example, and today we honor you and the memory of all who were lost in this country and on this continent."

The assembled crowd erupted in thunderous applause.

"Thank you, sir," Abby replied. "Thank you very much."

Jacob, however, could not speak. His eyes were filled with tears, and his hands were trembling.

Abby handed him a fresh handkerchief.

He took it and stared into her eyes, red and moist as well. "I love you," he whispered.

"I love you too," she whispered back.

Pulling himself together, Jacob wiped his eyes and cleared his throat. Then he turned to the prime minister. "Sir, you are most kind. May I introduce to you my Abigail?"

The premier, accompanied by his own wife, smiled warmly, and they both shook Abby's hand.

"I have wanted to meet you for quite some time, Mrs. Weisz," the first lady of Poland said softly. "I have heard and read a great deal about you. It is such an honor to finally meet you in person."

"The honor is all mine," Abby said graciously.

"We have a present for you, Mrs. Weisz," the prime minister said. "For both of you, really." He then handed Abby a small package wrapped up in brown paper and string.

Jacob's heart raced as he watched his wife's frail hands begin to unwrap it. Could it be? It wasn't possible.

But sure enough, when Abby got the paper off, there it was—the leather journal he had given her so long ago, filled with the poems he had written in Auschwitz.

It was now Abby's turn to be overcome with emotion. Tears streamed down her face as she opened the journal and touched its yellowed pages.

The first lady explained how the journal had been found by archivists and brought to her attention while they were preparing for this trip.

"It is beautiful," Abby said through her tears, clasping the journal to her chest. "Thank you so very much. From the bottom of my heart, I thank you."

After a moment, Jacob spoke again.

"Your Excellency, I would like to introduce you to one of my sons—our firstborn."

"It is an honor to meet you, sir," the prime minister said, shaking hands with the distinguished, gray-haired sixty-eight-year-old gentleman at Jacob and Abby's side.

"Likewise, Your Excellency."

"What's your name?" the premier asked when Jacob forgot to offer it.

"It's Luc, sir," the son replied. "Jean-Luc Weisz. I want to thank you for all you've done to welcome my parents back to Poland and to bring all of us here as well. I didn't think I'd ever come here. For years, my father forbade it. But here we are, and we're all deeply grateful."

They exchanged pleasantries for a few minutes and had no small number of pictures taken. Then Jacob and Abby and their wheelchairs and their family were loaded onto buses and given a police escort on the hour-long drive to the Auschwitz-Birkenau camp.

Abby chatted nervously with Luc and their other children on the sixty-five-kilometer journey. But Jacob said nothing. He just held Abby's hand and squeezed it tightly. He was doing this for her and for their family, but there was nothing in him that wanted to be back in that place again, and the closer he got, the more he dreaded it.

When they arrived, they were greeted by a larger delegation of Polish, Israeli, German, British, and American officials, including ambassadors from each of the countries, various Jewish scholars, prominent rabbis, pastors, priests, and journalists from across the globe. Jacob was, after all, the last living person ever to have successfully escaped from the world's most notorious death camp, and his return on the seventieth anniversary of his flight to freedom was making headlines all over the world.

Throughout the long day, Jacob endured the speeches and the photo opportunities. He accepted an award, though he had informed them before coming that he would not speak, and he did not. But Abby spoke, and she was quite eloquent, he thought. To the world he imagined she looked gray and wrinkled and frail. But to him she was still as beautiful as the day he had met her, and she always would be.

Then, as a family, they toured the Auschwitz camp. They toured the barracks and the dining hall and the Canada command and the medical clinic where Abby had worked. They visited the home of Rudolf Hoess and saw the gallows where Max was hanged. At Abby's insistence, there was no guide or foreign officials or any media for this portion of the day. This was just for them as a family, and wherever they went, Abby told them stories of what had happened there.

Finally their children wheeled Jacob and Abby into the gas chamber. There they did not speak. They just sat quietly.

Then they were wheeled next door to the crematorium, where the ovens were still visible. They did not speak there either. What was there to say?

Eventually they toured the Birkenau camp as well. They saw the train tracks and even a cattle car that was still there. They visited some of the dilapidated barracks and the ruins of the large gas chambers and crematoriums, blown up by the Germans in the last weeks before liberation when they heard that the Soviets were rapidly approaching from the east. Most of what had once been there was gone. The bakery was gone, and so, of course, was the woodpile from which Jacob and Luc had made their escape. But the memories came flooding back, and Jacob continually fought back tears.

It was June, and though it was warm, Jacob and Abby were both developing a nagging cough, and their son Jean-Luc was becoming concerned for their health. So as the sun began to set, they all decided they had seen enough. They met again briefly with the prime minister and the various officials. They said their thank-yous and their good-byes. Then they were bundled back up and put back on the buses to return to Kraków.

On the bus ride, no one said a word. Certainly not Jacob. He just sipped a cup of hot tea Luc had given him and held Abby's hand as he stared out at the beautiful countryside passing by.

Soon Abby fell asleep. It had been a big day, and she had done nearly all of the talking. But as she slept so peacefully, Jacob kept finding himself staring at her. He still couldn't believe his good fortune—how he had found her in a Red Cross refugee camp soon after her liberation, how he had sat at her bedside night and day for months, feeding her and reading to her and telling her the news of Hitler's suicide and VE-day.

But in the end, it had not been he who rescued her. It had been she who rescued him. For it was Abby, more than anyone else, who had helped Jacob Weisz survive the traumas of the Holocaust. And not just in the camp, but over the last seven decades of their life together. It was she who had helped him regain his faith in humanity and eventually his faith in God.

Abigail Cohen Weisz loved to say she had never lost faith in the God of Abraham, Isaac, and Jacob—not even in Auschwitz. To the contrary, she loved him more than ever. Indeed, she loved to remind her husband and their children that the Jews had suffered for thousands of years—under Pharaoh, under the Babylonians and the Persians and the Greeks and the Romans. That didn't prove there was no God. Rather, she argued, the survival of the Jews throughout the ages—through all the attempts to exterminate them—proved there most certainly was—and *is*—a God, and not just any God but the God of Israel, who loved them, as the prophet Jeremiah once wrote, with an "everlasting love" and continued to draw his people to him with everlasting kindness.

It was she who reminded Jacob of the many ways God had rescued them. It was she who reminded him of Max and Josef and Jean-Luc Leclerc, all of whom had in one way or another given their lives that they might live. Not every survivor shared her sense of optimism and hope for the future. Jacob certainly hadn't. But by her simple faith and constant love, she wooed him.

It had taken Jacob quite some time, but after the birth of their first son, Luc, he had begun to reconsider his skepticism. Over the decades, he had read from the book of Psalms Abby had given him. Every morning when he woke up and every night before he went to sleep, he had searched the Psalms and the prophets and the rest of the Scriptures long and hard. From time to time, he would even pick up the Bible Abby had given to Luc. And eventually he had come to believe that Abby was right. God was not only real but had, in fact, shown himself to Jacob in countless ways, large and small, in the camp and beyond.

In fact, the more Jacob had read the Scriptures, the more his hunger for God's Word had grown. And the more Jacob realized that the Lord had rescued him—and rescued him for a purpose—the more he realized that Abby's great faith had become his own.

The God of the Bible was no longer simply the God of Abraham and Isaac.

Now he was the God of Jacob as well.

AUTHOR'S NOTE

In many ways, this is the most difficult book I've ever written. It is the first work of historical fiction I have ever attempted, and it has been a deeply personal project.

To write about the events of the Holocaust is to step onto sacred ground. To create a work of fiction in hopes of helping people understand the truth of what really happened—and to try to inspire people to begin their own journey to learn the facts, the truth, the testimonies of those who were there—is a sensitive endeavor. Of this I am keenly aware.

So far as I know, none of my relatives were murdered at Auschwitz or in the other Nazi death camps. As the descendant of Orthodox Jews who escaped the pogroms of czarist Russia in the early years of the twentieth century, I realize that I have been very fortunate. By God's grace, my paternal grandparents and great-grandparents, after fleeing Russia, did not settle in Poland or Germany or Austria. Instead, they made it to America, where they found safety and freedom several decades before Adolf Hitler rose to power. Other relatives of mine, including those on my Gentile mother's side of the family, are originally from Germany. But they, too, immigrated to America before the events of World War II unfolded. Had they stayed in Europe, their story likely would have turned out very differently. Indeed, often I have wondered what would have happened to our family if they had made different choices.

In November of 2011, on a cold, dark, misty day, I traveled to Poland with two couples who are friends of mine. One of the men is the pastor of a church in the U.S. The other pastors a church in Germany. Neither had been to Auschwitz-Birkenau before. Nor had I. Together, we walked the grounds of the camps. We saw the barbed wire and the guard towers. We stood inside a gas chamber. We saw the ovens. We learned the history. We asked many questions, and we wept.

Before leaving Auschwitz that day, I purchased a book titled *London Has Been Informed*. The book details several of the dramatic, real-life escapes from Auschwitz and the stories of real heroes who risked their lives to bring news of the horrors of the death camps to the Jewish communities in Hungary and to the Allies. Interestingly, our tour guide had not mentioned anything about these escapes. Intrigued, I began to track down whatever books and documentary films I could find, not simply about the Holocaust but about these escapes and their importance. I also wanted to learn more about the "Auschwitz Protocol," the actual document written by several of these escapees to explain to the world what Hitler and the Nazis were doing to exterminate the Jewish people. To this end, I was blessed to meet with experts and scholars at Yad Vashem—the world center for Holocaust research—who spent many hours answering my questions and giving me their insights, for which I am very grateful.

On a parallel track, I spent time researching what Yad Vashem calls the "Righteous Gentiles." I found myself intrigued with the stories of Christians—both Protestants and Catholics—who risked their lives to protect and rescue Jewish men, women, and children during the Holocaust. Some of these Christians, including pastors and priests, were arrested by the Nazis and sent to concentration camps. Indeed, some of them laid down their lives that others might live.

Le Chambon is a real town in France. An article on the website of the United States Holocaust Memorial Museum notes, "From December 1940 to September 1944, the inhabitants of the French village of Le Chambon-sur-Lignon (population 5,000) and the villages on the surrounding plateau (population 24,000) provided refuge for an estimated 5,000 people. This number included an estimated 3,000–3,500 Jews who were fleeing from the Vichy authorities and the Germans."

The article describes how a local pastor and his assistant led the residents as they "offered shelter in private homes, in hotels, on farms, and in schools. They forged identification and ration cards for the refugees and in some cases guided them across the border to neutral Switzerland." The inhabitants of Le Chambon and the nearby villages were recognized for their exceptional efforts by the State of Israel in 1990, when they were named Righteous among the Nations. You can find the text of the article at http://www.ushmm.org/wlc/en/article.php?ModuleId=10007518.

Jacob Weisz and Jean-Luc Leclerc are fictional characters, but their stories are inspired by the heroic lives of numerous real men, both Jews and Christians.

Other elements in the story are factual. Among them:

- The letters read by Jacob's fellow prisoners in the train car are based on actual letters of warning sent by inmates to their loved ones.
- The lessons for a successful escape given to Jacob by Steinberger are taken more or less verbatim from Rudolf Vrba's book *I Escaped from Auschwitz*, pages 213–215.
- The BBC broadcast Jacob hears in chapter 103 is taken from the transcript of the actual radio announcement on January 27, 1945. You can find it at http://news.bbc.co.uk/onthisday/hi/dates/stories/january/27/newsid_3520000/3520986.stm.
- The suicide note left by one of the Jewish leaders in the Warsaw ghetto in chapter 44 is a real document, though I have taken a minor liberty with the timing. The real note was written on May 11, 1943, whereas in the book I have that scene taking place on April 24. You can find the full text of the note at http://www.jewishvirtuallibrary.org/jsource/Holocaust/Bund.html.
- Dr. Mengele was a real-life monster who performed sadistic experiments on live prisoners at Auschwitz from May 30, 1943, until January 1945, when he fled upon learning of the advancing Soviet army. Again, I adjusted the timing slightly; I have him already active at Auschwitz on April 25, 1943. My purpose in occasionally making minor alterations like this was to represent the conditions of life at Auschwitz and try to help the reader get a better sense of what it would be like to suffer in—and then try to escape from—that actual living hell. I hope you will do your own research to better understand the facts, the timing, and the implications.

Among the books and films I studied during this project and that I highly recommend:

- *London Has Been Informed: Reports by Auschwitz Escapees,* edited by Henryk Świebocki
- *I Escaped from Auschwitz* by Rudolf Vrba
- *Escape from Hell: The True Story of the Auschwitz Protocol* by Alfred Wetzler
- *The Auschwitz Volunteer: Beyond Bravery* by Witold Pilecki
- *Secrets of the Dead: Escape from Auschwitz*, PBS Home Video
- The Night Trilogy: *Night*, *Dawn*, and *Day* by Elie Wiesel
- *The Rise and Fall of the Third Reich: A History of Nazi Germany* by William L. Shirer
- *The Hiding Place* by Corrie Ten Boom
- *Lest Innocent Blood Be Shed: The Story of the Village of Le Chambon and How Goodness Happened There* by Philip P. Haille
- *Weapons of the Spirit*, a documentary film by Pierre Sauvage about the rescue efforts of the people of Le Chambon
- *Bonhoeffer: Pastor, Martyr, Prophet, Spy* by Eric Metaxas
- *When Light Pierced the Darkness: Christian Rescue of Jews in Nazi-Occupied Poland* by Nechama Tec
- *Silent Rebels: The True Story of the Raid on the Twentieth Train to Auschwitz* by Marion Schreiber
- *The Righteous: The Unsung Heroes of the Holocaust* by Martin Gilbert
- *Auschwitz and the Allies* by Martin Gilbert
- *The Bombing of Auschwitz: Should the Allies Have Attempted It?* edited by Michael J. Neufeld and Michael Berenbaum
- *Commandant of Auschwitz* by Rudolf Hoess

In addition to these writers and film producers, I am deeply grateful to all those who helped me in my research. I feel special heartfelt gratitude to the staff and scholars at Yad Vashem and Christian Friends of Yad Vashem for their time, insights, and kindness. These include Dr. Susanna Kokkonen, Dr. David Silverklang, Dr. Robert Rozett, and Dr. Yehuda Bauer.

Special thanks in this effort also go to the great team at Tyndale House Publishers, including Mark Taylor, Jeff Johnson, Ron Beers,

Karen Watson, Jeremy Taylor, Jan Stob, Cheryl Kerwin, Todd Starowitz, and Dean Renninger. I am deeply grateful to them for their ongoing support, partnership, and abiding friendship.

Thanks to Scott Miller, my good friend and superb literary agent at Trident Media Group.

Thanks so much to my parents, Len and Mary Rosenberg, for all their love and support on this project and so many others. Thanks to the November Communications team—June Meyers and Nancy Pierce—for their love and tireless assistance. Thanks as well to my extended family and close friends.

Many, many thanks to my dear and wonderful wife, Lynn, and to our four wonderful sons, Caleb, Jacob, Jonah, and Noah, for your love, your prayers, your patience, and your boundless encouragement. What a joy it is to do life with you guys. I am blessed beyond words.

Most of all, I'm grateful to my Lord—the God of Abraham, Isaac, and Jacob—for sustaining me and for giving me the opportunity to share his love with others.

ABOUT THE AUTHOR

Joel C. Rosenberg is the *New York Times* bestselling author of six novels—*The Last Jihad, The Last Days, The Ezekiel Option, The Copper Scroll, Dead Heat,* and *The Twelfth Imam*—and two nonfiction books, *Epicenter* and *Inside the Revolution*, with nearly 3 million total copies in print. *The Ezekiel Option* received the Gold Medallion award as the "Best Novel of 2006" from the Evangelical Christian Publishers Association. Joel is the producer of two documentary films based on his nonfiction books. He is also the founder of The Joshua Fund, a nonprofit educational and charitable organization to mobilize Christians to "bless Israel and her neighbors in the name of Jesus" with food, clothing, medical supplies, and other humanitarian relief.

As a communications advisor, Joel has worked with a number of U.S. and Israeli leaders, including Steve Forbes, Rush Limbaugh, Natan Sharansky, and Benjamin Netanyahu. As an author, he has been interviewed on hundreds of radio and TV programs, including ABC's *Nightline, CNN Headline News*, FOX News Channel, The History Channel, MSNBC, *The Rush Limbaugh Show, The Sean Hannity Show*, and *Glenn Beck*. He has been profiled by the *New York Times*, the *Washington Times*, the *Jerusalem Post*, and *World* magazine. He has addressed audiences all over the world, including those in Israel, Iraq,

Jordan, Egypt, Turkey, Russia, and the Philippines. He has also spoken at the White House, the Pentagon, and to members of Congress.

In 2008, Joel designed and hosted the first Epicenter Conference in Jerusalem. The event drew two thousand Christians who wanted to "learn, pray, give, and go" to the Lord's work in Israel and the Middle East. Subsequent Epicenter Conferences have been held in San Diego (2009); Manila, Philippines (2010); and Philadelphia (2010). The live webcast of the Philadelphia conference drew some thirty-four thousand people from more than ninety countries to listen to speakers such as Israeli Vice Prime Minister Moshe Yaalon; pastors from the U.S., Israel, and Iran; Lt. General (ret.) Jerry Boykin; Kay Arthur; Janet Parshall; Tony Perkins; and Mosab Hassan Yousef, the son of one of the founders of Hamas who has renounced Islam and terrorism and become a follower of Jesus Christ and a friend of both Israelis and Palestinians.

The son of a Jewish father and a Gentile mother, Joel is an evangelical Christian with a passion to make disciples of all nations and teach Bible prophecy. A graduate of Syracuse University with a BFA in filmmaking, he is married, has four sons, and lives near Washington, DC.

To visit Joel's weblog—or sign up for his free weekly "Flash Traffic" e-mails—please visit www.joelrosenberg.com.

Please also visit these other websites:

www.joshuafund.net
www.epicenterconference.com

and Joel's "Epicenter Team" and the Joel C. Rosenberg public profile page on Facebook.